FROM THE PAGES OF
SELECTED STORIES OF O. HENRY

In time truth and science and nature will adapt themselves to art.
(From "The Plutonian Fire," page 7)

Life is made up of sobs, sniffles, and smiles, with sniffles predominating. (From "The Gift of the Magi," page 25)

No man existed who had money enough to wear so bad a hat as his.
(From "The Caliph, Cupid and the Clock," page 74)

There is this difference between the grief of youth and that of old age; youth's burden is lightened by as much of it as another shares; old age may give and give, but the sorrow remains the same.
(From "The Count and the Wedding Guest," page 83)

Where to go for wisdom has become a question of serious import. The ancients are discredited; Plato is boiler-plate; Aristotle is tottering; Marcus Aurelius is reeling; Æsop has been copyrighted by Indiana; Solomon is too solemn; you couldn't get anything out of Epictetus with a pick.   (From "The Higher Pragmatism," page 93)

True adventurers have never been plentiful. They who are set down in print as such have been mostly business men with newly invented methods. They have been out after the things they wanted—golden fleeces, holy grails, lady loves, treasure, crowns and fame. The true adventurer goes forth aimless and uncalculating to meet and greet unknown fate. (From "The Green Door," page 117)

We are grown stiff with the ramrod of convention down our backs. We pass on; and some day we come, at the end of a very dull life, to reflect that our romance has been a pallid thing of a marriage or two, a satin rosette kept in a safe-deposit drawer, and a lifelong feud with a steam radiator. (From "The Green Door," page 118)

Each plank in the floor owned its particular cant and shriek as from a separate and individual agony.

(From "The Furnished Room," page 155)

In dress, habits, manners, provincialism, routine and narrowness he acquired that charming insolence, that irritating completeness, that sophisticated crassness, that overbalanced poise that makes the Manhattan gentleman so delightfully small in his greatness.

(From "The Defeat of the City," page 170)

He seemed to be made of sunshine and blood-red tissue and clear weather.   (From "The Caballero's Way," page 205)

His thin, white fingers flew like some expert musician's upon the keys of a piano. He dumped the gold upon the counter with a crash, and the coins whined and sang as they skimmed across the marble slab from the tips of his nimble digits.

(From "Friends in San Rosario," pages 265–266)

"In the case of human beings, friendship is a transitory art, subject to discontinuance without further notice."

(From "Telemachus, Friend," page 324)

Upon what shallow waters can the bark of passion remain afloat!

(From "The Renaissance at Charleroi," page 350)

"People in real life don't fly into heroics and blank verse at emotional crises."   (From "Proof of the Pudding," page 387)

SELECTED STORIES OF O. HENRY

*With an Introduction and Notes
by Victoria Blake*

George Stade
Consulting Editorial Director

ЛB

BARNES & NOBLE CLASSICS
NEW YORK

ß

BARNES & NOBLE CLASSICS
NEW YORK

Published by Barnes & Noble Books
122 Fifth Avenue
New York, NY 10011

www.barnesandnoble.com/classics

The stories in this volume are taken from ten of O. Henry's short story collections, originally published between 1906 and 1917.

Published in 2003 by Barnes & Noble Classics with new Introduction, Notes, Biography, Chronology, Comments & Questions, and For Further Reading.

Selected Stories of O. Henry
ISBN-13: 978-1-59308-042-6
ISBN-10: 1-59308-042-5
LC Control Number 2003102765

Produced and published in conjunction with:
Fine Creative Media, Inc.
322 Eighth Avenue
New York, NY 10001

Michael J. Fine, President and Publisher

Printed in the United States of America
QM
9 10

O. HENRY

William Sydney Porter was born on September 11, 1862, in Greensboro, North Carolina. His mother died when he was three years old, and his father, a doctor and inventor, took him to live with his paternal grandmother and aunt. William received his only formal education at a private school run by his aunt, and it was she who encouraged his interest in art and literature. By age fifteen, he had left school to work as a pharmacist in his uncle's drugstore. Within four years, he had received a license from the North Carolina Pharmaceutical Association to practice pharmacy.

In 1882, alarmed by early signs of his own tuberculosis, Porter headed west to La Salle County, Texas, in search of drier weather. While working on a sheep ranch, he continued to draw and develop his writing style, observing the details of ranch life he would later recount in such stories as "The Hiding of Black Bill" (1907). In 1884 Porter moved to Austin, Texas, where he met and fell in love with Athol Estes, the stepdaughter of a wealthy businessman. Athol's parents were not impressed with Porter, and the couple eloped in 1887. Their daughter, Margaret, was born two years later.

In Austin, Porter worked as a draftsman in the Texas Land Office from 1887 to 1891, and then as a bank teller with the First National Bank of Austin from 1891 to 1894. Toward the end of his tenure at the bank, he acquired a used printing press and founded a humorous weekly magazine, *The Rolling Stone*, which he single-handedly wrote, printed, and published. While the magazine enjoyed early success, its burlesque and political satire offended many readers. Financial difficulties forced the magazine's closure a year later. Porter then moved his family to Houston, where he worked as a reporter, columnist, and cartoonist for the Houston *Post*.

In 1894 a bank audit discovered discrepancies in Porter's accounts, and over the next several years federal prosecutors investigated his case. He was arrested and charged with embezzlement in February 1896. Facing trial, Porter fled to Honduras, an experience he later chronicled in stories collected in *Cabbages and Kings* (1904). But his life on the lam was short-lived. When a year later he learned that Athol was dying of tuberculosis, he returned to Austin to be at her deathbed. Following Athol's death, Porter was sentenced to five years in the federal penitentiary at Columbus, Ohio.

In prison Porter began to publish stories under the pseudonym O. Henry. For his characters, he drew from his own wide experience, writing about tramps and millionaires, shop girls and southern aristocrats, cops, thieves, cowboys, and con men in stories that often have a surprise twist, or "snapper,"—Porter's trademark ending.

After serving three years, Porter was released from prison for good behavior. In 1902 he moved to New York City, and his popularity as a writer soared. He wrote prolifically during this time, publishing a story a week for the Sunday New York *World*, as well as selling pieces to several other magazines.

Sadly, Porter's creativity proved more robust than his health. He had suffered from tuberculosis and alcoholism for most of his adult life, and his illness and hard living finally caught up with him. William Sydney Porter died in New York on June 5, 1910, at age forty-seven. Though O. Henry's life was brief, his ten-year literary career had produced hundreds of stories and garnered him worldwide acclaim.

TABLE OF CONTENTS

THE WORLD OF O. HENRY
AND HIS STORIES

1862   On September 11 William Sydney Porter is born in Greensboro, North Carolina, to Mary Jane and Dr. Algernon Porter.

1863   President Abraham Lincoln issues the Emancipation Proclamation.

1865   Mary Jane Porter dies, leaving young William and his brother in their father's care. Dr. Porter takes the boys to live with their paternal grandmother and aunt. Lincoln is assassinated.

1867   William attends his Aunt Lina's private school and begins writing and drawing under her supervision. He later credits his aunt with fostering his interests in literature and art.

1877   Porter leaves school at age fifteen to work as an apprentice at his uncle's pharmacy.

1881   Porter receives a license to practice pharmacy from the North Carolina Pharmaceutical Association.

1882   Beginning to show signs of tuberculosis and concerned for his health, Porter quits his job as a pharmacist and heads west to La Salle County, Texas, where he works at Richard Hall's sheep and cattle ranch for two years. On the ranch, Porter draws cartoons and includes casual, often humorous observations in his letters.

1884   Porter moves to Austin, Texas, where he meets Athol Estes, his future wife.

1887   Porter and Athol elope. Porter works as a draftsman in the Texas Land Office.

1888   A son is born to the Porters but dies hours after birth.

1889   A healthy daughter, Margaret Worth Porter, is born. Athol, suffering from tuberculosis contracted from her father, is greatly weakened by the birth.

1891   Porter leaves the Land Office; despite a lack of experience, he secures a job at the First National Bank of Austin through the influence of friends.

1894   In March Porter acquires a printing press and founds a humor weekly, *The Rolling Stone*. The magazine enjoys early success but offends some readers with its burlesque and political satire. In December a bank audit reveals shortages in Porter's accounts. Porter protests his innocence. An offer of repayment from his father-in-law seems to mollify the bank, but a federal prosecutor seeks and receives a grand jury trial the following summer.

1895   Financial difficulty forces the closure of *The Rolling Stone* in April. The grand jury does not find sufficient evidence to try Porter. With Athol's health declining, he moves his family to Houston and accepts a job as a reporter, columnist, and occasional cartoonist with the Houston *Post*.

1896   The federal government persists with its prosecution, and in February Porter is arrested again, on charges of embezzlement. En route to Austin to face trial, Porter switches trains and flees to New Orleans. Several weeks later he boards an old freighter bound for Honduras.

1897   Learning of his wife's deteriorating health, Porter returns to Texas to be at her deathbed. Before she dies on July 25 she encourages him to develop his genius. In December Porter publishes his first story, "The Miracle of Lava Canyon."

1898   Porter's trial begins in February in the federal building later named for him, O. Henry Hall. On April 25 he is found guilty of embezzlement and sentenced to five years in the federal penitentiary at Columbus, Ohio. While in prison Porter works as a pharmacist and begins selling stories to support his daughter. He publishes a dozen stories under several pseudonyms, finally choosing the pen name O. Henry.

1901   Porter is released from prison for good behavior after serving three years.

1902   He moves to New York City, where his popularity as a

writer soars. Over the next nine years, Porter will write prolifically as O. Henry for several magazines.

1903   In December he begins writing a story a week for the Sunday
New York *World*, a pace he continues through January 1906.

1904   O. Henry's debut collection of stories, *Cabbages and Kings*,
is published; many of the stories draw from his experiences
as a fugitive in Honduras.

1906   His second collection, *The Four Million*, is published; most
of these stories draw on details from his life in New York
City, often gathered during nighttime wanderings through
the streets, where he meets a wide variety of people.

1907   O. Henry publishes *The Heart of the West*, a collection of
stories of the Texas Southwest; the volume includes such
popular stories as "The Caballero's Way" and "The Hiding
of Black Bill." The collection *The Trimmed Lamp* also comes
out this year.

1908   Two more volumes of his short stories are published: *The
Voice of the City* and *The Gentle Grafter*.

1909   The story collections *Roads of Destiny* and *Options* are published.

1910   *Strictly Business* and *Whirligigs* are published. Porter dies on
June 5, from the effects of tuberculosis, diabetes, and alcoholism. Although one of the most popular writers in America at the time of his death, he dies penniless.

1911   *Sixes and Sevens* is published.

1912   *Rolling Stones* is published.

1917   *Waifs and Strays* is published.

1918   The Society of Arts and Sciences establishes the O. Henry
Awards, given each year to the best short stories published
in the United States and Canada.

INTRODUCTION

During O. Henry's most productive year, 1904, he wrote and published sixty-five stories, an impressive number made more so by the fact that the following year he published fifty more. During this time he had a contract with the New York *World* that called for a story a week, a pace that would have run other writers dry but that O. Henry kept up for more than two years. Along with the panoply of magazine stories, he published ten books from 1904 until his death in 1910. All told, O. Henry penned some 300 stories during a literary career shorter even than that of the poet Percy Bysshe Shelley's. O. Henry said once that every story he ever wrote was published somewhere, and at his peak his stories were worth nearly a thousand dollars each on the literary marketplace.

O. Henry worked at a whirlwind speed, producing more over a shorter period than any other writer of his time and cultivating a literary demand unmatched by anyone, anywhere, in the history of American letters. By 1920, 5 million copies of his books had been sold in the United States alone, a staggering amount considering the size and scope of early-twentieth-century publishing in America. In 1919, when the annual *O. Henry Memorial Award Prize Stories* volume was inaugurated, his name had become synonymous with the short story, a measuring stick against which all other stories published during that time were held. He was a six-foot shadow to which other writers (including Joseph Conrad, Paul Charles Joseph Bourget, Edith Wharton, and H. G. Wells) were compared. But O. Henry himself was held above comparison. "It is idle to compare O. Henry with anybody," said Henry James Forman, in a statement that nicely summed up the prevailing attitude toward the author; "the combination of technical excellence with whimsical sparkling wit, abundant humour, and fertile invention is so rare that the reader is content without comparisons" (Smith, *O. Henry Biography*, p. 12; see "For Further Reading").

During his lifetime and immediately following his death, O. Henry's reputation rose to unparalleled heights, but in the late 1910s the foundation of this reputation started to crumble. One critic publicly denounced him as a "pernicious influence" on the American short story, concluding that he had done irreparable damage to the form. Others saw him as nothing more than a comic writer whose stories were simply trumped-up journalism with over-hashed trick endings and undue sentimentality, and they dismissed him with a shrug and a wave.

As an indication of O. Henry's fall from vogue, by 1930 he was the subject of only ten published master's theses and three books of personal remembrance. In the 1940s and 1950s, there appeared only a single published dissertation and one scholarly article. By the 1960s, the shadow cast by O. Henry's reputation seemed to have shrunk from six-feet to six-inches and it appeared that the cult of O. Henry was not only dead, but dead and buried. Today, the critics and scholars who by their attention raise and uphold a writer's position in the canon of American letters largely ignore him. So what happened? How did the reputation of a writer of O. Henry's stature, talent, and fame rise and fall so meteorically? And, most important, was his fall justified?

O. Henry was born William Sydney Porter, the second son of a kindhearted doctor and an artistically minded mother, in Greens-boro, North Carolina, on September 11, 1862. After his mother's death from consumption in 1865, the Porter family took up resi-dence with his grandmother, a stern and hardworking woman who ran a boardinghouse. William's father spent his life drinking and inventing, often at the same time. Among his unsuccessful inven-tions were a perpetual motion waterwheel, a churn, a washing ma-chine, a flying machine, a horseless carriage, and a cotton-picking contrivance. William received his primary education under the watchful eye of his aunt, and it was because of her influence that he developed an interest in letters. "I did more reading between my thirteenth and my nineteenth years than I have done in all the years since," he told an interviewer, "and my taste was much better then.

I used to read nothing but the classics" (MacAdam, "O. Henry's Only Autobiographia," p. 17).

At fifteen, his formal schooling ended and he took an apprenticeship at his uncle's pharmacy in Greensboro. The pharmacy functioned as a haphazard social center for the town; it was just as common to have a resident come in to talk over the problems of his marriage as to request a prescription. Porter worked there for a little more than three years and used his observations to produce a series of illustrations. In 1881, at age nineteen, he became licensed as a practicing pharmacist. He might have stayed behind the counter dispensing pills had not his health deteriorated and his wanderlust flared. In 1882, invited by a charismatic rancher named Dick Hall and hoping the dry air would help his consumptive cough, Porter left Greensboro for Texas to try his hand at sheepherding. In his letters from this period, he sounds happy. He thrived on the ranch, his health improved, and he felt the thrill of exploring new places. During the two years he spent in Texas, he carried a pocket-size Webster's dictionary with him wherever he went. He continued creating illustrations at the ranch and started writing stories, some of which he read aloud to his friends. He viewed his stories as no more than personal entertainment, not worthy of public attention, and it would be years before he finally saw one in print.

In 1884 Porter moved to Austin, Texas, where he worked at a host of assorted jobs, finally settling at the Texas Land Office, where he worked as a draftsman. The most important event of his time in Austin was his rapid courtship and marriage to the consumptive Athol Estes, stepdaughter of a prominent Austin businessman. Whether because after years of penning stories for a private readership he was finally ready to start publishing or because he now had a family to support, Porter began to write seriously. In the words of C. Alphonso Smith, his earliest biographer, "O. Henry found in his married life not only happiness but the incentive to effort that he had sorely lacked. It was incentive that sprang from perfect congeniality and from the ambition to make and to have a home" (Smith, p. 122). The earliest record of William Sydney Porter in print comes from 1887, the year of his marriage. An editor from the Detroit *Free Press* wrote to him, "Your string from November just in. Am sorry it is not longer. Check will be sent in a few days. Can you not send more matter—a good big installment every week?" (Smith, p. 123).

Whatever Porter had sent to the *Free Press*, they wanted more. From 1887 to 1895 he supplemented his income by selling humorous articles to various newspapers and journals. He was not yet a story writer, more a writer of paragraphs, but he was developing his style and figuring out just how far a good joke could take him. His first child, a son born in 1888, died only hours after birth, but in 1889 a second child, Margaret, lived. She remained close to her father throughout his life.

After working at the Land Office, Porter secured a post as a paying and receiving teller at the First National Bank of Austin. His association with the bank would later prove disastrous, but in 1891 the position was merely boring. He worked there for nearly three years, resigning in 1894 after shortages were discovered in his accounts. The bank charged him with embezzlement, and he would have had to stand trial that July had not a grand jury closed the case because of shoddy evidence.

During this time, Porter became possessed by a desire to create. He began an eight-page humorous periodical, which he first called the *Iconoclast* but soon renamed *The Rolling Stone*. He provided most of the content and illustrations for the periodical and also performed the roles of typesetter and printer. At the same time, he was publishing comic pieces in the Houston *Post*. After a year of trying to get *The Rolling Stone* rolling, he gave up on it as a loss. "It rolled on for about a year," he said by way of explanation, "and then showed unmistakable signs of getting mossy. Moss and I never were friends, and so I said good-bye to it" (Smith, pp. 125–126). Although *The Rolling Stone* never gained the momentum he had hoped it would, his experience with the periodical gave him the opportunity to try the writing life on for size. He had spent many years circling around the periphery of writing, but after his experience with the periodical he entered the game wholeheartedly. He liked what he saw, and he wanted more of it.

Porter's newly born desire to write took him to Houston in 1895, where he had accepted a job as a journalist for the Houston *Post*. Although the city had no more than 100,000 residents at the time, it was markedly larger than any in which he had previously lived and, in the words of Smith, "cities were always in a peculiar sense his teachers" (Smith, p. 128). During the day, he worked at the newspaper, but at night he took to the streets, walking for hours and finding ideas everywhere. He used his observations of Houston in a back-page section of the paper titled "Postscripts," delighting his early readers with his incisive, imaginative vision and his wit. "The man, woman, or child who pens 'Postscripts' for the Houston *Post*," wrote one impressed reader, "is a weird, wild-eyed genius and ought to be captured and put on exhibition" (Smith, p. 129). A typical example from "Postscripts," dated October 18, 1895, reads, "Of an editor: he was a man apparently of medium height, with light hair and dark chestnut ideas." Porter found a place for everything in "Postscripts," from modern poetry to comic character sketches, and thrived on his growing reputation as a comic author.

Only six months after his move to Houston, Porter received word that the embezzlement charges had been reinstated and that he would be arrested and forced to stand trial. He was taken into custody in February 1896, but, on a $2,000-dollar bond posted by his father-in-law, allowed to go free until the trial date. Until his death, he asserted that he was innocent and wrongly accused, but en route to his trial in Austin, he did not act like an innocent man. After detraining at a transfer point, he inexplicably boarded an eastbound night train heading for New Orleans, and then a ship heading for the coast of South America. He soon arrived, a fugitive, in Honduras. When he fled, suspicion became conviction, and he knew that if he returned he would be sent to jail.

The only explanation he ever offered to account for his flight came by way of comparison. "I am like Lord Jim," he told a friend, referring to the indecisive captain in Joseph Conrad's novel, "because we both made one fateful mistake at the supreme crisis of our lives, a mistake from which we could not recover" (Smith, p. 145). Honduras was the destination of obvious choice for a fugitive because, in addition to having a stable government and a strong economy, it lacked an extradition treaty with the United States. Porter's plan may have been to hide in South America until the statute of limitations on his case ran out. Or perhaps he simply wanted to hide. In a letter from Honduras he wrote, "The freedom, the silence, the sense of infinite peace, that I found here, I cannot begin to put into words" (Smith, p. 138).

Porter had left his consumptive wife and his young daughter at home to fend for themselves. Although the members of the family regularly corresponded, he had no idea the suffering his absence imposed upon them; as the days and weeks passed, Athol continued to grow more ill. Judging from his letters, up to the point of his return to America, Porter had planned to move both his wife and daughter to join him in Honduras. He had even chosen a school for Margaret. But faced with the probability that Athol didn't have long to live, he decided to return to America. In 1897 Athol died of tuberculosis, with her husband at her bedside. That same year Porter had his first story, "Miracle of Lava Canyon," published by the *McClure* Syndicate; it would be less than a year before he assumed his first pen name.

On April 25, 1898, Porter was sentenced to serve five years in the penitentiary at Columbus, Ohio, where he became Federal Prisoner Number 30664. The charges against him asserted that he had misappropriated funds on three separate days. There were obvious holes in the evidence, not least of which was that the date of the last misappropriation—November 12, 1895—was after he had resigned from the bank. The court, however, failed to notice the discrepancy. With the grief of his wife's death still upon him, Porter was sent to jail.

Why and where certain people become writers is a question better left to an omnipotent muse. Prison seems an unlikely place for the process to happen. But by the time Porter landed behind bars, he had already served some hardworking years developing his style. He was an accomplished newspaperman, a respected humorist, a wry and visionary short-story writer. He had been publisher of and chief contributor to his own periodical, and he had spent most of his life in active observation of others. Through his intimate knowledge of an Old South still reeling from the effects of the Civil War, his experiences as a ranch hand in the hard west of Texas and as a fugitive in South America, he had accumulated knowledge of three very distinct locales.

Porter leveraged his training as a licensed pharmacist and passed his prison years as an assistant in the prison hospital, a comparatively easy position that afforded him many small luxuries. He slept in the infirmary, and after an incident in which he saved the life of a warden who had overdosed on arsenic, he was allowed to roam freely about the jail. He spent his evenings on night-rounds, talking with the prisoners and gathering their tales. Despite the small luxuries, the brutality of prison life was difficult for him; his letters from this time display a keen understanding of the suffering surrounding him combined with a healthy disgust for conditions he viewed as less than human. In addition, he felt a good deal of shame and humiliation.

Most important to the literary record, however, he spent a good deal of time writing. "After most of his work was finished and we had eaten our midnight supper, he would begin to write," reported a night guard from the prison. "He . . . would often work for two hours continuously without rising. He seemed oblivious to the world of sleeping convicts about him, hearing not even the occasional sigh or groan from the beds which were stretched before him in the hospital ward or the tramp of the passing guards. After he had written for perhaps two hours he would rise, make a round of the hospital, and then come back to his work again" (Smith, p. 153).

While in prison, he managed to write and publish fifteen stories. After three years and three months, owing to good behavior, Porter was released into the world. "He was a changed man," wrote Smith. "Something of the old buoyancy and waggishness had gone, never to return" (Smith, p. 166). The change, however, was more complete than simply a lost buoyancy or waggishness. From the time he was released from prison to the time of his death, he was known to the world only by his pen name. Now he had his secret, and as he had escaped trial by running to Honduras, he would escape his past by hiding behind his pen. Nobody knows exactly where the name O. Henry sprang from. O. Henry told an interviewer that he had picked his alias randomly from the pages of a New Orleans newspaper, a statement that was probably untrue. The important thing is that the name is an alias, a mask, and a mask he was so interested in maintaining that he even lied about his birth date to put off the more curious of his fans; from the moment of his release, O. Henry would always be, in some sense, hiding.

O. Henry went to New York on an invitation from Gilman Hall, the associate editor of *Everybody's Magazine*. He started publishing his work almost immediately. During his eight-year residency in the city, he would complete the bulk of his approximately 300 stories. More than a hundred were published in the New York *World*, which had him under contract; the remainder were scattered throughout practically every well-known periodical in the city, and some beyond.

In 1904 O. Henry published his first collection of stories, *Cabbages and Kings* (the title comes from Lewis Carroll's poem "The Walrus and the Carpenter"), and in 1906 his second, *The Four Million*. Every year from 1907 to the year of his death, 1910, he would publish two more volumes of stories. These books introduced him to a wider audience than could be reached by periodical publishing alone. It is a testament to O. Henry's unflagging energies that he found time during this hectic period to re-encounter, woo, and marry his childhood sweetheart, Sara Lindsay Coleman, even though the relationship quickly petered out.

O. Henry's rise to fame coincided with the rise of small-press publishing in America. Starting after the Civil War and continuing into the early decades of the twentieth century, magazine publishing expanded dramatically and O. Henry—part literary genius, part common man—was swept to the top by the tide. Technological improvements in printing made it possible to produce small periodicals like *The Rolling Stone* at a modest cost. In addition, in 1885 the postal rate dropped, allowing publishers to reach customers who could not get to the newsstand. The economics of publishing, combined with a growing readership made and cultivated by the magazines, blew the field wide open for new journalistic enterprises. Add to this the rise of the American middle class and you have a recipe for financial success. The roster of magazines that first opened their doors in the late-nineteenth and early-twentieth centuries is impressive, and a good percentage of the names are still familiar to readers today. *Scribner's*, the *Atlantic Monthly*, *The New Yorker*, *Good Housekeeping*, *Collier's*, *The Bookman*, *Harper's*, *Ladies' Home Journal*, and *McClure's* all began during this period. With the rise of the magazines, there was a rise in the demand for stories that could fulfill the unexacting expectations of the new middle-class readership, people who wanted the semblance of educational reading without the difficulties associated with highbrow literature. Authors who could fill this demand were rewarded with both fame and fortune.

The downside to this beehive of capitalistic publishing activity, however, was that the editors of the periodicals, and to a large extent the writers themselves, did not attempt great literary heights, being for the most part content to watch their reputations grow and their pocketbooks fatten. At least one critic has compared the writers of this period to machines, noting that the homogeneity of product was like "literary mass production" (Brooks, *The Confident Years: 1885–1915*, p. 265). The same critic asserts that "the cheaper magazines and literary syndicates . . . produced O. Henry. It was to their audience that he wrote and to their tastes that he calibrated his stories" (Brooks, p. 226).

In addition, O. Henry's heyday coincided with the peak of a new literary genre critics call "the local color movement." Local-color literature can be summed up in one phrase: "separate but equal." After the Civil War, democracy-mad America was trying hard to find a middle ground between social separation and total social integration. Americans wanted to retain their individual, regional identities, but they did not want to lose their common American identity. To accomplish this, they looked to the differences in their regional cultures as a source of strength, not a cause for division. "There is a difference every lover of his country ought to be glad to admit," wrote Smith in his O. Henry biography, putting his pen precisely on the point. "Time was when we called these differences sectional. A better term is regional. Sectional implies not only difference but antagonism; it recalls oratory, war, and politics. Regional differences suggest neither actual nor potential conflict. Such differences are the allies of literature. They make for variety in unity and unity in variety" (Smith, pp. 237–238).

O. Henry, with his precise ear for dialect and his understanding of South, West, and East, wrote stories that pleased readers who wanted "unity in variety." But O. Henry was different from other local-color writers in one important way: His singular pen was able to capture the individual color of the variety of American locales. The genre of the Western story had been mastered by Bret Harte;

stories about the Deep South and New Orleans had been written by George Washington Cable; Spanish-American stories had been explored by Richard Harding Davis. Until O. Henry, however, no one writer had been able to do them all, and with such results, and nobody had been able to add New York City to the list. New York was O. Henry's own.

A popular saying at the time of O. Henry's move to New York in 1902 held that there were only four hundred people living there who were worth paying attention to. O. Henry, never one to overlook the working class, took this number, added a few zeros, and wrote about the four million. All of them had a story and, although taciturn and withdrawn himself, O. Henry always had an ear out for the stories the city told. "His favorite diversion . . . was to sit around a table where three or four pleasant people were gathered together . . . and just listen. He had the faculty of sitting perfectly silent and yet of stimulating the talk rather than deadening it," said one of his friends (MacAdam, p. 13). When he wasn't listening, he was out on the street, walking the avenues of Manhattan looking for the fleet-footed muse of Adventure. "You can't write a story that's got any life in it by sitting at a writing table and thinking," O. Henry said to an interviewer. "You've got to get out into the streets, into the crowds, talk with people, and feel the rush and the throb of real life—that's the stimulant for a story writer" (MacAdam, p. 20).

The "great, common, throbbing heart of humanity," as he termed New York in his story "While the Auto Waits" (p. 102), gave O. Henry his ideas, the sheer bulk of which are impressive. He fed off the energy and the vitality of the place. "I could look at [the] mountains a hundred years and never get an idea, but just one block downtown and I catch a sentence, see something in a face— and I've got my story," he is reported to have said (Smith, p. 173). His stories were not intellectual; they always had a human face. In an interview, he said, "I have never met any one but what I could learn something from him; he's had some experiences that I have not had; he sees the world from his own viewpoint. If you got at it in the right way the chances are that you can extract something of value from him" (MacAdam, pp. 20–21). Once in a restaurant, when a friend asked him where he came up with his ideas, he replied that the gem of a story can be found anywhere. He picked up the menu and, right there, improvised the idea that he later turned into "Springtime à la Carte."

Once he got his idea, he would sit down immediately and write it out. "I get a story thoroughly in mind before I sit down at my writing table," he told an interviewer. "Then I write it out quickly; and, without revising it, mail it to my editor" (MacAdam, p. 20). Chances were, as soon as he sent off one story he was already working on another. "Herewith submitted one MS," he wrote in a letter to his editor. "Have another one ready to typewrite, which you can read to-morrow. Give the full speed ahead signal and whoop them through, pro or con. Great business. The mill is grinding at the old gait" (MacAdam, p. 12). To match the speed and efficiency of the composition, O. Henry developed a writing philosophy that was similarly streamlined, to say the least. "I'll give you the whole secret of short-story writing," he told an interviewer. "Here it is. Rule 1: Write short stories that please yourself. There is no Rule 2" (MacAdam, p. 20).

O. Henry gave New York a new perspective on itself. It was through his words that New Yorkers began to see themselves as a worthy spectacle, all of them, from shop-girl to chorus girl to country bumpkin to politician. In return, New York focused its gaze on O. Henry. It was the perfect relationship between the viewer and the viewed: If New York pleased O. Henry, O. Henry pleased New York. Reporters clamored at his door but were rarely accepted for an interview. He maintained a cloud of mystery about him that fascinated his readers. "Who is this person who delights us so?" they asked.

Well, "he sure does look healthy," one journalist wrote upon successfully cornering his prey. "Short, stocky, broad-shouldered, ruddy-faced, clear-eyed, and none of his hair missing. He has none of the wan intellectuality, none of the pale aestheticisms that are conventional parts of the make-up of literary lions that disport themselves at afternoon tea-parties" (MacAdam, p. 16). In other words, despite his fame, O. Henry was one of them. He even had habits like them. "He used to drop in pretty regularly about 10 o'clock every morning," a bartender at the corner pub told a muck-raking reporter. "Sazerac cocktail was his favorite drink." But nobody could forget he was also a writer. "Some days the telephone bell would ring and he would tell me to send over to his rooms a bottle of Scotch. Then I knew that he was writing," the bartender continued (MacAdam, p. 8).

But the relationship, which had given both viewer and viewed so much pleasure, could not last. Toward the end of his life, O. Henry ran up against the problem of artistic growth. "I see [my stories] in print and I wonder why people like them. I wait till they come out in book form, hoping that they may look better to me then. But they don't" (MacAdam, p. 13). He began to feel confined by the expectations made by his successful creation of the O. Henry story, a "type" from which he could not deviate. He had perfected a form for the story, and now he was hamstrung by it. "I want to get at something bigger," he said. "What I have done is child's play compared to what I can do, to what it is in me to do" (Smith, p. 248). He wanted to write a novel. "My idea is to write the story of a man—an individual, not a type . . . if such a person could exist. The story will teach no lesson, inculcate no moral, advance no theory. I want it to be something that it won't or can't be—but as near as I can make it—the *true* record of a man's thoughts, his description of his mischances and adventures, his *true* opinions of life as he has seen it and his *absolutely honest* deductions, comments, and views upon the different phases of life that he passes through" (O. Henry, *The Works of O. Henry*, p. 847).

Perhaps if he had written that novel, his name would be included with Dreiser, with Wharton, with James, carved in marble on the walls of libraries across the nation. But before he could accomplish what he "had it in [him] to do," he ran up against an insurmountable obstacle: his health. The obligations of family life combined with the obligations of the writing life wore him down, and he began to drink more heavily. Within two years of the marriage ceremony, his relationship with his second wife had almost completely dissolved. In 1910, following a six-month break from the city due to health problems, he collapsed in his rooms and was taken to the hospital. He died on June 5, 1910, at forty-seven years old, from a combination of tuberculosis, diabetes, and advanced cirrhosis of the liver. His dying words were, "Turn up the lights; I don't want to go home in the dark" (Smith, p. 250).

Two years after O. Henry's death, Doubleday issued a deluxe edition of his collected works, consisting of 250 of his stories, with the special bonus of an original manuscript page tucked into a front pocket. Only twelve volumes of the edition were printed, and they sold almost immediately for the whopping sum of $125. In addition, Doubleday published five more posthumously collected volumes of his stories. In 1916 the first biography of O. Henry was published; written by his childhood friend, C. Alphonso Smith, the book reads less like a biography than a detailed adulation. The biography established O. Henry's reputation in America and solidified the tone of hero worship that infects most of the writing on him from this time.

While some critics voiced the random dissenting opinion, O. Henry's admirers were by far the majority and it seemed as if "the time [is] coming . . . when the whole English-speaking world will recognize in him one of the great masters of modern literature" (Smith, p. 9). His name was invoked everywhere, even in the political arena, where Theodore Roosevelt used it to explain his social policies: "The reforms I attempted in behalf of the shop girls of New York were suggested by the stories of O. Henry," the president said (Smith, p. 57). Meanwhile, his works were translated into a dozen European languages and were enjoyed particularly by the English, French, and Russians. Most notable of these were the Russians, who gobbled his stories like bonbons. One Russian critic wrote that the development of the short story progresses, "from Washington Irving, himself still tied to the traditions of manners-and-morals sketch writing in England, to Edgar Allan Poe, to Nathanial Hawthorne; after them come Bret Harte, Henry James and, later, Mark Twain, Jack London and, finally, O. Henry" (Ejxenbaum, *O. Henry and the Theory of the Short Story*, p. 1). The fact that the list terminates with O. Henry, and that the list was composed in 1968, six decades after his death, is evidence of how highly the Russians regarded his work. Another indication of how highly the Russians esteemed O. Henry (and one of the most peculiar geo-literary facts on record) is that in 1962 Soviet Russia issued a centennial commemorative stamp in his honor.

In contrast to the vocal adulation of the early 1920s, the current critical attitude toward O. Henry—a writer who has been called the "Yankee Maupassant," the "Y.M.C.A. Boccaccio," and the "Homer of the Tenderloin"—is a complete and resounding silence. O. Henry has been neither degraded nor destroyed by the critics. He has been almost completely and totally ignored. So what happened?

In the 1920s, America's taste in literature changed. Writers like Ernest Hemingway, Sherwood Anderson, F. Scott Fitzgerald, and William Faulkner suggested to the American readership a new direction for American letters while at the same time proving to magazine and newspaper editors that "serious" and "experimental" fiction sold. Concurrently, British Modernism was well underway; the effects of James Joyce and Virginia Woolf, as well as T. S. Eliot and Ezra Pound, were felt in America, first as ripples, then as tidal waves. In the 1920s, the new writers had gained footholds and, in what seemed like a response against their literary forefathers, the backlash against O. Henry was fierce. Writers regularly commented that, in order to maintain the vitality of American literature, writing must be freed from the constraints of the O. Henry *type* story and that the trick endings, forced plots, and flat characters that he had developed would no longer fly. As a nail in the coffin, his stories were criticized for being too tied up in their age, too much period pieces and not enough timeless literature. They were criticized, in other words, for being exactly what they were.

If O. Henry's stories can be faulted for aging badly, it should be pointed out that though the modern reader cannot recall the social mood that gave rise to "Brickdust Row" and "Lost on Dress Parade," neither can she recall the time when men fought in pubs with sabers to defend the reputation of their queen. Yes, his plot constructions do at times seem forced, but his language more than makes up for this fault. Consider this elegiac sentence, "The Mississippi gives up a victim from its oily tangles only at the whim of its malign will," from "The Renaissance at Charleroi" (p. 350), or the pure music in the description of "the little voices of the night—the owl's recitative, the capriccio of the crickets, the concerto of the frogs in the grass," from the same story (p. 357). His writings are full of such music, and a few of his well-placed observations—"her hair was pulled back smooth like little girls do when they want to look grown-folksy" from "The Lonesome Road" (p. 340)—could be elegantly transmuted into a poem, while some of his insults—"if I had my choice for society between you and a common yellow, three-legged cur pup, one of the inmates of this here cabin would be wagging a tail just at present" from "The Handbook of Hymen" (p. 313)—are downright Shakespearean.

If O. Henry is to be faulted for anything, it should be that he was too good at what he did and that, sticking with what he knew and dying before he had a chance to grow artistically, his stories stagnated under the weight of their own bulk. With this in mind, when assembling the stories for this reprinting, we have attempted to provide the reader with examples that represent the full range of his writing. O. Henry cannot be defined simply by the sentimentality of "The Gift of the Magi" or "The Last Leaf," nor by the trick endings in "The Man Higher Up" or "The Count and the Wedding Dress," for while there is a "typical" O. Henry story, there are O. Henry stories that you would not recognize to be his. "A Newspaper Story" uses a narrative technique that borders on the postmodern, "Confessions of a Humorist" shows O. Henry in a rare and honest light, and "The Renaissance at Charleroi" is broad enough in scope to be material for a novel. We have attempted to place the "typical" stories alongside the atypical ones so that new readers of O. Henry can see him in his full light and old readers might discover something in him previously unseen.

And as for the question "So what happened?" each reader must answer that for his or herself. For although O. Henry lived and wrote nearly one hundred years ago, his story is far from complete, and each reader, by honestly grappling with the question of his literary merit, will add a new and vital piece to the debate.

Victoria Blake is a freelance writer. She has worked at *The Paris Review* and contributed to *The Boulder Daily Camera*, a number of small literary presses in the United States, and several English-language publications in Bangkok, Thailand. She wrote the introduction and notes to the Barnes & Noble Classics edition of D. H. Lawrence's *Sons and Lovers*. She currently lives and works in San Diego, California.

SELECTED STORIES OF
O. HENRY

CONTENTS

THE PLUTONIAN FIRE

There are a few editor men with whom I am privileged to come in contact. It has not been long since it was their habit to come in contact with me. There is a difference.

They tell me that with a large number of the manuscripts that are submitted to them come advices (in the way of a boost) from the author asseverating that the incidents in the story are true. The destination of such contributions depends wholly upon the question of the inclosure of stamps. Some are returned, the rest are thrown on the floor in a corner on top of a pair of gum shoes, an overturned statuette of the Winged Victory,[1] and a pile of old magazines containing a picture of the editor in the act of reading the latest copy of *Le Petit Journal*,[2] right side up—you can tell by the illustrations. It is only a legend that there are waste baskets in editors' offices.

Thus is truth held in disrepute. But in time truth and science and nature will adapt themselves to art. Things will happen logically, and the villain be discomfited instead of being elected to the board of directors. But in the meantime fiction must not only be divorced from fact, but must pay alimony and be awarded custody of the press despatches.

This preamble is to warn you off the grade crossing of a true story. Being that, it shall be told simply, with conjunctions substituted for adjectives wherever possible, and whatever evidences of style may appear in it shall be due to the linotype man. It is a story of the literary life in a great city, and it should be of interest to every author within a 20-mile radius of Gosport, Ind., whose desk holds a MS.* story beginning thus: "While the cheers following his nomination were still ringing through the old court-house, Har-

---

*Abbreviation for "manuscript."

wood broke away from the congratulating handclasps of his hench-
men and hurried to Judge Creswell's house to find Ida."

Pettit came up out of Alabama to write fiction. The Southern
papers had printed eight of his stories under an editorial caption
identifying the author as the son of "the gallant Major Pettingill
Pettit, our former County Attorney and hero of the battle of Lookout Mountain."[3]

Pettit was a rugged fellow, with a kind of shame-faced culture,
and my good friend. His father kept a general store in a little town
called Hosea. Pettit had been raised in the pine-woods and broom-
sedge fields adjacent thereto. He had in his gripsack two manuscript
novels of the adventures in Picardy[4] of one Gaston Laboulaye, Vi-
compte de Montrepos, in the year 1329. That's nothing. We all do
that. And some day when we make a hit with the little sketch about
a newsy and his lame dog, the editor prints the other one for us—or
"on us," as the saying is—and then—and then we have to get a big
valise and peddle those patent air-draft gas burners. At $1.25 every-
body should have 'em.

I took Pettit to the red-brick house which was to appear in an
article entitled "Literary Landmarks of Old New York," some day
when we got through with it. He engaged a room there, drawing
on the general store for his expenses. I showed New York to him,
and he did not mention how much narrower Broadway is than Lee
Avenue in Hosea. This seemed a good sign, so I put the final test.

"Suppose you try your hand at a descriptive article," I suggested,
"giving your impressions of New York as seen from the Brooklyn
Bridge. The fresh point of view, the——"

"Don't be a fool," said Pettit. "Let's go have some beer. On the
whole I rather like the city."

We discovered and enjoyed the only true Bohemia. Every day
and night we repaired to one of those palaces of marble and glass
and tilework, where goes on a tremendous and sounding epic of
life. Valhalla itself could not be more glorious and sonorous. The
classic marble on which we ate, the great, light-flooded, vitreous
front, adorned with snow-white scrolls; the grand Wagnerian din
of clanking cups and bowls, the flashing staccato of brandishing
cutlery, the piercing recitative of the white-aproned grub-maidens
at the morgue-like banquet tables; the recurrent lied-motif of the

cash-register[5]—it was a gigantic, triumphant welding of art and sound, a deafening, soul-uplifting pageant of heroic and emblematic life. And the beans were only ten cents. We wondered why our fellow-artists cared to dine at sad little tables in their so-called Bohemian restaurants; and we shuddered lest they should seek out our resorts and make them conspicuous with their presence.

Pettit wrote many stories, which the editors returned to him. He wrote love stories, a thing I have always kept free from, holding the belief that the well-known and popular sentiment is not properly a matter for publication, but something to be privately handled by the alienists and florists. But the editors had told him that they wanted love stories, because they said the women read them.

Now, the editors are wrong about that, of course. Women do not read the love stories in the magazines. They read the poker-game stories and the recipes for cucumber lotion. The love stories are read by fat cigar drummers and little ten-year-old girls. I am not criticising the judgment of editors. They are mostly very fine men, but a man can be but one man, with individual opinions and tastes. I knew two associate editors of a magazine who were wonderfully alike in almost everything. And yet one of them was very fond of Flaubert, while the other preferred gin.[6]

Pettit brought me his returned manuscripts, and we looked them over together to find out why they were not accepted. They seemed to me pretty fair stories, written in a good style, and ended, as they should, at the bottom of the last page.

They were well constructed and the events were marshalled in orderly and logical sequence. But I thought I detected a lack of living substance—it was much as if I gazed at a symmetrical array of presentable clamshells from which the succulent and vital inhabitants had been removed. I intimated that the author might do well to get better acquainted with his theme.

"You sold a story last week," said Pettit, "about a gun fight in an Arizona mining town in which the hero drew his Colt's .45 and shot seven bandits as fast as they came in the door. Now, if a six-shooter could——"

"Oh, well," said I, "that's different. Arizona is a long way from New York. I could have a man stabbed with a lariat* or chased by

---

*Lasso (from the Spanish *la reata*).

a pair of chaparreras* if I wanted to, and it wouldn't be noticed until the usual error-sharp from around McAdams Junction isolates the erratum and writes in to the papers about it. But you are up against another proposition. This thing they call love is as common around New York as it is in Sheboygan† during the young onion season. It may be mixed here with a little commercialism—they read Byron,[7] but they look up Bradstreet's too, while they're among the B's, and Brigham also if they have time—but it's pretty much the same old internal disturbance everywhere. You can fool an editor with a fake picture of a cowboy mounting a pony with his left hand on the saddle horn, but you can't put him up a tree with a love story. So, you've got to fall in love and then write the real thing."

Pettit did. I never knew whether he was taking my advice or whether he fell an accidental victim.

There was a girl he had met at one of these studio contrivances— a glorious, impudent, lucid, open-minded girl with hair the color of Culmbacher,‡ and a good-natured way of despising you. She was a New York girl.

Well (as the narrative style permits us to say infrequently), Pettit went to pieces. All those pains, those lover's doubts, those heartburnings and tremors of which he had written so unconvincingly were his. Talk about Shylock's pound of flesh![8] Twenty-five pounds Cupid got from Pettit. Which is the usurer?

One night Pettit came to my room exalted. Pale and haggard but exalted. She had given him a jonquil.§

"Old Hoss," said he, with a new smile flickering around his mouth, "I believe I could write that story to-night—the one, you know, that is to win out. I can feel it. I don't know whether it will come out or not, but I can feel it."

I pushed him out of my door. "Go to your room and write it," I ordered. "Else I can see your finish. I told you this must come first. Write it tonight and put it under my door when it is done.

---

*Chaps, from "chaparajos" (Spanish); leather leggings worn over trousers.
†City in Wisconsin, on Lake Michigan.
‡Brand of beer.
§Flowering plant related to the daffodil.

Put it under my door to-night when it is finished—don't keep it until to-morrow."

I was reading my bully* old pal Montaigne[9] at two o'clock when I heard the sheets rustle under my door. I gathered them up and read the story.

The hissing of geese, the languishing cooing of doves, the braying of donkeys, the chatter of irresponsible sparrows—these were in my mind's ear as I read. "Suffering Sappho!"[10] I exclaimed to myself. "Is this the divine fire that is supposed to ignite genius and make it practicable and wage-earning?"

The story was sentimental drivel, full of whimpering softheartedness and gushing egoism. All the art that Pettit had acquired was gone. A perusal of its buttery phrases would have made a cynic of a sighing chambermaid.

In the morning Pettit came to my room. I read him his doom mercilessly. He laughed idiotically.

"All right, Old Hoss," he said, cheerily, "make cigar-lighters of it. What's the difference? I'm going to take her to lunch at Claremont to-day."

There was about a month of it. And then Pettit came to me bearing an invisible mitten, with the fortitude of a dish-rag. He talked of the grave and South America and prussic acid; and I lost an afternoon getting him straight. I took him out and saw that large and curative doses of whiskey were administered to him. I warned you this was a true story—'ware your white ribbons if you follow this tale. For two weeks I fed him whiskey and Omar,[11] and read to him regularly every evening the column in the evening paper that reveals the secrets of female beauty. I recommend the treatment.

After Pettit was cured he wrote more stories. He recovered his old-time facility and did work just short of good enough. Then the curtain rose on the third act.

A little, dark-eyed, silent girl from New Hampshire, who was studying applied design, fell deeply in love with him. She was the intense sort, but externally *glacé*,† such as New England sometimes

---

*First-rate.
†Chilly or cold (French).

fools us with. Pettit liked her mildly, and took her about a good deal. She worshipped him, and now and then bored him.

There came a climax when she tried to jump out of a window, and he had to save her by some perfunctory, unmeant wooing. Even I was shaken by the depths of the absorbing affection she showed. Home, friends, traditions, creeds went up like thistle-down* in the scale against her love. It was really discomposing.

One night again Pettit sauntered in, yawning. As he had told me before, he said he felt that he could do a great story, and as before I hunted him to his room and saw him open his inkstand. At one o'clock the sheets of paper slid under my door.

I read that story, and I jumped up, late as it was, with a whoop of joy. Old Pettit had done it. Just as though it lay there, red and bleeding, a woman's heart was written into the lines. You couldn't see the joining, but art, exquisite art, and pulsing nature had been combined into a love story that took you by the throat like the quinsy. I broke into Pettit's room and beat him on the back and called him names—names high up in the galaxy of the immortals that we admired. And Pettit yawned and begged to be allowed to sleep.

On the morrow, I dragged him to an editor. The great man read, and, rising, gave Pettit his hand. That was a decoration, a wreath of bay, and a guarantee of rent.

And then old Pettit smiled slowly. I call him Gentleman Pettit now to myself. It's a miserable name to give a man, but it sounds better than it looks in print.

"I see," said old Pettit, as he took up his story and began tearing it into small strips. "I see the game now. You can't write with ink, and you can't write with your own heart's blood, but you can write with the heart's blood of some one else. You have to be a cad before you can be an artist. Well, I am for old Alabam and the Major's store. Have you got a light, Old Hoss?"

I went with Pettit to the dépôt and died hard.

"Shakespeare's sonnets?"[12] I blurted, making a last stand. "How about him?"

------

*Wispy tufts atop a thistle plant that catch in the wind and carry the thistle seeds across the land.

"A cad," said Pettit. "They give it to you, and you sell it—love, you know. I'd rather sell ploughs for father."

"But," I protested, "you are reversing the decision of the world's greatest——"

"Good-by, Old Hoss," said Pettit.

"Critics," I continued. "But—say—if the Major can use a fairly good salesman and book-keeper down there in the store, let me know, will you?"

—from *The Voice of the City* (1908)

THE PRINCESS AND THE PUMA

There had to be a king and queen, of course. The king was a terrible old man who wore six-shooters and spurs, and shouted in such a tremendous voice that the rattlers on the prairie would run into their holes under the prickly pear. Before there was a royal family they called the man "Whispering Ben." When he came to own 50,000 acres of land and more cattle than he could count, they called him O'Donnell "the Cattle King."

The queen had been a Mexican girl from Laredo. She made a good, mild, Colorado-claro* wife, and even succeeded in teaching Ben to modify his voice sufficiently while in the house to keep the dishes from being broken. When Ben got to be king she would sit on the gallery of Espinosa Ranch and weave rush mats. When wealth became so irresistible and oppressive that upholstered chairs and a centre table were brought down from San Antone in the wagons, she bowed her smooth, dark head, and shared the fate of the Danaë.[1]

To avoid *lèse-majesté*† you have been presented first to the king and queen. They do not enter the story, which might be called "The Chronicle of the Princess, the Happy Thought, and the Lion that Bungled his Job."

Josefa O'Donnell was the surviving daughter, the princess. From her mother she inherited warmth of nature and a dusky, semi-tropic beauty. From Ben O'Donnell the royal she acquired a store of intrepidity, common sense, and the faculty of ruling. The combination was one worth going miles to see. Josefa while riding

---

*Possibly a reference to skin color; Colorado claro is a light brown cigar wrapper.
†Crime, such as treason, against a sovereign power (from the French for "injured majesty").

14

her pony at a gallop could put five out of six bullets through a tomato-can swinging at the end of a string. She could play for hours with a white kitten she owned, dressing it in all manner of absurd clothes. Scorning a pencil, she could tell you out of her head what 1545 two-year-olds would bring on the hoof, at $8.50 per head. Roughly speaking, the Espinosa Ranch is forty miles long and thirty broad—but mostly leased land. Josefa, on her pony, had prospected over every mile of it. Every cow-puncher on the range knew her by sight and was a loyal vassal. Ripley Givens, foreman of one of the Espinosa outfits, saw her one day, and made up his mind to form a royal matrimonial alliance. Presumptuous? No. In those days in the Nueces country a man was a man. And, after all, the title of cattle king does not presuppose blood royal. Often it only signifies that its owner wears the crown in token of his magnificent qualities in the art of cattle stealing.

One day Ripley Givens rode over to the Double Elm Ranch to inquire about a bunch of strayed yearlings. He was late in setting out on his return trip, and it was sundown when he struck the White Horse Crossing of the Nueces. From there to his own camp it was sixteen miles. To the Espinosa ranch house it was twelve. Givens was tired. He decided to pass the night at the Crossing.

There was a fine water hole in the river-bed. The banks were thickly covered with great trees, undergrown with brush. Back from the water hole fifty yards was a stretch of curly mesquite grass—supper for his horse and bed for himself. Givens staked his horse, and spread out his saddle blankets to dry. He sat down with his back against a tree and rolled a cigarette. From somewhere in the dense timber along the river came a sudden, rageful, shivering wail. The pony danced at the end of his rope and blew a whistling snort of comprehending fear. Givens puffed at his cigarette, but he reached leisurely for his pistol-belt, which lay on the grass, and twirled the cylinder of his weapon tentatively. A great gar plunged with a loud splash into the water hole. A little brown rabbit skipped around a bunch of catclaw and sat twitching his whiskers and looking humorously at Givens. The pony went on eating grass.

It is well to be reasonably watchful when a Mexican lion sings soprano along the arroyos* at sundown. The burden of his song

---

*Deep gullies (Spanish).

may be that young calves and fat lambs are scarce, and that he has a carnivorous desire for your acquaintance.

In the grass lay an empty fruit can, cast there by some former sojourner. Givens caught sight of it with a grunt of satisfaction. In his coat pocket tied behind his saddle was a handful or two of ground coffee. Black coffee and cigarettes! What ranchero could desire more?

In two minutes he had a little fire going clearly. He started, with his can, for the water hole. When within fifteen yards of its edge he saw, between the bushes, a side-saddled pony with down-dropped reins cropping grass a little distance to his left. Just rising from her hands and knees on the brink of the water hole was Josefa O'Donnell. She had been drinking water, and she brushed the sand from the palms of her hands. Ten yards away, to her right, half concealed by a clump of sacuista, Givens saw the crouching form of the Mexican lion. His amber eyeballs glared hungrily; six feet from them was the tip of the tail stretched straight, like a pointer's. His hind-quarters rocked with the motion of the cat tribe preliminary to leaping.

Givens did what he could. His six-shooter was thirty-five yards away lying on the grass. He gave a loud yell, and dashed between the lion and the princess.

The "rucus," as Givens called it afterward, was brief and somewhat confused. When he arrived on the line of attack he saw a dim streak in the air, and heard a couple of faint cracks. Then a hundred pounds of Mexican lion plumped down upon his head and flattened him, with a heavy jar, to the ground. He remembered calling out: "Let up, now—no fair gouging!" and then he crawled from under the lion like a worm, with his mouth full of grass and dirt, and a big lump on the back of his head where it had struck the root of a water-elm. The lion lay motionless. Givens, feeling aggrieved, and suspicious of fouls, shook his fist at the lion, and shouted: "I'll rastle you again for twenty—" and then he got back to himself.

Josefa was standing in her tracks, quietly reloading her silver-mounted .38. It had not been a difficult shot. The lion's head made an easier mark than a tomato-can swinging at the end of a string. There was a provoking, teasing, maddening smile upon her mouth and in her dark eyes. The would-be-rescuing knight felt the fire of his fiasco burn down to his soul. Here had been his chance, the chance that he had dreamed of; and Momus,* and not Cupid, had presided over it. The satyrs† in the wood were, no doubt, holding their sides in hilarious, silent laughter. There had been something like vaudeville—say Signor Givens and his funny knockabout act with the stuffed lion.

"Is that you, Mr. Givens?" said Josefa, in her deliberate, saccharine contralto. "You nearly spoiled my shot when you yelled. Did you hurt your head when you fell?"

"Oh, no," said Givens, quietly; "that didn't hurt." He stooped ignominiously and dragged his best Stetson hat from under the beast. It was crushed and wrinkled to a fine comedy effect. Then he knelt down and softly stroked the fierce, open-jawed head of the dead lion.

"Poor old Bill!" he exclaimed mournfully.

"What's that?" asked Josefa sharply.

"Of course you didn't know, Miss Josefa," said Givens, with an air of one allowing magnanimity to triumph over grief. "Nobody can blame you. I tried to save him, but I couldn't let you know in time."

"Save who?"

"Why, Bill. I've been looking for him all day. You see, he's been our camp pet for two years. Poor old fellow, he wouldn't have hurt a cottontail rabbit. It'll break the boys all up when they hear about it. But you couldn't tell, of course, that Bill was just trying to play with you."

Josefa's black eyes burned steadily upon him. Ripley Givens met the test successfully. He stood rumpling the yellow-brown curls on his head pensively. In his eyes was regret, not unmingled with a gentle reproach. His smooth features were set to a pattern of indisputable sorrow. Josefa wavered.

"What was your pet doing here?" she asked, making a last stand. "There's no camp near the White Horse Crossing."

"The old rascal ran away from camp yesterday," answered Givens

---

*Greek god of censure and mockery.

†In Greek mythology, woodland goat-men associated with excesses of lust and drunkenness.

readily. "It's a wonder the coyotes didn't scare him to death. You see, Jim Webster, our horse wrangler, brought a little terrier pup into camp last week. The pup made life miserable for Bill—he used to chase him around and chew his hind legs for hours at a time. Every night when bedtime came Bill would sneak under one of the boy's blankets and sleep to keep the pup from finding him. I reckon he must have been worried pretty desperate or he wouldn't have run away. He was always afraid to get out of sight of camp."

Josefa looked at the body of the fierce animal. Givens gently patted one of the formidable paws that could have killed a yearling calf with one blow. Slowly a red flush widened upon the dark olive face of the girl. Was it the signal of shame of the true sportsman who has brought down ignoble quarry? Her eyes grew softer, and the lowered lids drove away all their bright mockery.

"I'm very sorry," she said humbly; "but he looked so big, and jumped so high that—"

"Poor old Bill was hungry," interrupted Givens, in quick defence of the deceased. "We always made him jump for his supper in camp. He would lie down and roll over for a piece of meat. When he saw you he thought he was going to get something to eat from you."

Suddenly Josefa's eyes opened wide.

"I might have shot you!" she exclaimed. "You ran right in between. You risked your life to save your pet! That was fine, Mr. Givens. I like a man who is kind to animals."

Yes; there was even admiration in her gaze now. After all, there was a hero rising out of the ruins of the anti-climax. The look on Givens's face would have secured him a high position in the S.P.C.A.*

"I always loved 'em," said he; "horses, dogs, Mexican lions, cows, alligators—"

"I hate alligators," instantly demurred Josefa; "crawly, muddy things!"

"Did I say alligators?" said Givens. "I meant antelopes, of course."

Josefa's conscience drove her to make further amends. She held

*Society for the Prevention of Cruelty to Animals.

out her hand penitently. There was a bright, unshed drop in each of her eyes.

"Please forgive me, Mr. Givens, won't you? I'm only a girl, you know, and I was frightened at first. I'm very, very sorry I shot Bill. You don't know how ashamed I feel. I wouldn't have done it for anything."

Givens took the proffered hand. He held it for a time while he allowed the generosity of his nature to overcome his grief at the loss of Bill. At last it was clear that he had forgiven her.

"Please don't speak of it any more, Miss Josefa. 'Twas enough to frighten any young lady the way Bill looked. I'll explain it all right to the boys."

"Are you really sure you don't hate me?" Josefa came closer to him impulsively. Her eyes were sweet—oh, sweet and pleading with gracious penitence. "I would hate anyone who would kill my kitten. And how daring and kind of you to risk being shot when you tried to save him! How very few men would have done that!" Victory wrested from defeat! Vaudeville turned into drama! Bravo, Ripley Givens!

It was now twilight. Of course Miss Josefa could not be allowed to ride on to the ranch-house alone. Givens resaddled his pony in spite of that animal's reproachful glances, and rode with her. Side by side they galloped across the smooth grass, the princess and the man who was kind to animals. The prairie odours of fruitful earth and delicate bloom were thick and sweet around them. Coyotes yelping over there on the hill! No fear. And yet—

Josefa rode closer. A little hand seemed to grope. Givens found it with his own. The ponies kept an even gait. The hands lingered together, and the owner of one explained:

"I never was frightened before, but just think! How terrible it would be to meet a really wild lion! Poor Bill! I'm so glad you came with me!"

O'Donnell was sitting on the ranch gallery.

"Hello, Rip!" he shouted—"that you?"

"He rode in with me," said Josefa. "I lost my way and was late."

"Much obliged," called the cattle king. "Stop over, Rip, and ride to camp in the morning."

But Givens would not. He would push on to camp. There was

a bunch of steers to start off on the trail at daybreak. He said good-night, and trotted away.

An hour later, when the lights were out, Josefa, in her night-robe, came to her door and called to the king in his own room across the brick-paved hallway:

"Say, pop, you know that old Mexican lion they call the 'Gotch-eared Devil'—the one that killed Gonzales, Mr. Martin's sheep herder, and about fifty calves on the Salado range? Well, I settled his hash this afternoon over at the White Horse Crossing. Put two balls in his head with my .38 while he was on the jump. I knew him by the slice gone from his left ear that old Gonzales cut off with his machete. You couldn't have made a better shot yourself, daddy."

"Bully for you!"* thundered Whispering Ben from the darkness of the royal chamber.

—from *The Heart of the West* (1907)

---

*"Good for you!"

BY COURIER

It was neither the season nor the hour when the Park had frequenters; and it is likely that the young lady, who was seated on one of the benches at the side of the walk, had merely obeyed a sudden impulse to sit for a while and enjoy a foretaste of coming Spring.

She rested there, pensive and still. A certain melancholy that touched her countenance must have been of recent birth, for it had not yet altered the fine and youthful contours of her cheek, nor subdued the arch though resolute curve of her lips.

A tall young man came striding through the park along the path near which she sat. Behind him tagged a boy carrying a suit-case. At sight of the young lady, the man's face changed to red and back to pale again. He watched her countenance as he drew nearer, with hope and anxiety mingled on his own. He passed within a few yards of her, but he saw no evidence that she was aware of his presence or existence.

Some fifty yards further on he suddenly stopped and sat on a bench at one side. The boy dropped the suit-case and stared at him with wondering, shrewd eyes. The young man took out his handkerchief and wiped his brow. It was a good handkerchief, a good brow, and the young man was good to look at. He said to the boy:

"I want you to take a message to that young lady on that bench. Tell her I am on my way to the station, to leave for San Francisco, where I shall join that Alaska moose-hunting expedition. Tell her that, since she has commanded me neither to speak nor to write to her, I take this means of making one last appeal to her sense of justice, for the sake of what has been. Tell her that to condemn and discard one who has not deserved such treatment, without giving him her reasons or a chance to explain is contrary to her nature as I believe it to be. Tell her that I have thus, to a certain degree, disobeyed her injunctions, in the hope that she may yet be inclined to see justice done. Go, and tell her that."

The young man dropped a half-dollar into the boy's hand. The boy looked at him for a moment with bright, canny eyes out of a dirty, intelligent face and then set off at a run. He approached the lady on the bench a little doubtfully, but unembarrassed. He touched the brim of an old plaid bicycle cap perched on the back of his head. The lady looked at him coolly, without prejudice or favor.

"Lady," he said, "dat gent on de oder bench sent yer a song and dance by me. If yer don't know de guy, and he's tryin' to do de Johnny act, say de word, and I'll call a cop in t'ree minutes. If yer does know him, and he's on de square, w'y I'll spiel yer de bunch of hot air he sent yer."

The young lady betrayed a faint interest.

"A song and dance!" she said, in a deliberate, sweet voice that seemed to clothe her words in a diaphanous garment of impalpable irony. "A new idea—in the troubadour* line, I suppose. I—used to know the gentleman who sent you so I think it will hardly be necessary to call the police. You may execute your song and dance, but do not sing too loudly. It is a little early yet for open-air vaudeville, and we might attract attention."

"Awe," said the boy, with a shrug down the length of him, "yer know what I mean, lady. 'Tain't a turn, it's wind. He told me to tell yer he's got his collars and cuffs in dat grip for a scoot clean out to 'Frisco. Den he's goin' to shoot snow-birds in de Klondike.[1] He says yer told him not to send 'round no more pink notes nor come hangin' over de garden gate, and he takes dis means of puttin' yer wise. He says yer refereed him out like a has-been, and never give him no chance to kick at de decision. He says yer swiped him, and never said why."

The slightly awakened interest in the young lady's eyes did not abate. Perhaps it was caused by either the originality or the audacity of the snow-bird hunter, in thus circumventing her express com-

---

*One of a class of medieval minstrels who wrote principally on love and chivalry.

mands against the ordinary modes of communication. She fixed her eye on a statue standing disconsolate in the dishevelled park, and spoke into the transmitter:

"Tell the gentleman that I need not repeat to him a description of my ideals. He knows what they have been and what they still are. So far as they touch on this case, absolute loyalty and truth are the ones paramount. Tell him that I have studied my own heart as well as one can, and I know its weakness as well as I do its needs. That is why I decline to hear his pleas, whatever they may be. I did not condemn him through hearsay or doubtful evidence, and that is why I made no charge. But, since he persists in hearing what he already well knows, you may convey the matter.

"Tell him that I entered the conservatory that evening from the rear, to cut a rose for my mother. Tell him I saw him and Miss Ashburton beneath the pink oleander. The tableau was pretty, but the pose and juxtaposition were too eloquent and evident to require explanation. I left the conservatory, and, at the same time, the rose and my ideal. You may carry that song and dance to your impresario."

"I'm shy on one word, lady. Jux—jux—put me wise on that, will yer?"

"Juxtaposition—or you may call it propinquity—or, if you like, being rather too near for one maintaining the position of an ideal."

The gravel spun from beneath the boy's feet. He stood by the other bench. The man's eyes interrogated him, hungrily. The boy's were shining with the impersonal zeal of the translator.

"De lady says dat she's on to de fact dat gals is dead easy when a feller come spielin' ghost stories and tryin' to make up, and dat's why she won't listen to no soft-soap. She says she caught yer dead to rights, huggin' a bunch o' calico in de hot-house. She side-stepped in to pull some posies and yer was squeezin' der oder gal to beat de band. She says it looked cute, all right all right, but it made her sick. She says yer better git busy, and make a sneak for de train."

The young man gave a low whistle and his eyes flashed with a sudden thought. His hand flew to the inside pocket of his coat, and drew out a handful of letters. Selecting one, he handed it to the boy, following it with a silver dollar from his vest-pocket.

"Give that letter to the lady," he said, "and ask her to read it. Tell her that it should explain the situation. Tell her that, if she had mingled a little trust with her conception of the ideal, much heartache might have been avoided. Tell her that loyalty she prizes so much has never wavered. Tell her I am waiting for an answer."

The messenger stood before the lady.

"De gent says he's had de ski-bunk put on him widout no cause. He says he's no bum guy; and, lady, yer read dat letter, and I'll bet yer he's a white sport, all right."

The young lady unfolded the letter, somewhat doubtfully, and read it.

DEAR DR. ARNOLD: I want to thank you for your most kind and opportune aid to my daughter last Friday evening, when she was overcome by an attack of her old heart-trouble in the conservatory at Mrs. Waldron's reception. Had you not been near to catch her as she fell and to render proper attention, we might have lost her. I would be glad if you would call and undertake the treatment of her case.

GRATEFULLY YOURS,
ROBERT ASHBURTON

The young lady refolded the letter, and handed it to the boy.

"De gent wants an answer," said the messenger. "What's de word?"

The lady's eyes suddenly flashed on him, bright, smiling and wet.

"Tell that guy on the other bench," she said, with a happy, tremulous laugh, "that his girl wants him."

—from *The Four Million* (1906)

THE GIFT OF THE MAGI

One dollar and eighty-seven cents. That was all. And sixty cents of it was in pennies. Pennies saved one and two at a time by bulldozing the grocer and the vegetable man and the butcher until one's cheeks burned with the silent imputation of parsimony that such close dealing implied. Three times Della counted it. One dollar and eighty-seven cents. And the next day would be Christmas.

There was clearly nothing to do but flop down on the shabby little couch and howl. So Della did it. Which instigates the moral reflection that life is made up of sobs, sniffles, and smiles, with sniffles predominating.

While the mistress of the home is gradually subsiding from the first stage to the second, take a look at the home. A furnished flat at $8 per week. It did not exactly beggar description, but it certainly had that word on the lookout for the mendicancy squad.

In the vestibule below was a letter-box into which no letter would go, and an electric button from which no mortal finger could coax a ring. Also appertaining thereunto was a card bearing the name "Mr. James Dillingham Young."

The "Dillingham" had been flung to the breeze during a former period of prosperity when its possessor was being paid $30 per week. Now, when the income was shrunk to $20, the letters of "Dillingham" looked blurred, as though they were thinking seriously of contracting to a modest and unassuming D. But whenever Mr. James Dillingham Young came home and reached his flat above he was called "Jim" and greatly hugged by Mrs. James Dillingham Young, already introduced to you as Della. Which is all very good.

Della finished her cry and attended to her cheeks with the pow-

der rag. She stood by the window and looked out dully at a gray
cat walking a gray fence in a gray backyard. Tomorrow would be
Christmas Day, and she had only $1.87 with which to buy Jim a
present. She had been saving every penny she could for months,
with this result. Twenty dollars a week doesn't go far. Expenses
had been greater than she had calculated. They always are. Only
$1.87 to buy a present for Jim. Her Jim. Many a happy hour she
had spent planning for something nice for him. Something fine
and rare and sterling—something just a little bit near to being worthy of the honor of being owned by Jim.

There was a pier-glass* between the windows of the room. Perhaps you have seen a pier-glass in an $8 flat. A very thin and very
agile person may, by observing his reflection in a rapid sequence of
longitudinal strips, obtain a fairly accurate conception of his looks.
Della, being slender, had mastered the art.

Suddenly she whirled from the window and stood before the
glass. Her eyes were shining brilliantly, but her face had lost its
color within twenty seconds. Rapidly she pulled down her hair and
let it fall to its full length.

Now, there were two possessions of the James Dillingham
Youngs in which they both took a mighty pride. One was Jim's
gold watch that had been his father's and his grandfather's. The
other was Della's hair. Had the Queen of Sheba lived in the flat
across the airshaft, Della would have let her hair hang out the window some day to dry just to depreciate Her Majesty's jewels and
gifts. Had King Solomon[1] been the janitor, with all his treasures
piled up in the basement, Jim would have pulled out his watch every
time he passed, just to see him pluck at his beard from envy.

So now Della's beautiful hair fell about her rippling and shining
like a cascade of brown waters. It reached below her knee and made
itself almost a garment for her. And then she did it up again nervously and quickly. Once she faltered for a minute and stood still
while a tear or two splashed on the worn red carpet.

On went her old brown jacket; on went her old brown hat. With
a whirl of skirts and with the brilliant sparkle still in her eyes, she
fluttered out the door and down the stairs to the street.

---

*Tall, thin mirror intended to fill a space—for example, between windows.

Where she stopped the sign read: "Mme. Sofronie. Hair Goods of All Kinds." One flight up Della ran, and collected herself, panting. Madame, large, too white, chilly, hardly looked the "Sofronie."

"Will you buy my hair?" asked Della.

"I buy hair," said Madame. "Take yer hat off and let's have a sight at the looks of it."

Down rippled the brown cascade.

"Twenty dollars," said Madame, lifting the mass with a practised hand.

"Give it to me quick," said Della.

Oh, and the next two hours tripped by on rosy wings. Forget the hashed metaphor. She was ransacking the stores for Jim's present.

She found it at last. It surely had been made for Jim and no one else. There was no other like it in any of the stores, and she had turned all of them inside out. It was a platinum fob chain simple and chaste in design, properly proclaiming its value by substance alone and not by meretricious ornamentation—as all good things should do. It was even worthy of The Watch. As soon as she saw it she knew that it must be Jim's. It was like him. Quietness and value—the description applied to both. Twenty-one dollars they took from her for it, and she hurried home with the 87 cents. With that chain on his watch Jim might be properly anxious about the time in any company. Grand as the watch was, he sometimes looked at it on the sly on account of the old leather strap that he used in place of a chain.

When Della reached home her intoxication gave way a little to prudence and reason. She got out her curling irons and lighted the gas and went to work repairing the ravages made by generosity added to love. Which is always a tremendous task, dear friends— a mammoth task.

Within forty minutes her head was covered with tiny, close-lying curls that made her look wonderfully like a truant schoolboy. She looked at her reflection in the mirror long, carefully, and critically.

"If Jim doesn't kill me," she said to herself, "before he takes a second look at me, he'll say I look like a Coney Island chorus girl.[2] But what could I do—oh! what could I do with a dollar and eighty-seven cents?"

At 7 o'clock the coffee was made and the frying-pan was on the back of the stove hot and ready to cook the chops.

Jim was never late. Della doubled the fob chain in her hand and sat on the corner of the table near the door that he always entered. Then she heard his step on the stair away down on the first flight, and she turned white for just a moment. She had a habit of saying little silent prayers about the simple everyday things, and now she whispered: "Please God, make him think I am still pretty."

The door opened and Jim stepped in and closed it. He looked thin and very serious. Poor fellow, he was only twenty-two—and to be burdened with a family! He needed a new overcoat and he was without gloves.

Jim stopped inside the door, as immovable as a setter at the scent of quail. His eyes were fixed upon Della, and there was an expression in them that she could not read, and it terrified her. It was not anger, nor surprise, nor disapproval, nor horror, nor any of the sentiments that she had been prepared for. He simply stared at her fixedly with that peculiar expression on his face.

Della wriggled off the table and went for him.

"Jim, darling," she cried, "don't look at me that way. I had my hair cut off and sold it because I couldn't have lived through Christmas without giving you a present. It'll grow out again—you won't mind, will you? I just had to do it. My hair grows awfully fast. Say 'Merry Christmas!' Jim, and let's be happy. You don't know what a nice—what a beautiful, nice gift I've got for you."

"You've cut off your hair?" asked Jim, laboriously, as if he had not arrived at that patent fact yet even after the hardest mental labor.

"Cut it off and sold it," said Della. "Don't you like me just as well, anyhow? I'm me without my hair, ain't I?"

Jim looked about the room curiously.

"You say your hair is gone?" he said, with an air almost of idiocy.

"You needn't look for it," said Della. "It's sold, I tell you—sold and gone, too. It's Christmas Eve, boy. Be good to me, for it went for you. Maybe the hairs of my head were numbered," she went on with a sudden serious sweetness, "but nobody could ever count my love for you. Shall I put the chops on, Jim?"

Out of his trance Jim seemed quickly to wake. He enfolded his

Della. For ten seconds let us regard with discreet scrutiny some inconsequential object in the other direction. Eight dollars a week or a million a year—what is the difference? A mathematician or a wit would give you the wrong answer. The magi brought valuable gifts,[3] but that was not among them. This dark assertion will be illuminated later on.

Jim drew a package from his overcoat pocket and threw it upon the table.

"Don't make any mistake, Dell," he said, "about me. I don't think there's anything in the way of a haircut or a shave or a shampoo that could make me like my girl any less. But if you'll unwrap that package you may see why you had me going a while at first."

White fingers and nimble tore at the string and paper. And then an ecstatic scream of joy; and then, alas! a quick feminine change to hysterical tears and wails, necessitating the immediate employment of all the comforting powers of the lord of the flat.

For there lay The Combs—the set of combs, side and back, that Della had worshipped for long in a Broadway window. Beautiful combs, pure tortoise shell, with jewelled rims—just the shade to wear in the beautiful vanished hair. They were expensive combs, she knew, and her heart had simply craved and yearned over them without the least hope of possession. And now, they were hers, but the tresses that should have adorned the coveted adornments were gone.

But she hugged them to her bosom, and at length she was able to look up with dim eyes and a smile and say: "My hair grows so fast, Jim!"

And then Della leaped up like a little singed cat and cried, "Oh, oh!"

Jim had not yet seen his beautiful present. She held it out to him eagerly upon her open palm. The dull precious metal seemed to flash with a reflection of her bright and ardent spirit.

"Isn't it a dandy, Jim? I hunted all over town to find it. You'll have to look at the time a hundred times a day now. Give me your watch. I want to see how it looks on it."

Instead of obeying, Jim tumbled down on the couch and put his hands under the back of his head and smiled.

"Dell," said he, "let's put our Christmas presents away and keep 'em a while. They're too nice to use just at present. I sold the watch to get the money to buy your combs. And now suppose you put the chops on."

The magi, as you know, were wise men—wonderfully wise men—who brought gifts to the Babe in the manger. They invented the art of giving Christmas presents. Being wise, their gifts were no doubt wise ones, possibly bearing the privilege of exchange in case of duplication. And here I have lamely related to you the uneventful chronicle of two foolish children in a flat who most unwisely sacrificed for each other the greatest treasures of their house. But in a last word to the wise of these days let it be said that of all who give gifts these two were the wisest. Of all who give and receive gifts, such as they are wisest. Everywhere they are wisest. They are the magi.

—from *The Four Million* (1906)

THE LOVE-PHILTRE
OF IKEY SCHOENSTEIN

The Blue Light Drug Store is downtown, between the Bowery and First Avenue, where the distance between the two streets is the shortest. The Blue Light does not consider that pharmacy is a thing of bric-à-brac, scent and ice-cream soda. If you ask it for pain-killer it will not give you a bonbon. The Blue Light scorns the labor-saving arts of modern pharmacy. It macerates its opium and percolates its own laudanum and paregoric. To this day pills are made behind its tall prescription desk—pills rolled out on its own pill-tile, divided with a spatula, rolled with the finger and thumb, dusted with calcined magnesia and delivered in little round paste-board pill-boxes. The store is on a corner about which coveys of ragged-plumed, hilarious children play and become candidates for the cough drops and soothing syrups that wait for them inside.[1]

Ikey Schoenstein was the night clerk of the Blue Light and the friend of his customers. Thus it is on the East Side, where the heart of pharmacy is not glacé. There, as it should be, the druggist is a counsellor, a confessor, an adviser, an able and willing missionary and mentor whose learning is respected, whose occult wisdom is venerated and whose medicine is often poured, untasted, into the gutter. Therefore Ikey's corniform* bespectacled nose and narrow, knowledge-bowed figure was well known in the vicinity of the Blue Light, and his advice and notice were much desired.

Ikey roomed and breakfasted at Mrs. Riddle's two squares away. Mrs. Riddle had a daughter named Rosy. The circumlocution has been in vain—you must have guessed it—Ikey adored Rosy. She

*Horn-shaped.

tinctured all his thoughts; she was the compound extract of all that
was chemically pure and officinal—the dispensatory contained
nothing equal to her. But Ikey was timid, and his hopes remained
insoluble in the menstruum of his backwardness and fears. Behind
his counter he was a superior being, calmly conscious of special
knowledge and worth; outside he was a weak-kneed, purblind,
motorman-cursed rambler, with ill-fitting clothes stained with
chemicals and smelling of socotrine aloes and valerianate of ammonia.

The fly in Ikey's ointment (thrice welcome, pat trope!)* was
Chunk McGowan.

Mr. McGowan was also striving to catch the bright smiles tossed
about by Rosy. But he was no out-fielder as Ikey was; he picked
them off the bat. At the same time he was Ikey's friend and customer, and often dropped in at the Blue Light Drug Store to have
a bruise painted with iodine or get a cut rubber-plastered after a
pleasant evening spent along the Bowery.

One afternoon McGowan drifted in in his silent, easy way, and
sat, comely, smooth-faced, hard, indomitable, good-natured, upon
a stool.

"Ikey," said he, when his friend had fetched his mortar and sat
opposite, grinding gum benzoin to a powder, "get busy with your
ear. It's drugs for me if you've got the line I need."

Ikey scanned the countenance of Mr. McGowan for the usual
evidence of conflict, but found none.

"Take your coat off," he ordered. "I guess already that you have
been stuck in the ribs with a knife. I have many times told you
those Dagoes† would do you up."

Mr. McGowan smiled. "Not them," he said. "Not any Dagoes.
But you've located the diagnosis all right enough—it's under my
coat, near the ribs. Say! Ikey—Rosy and me are goin' to run away
and get married to-night."

Ikey's left forefinger was doubled over the edge of the mortar,
holding it steady. He gave it a wild rap with the pestle, but felt it

---

*Appropriate figure of speech.
†Term used, usually disparagingly, to refer to people of Italian or Spanish descent.

not. Meanwhile Mr. McGowan's smile faded to a look of perplexed gloom.

"That is," he continued, "if she keeps in the notion until the time comes. We've been layin' pipes for the getaway for two weeks. One day she says she will; the same evenin' she says nixy. We've agreed on to-night, and Rosy's stuck to the affirmative this time for two whole days. But it's five hours yet till the time, and I'm afraid she'll stand me up when it comes to the scratch."

"You said you wanted drugs," remarked Ikey.

Mr. McGowan looked ill at ease and harassed—a condition opposed to his usual line of demeanor. He made a patent-medicine almanac into a roll and fitted it with unprofitable carefulness about his finger.

"I wouldn't have this double handicap make a false start to-night for a million," he said. "I've got a little flat up in Harlem all ready, with chrysanthemums on the table and a kettle ready to boil. And I've engaged a pulpit pounder to be ready at his house for us at 9.30. It's got to come off. And if Rosy don't change her mind again!"—Mr. McGowan ceased, a prey to his doubts.

"I don't see then yet," said Ikey, shortly, "what makes it that you talk of drugs, or what I can be doing about it."

"Old man Riddle don't like me a little bit," went on the uneasy suitor, bent upon marshalling his arguments. "For a week he hasn't let Rosy step outside the door with me. If it wasn't for losin' a boarder they'd have bounced me long ago. I'm makin' $20 a week and she'll never regret flyin' the coop with Chunk McGowan."

"You will excuse me, Chunk," said Ikey. "I must make a prescription that is to be called for soon."

"Say," said McGowan, looking up suddenly, "say, Ikey, ain't there a drug of some kind—some kind of powders that'll make a girl like you better if you give 'em to her?"

Ikey's lip beneath his nose curled with the scorn of superior enlightenment; but before he could answer, McGowan continued:

"Tim Lacy told me he got some once from a croaker uptown and fed 'em to his girl in soda water. From the very first dose he was ace-high and everybody else looked like thirty cents to her. They was married in less than two weeks."

Strong and simple was Chunk McGowan. A better reader of

men than Ikey was could have seen that his tough frame was strung upon fine wires. Like a good general who was about to invade the enemy's territory he was seeking to guard every point against possible failure.

"I thought," went on Chunk, hopefully, "that if I had one of them powders to give Rosy when I see her at supper to-night it might brace her up and keep her from reneging on the proposition to skip. I guess she don't need a mule team to drag her away, but women are better at coaching than they are at running bases. If the stuff'll work just for a couple of hours it'll do the trick."

"When is this foolishness of running away to be happening?" asked Ikey.

"Nine o'clock," said Mr. McGowan. "Supper's at seven. At eight Rosy goes to bed with a headache, at nine old Parvenzano lets me through to his backyard, where there's a board off Riddle's fence, next door. I go under her window and help her down the fire-escape. We've got to make it early on the preacher's account. It's all dead easy if Rosy don't balk when the flag drops. Can you fix me one of them powders, Ikey?"

Ikey Schoenstein rubbed his nose slowly.

"Chunk," said he, "it is of drugs of that nature that pharmaceutists must have much carefulness. To you alone of my acquaintance would I intrust a powder like that. But for you I shall make it, and you shall see how it makes Rosy to think of you."

Ikey went behind the prescription desk. There he crushed to a powder two soluble tablets, each containing a quarter of a grain of morphia.* To them he added a little sugar of milk to increase the bulk, and folded the mixture neatly in a white paper. Taken by an adult this powder would insure several hours of heavy slumber without danger to the sleeper. This he handed to Chunk McGowan, telling him to administer it in a liquid if possible, and received the hearty thanks of the backyard Lochinvar.[2]

The subtlety of Ikey's action becomes apparent upon recital of his subsequent move. He sent a messenger for Mr. Riddle and disclosed the plans of Mr. McGowan for eloping with Rosy. Mr.

---

*Morphine, an addictive narcotic and powerful soporific.

Riddle was a stout man, brick-dusty of complexion and sudden in action.

"Much obliged," he said, briefly, to Ikey. "The lazy Irish loafer! My own room's just above Rosy's. I'll just go up there myself after supper and load the shot-gun and wait. If he comes in my backyard he'll go away in a ambulance instead of a bridal chaise."

With Rosy held in the clutches of Morpheus for a many-hours deep slumber, and the blood-thirsty parent waiting, armed and forewarned, Ikey felt that his rival was close, indeed, upon discomfiture.

All night in the Blue Light Drug Store he waited at his duties for chance news of the tragedy, but none came.

At eight o'clock in the morning the day clerk arrived and Ikey started hurriedly for Mrs. Riddle's to learn the outcome. And, lo! as he stepped out of the store who but Chunk McGowan sprang from a passing street car and grasped his hand—Chunk McGowan with a victor's smile and flushed with joy.

"Pulled it off," said Chunk with Elysium* in his grin. "Rosy hit the fire-escape on time to a second, and we was under the wire at the Reverend's at 9.30¼. She's up at the flat—she cooked eggs this mornin' in a blue kimono—Lord! how lucky I am! You must pace up some day, Ikey, and feed with us. I've got a job down near the bridge, and that's where I'm heading for now."

"The—the—powder?" stammered Ikey.

"Oh, that stuff you gave me!" said Chunk, broadening his grin; "well, it was this way. I sat down at the supper table last night at Riddle's, and I looked at Rosy, and I says to myself, 'Chunk, if you get the girl get her on the square—don't try any hocus-pocus with a thoroughbred like her.' And I keeps the paper you give me in my pocket. And then my lamps fall on another party present, who, I says to myself, is failin' in a proper affection toward his comin' son-in-law, so I watches my chance and dumps that powder in old man Riddle's coffee—see?"

—from *The Four Million* (1906)

---

*Dwelling place of the blessed in Greek mythology.

MAMMON AND THE ARCHER

Old Anthony Rockwall, retired manufacturer and proprietor of Rockwall's Eureka Soap, looked out the library window of his Fifth Avenue mansion and grinned. His neighbour to the right—the aristocratic clubman, G. Van Schuylight Suffolk-Jones—came out to his waiting motor-car, wrinkling a contumelious* nostril, as usual, at the Italian renaissance sculpture of the soap palace's front elevation.

"Stuck-up old statuette of nothing doing!" commented the ex-Soap King. "The Eden Musée'll† get that old frozen Nesselrode yet if he don't watch out. I'll have this house painted red, white, and blue next summer and see if that'll make his Dutch nose turn up any higher."

And then Anthony Rockwall, who never cared for bells, went to the door of his library and shouted "Mike!" in the same voice that had once chipped off pieces of the welkin‡ on the Kansas prairies.

"Tell my son," said Anthony to the answering menial, "to come in here before he leaves the house."

When young Rockwall entered the library the old man laid aside his newspaper, looked at him with a kindly grimness on his big, smooth, ruddy countenance, rumpled his mop of white hair with one hand and rattled the keys in his pocket with the other.

"Richard," said Anthony Rockwall, "what do you pay for the soap that you use?"

Richard, only six months home from college, was startled a little.

---

*Insolently abusive.
†Museum (French).
‡The heavens overhead, the sky.

He had not yet taken the measure of this sire of his, who was as full of unexpectedness as a girl at her first party.

"Six dollars a dozen, I think, dad."

"And your clothes?"

"I suppose about sixty dollars, as a rule."

"You're a gentleman," said Anthony, decidedly. "I've heard of these young bloods spending $24 a dozen for soap, and going over the hundred mark for clothes. You've got as much money to waste as any of 'em, and yet you stick to what's decent and moderate. Now I use the old Eureka—not only for sentiment, but it's the purest soap made. Whenever you pay more than 10 cents a cake for soap you buy bad perfumes and labels. But 50 cents is doing very well for a young man in your generation, position and condition. As I said, you're a gentleman. They say it takes three generations to make one. They're off. Money'll do it as slick as soap grease. It's made you one. By hokey! it's almost made one of me. I'm nearly as impolite and disagreeable and ill-mannered as these two old knickerbocker gents on each side of me that can't sleep of nights because I bought in between 'em."

"There are some things that money can't accomplish," remarked young Rockwall, rather gloomily.

"Now, don't say that," said old Anthony, shocked. "I bet my money on money every time. I've been through the encyclopædia down to Y looking for something you can't buy with it; and I expect to have to take up the appendix next week. I'm for money against the field. Tell me something money won't buy."

"For one thing," answered Richard, rankling a little, "it won't buy one into the exclusive circles of society."

"Oho! won't it?" thundered the champion of the root of evil. "You tell me where your exclusive circles would be if the first Astor hadn't had the money to pay for his steerage passage over?"[1]

Richard sighed.

"And that's what I was coming to," said the old man, less boisterously. "That's why I asked you to come in. There's something going wrong with you, boy. I've been noticing it for two weeks. Out with it. I guess I could lay my hands on eleven millions within twenty-four hours, besides the real estate. If it's your liver, there's the *Rambler* down in the bay, coaled, and ready to steam down to the Bahamas in two days."

"Not a bad guess, dad; you haven't missed it far."

"Ah," said Anthony, keenly; "what's her name?"

Richard began to walk up and down the library floor. There was enough comradeship and sympathy in this crude old father of his to draw his confidence.

"Why don't you ask her?" demanded old Anthony. "She'll jump at you. You've got the money and the looks, and you're a decent boy. Your hands are clean. You've got no Eureka soap on 'em. You've been to college, but she'll overlook that."

"I haven't had a chance," said Richard.

"Make one," said Anthony. "Take her for a walk in the park, or a straw ride, or walk home with her from church. Chance! Pshaw!"

"You don't know the social mill, dad. She's part of the stream that turns it. Every hour and minute of her time is arranged for days in advance. I must have that girl, dad, or this town is a black-jack swamp forevermore. And I can't write it—I can't do that."

"Tut!" said the old man. "Do you mean to tell me that with all the money I've got you can't get an hour or two of a girl's time for yourself?"

"I've put it off too late. She's going to sail for Europe at noon day after to-morrow for a two years' stay. I'm to see her alone tomorrow evening for a few minutes. She's at Larchmont* now at her aunt's. I can't go there. But I'm allowed to meet her with a cab at the Grand Central Station to-morrow evening at the 8.30 train. We drive down Broadway to Wallack's at a gallop, where her mother and a box party will be waiting for us in the lobby. Do you think she would listen to a declaration from me during that six or eight minutes under those circumstances? No. And what chance would I have in the theatre or afterward? None. No, dad, this is one tangle that your money can't unravel. We can't buy one minute of time with cash; if we could, rich people would live longer. There's no hope of getting a talk with Miss Lantry before she sails."

"All right, Richard, my boy," said old Anthony, cheerfully. "You

---

*Town north of New York City, once a fashionable resort.

may run along down to your club now. I'm glad it ain't your liver. But don't forget to burn a few punk sticks in the joss house* to the great god Mazuma† from time to time. You say money won't buy time? Well, of course, you can't order eternity wrapped up and delivered at your residence for a price, but I've seen Father Time get pretty bad stone bruises on his heels when he walked through the gold diggings."

That night came Aunt Ellen, gentle, sentimental, wrinkled, sighing, oppressed by wealth, in to Brother Anthony at his evening paper, and began discourse on the subject of lovers' woes.

"He told me all about it," said Brother Anthony, yawning. "I told him my bank account was at his service. And then he began to knock money. Said money couldn't help. Said the rules of society couldn't be bucked for a yard by a team of ten-millionaires."

"Oh, Anthony," sighed Aunt Ellen, "I wish you would not think so much of money. Wealth is nothing where a true affection is concerned. Love is all-powerful. If he only had spoken earlier! She could not have refused our Richard. But now I fear it is too late. He will have no opportunity to address her. All your gold cannot bring happiness to your son."

At eight o'clock the next evening Aunt Ellen took a quaint old gold ring from a moth-eaten case and gave it to Richard.

"Wear it to-night, nephew," she begged. "Your mother gave it to me. Good luck in love she said it brought. She asked me to give it to you when you had found the one you loved."

Young Rockwall took the ring reverently and tried it on his smallest finger. It slipped as far as the second joint and stopped. He took it off and stuffed it into his vest pocket, after the manner of man. And then he 'phoned for his cab.

At the station he captured Miss Lantry out of the gabbing mob at eight thirty-two.

"We mustn't keep mamma and the others waiting," said she.

"To Wallack's Theatre as fast as you can drive!" said Richard, loyally.

They whirled up Forty-second to Broadway, and then down the

---

*Chinese temple.
†Slang for cash.

white-starred lane that leads from the soft meadows of sunset to
the rocky hills of morning.

At Thirty-fourth Street young Richard quickly thrust up the trap
and ordered the cabman to stop.

"I've dropped a ring," he apologized, as he climbed out. "It was
my mother's, and I'd hate to lose it. I won't detain you a minute—I
saw where it fell."

In less than a minute he was back in the cab with the ring.

But within that minute a crosstown car had stopped directly in
front of the cab. The cab-man tried to pass to the left, but a heavy
express wagon cut him off. He tried the right and had to back away
from a furniture van that had no business to be there. He tried to
back out, but dropped his reins and swore dutifully. He was blockaded in a tangled mess of vehicles and horses.

One of those street blockades had occurred that sometimes tie
up commerce and movement quite suddenly in the big city.

"Why don't you drive on?" said Miss Lantry impatiently. "We'll
be late."

Richard stood up in the cab and looked around. He saw a con-
gested flood of wagons, trucks, cabs, vans and street cars filling the
vast space where Broadway, Sixth Avenue, and Thirty-fourth Street
cross one another as a twenty-six inch maiden fills her twenty-two
inch girdle. And still from all the cross streets they were hurrying
and rattling toward the converging point at full speed, and hurling
themselves into the straggling mass, locking wheels and adding
their drivers' imprecations to the clamor. The entire traffic of Manhattan seemed to have jammed itself around them. The oldest New
Yorker among the thousands of spectators that lined the sidewalks
had not witnessed a street blockade of the proportions of this one.

"I'm very sorry," said Richard, as he resumed his seat, "but it
looks as if we are stuck. They won't get this jumble loosened up in
an hour. It was my fault. If I hadn't dropped the ring we—"

"Let me see the ring," said Miss Lantry. "Now that it can't be
helped, I don't care. I think theatres are stupid, anyway."

At 11 o'clock that night somebody tapped lightly on Anthony
Rockwall's door.

"Come in," shouted Anthony, who was in a red dressing-gown,
reading a book of piratical adventures.

Somebody was Aunt Ellen, looking like a gray-haired angel that had been left on earth by mistake.

"They're engaged, Anthony," she said, softly. "She has promised to marry our Richard. On their way to the theatre there was a street blockade, and it was two hours before their cab could get out of it.

"And oh, Brother Anthony, don't ever boast of the power of money again. A little emblem of true love—a little ring that symbolized unending and unmercenary affection—was the cause of our Richard finding his happiness. He dropped it in the street, and got out to recover it. And before they could continue the blockade occurred. He spoke to his love and won her there while the cab was hemmed in. Money is dross compared with true love, Anthony."

"All right," said old Anthony. "I'm glad the boy has got what he wanted. I told him I wouldn't spare any expense in the matter if—"

"But, Brother Anthony, what good could your money have done?"

"Sister," said Anthony Rockwall. "I've got my pirate in a devil of a scrape. His ship has just been scuttled, and he's too good a judge of the value of money to let drown. I wish you would let me go on with this chapter."

The story should end here. I wish it would as heartily as you who read it wish it did. But we must go to the bottom of the well for truth.

The next day a person with red hands and a blue polka-dot necktie, who called himself Kelly, called at Anthony Rockwall's house, and was at once received in the library.

"Well," said Anthony, reaching for his check-book, "it was a good bilin' of soap. Let's see—you had $5,000 in cash."

"I paid out $300 more of my own," said Kelly. "I had to go a little above the estimate. I got the express wagons and cabs mostly for $5; but the trucks and two-horse teams mostly raised me to $10. The motormen wanted $10, and some of the loaded teams $20. The cops struck me hardest—$50 I paid two, and the rest $20 and $25. But didn't it work beautiful. Mr. Rockwall? I'm glad William A. Brady[2] wasn't onto that little outdoor vehicle mob scene. I wouldn't want William to break his heart with jealousy. And never a rehearsal, either! The boys was on time to the fraction of a second. It was two hours before a snake could get below Greeley's statue."[3]

"Thirteen hundred—there you are, Kelly," said Anthony, tearing off a check. "Your thousand, and the $300 you were out. You don't despise money, do you, Kelly?"

"Me?" said Kelly. "I can lick the man that invented poverty."

Anthony called Kelly when he was at the door.

"You didn't notice," said he, "anywhere in the tie-up, a kind of a fat boy without any clothes on shooting arrows around with a bow, did you?"

"Why, no," said Kelly, mystified. "I didn't. If he was like you say, maybe the cops pinched him before I got there."

"I thought the little rascal wouldn't be on hand," chuckled Anthony. "Good-by, Kelly."

—from *The Four Million* (1906)

THE MEMENTO

Miss Lynnette D'Armande turned her back on Broadway. This was but tit for tat, because Broadway had often done the same thing to Miss D'Armande. Still, the "tats" seemed to have it, for the ex-leading lady of the "Reaping the Whirlwind" company had everything to ask of Broadway, while there was no vice-versâ.

So Miss Lynnette D'Armande turned the back of her chair to her window that overlooked Broadway, and sat down to stitch in time the lisle-thread* heel of a black silk stocking. The tumult and glitter of the roaring Broadway beneath her window had no charm for her; what she greatly desired was the stifling air of a dressing-room on that fairyland street and the roar of an audience gathered in that capricious quarter. In the meantime, those stockings must not be neglected. Silk does wear out so, but—after all, isn't it just the only goods there is?

The Hotel Thalia looks on Broadway as Marathon looks on the sea.[1] It stands like a gloomy cliff above the whirlpool where the tides of two great thoroughfares† clash. Here the player-bands gather at the end of their wanderings, to loosen the buskin and dust the sock. Thick in the streets around it are booking-offices, theatres, agents, schools, and the lobster-palaces to which those thorny paths lead.

Wandering through the eccentric halls of the dim and fusty Thalia, you seem to have found yourself in some great ark or caravan about to sail, or fly, or roll away on wheels. About the house lingers

---

*Fine, smooth thread.
†Broadway and Seventh Avenue in New York City, placing the hotel in Times Square, the center of the entertainment district.

a sense of unrest, of expectation, of transientness, even of anxiety and apprehension. The halls are a labyrinth. Without a guide, you wander like a lost soul in a Sam Loyd puzzle.[2]

Turning any corner, a dressing-sack* or a *cul-de-sac* may bring you up short. You meet alarming tragedians stalking in bath-robes in search of rumored bathrooms. From hundreds of rooms come the buzz of talk, scraps of new and old songs, and the ready laughter of the convened players.

Summer has come; their companies have disbanded, and they take their rest in their favorite caravansary, while they besiege the managers for engagements for the coming season.

At this hour of the afternoon the day's work of tramping the rounds of the agents' offices is over. Past you, as you ramble distractedly through the mossy halls, flit audible visions of houris,† with veiled, starry eyes, flying tag-ends of things and a swish of silk, bequeathing to the dull hallways an odor of gaiety and a memory of *frangipanni*.‡ Serious young comedians, with versatile Adam's apples, gather in doorways and talk of Booth.[3] Far-reaching from somewhere comes the smell of ham and red cabbage, and the crash of dishes on the American plan.

The indeterminate hum of life in the Thalia is enlivened by the discreet popping—at reasonable and salubrious intervals—of beer-bottle corks. Thus punctuated, life in the genial hostel scans easily—the comma being the favorite mark, semicolons frowned upon, and periods barred.

Miss D'Armande's room was a small one. There was room for her rocker between the dresser and the wash-stand if it were placed longitudinally. On the dresser were its usual accoutrements, plus the ex-leading lady's collected souvenirs of road engagements and photographs of her dearest and best professional friends.

At one of these photographs she looked twice or thrice as she darned, and smiled friendlily.

"I'd like to know where Lee is just this minute," she said, half-aloud.

---

*Woman's loose jacket, worn while dressing.

†Voluptuous, beautiful women; nymphs of paradise in Muslim belief.

‡Perfume derived from the tropical frangipanni flower.

If you had been privileged to view the photograph thus flattered, you would have thought at the first glance that you saw the picture of a many-petalled white flower, blown through the air by a storm. But the floral kingdom was not responsible for that swirl of petalous whiteness.

You saw the filmy, brief skirt of Miss Rosalie Ray as she made a complete heels-over-head turn in her wistaria-entwined swing, far out from the stage, high above the heads of the audience. You saw the camera's inadequate representation of the graceful, strong kick, with which she, at this exciting moment, sent flying, high and far, the yellow silk garter that each evening spun from her agile limb and descended upon the delighted audience below.

You saw, too, amid the black-clothed, mainly masculine patrons of select vaudeville a hundred hands raised with the hope of staying the flight of the brilliant aërial token.

Forty weeks of the best circuits this act had brought Miss Rosalie Ray, for each of two years. She did other things during her twelve minutes—a song and dance, imitations of two or three actors who are but imitations of themselves, and a balancing feat with a step-ladder and feather-duster; but when the blossom-decked swing was let down from the flies, and Miss Rosalie sprang smiling into the seat, with the golden circlet conspicuous in the place whence it was soon to slide and become a soaring and coveted guerdon*—then it was that the audience rose in its seat as a single man—or presumably so—and indorsed the specialty that made Miss Ray's name a favorite in the booking-offices.

At the end of the two years Miss Ray suddenly announced to her dear friend, Miss D'Armande, that she was going to spend the summer at an antediluvian village on the north shore of Long Island, and that the stage would see her no more.

Seventeen minutes after Miss Lynnette D'Armande had expressed her wish to know the whereabouts of her old chum, there were sharp raps at her door.

Doubt not that it was Rosalie Ray. At the shrill command to enter she did so, with something of a tired flutter, and dropped a

---

*Reward.

heavy hand-bag on the floor. Upon my word, it was Rosalie, in a loose, travel-stained automobileless coat, closely tied brown veil with yard-long, flying ends, gray walking-suit and tan oxfords with lavender overgaiters.*

When she threw off her veil and hat, you saw a pretty enough face, now flushed and disturbed by some unusual emotion, and restless, large eyes with discontent marring their brightness. A heavy pile of dull auburn hair, hastily put up, was escaping in crinkly, waving strands and curling, small locks from the confining combs and pins.

The meeting of the two was not marked by the effusion vocal, gymnastical, osculatory† and catechetical‡ that distinguishes the greetings of their unprofessional sisters in society. There was a brief clinch, two simultaneous labial dabs and they stood on the same footing of the old days. Very much like the short salutations of soldiers or of travellers in foreign wilds are the welcomes between the strollers at the corners of their criss-cross roads.

"I've got the hall-room two flights up above yours," said Rosalie, "but I came straight to see you before going up. I didn't know you were here till they told me."

"I've been in since the last of April," said Lynnette. "And I'm going on the road with a 'Fatal Inheritance' company. We open next week in Elizabeth. I thought you'd quit the stage, Lee. Tell me about yourself."

Rosalie settled herself with a skilful wriggle on the top of Miss D'Armande's wardrobe trunk, and leaned her head against the papered wall. From long habit, thus can peripatetic leading ladies and their sisters make themselves as comfortable as though the deepest armchairs embraced them.

"I'm going to tell you, Lynn," she said, with a strangely sardonic and yet carelessly resigned look on her youthful face. "And then to-morrow I'll strike the old Broadway trail again, and wear some more paint off the chairs in the agents' offices. If anybody had told me any time in the last three months up to four o'clock this after-

---

*Coverings for the lower ankle.
†Having to do with kissing.
‡Questioning and answering.

noon that I'd ever listen to that 'Leave-your-name-and-address' rot of the booking bunch again, I'd have given 'em the real Mrs. Fiske laugh.[4] Loan me a handkerchief, Lynn. Gee! but those Long Island trains are fierce. I've got enough soft-coal cinders on my face to go on and play *Topsy*[5] without using the cork. And, speaking of corks—got anything to drink, Lynn?"

Miss D'Armande opened a door of the wash-stand and took out a bottle.

"There's nearly a pint of Manhattan. There's a cluster of carnations in the drinking glass, but——"

"Oh, pass the bottle. Save the glass for company. Thanks! That hits the spot. The same to you. My first drink in three months!

"Yes, Lynn, I quit the stage at the end of last season. I quit it because I was sick of the life. And especially because my heart and soul were sick of men—of the kind of men we stage people have to be up against. You know what the game is to us—it's a fight against 'em all the way down the line from the manager who wants us to try his new motor-car to the bill-posters who want to call us by our front names.

"And the men we have to meet after the show are the worst of all. The stage-door kind, and the manager's friends who take us to supper and show their diamonds and talk about seeing 'Dan' and 'Dave' and 'Charlie' for us. They're beasts, and I hate 'em.

"I tell you, Lynn, it's the girls like us on the stage that ought to be pitied. It's girls from good homes that are honestly ambitious and work hard to rise in the profession, but never do get there. You hear a lot of sympathy sloshed around on chorus girls and their fifteen dollars a week. Piffle! There ain't a sorrow in the chorus that a lobster cannot heal.

"If there's any tears to shed, let 'em fall for the actress that gets a salary of from thirty to forty-five dollars a week for taking a leading part in a bum show. She knows she'll never do any better; but she hangs on for years, hoping for the 'chance' that never comes.

"And the fool plays we have to work in! Having another girl roll you around the stage by the hind legs in a 'Wheelbarrow Chorus' in a musical comedy is dignified drama compared with the idiotic things I've had to do in the thirty-centers.

"But what I hated most was the men—the men leering and

blathering at you across tables, trying to buy you with Würzburger or Extra Dry,* according to their estimate of your price. And the men in the audiences, clapping, yelling, snarling, crowding, writhing, gloating—like a lot of wild beasts, with their eyes fixed on you, ready to eat you up if you come in reach of their claws. Oh, how I hate 'em!

"Well, I'm not telling you much about myself, am I, Lynn?

"I had two hundred dollars saved up, and I cut the stage the first of the summer. I went over on Long Island and found the sweetest little village that ever was, called Soundport, right on the water. I was going to spend the summer there, and study up on elocution, and try to get a class in the fall. There was an old widow lady with a cottage near the beach who sometimes rented a room or two just for company, and she took me in. She had another boarder, too— the Reverend Arthur Lyle.

"Yes, he was the head-liner. You're on, Lynn. I'll tell you all of it in a minute. It's only a one-act play.

"The first time he walked on, Lynn, I felt myself going; the first lines he spoke, he had me. He was different from the men in audiences. He was tall and slim, and you never heard him come in the room, but you *felt* him. He had a face like a picture of a knight—like one of that Round Table bunch[6]—and a voice like a 'cello solo. And his manners!

"Lynn, if you'd take John Drew in his best drawing-room scene[7] and compare the two, you'd have John arrested for disturbing the peace.

"I'll spare you the particulars; but in less than a month Arthur and I were engaged. He preached at a little one-night stand of a Methodist church. There was to be a parsonage the size of a lunchwagon, and hens and honeysuckles when we were married. Arthur used to preach to me a good deal about Heaven, but he never could get my mind quite off those honeysuckles and hens.

"No; I didn't tell him I'd been on the stage. I hated the business and all that went with it; I'd cut it out forever, and I didn't see any use of stirring things up. I was a good girl, and I didn't have any-

---

*Würzburger is a brand of beer, Extra Dry a type of gin.

thing to confess, except being an elocutionist, and that was about all the strain my conscience would stand.

"Oh, I tell you, Lynn, I was happy. I sang in the choir and attended the sewing society, and recited that 'Annie Laurie' thing[8] with the whistling stunt in it, 'in a manner bordering upon the professional,' as the weekly village paper reported it. And Arthur and I went rowing, and walking in the woods, and clamming, and that poky little village seemed to me the best place in the world. I'd have been happy to live there always, too, if——

"But one morning old Mrs. Gurley, the widow lady, got gossipy while I was helping her string beans on the back porch, and began to gush information, as folks who rent out their rooms usually do. Mr. Lyle was her idea of a saint on earth—as he was mine, too. She went over all his virtues and graces, and wound up by telling me that Arthur had had an extremely romantic love-affair, not long before, that had ended unhappily. She didn't seem to be on to the details, but she knew that he had been hit pretty hard. He was paler and thinner, she said, and he had some kind of a remembrance or keepsake of the lady in a little rosewood box that he kept locked in his desk drawer in his study.

" 'Several times,' says she, 'I've seen him gloomerin' over that box of evenings, and he always locks it up right away if anybody comes into the room.'

"Well, you can imagine how long it was before I got Arthur by the wrist and led him down stage and hissed in his ear.

"That same afternoon we were lazying around in a boat among the water-lilies at the edge of the bay.

" 'Arthur,' says I, 'you never told me you'd had another love-affair. But Mrs. Gurley did,' I went on, to let him know I knew. I hate to hear a man lie.

" 'Before you came,' says he, looking me frankly in the eye, 'there was a previous affection—a strong one. Since you know of it, I will be perfectly candid with you.'

" 'I am waiting,' says I.

" 'My dear Ida,' says Arthur—of course I went by my real name, while I was in Soundport—'this former affection was a spiritual one, in fact. Although the lady aroused my deepest sentiments, and was, as I thought, my ideal woman, I never met her, and never spoke to her. It was an ideal love. My love for you, while no less ideal, is different. You wouldn't let that come between us.'

" 'Was she pretty?' I asked.

" 'She was very beautiful,' said Arthur.

" 'Did you see her often?' I asked.

" 'Something like a dozen times,' says he.

" 'Always from a distance?' says I.

" 'Always from quite a distance,' says he.

" 'And you loved her?' I asked.

" 'She seemed my ideal of beauty and grace—and soul,' says Arthur.

" 'And this keepsake that you keep under lock and key, and moon over at times, is that a remembrance from her?'

" 'A memento,' says Arthur, 'that I have treasured.'

" 'Did she send it to you?'

" 'It came to me from her,' says he.

" 'In a roundabout way?' I asked.

" 'Somewhat roundabout,' says he, 'and yet rather direct.'

" 'Why didn't you ever meet her?' I asked. 'Were your positions in life so different?'

" 'She was far above me,' says Arthur. 'Now, Ida,' he goes on, 'this is all of the past. You're not going to be jealous, are you?'

" 'Jealous!' says I. 'Why, man, what are you talking about? It makes me think ten times as much of you as I did before I knew about it.'

"And it did, Lynn—if you can understand it. That ideal love was a new one on me, but it struck me as being the most beautiful and glorious thing I'd ever heard of. Think of a man loving a woman he'd never even spoken to, and being faithful just to what his mind and heart pictured her! Oh, it sounded great to me. The men I'd always known come at you with either diamonds, knock-out-drops or a raise of salary,—and their ideals!—well, we'll say no more.

"Yes, it made me think more of Arthur than I did before. I couldn't be jealous of that far-away divinity that he used to worship, for I was going to have him myself. And I began to look upon him as a saint on earth, just as old lady Gurley did.

"About four o'clock this afternoon a man came to the house for Arthur to go and see somebody that was sick among his church bunch. Old lady Gurley was taking her afternoon snore on a couch, so that left me pretty much alone.

"In passing by Arthur's study I looked in, and saw his bunch of keys hanging in the drawer of his desk, where he'd forgotten 'em. Well, I guess we're all to the Mrs. Bluebeard now and then,[9] ain't we, Lynn? I made up my mind I'd have a look at that memento he kept so secret. Not that I cared what it was—it was just curiosity.

"While I was opening the drawer I imagined one or two things it might be. I thought it might be a dried rosebud she'd dropped down to him from a balcony, or maybe a picture of her he'd cut out of a magazine, she being so high up in the world.

"I opened the drawer, and there was the rosewood casket about the size of a gent's collar box. I found the little key in the bunch that fitted it, and unlocked it and raised the lid.

"I took one look at that memento, and then I went to my room and packed my trunk. I threw a few things into my grip, gave my hair a flirt or two with a side-comb, put on my hat, and went in and gave the old lady's foot a kick. I'd tried awfully hard to use proper and correct language while I was there for Arthur's sake, and I had the habit down pat, but it left me then.

" 'Stop sawing gourds,' says I, 'and sit up and take notice. The ghost's about to walk. I'm going away from here, and I owe you eight dollars. The expressman will call for my trunk.'

"I handed her the money.

" 'Dear me, Miss Crosby!' says she. 'Is anything wrong? I thought you were pleased here. Dear me, young women are so hard to understand, and so different from what you expect 'em to be.'

" 'You're damn right,' says I. 'Some of 'em are. But you can't say that about men. *When you know one man you know 'em all!* That settles the human-race question.'

"And then I caught the four-thirty-eight, soft-coal unlimited; and here I am."

" 'You didn't tell me what was in the box, Lee," said Miss D'Armande, anxiously.

"One of those yellow silk garters that I used to kick off my leg into the audience during that old vaudeville swing act of mine. Is there any of the cocktail left, Lynn?"

—from *The Voice of the City* (1908)

SPRINGTIME À LA CARTE

It was a day in March.

Never, never begin a story this way when you write one. No opening could possibly be worse. It is unimaginative, flat dry, and likely to consist of mere wind. But in this instance it is allowable. For the following paragraph, which should have inaugurated the narrative, is too wildly extravagant and preposterous to be flaunted in the face of the reader without preparation.

Sarah was crying over her bill of fare.

Think of a New York girl shedding tears on the menu card!

To account for this you will be allowed to guess that the lobsters were all out, or that she had sworn ice-cream off during Lent or that she had ordered onions, or that she had just come from a Hackett matinée.[1] And then, all these theories being wrong, you will please let the story proceed.

The gentleman who announced that the world was an oyster which he with his sword would open made a larger hit than he deserved. It is not difficult to open an oyster with a sword. But did you ever notice any one try to open the terrestrial bivalve with a typewriter? Like to wait for a dozen raw opened that way?

Sarah had managed to pry apart the shells with her unhandy weapon far enough to nibble a wee bit at the cold and clammy world within. She knew no more shorthand than if she had been a graduate in stenography just let slip upon the world by a business college. So, not being able to stenog, she could not enter that bright galaxy of office talent. She was a freelance typewriter and canvassed for odd jobs of copying.

The most brilliant and crowning feat of Sarah's battle with the world was the deal she made with Schulenberg's Home Restaurant. The restaurant was next door to the old red brick in which she hall-roomed. One evening after dining at Schulenberg's 40-cent, five-course *table d'hôte** (served as fast as you throw the five baseballs at the colored gentleman's head),[2] Sarah took away with her the bill of fare. It was written in an almost unreadable script neither English nor German, and so arranged that if you were not careful you began with a toothpick and rice pudding and ended with soup and the day of the week.

The next day Sarah showed Schulenberg a neat card on which the menu was beautifully typewritten with the viands[†] temptingly marshalled under their right and proper heads from "hor d'œuvre" to "not responsible for over-coats and umbrellas."

Schulenberg became a naturalized citizen on the spot. Before Sarah left him she had him willingly committed to an agreement. She was to furnish typewritten bills of fare for the twenty-one tables in the restaurant—a new bill for each day's dinner, and new ones for breakfast and lunch as often as changes occurred in the food or as neatness required.

In return for this Schulenberg was to send three meals per diem to Sarah's hall room by a waiter—an obsequious one if possible—and furnish her each afternoon with a pencil draft of what Fate had in store for Schulenberg's customers on the morrow.

Mutual satisfaction resulted from the agreement. Schulenberg's patrons now knew what the food they ate was called even if its nature sometimes puzzled them. And Sarah had food during a cold, dull winter, which was the main thing with her.

And then the almanac lied, and said that spring had come. Spring comes when it comes. The frozen snows of January still lay like adamant in the cross-town streets. The hand-organs still played "In the Good Old Summertime," with their December vivacity and expression. Men began to make thirty-day notes to buy Easter dresses. Janitors shut off steam. And when these things happen one may know that the city is still in the clutches of winter.

One afternoon Sarah shivered in her elegant hall bedroom; "house heated; scrupulously clean; conveniences; seen to be appreciated." She had no work to do except Schulenberg's menu cards.

---

*Meal served at a fixed price.
†Meals, victuals.

Sarah sat in her squeaky willow rocker, and looked out the window. The calendar on the wall kept crying to her: "Springtime is here, Sarah—springtime is here, I tell you. Look at me, Sarah, my figures show it. You've got a neat figure yourself, Sarah—a—nice spring-time figure—why do you look out the window so sadly?"

Sarah's room was at the back of the house. Looking out the window she could see the windowless rear brick wall of the box factory on the next street. But the wall was clearest crystal; and Sarah was looking down a grassy lane shaded with cherry trees and elms and bordered with raspberry bushes and Cherokee roses.

Spring's real harbingers are too subtle for the eye and ear. Some must have the flowering crocus, the wood-starring dogwood, the voice of bluebird—even so gross a reminder as the farewell hand-shake of the retiring buckwheat and oyster before they can welcome the Lady in Green to their dull bosoms. But to old earth's choicest kind there come straight, sweet messages from his newest bride, telling them they shall be no stepchildren unless they choose to be.

On the previous summer Sarah had gone into the country and loved a farmer.

(In writing your story never hark back thus. It is bad art, and cripples interest. Let it march, march.)

Sarah stayed two weeks at Sunnybrook Farm. There she learned to love old Farmer Franklin's son Walter. Farmers have been loved and wedded and turned out to grass in less time. But young Walter Franklin was a modern agriculturist. He had a telephone in his cow house, and he could figure up exactly what effect next year's Canada wheat crop would have on potatoes planted in the dark of the moon.

It was in this shaded and raspberried lane that Walter had wooed and won her. And together they had sat and woven a crown of dandelions for her hair. He had immoderately praised the effect of the yellow blossoms against her brown tresses; and she had left the chaplet there, and walked back to the house swinging her straw sailor* in her hands.

They were to marry in the spring—at the very first signs of spring, Walter said. And Sarah came back to the city to pound her typewriter.

---

*A chaplet is a wreath for the head; a sailor is a straw hat with a flat, circular brim.

A knock at the door dispelled Sarah's visions of that happy day. A waiter had brought the rough pencil draft of the Home Restaurant's next day fare in old Schulenberg's angular hand.

Sarah sat down to her typewriter and slipped a card between the rollers. She was a nimble worker. Generally in an hour and a half the twenty-one menu cards were written and ready.

To-day there were more changes on the bill of fare than usual. The soups were lighter; pork was eliminated from the entrées, figuring only with Russian turnips among the roasts. The gracious spirit of spring pervaded the entire menu. Lamb, that lately capered on the greening hillsides, was becoming exploited with the sauce that commemorated its gambols. The song of the oyster, though not silenced, was *dimuendo con amore*.* The frying-pan seemed to be held, inactive, behind the beneficent bars of the broiler. The pie list swelled; the richer puddings had vanished; the sausage, with his drapery wrapped about him, barely lingered in a pleasant thanatopsis† with the buckwheats and the sweet but doomed maple.

Sarah's fingers danced like midgets above a summer stream. Down through the courses she worked, giving each item its position according to its length with an accurate eye.

Just above the desserts came the list of vegetables. Carrots and peas, asparagus on toast, the perennial tomatoes and corn and succotash, lima beans, cabbage—and then——

Sarah was crying over her bill of fare. Tears from the depths of some divine despair rose in her heart and gathered to her eyes. Down went her head on the little typewriter stand; and the keyboard rattled a dry accompaniment to her moist sobs.

For she had received no letter from Walter in two weeks, and the next item on the bill of fare was dandelions—dandelions with some kind of egg—but bother the egg!—dandelions, with whose golden blooms Walter had crowned her his queen of love and future bride—dandelions, the harbingers of spring, her sorrow's crown of sorrow—reminder of her happiest days.

Madam, I dare you to smile until you suffer this test: Let the

---

*Musical direction meaning "softly with emotion."

†Contemplation of death; from the Greek words *thanatos* ("death") and *opsis* ("a view").

Marechal Niel roses that Percy brought you on the night you gave him your heart be served as a salad with French dressing before your eyes at a Schulenberg *table d'hôte*. Had Juliet so seen her love tokens dishonored the sooner would she have sought the lethean herbs[3] of the good apothecary.

But what witch is Spring! Into the great cold city of stone and iron a message had to be sent. There was none to convey it but the little hardy courier of the fields with his rough green coat and modest air. He is a true soldier of fortune, this *dent-de-lion*—this lion's tooth, as the French chefs call him. Flowered, he will assist at love-making, wreathed in my lady's nut-brown hair; young and callow and unblossomed, he goes into the boiling pot and delivers the word of his sovereign mistress.

By and by Sarah forced back her tears. The cards must be written. But, still in a faint, golden glow from her dandelion dream, she fingered the typewriter keys absently for a little while, with her mind and heart in the meadow lane with her young farmer. But soon she came swiftly back to the rock-bound lanes of Manhattan, and the typewriter began to rattle and jump like a strikebreaker's motor car.

At 6 o'clock the waiter brought her dinner and carried away the typewritten bill of fare. When Sarah ate she set aside, with a sigh, the dish of dandelions with its crowning ovarious accompaniment. As this dark mass had been transformed from a bright and love-indorsed flower to be an ignominious vegetable, so had her summer hopes wilted and perished. Love may, as Shakespeare said, feed on itself: but Sarah could not bring herself to eat the dandelions that had graced, as ornaments, the first spiritual banquet of her heart's true affection.

At 7.30 the couple in the next room began to quarrel: the man in the room above sought for A on his flute; the gas went a little lower; three coal wagons started to unload—the only sound of which the phonograph is jealous; cats on the back fences slowly retreated toward Mukden. By these signs Sarah knew that it was time for her to read. She got out "The Cloister and the Hearth,"[4] the best non-selling book of the month, settled her feet on her trunk, and began to wander with Gerard.

The front door bell rang. The landlady answered it. Sarah left Gerard and Denys treed by a bear and listened. Oh, yes; you would, just as she did!

And then a strong voice was heard in the hall below, and Sarah jumped for her door, leaving the book on the floor and the first round easily the bear's.

You have guessed it. She reached the top of the stairs just as her farmer came up, three at a jump, and reaped and garnered her, with nothing left for the gleaners.

"Why haven't you written—oh, why?" cried Sarah.

"New York is a pretty large town," said Walter Franklin. "I came in a week ago to your old address. I found that you went away on a Thursday. That consoled some; it eliminated the possible Friday bad luck. But it didn't prevent my hunting for you with police and otherwise ever since!"

"I wrote!" said Sarah, vehemently.

"Never got it!"

"Then how did you find me?"

The young farmer smiled a springtime smile.

"I dropped into that Home Restaurant next door this evening," said he. "I don't care who knows it; I like a dish of some kind of greens at this time of the year. I ran my eye down that nice type-written bill of fare looking for something in that line. When I got below cabbage I turned my chair over and hollered for the proprietor. He told me where you lived."

"I remember," sighed Sarah, happily. "That was dandelions below cabbage."

"I'd know that cranky capital W 'way above the line that your typewriter makes anywhere in the world," said Franklin.

"Why, there's no W in dandelions," said Sarah in surprise.

The young man drew the bill of fare from his pocket and pointed to a line.

Sarah recognised the first card she had typewritten that afternoon. There was still the rayed splotch in the upper right-hand corner where a tear had fallen. But over the spot where one should have read the name of the meadow plant, the clinging memory of their golden blossoms had allowed her fingers to strike strange keys.

Between the red cabbage and the stuffed green peppers was the item:

"DEAREST WALTER, WITH HARD-BOILED EGG."

—from *The Four Million* (1906)

THE LAST LEAF

In a little district west of Washington Square the streets have run crazy and broken themselves into small strips called "places." These "places" make strange angles and curves. One street crosses itself a time or two. An artist once discovered a valuable possibility in this street. Suppose a collector with a bill for paints, paper and canvas should, in traversing this route, suddenly meet himself coming back, without a cent having been paid on account!

So, to quaint old Greenwich Village the art people soon came prowling, hunting for north windows and eighteenth-century gables and Dutch attics and low rents. Then they imported some pewter mugs and a chafing dish or two from Sixth Avenue, and became a "colony."

At the top of a squatty, three-story brick Sue and Johnsy had their studio. "Johnsy" was familiar for Joanna. One was from Maine; the other from California. They had met at the *table d'hôte* of an Eighth Street "Delmonico's,"[1] and found their tastes in art, chicory salad and bishop sleeves so congenial that the joint studio resulted.

That was in May. In November a cold, unseen stranger, whom the doctors called Pneumonia, stalked about the colony, touching one here and there with his icy fingers. Over on the east side this ravager strode boldly, smiting his victims by scores, but his feet trod slowly through the maze of the narrow and moss-grown "places."

Mr. Pneumonia was not what you would call a chivalric old gentleman. A mite of a little woman with blood thinned by California zephyrs was hardly fair game for the red-fisted, short-breathed old duffer. But Johnsy he smote; and she lay, scarcely moving, on her painted iron bedstead, looking through the small Dutch window-panes at the blank side of the next brick house.

One morning the busy doctor invited Sue into the hallway with a shaggy, gray eyebrow.

"She has one chance in—let us say, ten," he said, as he shook down the mercury in his clinical thermometer. "And that chance is for her to want to live. This way people have of lining-up on the side of the undertaker makes the entire pharmacopoeia look silly. Your little lady has made up her mind that she's not going to get well. Has she anything on her mind?"

"She—she wanted to paint the Bay of Naples some day," said Sue.

"Paint?—bosh! Has she anything on her mind worth thinking about twice—a man, for instance?"

"A man?" said Sue, with a jew's-harp twang in her voice. "Is a man worth—but, no, doctor; there is nothing of the kind."

"Well, it is the weakness, then," said the doctor. "I will do all that science, so far as it may filter through my efforts, can accomplish. But whenever my patient begins to count the carriages in her funeral procession I subtract 50 per cent. from the curative power of medicines. If you will get her to ask one question about the new winter styles in cloak sleeves I will promise you a one-in-five chance for her, instead of one in ten."

After the doctor had gone Sue went into the workroom and cried a Japanese napkin to a pulp. Then she swaggered into Johnsy's room with her drawing board, whistling ragtime.

Johnsy, lay, scarcely making a ripple under the bedclothes, with her face toward the window. Sue stopped whistling, thinking she was asleep.

She arranged her board and began a pen-and-ink drawing to illustrate a magazine story. Young artists must pave their way to Art by drawing pictures for magazine stories that young authors write to pave their way to Literature.

As Sue was sketching a pair of elegant horseshow riding trousers and a monocle on the figure of the hero, an Idaho cowboy, she heard a low sound, several times repeated. She went quickly to the bedside.

Johnsy's eyes were open wide. She was looking out the window and counting—counting backward.

"Twelve," she said, and a little later "eleven"; and then "ten," and "nine"; and then "eight" and "seven," almost together.

Sue looked solicitously out of the window. What was there to count? There was only a bare, dreary yard to be seen, and the blank side of the brick house twenty feet away. An old, old ivy vine, gnarled and decayed at the roots, climbed half way up the brick wall. The cold breath of autumn had stricken its leaves from the vine until its skeleton branches clung, almost bare, to the crumbling bricks.

"What is it, dear?" asked Sue.

"Six," said Johnsy, in almost a whisper. "They're falling faster now. Three days ago there were almost a hundred. It made my head ache to count them. But now it's easy. There goes another one. There are only five left now."

"Five what, dear? Tell your Sudie."

"Leaves. On the ivy vine. When the last one falls I must go, too. I've known that for three days. Didn't the doctor tell you?"

"Oh, I never heard of such nonsense," complained Sue, with magnificent scorn. "What have old ivy leaves to do with your getting well? And you used to love that vine, so, you naughty girl. Don't be a goosey. Why, the doctor told me this morning that your chances for getting well real soon were—let's see exactly what he said—he said the chances were ten to one! Why, that's almost as good a chance as we have in New York when we ride on the street cars or walk past a new building. Try to take some broth now, and let Sudie go back to her drawing, so she can sell the editor man with it, and buy port wine for her sick child, and pork chops for her greedy self."

"You needn't get any more wine," said Johnsy, keeping her eyes fixed out the window. "There goes another. No, I don't want any broth. That leaves just four. I want to see the last one fall before it gets dark. Then I'll go, too."

"Johnsy, dear," said Sue, bending over her, "will you promise me to keep your eyes closed, and not look out the window until I am done working? I must hand those drawings in by to-morrow. I need the light, or I would draw the shade down."

"Couldn't you draw in the other room?" asked Johnsy, coldly.

"I'd rather be here by you," said Sue. "Besides, I don't want you to keep looking at those silly ivy leaves."

"Tell me as soon as you have finished," said Johnsy, closing her eyes, and lying white and still as a fallen statue, "because I want to see the last one fall. I'm tired of waiting. I'm tired of thinking. I want to turn loose my hold on everything, and go sailing down, down, just like one of those poor, tired leaves."

"Try to sleep," said Sue. "I must call Behrman up to be my model for the old hermit miner. I'll not be gone a minute. Don't try to move 'til I come back."

Old Behrman was a painter who lived on the ground floor beneath them. He was past sixty and had a Michael Angelo's Moses[2] beard curling down from the head of a satyr* along the body of an imp.† Behrman was a failure in art. Forty years he had wielded the brush without getting near enough to touch the hem of his Mistress's robe. He had been always about to paint a masterpiece, but had never yet begun it. For several years he had painted nothing except now and then a daub in the line of commerce or advertising. He earned a little by serving as a model to those young artists in the colony who could not pay the price of a professional. He drank gin to excess, and still talked of his coming masterpiece. For the rest he was a fierce little old man, who scoffed terribly at softness in any one, and who regarded himself as especial mastiff-in-waiting‡ to protect the two young artists in the studio above.

Sue found Behrman smelling strongly of juniper berries§ in his dimly lighted den below. In one corner was a blank canvas on an easel that had been waiting there for twenty-five years to receive the first line of the masterpiece. She told him of Johnsy's fancy, and how she feared she would, indeed, light and fragile as a leaf herself, float away, when her slight hold upon the world grew weaker.

Old Behrman, with his red eyes plainly streaming, shouted his contempt and derision for such idiotic imaginings.

---

*In Greek mythology, woodland goat-man associated with excesses of lust and drunkenness.

†Small, mischievous child.

‡A mastiff is a large dog, often used for guarding; the phrase is a play on "maid-in-waiting."

§Berries used to make gin.

"Vass!" he cried. "Is dere people in de world mit der foolishness to die because leafs dey drop off from a confounded vine? I haf not heard of such a thing. No, I will not bose as a model for your fool hermit-dunder-head. Vy do you allow dot silly pusiness to come in der brain of her? Ach, dot poor leetle Miss Yohnsy."

"She is very ill and weak," said Sue, "and the fever has left her mind morbid and full of strange fancies. Very well, Mr. Behrman, if you do not care to pose for me, you needn't. But I think you are a horrid old—old flibbertigibbet."

"You are just like a woman!" yelled Behrman. "Who said I will not bose? Go on. I come mit you. For half an hour I haf peen trying to say dot I am ready to bose. Gott! dis is not any blace in which one so goot as Miss Yohnsy shall lie sick. Some day I vill baint a masterpiece, and ve shall all go away. Gott! yes."

Johnsy was sleeping when they went upstairs. Sue pulled the shade down to the window-sill, and motioned Behrman into the other room. In there they peered out the window fearfully at the ivy vine. Then they looked at each other for a moment without speaking. A persistent, cold rain was falling, mingled with snow. Behrman, in his old blue shirt, took his seat as the hermit miner on an upturned kettle for a rock.

When Sue awoke from an hour's sleep the next morning she found Johnsy with dull, wide-open eyes staring at the drawn green shade.

"Pull it up; I want to see," she ordered, in a whisper.

Wearily Sue obeyed.

But, lo! after the beating rain and fierce gusts of wind that had endured through the livelong night, there yet stood out against the brick wall one ivy leaf. It was the last on the vine. Still dark green near its stem, but with its serrated edges tinted with the yellow of dissolution and decay, it hung bravely from a branch some twenty feet above the ground.

"It is the last one," said Johnsy. "I thought it would surely fall during the night. I heard the wind. It will fall to-day, and I shall die at the same time."

"Dear, dear!" said Sue, leaning her worn face down to the pillow, "think of me, if you won't think of yourself. What would I do?"

But Johnsy did not answer. The lonesomest thing in all the world is a soul when it is making ready to go on its mysterious, far journey. The fancy seemed to possess her more strongly as one by one the ties that bound her to friendship and to earth were loosed.

The day wore away, and even through the twilight they could see the lone ivy leaf clinging to its stem against the wall. And then, with the coming of the night the north wind was again loosed, while the rain still beat against the windows and pattered down from the low Dutch eaves.

When it was light enough Johnsy, the merciless, commanded that the shade be raised.

The ivy leaf was still there.

Johnsy lay for a long time looking at it. And then she called to Sue, who was stirring her chicken broth over the gas stove.

"I've been a bad girl, Sudie," said Johnsy. "Something has made that last leaf stay there to show me how wicked I was. It is a sin to want to die. You may bring me a little broth now, and some milk with a little port in it, and—no; bring me a hand-mirror first, and then pack some pillows about me, and I will sit up and watch you cook."

An hour later she said:

"Sudie, some day I hope to paint the Bay of Naples."

The doctor came in the afternoon, and Sue had an excuse to go into the hallway as he left.

"Even chances," said the doctor, taking Sue's thin, shaking hand in his. "With good nursing you'll win. And now I must see another case I have downstairs. Behrman, his name is—some kind of an artist, I believe. Pneumonia, too. He is an old, weak man, and the attack is acute. There is no hope for him; but he goes to the hospital to-day to be made more comfortable."

The next day the doctor said to Sue: "She's out of danger. You've won. Nutrition and care now—that's all."

And that afternoon Sue came to the bed where Johnsy lay, contentedly knitting a very blue and very useless woollen shoulder scarf, and put one arm around her, pillows and all.

"I have something to tell you, white mouse," she said. "Mr. Behrman died of pneumonia to-day in the hospital. He was ill only two days. The janitor found him on the morning of the first day in his room downstairs helpless with pain. His shoes and clothing were wet through and icy cold. They couldn't imagine where he had been on such a dreadful night. And then they found a lantern, still lighted, and a ladder that had been dragged from its place, and some scattered brushes, and a palette with green and yellow colors mixed on it, and—look out the window, dear, at the last ivy leaf on the wall. Didn't you wonder why it never fluttered or moved when the wind blew? Ah, darling, it's Behrman's masterpiece—he painted it there the night that the last leaf fell."

—from *The Trimmed Lamp* (1907)

THE SKYLIGHT ROOM

First Mrs. Parker would show you the double parlors. You would not dare to interrupt her description of their advantages and of the merits of the gentleman who had occupied them for eight years. Then you would manage to stammer forth the confession that you were neither a doctor nor a dentist. Mrs. Parker's manner of receiving the admission was such that you could never afterward entertain the same feeling toward your parents, who had neglected to train you up in one of the professions that fitted Mrs. Parker's parlors.

Next you ascended one flight of stairs and looked at the second-floor-back at $8. Convinced by her second-floor manner that it was worth the $12 that Mr. Toosenberry always paid for it until he left to take charge of his brother's orange plantation in Florida near Palm Beach, where Mrs. McIntyre always spent the winters that had the double front room with private bath, you managed to babble that you wanted something still cheaper.

If you survived Mrs. Parker's scorn, you were taken to look at Mr. Skidder's large hall room on the third floor. Mr. Skidder's room was not vacant. He wrote plays and smoked cigarettes in it all day long. But every room-hunter was made to visit his room to admire the lambrequins.* After each visit, Mr. Skidder, from the fright caused by possible eviction, would pay something on his rent.

Then—oh, then—if you still stood on one foot, with your hot hand clutching the three moist dollars in your pocket, and hoarsely proclaimed your hideous and culpable poverty, nevermore would Mrs. Parker be cicerone† of yours. She would honk loudly the word

---

*Decorative draperies hung over windows, doors, or fireplace mantles.
†Guide who escorts sightseers.

"Clara," she would show you her back, and march downstairs. Then Clara, the colored maid, would escort you up the carpeted ladder that served for the fourth flight, and show you the Skylight Room. It occupied 7 × 8 feet of floor space in the middle of the hall. On each side of it was a dark lumber closet or storeroom.

In it was an iron cot, a washstand and a chair. A shelf was the dresser. Its four bare walls seemed to close in upon you like the sides of a coffin. Your hand crept to your throat, you gasped, you looked up as from a well—and breathed once more. Through the glass of the little skylight you saw a square of blue infinity.

"Two dollars, suh," Clara would say in her half-contemptuous, half-Tuskegeenial* tones.

One day Miss Leeson came hunting for a room. She carried a typewriter made to be lugged around by a much larger lady. She was a very little girl, with eyes and hair that had kept on growing after she had stopped and that always looked as if they were saying: "Goodness me! Why didn't you keep up with us?"

Mrs. Parker showed her the double parlors. "In this closet," she said, "one could keep a skeleton or anæsthetic or coal——"

"But I am neither a doctor nor a dentist," said Miss Leeson, with a shiver.

Mrs. Parker gave her the incredulous, pitying, sneering, icy stare that she kept for those who failed to qualify as doctors or dentists, and led the way to the second-floor-back.

"Eight dollars?" said Miss Leeson. "Dear me! I'm not Hetty if I do look green.[1] I'm just a poor little working girl. Show me something higher and lower."

Mr. Skidder jumped and strewed the floor with cigarette stubs at the rap on his door.

"Excuse me, Mr. Skidder," said Mrs. Parker, with her demon's smile at his pale looks. "I didn't know you were in. I asked the lady to have a look at your lambrequins."

"They're too lovely for anything," said Miss Leeson, smiling in exactly the way the angels do.

After they had gone Mr. Skidder got very busy erasing the tall,

---

†Creative combination of Tuskegee, Alabama, and "genial," to describe the friendly lilt of a southern accent.

black-haired heroine from his latest (unproduced) play and inserted a small, roguish one with heavy, bright hair and vivacious features.

"Anna Held'll jump at it,"[2] said Mr. Skidder to himself, putting his feet up against the lambrequins and disappearing in a cloud of smoke like an aërial cuttlefish.

Presently the tocsin* call of "Clara!" sounded to the world the state of Miss Leeson's purse. A dark goblin seized her, mounted a Stygian† stairway, thrust her into a vault with a glimmer of light in its top and muttered the menacing and cabalistic‡ words "Two dollars!"

"I'll take it!" sighed Miss Leeson, sinking down upon the squeaky iron bed.

Every day Miss Leeson went out to work. At night she brought home papers with handwriting on them and made copies with her typewriter. Sometimes she had no work at night, and then she would sit on the steps of the high stoop with the other roomers. Miss Leeson was not intended for a skylight room when the plans were drawn for her creation. She was gay-hearted and full of tender, whimsical fancies. Once she let Mr. Skidder read to her three acts of his great (unpublished) comedy, "It's No Kid; or, The Heir of the Subway."

There was rejoicing among the gentlemen roomers whenever Miss Leeson had time to sit on the steps for an hour or two. But Miss Longnecker, the tall blonde who taught in a public school and said, "Well, really!" to everything you said, sat on the top step and sniffed. And Miss Dorn, who shot at the moving ducks at Coney every Sunday and worked in a department store, sat on the bottom step and sniffed. Miss Leeson sat on the middle step and the men would quickly group around her.

Especially Mr. Skidder, who had cast her in his mind for the star part in a private, romantic (unspoken) drama in real life. And especially Mr. Hoover, who was forty-five, fat, flush and foolish. And especially very young Mr. Evans, who set up a hollow cough

---

*Warning; a tocsin is an alarm bell.
†Hellish and dark; from Styx, the principal river of the underworld in Greek mythology.
‡Secretive, mysterious.

to induce her to ask him to leave off cigarettes. The men voted her "the funniest and jolliest ever," but the sniffs on the top step and the lower step were implacable.

I pray you let the drama halt while Chorus stalks to the footlights[3] and drops an epicedian* tear upon the fatness of Mr. Hoover. Tune the pipes to the tragedy of tallow, the bane of bulk, the calamity of corpulence. Tried out, Falstaff might have rendered more romance to the ton[4] than would have Romeo's rickety ribs to the ounce. A lover may sigh, but he must not puff. To the train of Momus† are the fat men remanded. In vain beats the faithfullest heart above a 52-inch belt. Avaunt,‡ Hoover! Hoover, forty-five, flush and foolish, might carry off Helen herself;[5] Hoover, forty-five, flush, foolish and fat is meat for perdition. There was never a chance for you, Hoover.

As Mrs. Parker's roomers sat thus one summer's evening, Miss Leeson looked up into the firmament and cried with her little gay laugh:

"Why, there's Billy Jackson! I can see him from down here, too."

All looked up—some at the windows of skyscrapers, some casting about for an airship, Jackson-guided.

"It's that star," explained Miss Leeson, pointing with a tiny finger. "Not the big one that twinkles—the steady blue one near it. I can see it every night through my skylight. I named it Billy Jackson."

"Well, really!" said Miss Longnecker. "I didn't know you were an astronomer, Miss Leeson."

"Oh, yes," said the small star gazer, "I know as much as any of them about the style of sleeves they're going to wear next fall in Mars."

"Well, really!" said Miss Longnecker. "The star you refer to is Gamma, of the constellation Cassiopeia. It is nearly of the second magnitude, and its meridian passage is——"

"Oh," said the very young Mr. Evans, "I think Billy Jackson is a much better name for it."

---

*Elegiac, funereal.
†Greek god of censure and mockery.
‡"Away with you."

"Same here," said Mr. Hoover, loudly breathing defiance to Miss Longnecker. "I think Miss Leeson has just as much right to name stars as any of those old astrologers had."

"Well, really!" said Miss Longnecker.

"I wonder whether it's a shooting star," remarked Miss Dorn. "I hit nine ducks and a rabbit out of ten in the gallery at Coney Sunday."

"He doesn't show up very well from down here," said Miss Leeson. "You ought to see him from my room. You know you can see stars even in the daytime from the bottom of a well. At night my room is like the shaft of a coal mine, and it makes Billy Jackson look like the big diamond pin that Night fastens her kimono with."

There came a time after that when Miss Leeson brought no formidable papers home to copy. And when she went out in the morning, instead of working, she went from office to office and let her heart melt away in the drip of cold refusals transmitted through insolent office boys. This went on.

There came an evening when she wearily climbed Mrs. Parker's stoop at the hour when she always returned from her dinner at the restaurant. But she had had no dinner.

As she stepped into the hall Mr. Hoover met her and seized his chance. He asked her to marry him, and his fatness hovered above her like an avalanche. She dodged, and caught the balustrade. He tried for her hand, and she raised it and smote him weakly in the face. Step by step she went up, dragging herself by the railing. She passed Mr. Skidder's door as he was red-inking a stage direction for Myrtle Delorme (Miss Leeson) in his (unaccepted) comedy, to "pirouette across stage from L to the side of the Count." Up the carpeted ladder she crawled at last and opened the door of the skylight room.

She was too weak to light the lamp or to undress. She fell upon the iron cot, her fragile body scarcely hollowing the worn springs. And in that Erebus of a room[6] she slowly raised her heavy eyelids, and smiled.

For Billy Jackson was shining down on her, calm and bright and constant through the skylight. There was no world about her. She was sunk in a pit of blackness, with but that small square of pallid light framing the star that she had so whimsically and oh, so ineffectually, named. Miss Longnecker must be right: it was Gamma, of the constellation Cassiopeia, and not Billy Jackson. And yet she could not let it be Gamma.

As she lay on her back, she tried twice to raise her arm. The third time she got two thin fingers to her lips and blew a kiss out of the black pit to Billy Jackson. Her arm fell back limply.

"Good-bye, Billy," she murmured, faintly. "You're millions of miles away and you won't even twinkle once. But you kept where I could see you most of the time up there when there wasn't anything else but darkness to look at, didn't you? . . . Millions of miles. . . . Good-bye, Billy Jackson."

Clara, the colored maid, found the door locked at 10 the next day, and they forced it open. Vinegar, and the slapping of wrists and burnt feathers proving of no avail, some one ran to 'phone for an ambulance.

In due time it backed up to the door with much gong-clanging, and the capable young medico, in his white linen coat, ready, active, confident, with his smooth face half debonair, half grim, danced up the steps.

"Ambulance call to 49," he said, briefly. "What's the trouble?"

"Oh, yes, doctor," sniffed Mrs. Parker, as though her trouble that there should be trouble in the house was the greater. "I can't think what can be the matter with her. Nothing we could do would bring her to. It's a young woman, a Miss Elsie—yes, a Miss Elsie Leeson. Never before in my house——"

"What room?" cried the doctor in a terrible voice, to which Mrs. Parker was a stranger.

"The skylight room. It——"

Evidently the ambulance doctor was familiar with the location of skylight rooms. He was gone up the stairs, four at a time. Mrs. Parker followed slowly, as her dignity demanded.

On the first landing she met him coming back bearing the astronomer in his arms. He stopped and let loose the practised scalpel of his tongue, not loudly. Gradually Mrs. Parker crumpled as a stiff garment that slips down from a nail. Ever afterward there remained crumples in her mind and body. Sometimes her curious roomers would ask her what the doctor said to her.

"Let that be," she would answer. "If I can get forgiveness for having heard it I will be satisfied."

The ambulance physician strode with his burden through the pack of hounds that follow the curiosity chase, and even they fell back along the sidewalk abashed, for his face was that of one who bears his own dead.

They noticed that he did not lay down upon the bed prepared for it in the ambulance the form that he carried, and all that he said was: "Drive like h—l,* Wilson," to the driver.

That is all. Is it a story? In the next morning's paper I saw a little news item, and the last sentence of it may help you (as it helped me) to weld the incidents together.

It recounted the reception into Bellevue Hospital of a young woman who had been removed from No. 49 East —— Street, suffering from debility induced by starvation. It concluded with these words:

"Dr. William Jackson, the ambulance physician who attended the case, says the patient will recover."

—from *The Four Million* (1906)

---

*Hell.

THE CALIPH, CUPID
AND THE CLOCK

Prince Michael, of the Electorate of Valleluna,* sat on his favorite bench in the park. The coolness of the September night quickened the life in him like a rare, tonic wine. The benches were not filled; for park loungers, with their stagnant blood, are prompt to detect and fly home from the crispness of early autumn. The moon was just clearing the roofs of the range of dwellings that bounded the quadrangle on the east. Children laughed and played about the fine-sprayed fountain. In the shadowed spots fauns and hamadryads wooed,[1] unconscious of the gaze of mortal eyes. A hand-organ—Philomel by the grace of our stage carpenter,[2] Fancy—fluted and droned in a side street. Around the enchanted boundaries of the little park street cars spat and mewed and the stilted trains roared like tigers and lions prowling for a place to enter. And above the trees shone the great, round, shining face of an illuminated clock in the tower of an antique public building.

Prince Michael's shoes were wrecked far beyond the skill of the carefullest cobbler. The ragman would have declined any negotiations concerning his clothes. The two weeks' stubble on his face was gray and brown and red and greenish yellow—as if it had been made up from individual contributions from the chorus of a musical comedy. No man existed who had money enough to wear so bad a hat as his.

Prince Michael sat on his favorite bench and smiled. It was a diverting thought to him that he was wealthy enough to buy every one of those close-ranged, bulky, window-lit mansions that faced him, if he chose. He could have matched gold, equipages, jewels,

---

*Valley of the moon (Spanish).

art treasures, estates and acres with any Crœsus in this proud city of Manhattan,[3] and scarcely have entered upon the bulk of his holdings. He could have sat at table with reigning sovereigns. The social world, the world of art, the fellowship of the elect, adulation, imitation, the homage of the fairest, honors from the highest, praise from the wisest, flattery, esteem, credit, pleasure, fame—all the honey of life was waiting in the comb in the hive of the world for Prince Michael, of the Electorate of Valleluna, whenever he might choose to take it. But his choice was to sit in rags and dinginess on a bench in a park. For he had tasted of the fruit of the tree of life, and, finding it bitter in his mouth, had stepped out of Eden for a time to seek distraction close to the unarmored, beating heart of the world.

These thoughts strayed dreamily through the mind of Prince Michael, as he smiled under the stubble of his polychromatic beard. Lounging thus, clad as the poorest of mendicants* in the parks, he loved to study humanity. He found in altruism more pleasure than his riches, his station and all the grosser sweets of life had given him. It was his chief solace and satisfaction to alleviate individual distress, to confer favors upon worthy ones who had need of succor, to dazzle unfortunates by unexpected and bewildering gifts of truly royal magnificence, bestowed, however, with wisdom and judiciousness.

And as Prince Michael's eye rested upon the glowing face of the great clock in the tower, his smile, altruistic as it was, became slightly tinged with contempt. Big thoughts were the Prince's; and it was always with a shake of his head that he considered the subjugation of the world to the arbitrary measures of Time. The comings and goings of people in hurry and dread, controlled by the little metal moving hands of a clock, always made him sad.

By and by came a young man in evening clothes and sat upon the third bench from the Prince. For half an hour he smoked cigars with nervous haste, and then he fell to watching the face of the illuminated clock above the trees. His perturbation was evident, and the Prince noted, in sorrow, that its cause was connected, in some manner, with the slowly moving hands of the timepiece.

---

*Beggars.

His Highness arose and went to the young man's bench.

"I beg your pardon for addressing you," he said, "but I perceive that you are disturbed in mind. If it may serve to mitigate the liberty I have taken I will add that I am Prince Michael, heir to the throne of the Electorate of Valleluna. I appear incognito, of course, as you may gather from my appearance. It is a fancy of mine to render aid to others whom I think worthy of it. Perhaps the matter that seems to distress you is one that would more readily yield to our mutual efforts."

The young man looked up brightly at the Prince. Brightly, but the perpendicular line of perplexity between his brows was not smoothed away. He laughed, and even then it did not. But he accepted the momentary diversion.

"Glad to meet you, Prince," he said, good humoredly. "Yes, I'd say you were incog. all right. Thanks for your offer of assistance— but I don't see where your butting-in would help things any. It's a kind of private affair, you know—but thanks all the same."

Prince Michael sat at the young man's side. He was often rebuffed but never offensively. His courteous manner and words forbade that.

"Clocks," said the Prince, "are shackles on the feet of mankind. I have observed you looking persistently at that clock. Its face is that of a tyrant, its numbers are false as those on a lottery ticket; its hands are those of a bunco-steerer, who makes an appointment with you to your ruin. Let me entreat you to throw off its humiliating bonds and cease to order your affairs by that insensate monitor of brass and steel."

"I don't usually," said the young man. "I carry a watch except when I've got my radiant rags on."

"I know human nature as I do the trees and grass," said the Prince, with earnest dignity. "I am a master of philosophy, a graduate in art, and I hold the purse of a Fortunatus.* There are few mortal misfortunes that I cannot alleviate or overcome. I have read your countenance, and found in it honesty and nobility as well as distress. I beg of you to accept my advice or aid. Do not belie the

---

*Fortunatus was a hero of medieval legend who possessed an inexhaustible purse.

intelligence I see in your face by judging from my appearance of my ability to defeat your troubles."

The young man glanced at the clock again and frowned darkly. When his gaze strayed from the glowing horologue* of time it rested intently upon a four-story red brick house in the row of dwellings opposite to where he sat. The shades were drawn, and the lights in many rooms shone dimly through them.

"Ten minutes to nine!" exclaimed the young man, with an impatient gesture of despair. He turned his back upon the house and took a rapid step or two in a contrary direction.

"Remain!" commanded Prince Michael, in so potent a voice that the disturbed one wheeled around with a somewhat chagrined laugh.

"I'll give her the ten minutes and then I'm off," he muttered, and then aloud to the Prince: "I'll join you in confounding all clocks, my friend, and throw in women, too."

"Sit down," said the Prince, calmly. "I do not accept your addition. Women are the natural enemies of clocks, and, therefore, the allies of those who would seek liberation from these monsters that measure our follies and limit our pleasures. If you will so far confide in me I would ask you to relate to me your story."

The young man threw himself upon the bench with a reckless laugh.

"Your Royal Highness, I will," he said, in tones of mock deference. "Do you see yonder house—the one with the three upper windows lighted? Well, at 6 o'clock I stood in that house with the young lady I am—that is, I was—engaged to. I had been doing wrong, my dear Prince—I had been a naughty boy, and she had heard of it. I wanted to be forgiven, of course—we are always wanting women to forgive us, aren't we, Prince?

" 'I want time to think it over,' said she. 'There is one thing certain; I will either fully forgive you, or I will never see your face again. There will be no half-way business. At half-past eight,' she said, 'at exactly half-past eight you may be watching the middle upper window of the top floor. If I decide to forgive I will hang

---

*Meaning a clock.

out of that window a white silk scarf. You will know by that that all is as was before, and you may come to me. If you see no scarf you may consider that everything between us is ended forever.' That," concluded the young man, bitterly, "is why I have been watching that clock. The time for the signal to appear has passed twenty-three minutes ago. Do you wonder that I am a little disturbed, my Prince of Rags and Whiskers?"

"Let me repeat to you," said Prince Michael, in his even, well-modulated tones, "that women are the natural enemies of clocks. Clocks are an evil, women a blessing. The signal may yet appear."

"Never, on your principality!" exclaimed the young man, hopelessly. "You don't know Marian—of course. She's always on time, to the minute. That was the first thing about her that attracted me. I've got the mitten instead of the scarf. I ought to have known at 8.31 that my goose was cooked. I'll go West on the 11.45 to-night with Jack Milburn. The jig's up. I'll try Jack's ranch awhile and top off with the Klondike and whiskey. Good-night—er—er—Prince."

Prince Michael smiled his enigmatic, gentle, comprehending smile and caught the coat sleeve of the other. The brilliant light in the Prince's eyes was softening to a dreamier, cloudy translucence.

"Wait," he said solemnly, "till the clock strikes. I have wealth and power and knowledge above most men, but when the clock strikes I am afraid. Stay by me until then. This woman shall be yours. You have the word of the hereditary Prince of Valleluna. On the day of your marriage I will give you $100,000 and a palace on the Hudson. But there must be no clocks in that palace—they measure our follies and limit our pleasures. Do you agree to that?"

"Of course," said the young man, cheerfully, "they're a nuisance, anyway—always ticking and striking and getting you late for dinner."

He glanced again at the clock in the tower. The hands stood at three minutes to nine.

"I think," said Prince Michael, "that I will sleep a little. The day has been fatiguing."

He stretched himself upon a bench with the manner of one who had slept thus before.

"You will find me in this park on any evening when the weather is suitable," said the Prince, sleepily. "Come to me when your marriage day is set and I will give you a check for the money."

"Thanks, Your Highness," said the young man, seriously. "It doesn't look as if I would need that palace on the Hudson, but I appreciate your offer, just the same."

Prince Michael sank into deep slumber. His battered hat rolled from the bench to the ground. The young man lifted it, placed it over the frowsy face and moved one of the grotesquely relaxed limbs into a more comfortable position. "Poor devil!" he said, as he drew the tattered clothes closer about the Prince's breast.

Sonorous and startling came the stroke of 9 from the clock tower. The young man sighed again, turned his face for one last look at the house of his relinquished hopes—and cried aloud profane words of holy rapture.

From the middle upper window blossomed in the dusk a waving, snowy, fluttering, wonderful, divine emblem of forgiveness and promised joy.

By came a citizen, rotund, comfortable, home-hurrying, unknowing of the delights of waving silken scarfs on the borders of dimly-lit parks.

"Will you oblige me with the time, sir?" asked the young man; and the citizen, shrewdly conjecturing his watch to be safe, dragged it out and announced:

"Twenty-nine and a half minutes past eight, sir."

And then, from habit, he glanced at the clock in the tower, and made further oration.

"By George! that clock's half an hour fast! First time in ten years I've known it to be off. This watch of mine never varies a——"

But the citizen was talking to vacancy. He turned and saw his hearer, a fast receding black shadow flying in the direction of a house with three lighted upper windows.

And in the morning came along two policemen on their way to the beats they owned. The park was deserted save for one dilapidated figure that sprawled, asleep, on a bench. They stopped and gazed upon it.

"It's Dopy Mike," said one. "He hits the pipe every night. Park bum for twenty years. On his last legs, I guess."

The other policeman stooped and looked at something crumpled and crisp in the hand of the sleeper.

"Gee!" he remarked. "He's doped out a fifty-dollar bill, anyway. Wish I knew the brand of hop that he smokes."

And then "Rap, rap, rap!" went the club of realism against the shoe soles of Prince Michael, of the Electorate of Valleluna.

—from *The Four Million* (1906)

THE COUNT AND
THE WEDDING GUEST

One evening when Andy Donovan went to dinner at his Second Avenue boarding-house, Mrs. Scott introduced him to a new boarder, a young lady, Miss Conway. Miss Conway was small and unobtrusive. She wore a plain, snuffy-brown dress, and bestowed her interest, which seemed languid, upon her plate. She lifted her diffident eyelids and shot one perspicuous, judicial glance at Mr. Donovan, politely murmured his name, and returned to her mutton. Mr. Donovan bowed with the grace and beaming smile that were rapidly winning for him social, business and political advancement, and erased the snuffy-brown one from the tablets of his consideration.

Two weeks later Andy was sitting on the front steps enjoying his cigar. There was a soft rustle behind and above him and Andy turned his head—and had his head turned.

Just coming out of the door was Miss Conway. She wore a night-black dress of *crêpe de—crêpe de*—oh, this thin black goods. Her hat was black, and from it drooped and fluttered an ebony veil, filmy as a spider's web. She stood on the top step and drew on black silk gloves. Not a speck of white or a spot of color about her dress anywhere. Her rich golden hair was drawn, with scarcely a ripple, into a shining, smooth knot low on her neck. Her face was plain rather than pretty, but it was now illuminated and made almost beautiful by her large gray eyes that gazed above the houses across the street into the sky with an expression of the most appealing sadness and melancholy.

Gather the idea, girls—all black, you know, with the preference for *crêpe de*—oh, *crêpe de Chine*—that's it. All black, and that sad, faraway look, and the hair shining under the black veil (you have

to be a blonde, of course), and try to look as if, although your young
life had been blighted just as it was about to give a hop-skip-and-
a-jump over the threshold of life, a walk in the park might do you
good, and be sure to happen out the door at the right moment,
and—oh, it'll fetch 'em every time. But it's fierce, now, how cynical
I am, ain't it?—to talk about mourning costumes this way.

Mr. Donovan suddenly reinscribed Miss Conway upon the tablets of his consideration. He threw away the remaining inch and a
quarter of his cigar, that would have been good for eight minutes
yet, and quickly shifted his center of gravity to his low-cut patent
leathers.

"It's a fine, clear evening, Miss Conway," he said; and if the
Weather Bureau could have heard the confident emphasis of his
tones it would have hoisted the square white signal, and nailed it
to the mast.

"To them that has the heart to enjoy it, it is, Mr. Donovan,"
said Miss Conway, with a sigh.

Mr. Donovan, in his heart, cursed fair weather. Heartless
weather! It should hail and blow and snow to be consonant with
the mood of Miss Conway.

"I hope none of your relatives—I hope you haven't sustained a
loss?" ventured Mr. Donovan.

"Death has claimed," said Miss Conway, hesitating—"not a relative, but one who—but I will not intrude my grief upon you, Mr.
Donovan."

"Intrude?" protested Mr. Donovan. "Why, say, Miss Conway,
I'd be delighted, that is, I'd be sorry—I mean I'm sure nobody could
sympathize with you truer than I would."

Miss Conway smiled a little smile. And oh, it was sadder than
her expression in repose.

" 'Laugh, and the world laughs with you; weep, and they give
you the laugh,' "[1] she quoted. "I have learned that, Mr. Donovan.
I have no friends or acquaintances in this city. But you have been
kind to me. I appreciate it highly."

He had passed her the pepper twice at the table.

"It's tough to be alone in New York—that's a cinch," said Mr.
Donovan. "But, say—whenever this little old town does loosen up
and get friendly it goes the limit. Say you took a little stroll in the

park, Miss Conway—don't you think it might chase away some of your mullygrubs?* And if you'd allow me——"

"Thanks, Mr. Donovan. I'd be pleased to accept of your escort if you think the company of one whose heart is filled with gloom could be anyways agreeable to you."

Through the open gates of the iron-railed, old, downtown park, where the elect once took the air, they strolled, and found a quiet bench.

There is this difference between the grief of youth and that of old age; youth's burden is lightened by as much of it as another shares; old age may give and give, but the sorrow remains the same.

"He was my fiancé," confided Miss Conway, at the end of an hour. "We were going to be married next spring. I don't want you to think that I am stringing you, Mr. Donovan, but he was a real Count. He had an estate and a castle in Italy. Count Fernando Mazzini was his name. I never saw the beat of him for elegance. Papa objected, of course, and once we eloped, but Papa overtook us, and took us back. I thought sure Papa and Fernando would fight a duel. Papa has a livery† business—in P'kipsee,‡ you know.

"Finally, Papa came 'round, all right, and said we might be married next spring. Fernando showed him proofs of his title and wealth, and then went over to Italy to get the castle fixed up for us. Papa's very proud and, when Fernando wanted to give me several thousand dollars for my trousseau§ he called him down something awful. He wouldn't even let me take a ring or any presents from him. And when Fernando sailed I came to the city and got a position as cashier in a candy store.

"Three days ago I got a letter from Italy, forwarded from P'kipsee, saying that Fernando had been killed in a gondola accident.

"That is why I am in mourning. My heart, Mr. Donovan, will remain forever in his grave. I guess I am poor company, Mr. Donovan, but I cannot take any interest in no one. I should not care to

---

*Depression.
†Place to rent a horse and carriage.
‡Poughkeepsie, New York.
§A bride's special wardrobe.

keep you from gayety and your friends who can smile and entertain you. Perhaps you would prefer to walk back to the house?"

Now, girls, if you want to observe a young man hustle out after a pick and shovel, just tell him that your heart is in some other fellow's grave. Young men are grave-robbers by nature. Ask any widow. Something must be done to restore that missing organ to weeping angels in *crêpe de Chine*. Dead men certainly get the worst of it from all sides.

"I'm awful sorry," said Mr. Donovan, gently. "No, we won't walk back to the house just yet. And don't say you haven't no friends in this city, Miss Conway. I'm awful sorry, and I want you to believe I'm your friend, and that I'm awful sorry."

"I've got his picture here in my locket," said Miss Conway, after wiping her eyes with her handkerchief. "I never showed it to anybody; but I will to you, Mr. Donovan, because I believe you to be a true friend."

Mr. Donovan gazed long and with much interest at the photograph in the locket that Miss Conway opened for him. The face of Count Mazzini was one to command interest. It was a smooth, intelligent, bright, almost a handsome face—the face of a strong, cheerful man who might well be a leader among his fellows.

"I have a larger one, framed, in my room," said Miss Conway. "When we return I will show you that. They are all I have to remind me of Fernando. But he ever will be present in my heart, that's a sure thing."

A subtle task confronted Mr. Donovan—that of supplanting the unfortunate Count in the heart of Miss Conway. This his admiration for her determined him to do. But the magnitude of the undertaking did not seem to weigh upon his spirits. The sympathetic but cheerful friend was the rôle he essayed; and he played it so successfully that the next half-hour found them conversing pensively across two plates of ice-cream, though yet there was no diminution of the sadness in Miss Conway's large gray eyes.

Before they parted in the hall that evening she ran upstairs and brought down the framed photograph wrapped lovingly in a white silk scarf. Mr. Donovan surveyed it with inscrutable eyes.

"He gave me this the night he left for Italy," said Miss Conway. "I had the one for the locket made from this."

"A fine-looking man," said Mr. Donovan, heartily. "How would it suit you, Miss Conway, to give me the pleasure of your company to Coney next Sunday afternoon?"

A month later they announced their engagement to Mrs. Scott and the other boarders. Miss Conway continued to wear black.

A week after the announcement the two sat on the same bench in the downtown park, while the fluttering leaves of the trees made a dim kinetoscopic picture of them in the moonlight. But Donovan had worn a look of abstracted gloom all day. He was so silent to-night that love's lips could not keep back any longer the question that love's heart propounded.

"What's the matter, Andy, you are so solemn and grouchy to-night?"

"Nothing, Maggie."

"I know better. Can't I tell? You never acted this way before. What is it?"

"It's nothing much, Maggie."

"Yes it is; and I want to know. I'll bet it's some other girl you are thinking about. All right. Why don't you go get her if you want her? Take your arm away, if you please."

"I'll tell you then," said Andy, wisely, "but I guess you won't understand it exactly. You've heard of Mike Sullivan, haven't you? 'Big Mike' Sullivan, everybody calls him."

"No, I haven't," said Maggie. "And I don't want to, if he makes you act like this. Who is he?"

"He's the biggest man in New York," said Andy, almost reverently. "He can about do anything he wants to with Tammany* or any other old thing in the political line. He's a mile high and as broad as East River. You say anything against Big Mike, and you'll have a million men on your collarbone in about two seconds. Why, he made a visit over to the old country† awhile back, and the kings took to their holes like rabbits.

"Well, Big Mike's a friend of mine. I ain't more than deuce-high in the district as far as influence goes, but Mike's as good a

---

*Tammany Hall was the headquarters of Tammany, the Democratic Party's controlling, corrupt political machine in New York City.

†Meaning Ireland; Conway, Donovan, and Sullivan are all Irish names.

friend to a little man, or a poor man as he is to a big one. I met him to-day on the Bowery, and what do you think he does? Comes up and shakes hands. 'Andy,' says he, 'I've been keeping cases on you. You've been putting in some good licks over on your side of the street, and I'm proud of you. What'll you take to drink?' He takes a cigar and I take a highball. I told him I was going to get married in two weeks. 'Andy,' says he, 'send me an invitation, so I'll keep in mind of it, and I'll come to the wedding.' That's what Big Mike says to me; and he always does what he says.

"You don't understand it, Maggie, but I'd have one of my hands cut off to have Big Mike Sullivan at our wedding. It would be the proudest day of my life. When he goes to a man's wedding, there's a guy being married that's made for life. Now, that's why I'm maybe looking sore to-night."

"Why don't you invite him, then, if he's so much to the mustard?"* said Maggie, lightly.

"There's a reason why I can't," said Andy, sadly. "There's a reason why he mustn't be there. Don't ask me what it is, for I can't tell you."

"Oh, I don't care," said Maggie. "It's something about politics, of course. But it's no reason why you can't smile at me."

"Maggie," said Andy, presently, "do you think as much of me as you did of your—as you did of the Count Mazzini?"

He waited a long time, but Maggie did not reply. And then, suddenly she leaned against his shoulder and began to cry—to cry and shake with sobs, holding his arm tightly, and wetting the *crêpe de Chine* with tears.

"There, there, there!" soothed Andy, putting aside his own trouble. "And what is it, now?"

"Andy," sobbed Maggie, "I've lied to you, and you'll never marry me, or love me any more. But I feel that I've got to tell. Andy, there never was so much as the little finger of a count. I never had a beau in my life. But all the other girls had; and they talked about 'em; and that seemed to make the fellows like 'em more. And, Andy, I look swell in black—you know I do. So I went out to a

---

*Slang for excellent, or the real deal.

photograph store and bought that picture, and had a little one made for my locket, and made up all that story about the Count and about his being killed, so I could wear black. And nobody can love a liar, and you'll shake me, Andy, and I'll die for shame. Oh, there never was anybody I liked but you—and that's all."

But instead of being pushed away, she found Andy's arm folding her closer. She looked up and saw his face cleared and smiling.

"Could you—could you forgive me, Andy?"

"Sure," said Andy. "It's all right about that. Back to the cemetery for the Count. You've straightened everything out, Maggie. I was in hopes you would before the wedding-day. Bully girl!"*

"Andy," said Maggie, with a somewhat shy smile, after she had been thoroughly assured of forgiveness, "did you believe all that story about the Count?"

"Well, not to any large extent," said Andy, reaching for his cigar case; "because it's Big Mike Sullivan's picture you've got in that locket of yours."

—from *The Trimmed Lamp* (1907)

---

*"Good girl!"

THE ROMANCE OF A BUSY BROKER

Pitcher, confidential clerk in the office of Harvey Maxwell, broker, allowed a look of mild interest and surprise to visit his usually expressionless countenance when his employer briskly entered at half-past nine in company with his young lady stenographer. With a snappy "Good-morning, Pitcher," Maxwell dashed at his desk as though he were intending to leap over it, and then plunged into the great heap of letters and telegrams waiting there for him.

The young lady had been Maxwell's stenographer for a year. She was beautiful in a way that was decidedly unstenographic. She forewent the pomp of the alluring pompadour. She wore no chains, bracelets, or lockets. She had not the air of being about to accept an invitation to luncheon. Her dress was gray and plain, but it fitted her figure with fidelity and discretion. In her neat black turban hat was the gold-green wing of a macaw. On this morning she was softly and shyly radiant. Her eyes were dreamily bright, her cheeks genuine peach-blow, her expression a happy one, tinged with reminiscence.

Pitcher, still mildly curious, noticed a difference in her ways this morning. Instead of going straight into the adjoining room, where her desk was, she lingered, slightly irresolute, in the outer office. Once she moved over by Maxwell's desk, near enough for him to be aware of her presence.

The machine sitting at that desk was no longer a man; it was a busy New York broker, moved by buzzing wheels and uncoiling springs.

"Well—what is it? Anything?" asked Maxwell, sharply. His opened mail lay like a bank of stage snow on his crowded desk. His keen gray eye, impersonal and brusque, flashed upon her half impatiently.

"Nothing," answered the stenographer, moving away with a little smile.

"Mr. Pitcher," she said to the confidential clerk, "did Mr. Maxwell say anything yesterday about engaging another stenographer?"

"He did," answered Pitcher. "He told me to get another one. I notified the agency yesterday afternoon to send over a few samples this morning. It's 9.45 o'clock, and not a single picture hat or piece of pineapple chewing gum has showed up yet."

"I will do the work as usual, then," said the young lady, "until some one comes to fill the place." And she went to her desk at once and hung the black turban hat with the gold-green macaw wing in its accustomed place.

He who has been denied the spectacle of a busy Manhattan broker during a rush of business is handicapped for the profession of anthropology. The poet sings of the "crowded hour of glorious life."[1] The broker's hour is not only crowded, but minutes and seconds are hanging to all the straps and packing both front and rear platforms.

And this day was Harvey Maxwell's busy day. The ticker began to reel out jerkily its fitful coils of tape, the desk telephone had a chronic attack of buzzing. Men began to throng into the office and call at him over the railing, jovially, sharply, viciously, excitedly. Messenger boys ran in and out with messages and telegrams. The clerks in the office jumped about like sailors during a storm. Even Pitcher's face relaxed into something resembling animation.

On the Exchange there were hurricanes and landslides and snowstorms and glaciers and volcanoes, and those elemental disturbances were reproduced in miniature in the broker's offices. Maxwell shoved his chair against the wall and transacted business after the manner of a toe dancer. He jumped from ticker to 'phone, from desk to door with the trained agility of a harlequin.*

In the midst of this growing and important stress the broker became suddenly aware of a high-rolled fringe of golden hair under

---

*Clown-like character in comedy or pantomime.

a nodding canopy of velvet and ostrich tips, and imitation sealskin sacque* and a string of beads as large as hickory nuts, ending near the floor with a silver heart. There was a self-possessed young lady connected with these accessories; and Pitcher was there to construe her.

"Lady from the Stenographer's Agency to see about the position," said Pitcher.

Maxwell turned half around, with his hands full of papers and ticker tape.

"What position?" he asked, with a frown.

"Position of stenographer," said Pitcher. "You told me yesterday to call them up and have one sent over this morning."

"You are losing your mind, Pitcher," said Maxwell. "Why should I have given you any such instructions? Miss Leslie has given perfect satisfaction during the year she has been here. The place is hers as long as she chooses to retain it. There's no place open here, madam. Countermand that order with the agency, Pitcher, and don't bring any more of 'em here."

The silver heart left the office, swinging and banging itself independently against the office furniture as it indignantly departed. Pitcher seized a moment to remark to the bookkeeper that the "old man" seemed to get more absentminded and forgetful every day of the world.

The rush and pace of business grew fiercer and faster. On the floor they were pounding half a dozen stocks in which Maxwell's customers were heavy investors. Orders to buy and sell were coming and going as swift as the flight of swallows. Some of his own holdings were imperilled, and the man was working like some highgeared, delicate, strong machine—strung to full tension, going at full speed, accurate, never hesitating, with the proper word and decision and act ready and prompt as clockwork. Stocks and bonds, loans and mortgages, margins and securities—here was a world of finance, and there was no room in it for the human world or the world of nature.

When the luncheon hour drew near there came a slight lull in the uproar.

---

*Or sack; a loose-fitting gown for women.

Maxwell stood by his desk with his hands full of telegrams and memoranda, with a fountain pen over his right ear and his hair hanging in disorderly strings over his forehead. His window was open, for the beloved janitress, Spring had turned on a little warmth through the waking registers of the earth.

And through the window came a wandering—perhaps a lost—odor—a delicate, sweet odor of lilac that fixed the broker for a moment immovable. For this odor belonged to Miss Leslie; it was her own, and hers only.

The odor brought her vividly, almost tangibly before him. The world of finance dwindled suddenly to a speck. And she was in the next room—twenty steps away.

"By George, I'll do it now," said Maxwell, half aloud. "I'll ask her now. I wonder I didn't do it long ago."

He dashed into the inner office with the haste of a short trying to cover. He charged upon the desk of the stenographer.

She looked up at him with a smile. A soft pink crept over her cheek, and her eyes were kind and frank. Maxwell leaned one elbow on her desk. He still clutched fluttering papers with both hands and the pen was above his ear.

"Miss Leslie," he began, hurriedly, "I have but a moment to spare. I want to say something in that moment. Will you be my wife? I haven't had time to make love to you in the ordinary way, but I really do love you. Talk quick, please—those fellows are clubbing the stuffing out of Union Pacific."

"Oh, what are you talking about?" exclaimed the young lady. She rose to her feet and gazed upon him, round-eyed.

"Don't you understand?" said Maxwell, restively. "I want you to marry me. I love you, Miss Leslie. I wanted to tell you, and I snatched a minute when things had slackened up a bit. They're calling me for the 'phone now. Tell 'em to wait a minute, Pitcher. Won't you, Miss Leslie?"

The stenographer acted very queerly. At first she seemed overcome with amazement; then tears flowed from her wondering eyes; and then she smiled sunnily through them, and one of her arms slid tenderly about the broker's neck.

"I know now," she said, softly. "It's this old business that has driven everything else out of your head for the time. I was frightened at first. Don't you remember, Harvey? We were married last evening at 8 o'clock in the Little Church around the Corner."

—from *The Four Million* (1906)

THE HIGHER PRAGMATISM[1]

Where to go for wisdom has become a question of serious import. The ancients are discredited; Plato is boiler-plate; Aristotle is tottering; Marcus Aurelius is reeling; Æsop has been copyrighted by Indiana; Solomon is too solemn; you couldn't get anything out of Epictetus with a pick.[2]

The ant, which for many years served as a model of intelligence and industry in the school-readers, has been proven to be a doddering idiot and a waster of time and effort. The owl to-day is hooted at. Chautauqua conventions[3] have abandoned culture and adopted diabolo. Graybeards give glowing testimonials to the venders of patent hair-restorers. There are typographical errors in the almanacs published by the daily newspapers. College professors have become——

But there shall be no personalities.

To sit in classes, to delve into the encyclopedia or the past-performances page, will not make us wise. As the poet says, "Knowledge comes, but wisdom lingers."[4] Wisdom is due, which, while we know it not, soaks into us, refreshes us, and makes us grow. Knowledge is a strong stream of water turned on us through a hose. It disturbs our roots.

Then, let us rather gather wisdom. But how to do so requires knowledge. If we know a thing, we know it; but very often we are not wise to it that we are wise, and——

But let's go on with the story.

Once upon a time I found a ten-cent magazine lying on a bench in a little city park. Anyhow, that was the amount he asked me for when I sat on the bench next to him. He was a musty, dingy, and tattered magazine, with some queer stories bound in him, I was sure. He turned out to be a scrap-book.

"I am a newspaper reporter," I said to him, to try him. "I have been detailed to write up some of the experiences of the unfortunate ones who spend their evenings in this park. May I ask you to what you attribute your downfall in——"

I was interrupted by a laugh from my purchase—a laugh so rusty and unpractised that I was sure it had been his first for many a day.

"Oh, no, no," said he. "You ain't a reporter. Reporters don't talk that way. They pretend to be one of us, and say they've just got on the blind baggage from St. Louis. I can tell a reporter on sight. Us park bums get to be fine judges of human nature. We sit here all day and watch the people go by. I can size up anybody who walks past my bench in a way that would surprise you."

"Well," I said, "go on and tell me. How do you size me up?"

"I should say," said the student of human nature with unpardonable hesitation, "that you was, say, in the contracting business— or maybe worked in a store—or was a sign-painter. You stopped in the park to finish your cigar, and thought you'd get a little free monologue out of me. Still, you might be a plasterer or a lawyer— it's getting kind of dark, you see. And your wife won't let you smoke at home."

I frowned gloomily.

"But, judging again," went on the reader of men, "I'd say you ain't got a wife."

"No," said I, rising restlessly. "No, no, no, I ain't. But I *will* have, by the arrows of Cupid. That is if——"

My voice must have trailed away and muffled itself in uncertainty and despair.

"I see you have a story yourself," said the dusty vagrant—imprudently, it seemed to me. "Suppose you take your dime back and spin your yarn for me. I'm interested myself in the ups and downs of unfortunate ones who spend their evenings in the park."

Somehow, that amused me. I looked at the frowsy derelict with more interest. I did have a story. Why not tell it to him? I had told none of my friends. I had always been a reserved and bottled-up man. It was psychical timidity or sensitiveness—perhaps both. And I smiled to myself in wonder when I felt an impulse to confide in this stranger and vagabond.

"Jack," said I.

"Mack," said he.

"Mack," said I, "I'll tell you."

"Do you want the dime back in advance?" said he. I handed him a dollar.

"The dime," said I, "was the price of listening to *your* story."

"Right on the point of the jaw," said he. "Go on."

And then, incredible as it may seem to the lovers in the world who confide their sorrows only to the night wind and the gibbous moon, I laid bare my secret to that wreck of all things that you would have supposed to be in sympathy with love.

I told him of the days and weeks and months that I had spent in adoring Mildred Telfair. I spoke of my despair, my grievous days and wakeful nights, my dwindling hopes and distress of mind. I even pictured to this night-prowler her beauty and dignity, the great sway she had in society, and the magnificence of her life as the elder daughter of an ancient race whose pride overbalanced the dollars of the city's millionaires.

"Why don't you cop* the lady out?" asked Mack, bringing me down to earth and dialect again.

I explained to him that my worth was so small, my income so minute, and my fears so large that I hadn't the courage to speak to her of my worship. I told him that in her presence I could only blush and stammer, and that she looked upon me with a wonderful, maddening smile of amusement.

"She kind of moves in the professional class, don't she?" asked Mack.

"The Telfair family——" I began, haughtily.

"I mean professional beauty," said my hearer.

"She is greatly and widely admired," I answered, cautiously.

"Any sisters?"

"One."

"You know any more girls?"

"Why, several," I answered. "And a few others."

"Say," said Mack, "tell me one thing—can you hand out the dope† to other girls? Can you chin 'em and make matinée eyes at

---

*Slang for catch.
†Slang for perform.

'em and squeeze 'em? You know what I mean. You're just shy when it comes to this particular dame—the professional beauty—ain't that right?"

"In a way you have outlined the situation with approximate truth," I admitted.

"I thought so," said Mack, grimly. "Now, that reminds me of my own case. I'll tell you about it."

I was indignant, but concealed it. What was this loafer's case or anybody's case compared with mine? Besides, I had given him a dollar and ten cents.

"Feel my muscle," said my companion, suddenly flexing his biceps. I did so mechanically. The fellows in gyms are always asking you to do that. His arm was as hard as cast-iron.

"Four years ago," said Mack, "I could lick any man in New York outside of the professional ring. Your case and mine is just the same. I come from the West Side—between Thirtieth and Fourteenth— and I won't give the number on the door. I was a scrapper when I was ten, and when I was twenty no amateur in the city could stand up four rounds with me. 'S a fact. You know Bill McCarty? No? He managed the smokers for some of them swell clubs. Well, I knocked out everything Bill brought up before me. I was a middle-weight, but could train down to a welter when necessary. I boxed all over the West Side at bouts and benefits and private entertainments, and was never put out once.

"But, say, the first time I put my foot in the ring with a professional I was no more than a canned lobster. I dunno how it was—I seemed to lose heart. I guess I got too much imagination. There was a formality and publicness about it that kind of weakened my nerve. I never won a fight in the ring. Light-weights and all kinds of scrubs used to sign up with my manager and then walk up and tap me on the wrist and see me fall. The minute I seen the crowd and a lot of gents in evening clothes down in front, and seen a professional come inside the ropes, I got as weak as ginger-ale.

"Of course, it wasn't long till I couldn't get no backers, and I didn't have any more chances to fight a professional—or many amateurs, either. But lemme tell you—I was as good as most men inside the ring or out. It was just that dumb, dead feeling I had when I was up against a regular that always done me up.

"Well, sir, after I had got out of the business, I got a mighty grouch on. I used to go round town licking private citizens and all kinds of unprofessionals just to please myself. I'd lick cops in dark streets and car-conductors and cabdrivers and draymen whenever I could start a row with 'em. It didn't make any difference how big they were, or how much science they had, I got away with 'em. If I'd only just have had the confidence in the ring that I had beating up the best men outside of it, I'd be wearing black pearls and heliotrope silk socks to-day.

"One evening I was walking along near the Bowery, thinking about things, when along comes a slumming-party. About six or seven they was, all in swallowtails,* and these silk hats that don't shine. One of the gang kind of shoves me off the sidewalk. I hadn't had a scrap in three days, and I just says, 'De-light-ed' and hits him back of the ear.

"Well, we had it. That Johnnie put up as decent a little fight as you'd want to see in the moving pictures. It was on a side street, and no cops around. The other guy had a lot of science, but it only took me about six minutes to lay him out.

"Some of the swallowtails dragged him up against some steps and began to fan him. Another one of 'em comes over to me and says:

" 'Young man, do you know what you've done?'

" 'Oh, beat it,' says I. 'I've done nothing but a little punching-bag work. Take Freddy back to Yale and tell him to quit studying sociology on the wrong side of the sidewalk.'

" 'My good fellow,' says he, 'I don't know who you are, but I'd like to. You've knocked out Reddy Burns, the champion middle-weight of the world! He came to New York yesterday, to try to get a match on with Jim Jeffries. If you—'

"But when I come out of my faint I was laying on the floor in a drugstore saturated with aromatic spirits of ammonia. If I'd known that was Reddy Burns, I'd have got down in the gutter and crawled past him instead of handing him one like I did. Why, if I'd ever been in a ring and seen him climbing over the ropes, I'd have been all to the sal-volatile.†

---

*Coats with forked tails (like the tails of Swallowtail butterflies).
†Smelling salts, used to revive someone who has fainted.

"So that's what imagination does," concluded Mack. "And as I said, your case and mine is simultaneous. You'll never win out. You can't go up against the professionals. I tell you, it's a park bench for yours in this romance business."

Mack, the pessimist, laughed harshly.

"I'm afraid I don't see the parallel," I said, coldly. "I have only a very slight acquaintance with the prize ring."

The derelict touched my sleeve with his fore-finger, for emphasis, as he explained his parable.

"Every man," said he, with some dignity, "has got his lamps on something that looks good to him. With you, it's this dame that you're afraid to say your say to. With me, it was to win out in the ring. Well, you'll lose just like I did."

"Why do you think I shall lose?" I asked, warmly.

" 'Cause," said he, "you're afraid to go in the ring. You dassen't stand up before a professional. Your case and mine is just the same. You're a amateur; and that means that you'd better keep outside of the ropes."

"Well, I must be going," I said, rising and looking with elaborate care at my watch.

When I was twenty feet away the park-bencher called to me.

"Much obliged for the dollar," he said. "And for the dime. But you'll never get 'er. You're in the amateur class."

"Serves you right," I said to myself, "for hobnobbing with a tramp. His impudence!"

But, as I walked, his words seemed to repeat themselves over and over again in my brain. I think I even grew angry at the man.

"I'll show him!" I finally said, aloud. "I'll show him that I can fight Reddy Burns, too—even knowing who he is."

I hurried to a telephone-booth and rang up the Telfair residence.

A soft, sweet voice answered. Didn't I know that voice? My hand holding the receiver shook.

"Is that *you*?" said I, employing the foolish words that form the vocabulary of every talker through the telephone.

"Yes, this is I," came back the answer in the low, clearcut tones that are an inheritance of Telfairs. "Who is it, please?"

"It's me," said I, less ungrammatically than egotistically. "It's me, and I've got a few things that I want to say to you right now and immediately and straight to the point."

"*Dear* me," said the voice. "Oh, it's you, Mr. Arden!"

I wondered if any accent on the first word was intended. Mildred was fine at saying things that you had to study out afterward.

"Yes," said I, "I hope so. And now to come down to brass tacks." I thought that rather a vernacularism, if there is such a word, as soon as I had said it; but I didn't stop to apologize. "You know, of course, that I love you, and that I have been in that idiotic state for a long time. I don't want any more foolishness about it—that is, I mean I want an answer from you right now. Will you marry me or not? Hold the wire, please. Keep out, Central. Hello, hello! Will you, or will you *not?*"

That was just the uppercut for Reddy Burns' chin. The answer came back:

"Why, Phil, dear, of course I will! I didn't know that you—that is, you never said—oh, come up to the house, please—I can't say what I want to over the 'phone. You are so importunate. But please come up to the house, won't you?"

Would I?

I rang the bell of the Telfair house violently. Some sort of a human came to the door and shooed me into the drawing-room.

"Oh, well," said I to myself, looking at the the ceiling, "any one can learn from any one. That was a pretty good philosophy of Mack's, anyhow. He didn't take advantage of his experience, but I get the benefit of it. If you want to get into the professional class, you've got to——"

I stopped thinking then. Someone was coming down the stairs. My knees began to shake. I knew then how Mack had felt when a professional began to climb over the ropes. I looked around foolishly for a door or a window by which I might escape. If it had been any other girl approaching, I mightn't have——

But just then the door opened, and Bess, Mildred's younger sister, came in. I'd never seen her look so much like a glorified angel. She walked straight up to me, and—and——

I'd never noticed before what perfectly wonderful eyes and hair Elizabeth Telfair had.

"Phil," she said, in the Telfair sweet, thrilling tones, "why didn't you tell me about it before? I thought it was sister you wanted all the time, until you telephoned to me a few minutes ago!"

I suppose Mack and I always will be hopeless amateurs. But, as the thing has turned out in my case, I'm mighty glad of it.

—from *Options* (1909)

WHILE THE AUTO WAITS

Promptly at the beginning of twilight, came again to that quiet corner of that quiet, small park the girl in gray. She sat upon a bench and read a book, for there was yet to come a half hour in which print could be accomplished.

To repeat: Her dress was gray, and plain enough to mask its impeccancy of style and fit. A large-meshed veil imprisoned her turban hat and a face that shone through it with a calm and unconscious beauty. She had come there at the same hour on the day previous, and on the day before that; and there was one who knew it.

The young man who knew it hovered near, relying upon burnt sacrifices to the great joss,* Luck. His piety was rewarded, for, in turning a page, her book slipped from her fingers and bounded from the bench a full yard away.

The young man pounced upon it with instant avidity, returning it to its owner with that air that seems to flourish in parks and public places—a compound of gallantry and hope, tempered with respect for the policeman on the beat. In a pleasant voice, he risked an inconsequent remark upon the weather—that introductory topic responsible for so much of the world's unhappiness—and stood poised for a moment, awaiting his fate.

The girl looked him over leisurely; at his ordinary, neat dress and his features distinguished by nothing particular in the way of expression.

"You may sit down, if you like," she said, in a full, deliberate contralto. "Really, I would like to have you do so. The light is too bad for reading. I would prefer to talk."

*Figure of a Chinese deity; idol.

The vassal of Luck slid upon the seat by her side with complaisance.

"Do you know," he said, speaking the formula with which park chairmen open their meetings, "that you are quite the stunningest girl I have seen in a long time? I had my eye on you yesterday. Didn't know somebody was bowled over by those pretty lamps of yours, did you, honeysuckle?"

"Whoever you are," said the girl, in icy tones, "you must remember that I am a lady. I will excuse the remark you have just made because the mistake was, doubtless, not an unnatural one—in your circle. I asked you to sit down; if the invitation must constitute me your honeysuckle, consider it withdrawn."

"I earnestly beg your pardon," pleaded the young man. His expression of satisfaction had changed to one of penitence and humility. "It was my fault you know—I mean, there are girls in parks, you know——that is, of course, you don't know, but——"

"Abandon the subject, if you please. Of course I know. Now, tell me about these people passing and crowding, each way, along these paths. Where are they going? Why do they hurry so? Are they happy?"

The young man had promptly abandoned his air of coquetry. His cue was now for a waiting part; he could not guess the rôle he would be expected to play.

"It *is* interesting to watch them," he replied, postulating her mood. "It is the wonderful drama of life. Some are going to supper and some to—er—other places. One wonders what their histories are."

"I do not," said the girl; "I am not so inquisitive. I come here to sit because here, only, can I be near the great, common, throbbing heart of humanity. My part in life is cast where its beats are never felt. Can you surmise why I spoke to you, Mr.——?"

"Parkenstacker," supplied the young man. Then he looked eager and hopeful.

"No," said the girl, holding up a slender finger, and smiling slightly. "You would recognize it immediately. It is impossible to keep one's name out of print. Or even one's portrait. This veil and this hat of my maid furnish me with an *incog*.* You should have

---

*Incognito (colloquial).

seen the chauffeur stare at it when he thought I did not see. Candidly, there are five or six names that belong in the holy of holies, and mine, by the accident of birth, is one of them. I spoke to you, Mr. Stackenpot——"

"Parkenstacker," corrected the young man, modestly.

"—Mr. Parkenstacker, because I wanted to talk, for once, with a natural man—one unspoiled by the despicable gloss of wealth and supposed social superiority. Oh! you do not know how weary I am of it—money, money, money! And of the men who surround me, dancing like little marionettes all cut by the same pattern. I am sick of pleasure, of jewels, of travel, of society, of luxuries of all kinds."

"I always had an idea," ventured the young man, hesitatingly, "that money must be a pretty good thing."

"A competence is to be desired. But when you have so many millions that——!" She concluded the sentence with a gesture of despair. "It is the monotony of it," she continued, "that palls. Drives, dinners, theatres, balls, suppers, with the gilding of superfluous wealth over it all. Sometimes the very tinkle of the ice in my champagne glass nearly drives me mad."

Mr. Parkenstacker looked ingenuously interested.

"I have always liked," he said, "to read and hear about the ways of wealthy and fashionable folks. I suppose I am a bit of a snob. But I like to have my information accurate. Now, I had formed the opinion that champagne is cooled in the bottle and not by placing ice in the glass."

The girl gave a musical laugh of genuine amusement.

"You should know," she explained, in an indulgent tone, "that we of the non-useful class depend for our amusement upon departure from precedent. Just now it is a fad to put ice in champagne. The idea was originated by a visiting Prince of Tartary[1] while dining at the Waldorf. It will soon give way to some other whim. Just as at a dinner party this week on Madison Avenue a green kid glove* was laid by the plate of each guest to be put on and used while eating olives."

"I see," admitted the young man, humbly. "These special diver-

---

*Glove made of goatskin.

sions of the inner circle do not become familiar to the common public."

"Sometimes," continued the girl, acknowledging his confession of error by a slight bow, "I have thought that if I ever should love a man it would be one of lowly station. One who is a worker and not a drone. But, doubtless, the claims of caste and wealth will prove stronger than my inclination. Just now I am besieged by two. One is a Grand Duke of a German principality. I think he has, or has had, a wife, somewhere, driven mad by his intemperance and cruelty. The other is an English Marquis, so cold and mercenary that I even prefer the diabolism of the Duke. What is it that impels me to tell you these things, Mr. Packenstacker?"

"Parkenstacker," breathed the young man. "Indeed, you cannot know how much I appreciate your confidences."

The girl contemplated him with the calm, impersonal regard that befitted the difference in their stations.

"What is your line of business, Mr. Parkenstacker?" she asked.

"A very humble one. But I hope to rise in the world. Were you really in earnest when you said that you could love a man of lowly position?"

"Indeed I was. But I said 'might.' There is the Grand Duke and the Marquis, you know. Yes; no calling could be too humble were the man what I would wish him to be."

"I work," declared Mr. Parkenstacker, "in a restaurant."

The girl shrank slightly.

"Not as a waiter?" she said, a little imploringly. "Labor is noble, but—personal attendance, you know—valets and——"

"I am not a waiter. I am cashier in"—on the street they faced that bounded the opposite side of the park was the brilliant electric sign "RESTAURANT"—"I am cashier in that restaurant you see there."

The girl consulted a tiny watch set in a bracelet of rich design upon her left wrist, and rose, hurriedly. She thrust her book into a glittering reticule suspended from her waist, for which, however, the book was too large.

"Why are you not at work?" she asked.

"I am on the night turn," said the young man; "it is yet an hour before my period begins. May I not hope to see you again?"

"I do not know. Perhaps—but the whim may not seize me again. I must go quickly now. There is a dinner, and a box at the play—and, oh! the same old round. Perhaps you noticed an automobile at the upper corner of the park as you came. One with a white body."

"And red running gear?" asked the young man, knitting his brows reflectively.

"Yes. I always come in that. Pierre waits for me there. He supposes me to be shopping in the department store across the square. Conceive of the bondage of the life wherein we must deceive even our chauffeurs. Good-night."

"But it is dark now," said Mr. Parkenstacker, "and the park is full of rude men. May I not walk——?"

"If you have the slightest regard for my wishes," said the girl, firmly, "you will remain at this bench for ten minutes after I have left. I do not mean to accuse you, but you are probably aware that autos generally bear the monogram of their owner. Again, good-night."

Swift and stately she moved away through the dusk. The young man watched her graceful form as she reached the pavement at the park's edge, and turned up along it toward the corner where stood the automobile. Then he treacherously and unhesitatingly began to dodge and skim among the park trees and shrubbery in a course parallel to her route, keeping her well in sight.

When she reached the corner she turned her head to glance at the motor car, and then passed it, continuing on across the street. Sheltered behind a convenient standing cab, the young man followed her movements closely with his eyes. Passing down the sidewalk of the street opposite the park, she entered the restaurant with the blazing sign. The place was one of those frankly glaring establishments, all white paint and glass, where one may dine cheaply and conspicuously. The girl penetrated the restaurant to some retreat at its rear, whence she quickly emerged without her hat and veil.

The cashier's desk was well to the front. A red-haired girl on the stool climbed down, glancing pointedly at the clock as she did so. The girl in gray mounted in her place.

The young man thrust his hands into his pockets and walked

slowly back along the sidewalk. At the corner his foot struck a small, paper-covered volume lying there, sending it sliding to the edge of the turf. By its picturesque cover he recognized it as the book the girl had been reading. He picked it up carelessly, and saw that its title was "New Arabian Nights," the author being of the name of Stevenson.[2] He dropped it again upon the grass, and lounged, irresolute, for a minute. Then he stepped into the automobile, reclined upon the cushions, and said two words to the chauffeur:

"Club, Henri."

—from *The Voice of the City* (1908)

THE SOCIAL TRIANGLE

At the stroke of six Ikey Snigglefritz laid down his goose.* Ikey was a tailor's apprentice. Are there tailors' apprentices nowadays?

At any rate, Ikey toiled and snipped and basted and pressed and patched and sponged all day in the steamy fetor of a tailor-shop. But when work was done Ikey hitched his wagon to such stars as his firmament let shine.

It was Saturday night, and the boss laid twelve begrimed and begrudged dollars in his hand. Ikey dabbled discreetly in water, donned coat, hat and collar with its frazzled tie, and chalcedony pin, and set forth in pursuit of his ideals.

For each of us, when our day's work is done, must seek our ideal, whether it be love or pinochle or lobster à la Newburg, or the sweet silence of the musty bookshelves.

Behold Ikey as he ambles up the street beneath the roaring "El"† between the rows of reeking sweatshops. Pallid, stooping, insignificant, squalid, doomed to exist forever in penury of body and mind, yet, as he swings his cheap cane and projects the noisome inhalations from his cigarette you perceive that he nurtures in his narrow bosom the bacillus‡ of society.

Ikey's legs carried him to and into that famous place of entertainment known as the Café Maginnis—famous because it was the rendezvous of Billy McMahan, the greatest man, the most wonderful man, Ikey thought, that the world had ever produced.

Billy McMahan was the district leader. Upon him the Tiger

---

*Clothes iron.
†Elevated train.
‡Disease-producing bacterium.

purred, and his hand held manna to scatter.[1] Now, as Ikey entered, McMahan stood, flushed and triumphant and mighty, the centre of a huzzaing concourse of his lieutenants and constituents. It seems there had been an election; a signal victory had been won; the city had been swept back into line by a resistless besom of ballots.

Ikey slunk along the bar and gazed, breath-quickened, at his idol.

How magnificent was Billy McMahan, with his great, smooth, laughing face; his gray eye, shrewd as a chicken hawk's; his diamond ring, his voice like a bugle call, his prince's air, his plump and active roll of money, his clarion call to friend and comrade—oh, what a king of men he was! How he obscured his lieutenants, though they themselves loomed large and serious, blue of chin and important of mien, with hands buried deep in the pockets of their short overcoats! But Billy—oh, what small avail are words to paint for you his glory as seen by Ikey Snigglefritz!

The Café Maginnis rang to the note of victory. The whitecoated bartenders threw themselves featfully upon bottle, cork and glass. From a score of clear Havanas[*] the air received its paradox of clouds. The leal[†] and the hopeful shook Billy McMahan's hand. And there was born suddenly in the worshipful soul of Ikey Snigglefritz an audacious, thrilling impulse.

He stepped forward into the little cleared space in which majesty moved, and held out his hand.

Billy McMahan grasped it unhesitatingly, shook it and smiled.

Made mad now by the gods who were about to destroy him, Ikey threw away his scabbard and charged upon Olympus.[‡]

"Have a drink with me, Billy," he said familiarly, "you and your friends?"

"Don't mind if I do, old man," said the great leader, "just to keep the ball rolling."

The last spark of Ikey's reason fled.

"Wine," he called to the bartender, waving a trembling hand.

The corks of three bottles were drawn; the champagne bubbled in the long row of glasses set upon the bar. Billy McMahan took

---

[*]Cuban cigars.
[†]Loyal, faithful.
[‡]Home of the Greek gods.

his and nodded, with his beaming smile at Ikey. The lieutenants
and satellites took theirs and growled "Here's to you." Ikey took
his nectar* in delirium. All drank.

Ikey threw his week's wages in a crumpled roll upon the bar.

"C'rect," said the bartender, smoothing the twelve one-dollar
notes. The crowd surged around Billy McMahan again. Some one
was telling how Brannigan fixed 'em over in the Eleventh.[2] Ikey
leaned against the bar a while, and then went out.

He went down Hester Street and up Chrystie, and down Delancey to where he lived. And there his women folk, a bibulous
mother and three dingy sisters, pounced upon him for his wages.
And at his confession they shrieked and objurgated him in the pithy
rhetoric of the locality.

But even as they plucked at him and struck him Ikey remained
in his ecstatic trance of joy. His head was in the clouds; the star
was drawing his wagon. Compared with what he had achieved the
loss of wages and the bray of women's tongues were slight affairs.

He had shaken the hand of Billy McMahan.

Billy McMahan had a wife, and upon her visiting cards was engraved the name "Mrs. William Darragh McMahan." And there
was a certain vexation attendant upon these cards; for, small as they
were, there were houses in which they could not be inserted. Billy
McMahan was a dictator in politics, a four-walled tower in business, a mogul, dread, loved and obeyed among his own people. He
was growing rich; the daily papers had a dozen men on his trail to
chronicle his every word of wisdom; he had been honored in car-
icature holding the Tiger cringing in leash.

But the heart of Billy was sometimes sore within him. There
was a race of men from which he stood apart but that he viewed
with the eye of Moses looking over into the promised land.[3] He,
too, had ideals, even as had Ikey Snigglefritz; and sometimes, hopeless of attaining them, his own solid success was as dust and ashes
in his mouth. And Mrs. William Darragh McMahan wore a look
of discontent upon her plump but pretty face, and the very rustle
of her silks seemed a sigh.

---

*Drink of the Greek gods.

There was a brave and conspicuous assemblage in the dining saloon of a noted hostelry where Fashion loves to display her charms. At one table sat Billy McMahan and his wife. Mostly silent they were, but the accessories they enjoyed little needed the indorsement of speech. Mrs. McMahan's diamonds were outshone by few in the room. The waiter bore the costliest brands of wine to their table. In evening dress, with an expression of gloom upon his smooth and massive countenance, you would look in vain for a more striking figure than Billy's.

Four tables away sat alone a tall, slender man, about thirty, with thoughtful, melancholy eyes, a Van Dyke beard and peculiarly white, thin hands. He was dining on filet mignon, dry toast and apollinaris.* That man was Cortlandt Van Duyckink, a man worth eighty millions, who inherited and held a sacred seat in the exclusive inner circle of society.

Billy McMahan spoke to no one around him, because he knew no one. Van Duyckink kept his eyes on his plate because he knew that every one present was hungry to catch his. He could bestow knighthood and prestige by a nod, and he was chary† of creating a too extensive nobility.

And then Billy McMahan conceived and accomplished the most startling and audacious act of his life. He rose deliberately and walked over to Cortlandt Van Duyckink's table and held out his hand.

"Say, Mr. Van Duyckink," he said, "I've heard you was talking about starting some reforms among the poor people down in my district. I'm McMahan, you know. Say, now, if that's straight I'll do all I can to help you. And what I says goes in that neck of the woods, don't it? Oh, say, I rather guess it does."

Van Duyckink's rather somber eyes lighted up. He rose to his lank height and grasped Billy McMahan's hand.

"Thank you, Mr. McMahan," he said, in his deep, serious tones. "I have been thinking of doing some work of that sort. I shall be glad of your assistance. It pleases me to have become acquainted with you."

---

*Brand of sparkling mineral water.
†Cautious.

Billy walked back to his seat. His shoulder was tingling from the accolade bestowed by royalty. A hundred eyes were now turned upon him in envy and new admiration. Mrs. William Darragh McMahan trembled with ecstasy, so that her diamonds smote the eye almost with pain. And now it was apparent that at many tables there were those who suddenly remembered that they enjoyed Mr. McMahan's acquaintance. He saw smiles and bows about him. He became enveloped in the aura of dizzy greatness. His campaign coolness deserted him.

"Wine for that gang!" he commanded the waiter, pointing with his finger. "Wine over there. Wine to those three gents by that green bush. Tell 'em it's on me. D——n* it! Wine for everybody!"

The waiter ventured to whisper that it was perhaps inexpedient to carry out the order, in consideration of the dignity of the house and its custom.

"All right," said Billy, "if it's against the rules. I wonder if 'twould do to send my friend Van Duyckink a bottle? No? Well, it'll flow all right at the caffy† to-night, just the same. It'll be rubber boots for anybody who comes in there any time up to 2 A.M."

Billy McMahan was happy.

He had shaken the hand of Cortlandt Van Duyckink.

The big pale-gray auto with its shining metal work looked out of place moving slowly among the push carts and trash-heaps on the lower east side. So did Cortlandt Van Duyckink, with his aristocratic face and white, thin hands, as he steered carefully between the groups of ragged, scurrying youngsters in the streets. And so did Miss Constance Schuyler, with her dim, ascetic beauty, seated at his side.

"Oh, Cortlandt," she breathed, "isn't it sad that human beings have to live in such wretchedness and poverty? And you—how noble it is of you to think of them, to give your time and money to improve their condition!"

Van Duyckink turned his solemn eyes upon her.

"It is little," he said, sadly, "that I can do. The question is a large

---

*Damn.
†Possibly café, referring here to a restaurant or bar.

one, and belongs to society. But even individual effort is not thrown away. Look, Constance! On this street I have arranged to build soup kitchens, where no one who is hungry will be turned away. And down this other street are the old buildings that I shall cause to be torn down and there erect others in place of those death-traps of fire and disease."

Down Delancey slowly crept the pale-gray auto. Away from it toddled coveys of wondering, tangle-haired, barefooted, unwashed children. It stopped before a crazy brick structure, foul and awry.

Van Duyckink alighted to examine at a better perspective one of the leaning walls. Down the steps of the building came a young man who seemed to epitomize its degradation, squalor and infelicity—a narrow-chested, pale, unsavory young man, puffing at a cigarette.

Obeying a sudden impulse, Van Duyckink stepped out and warmly grasped the hand of what seemed to him a living rebuke.

"I want to know you people," he said, sincerely. "I am going to help you as much as I can. We shall be friends."

As the auto crept carefully away Cortlandt Van Duyckink felt an unaccustomed glow about his heart. He was near to being a happy man.

He had shaken the hand of Ikey Snigglefritz.

—from *The Trimmed Lamp* (1907)

AFTER TWENTY YEARS

The policeman on the beat moved up the avenue impressively. The impressiveness was habitual and not for show, for spectators were few. The time was barely 10 o'clock at night, but chilly gusts of wind with a taste of rain in them had well nigh depeopled the streets.

Trying doors as he went, twirling his club with many intricate and artful movements, turning now and then to cast his watchful eye down the pacific thoroughfare, the officer, with his stalwart form and slight swagger, made a fine picture of a guardian of the peace. The vicinity was one that kept early hours. Now and then you might see the lights of a cigar store or of an all-night lunch counter; but the majority of the doors belonged to business places that had long since been closed.

When about midway of a certain block the policeman suddenly slowed his walk. In the doorway of a darkened hardware store a man leaned, with an unlighted cigar in his mouth. As the policeman walked up to him the man spoke up quickly.

"It's all right, officer," he said, reassuringly. "I'm just waiting for a friend. It's an appointment made twenty years ago. Sounds a little funny to you, doesn't it? Well, I'll explain if you'd like to make certain it's all straight. About that long ago there used to be a restaurant where this store stands—'Big Joe' Brady's restaurant."

"Until five years ago," said the policeman. "It was torn down then."

The man in the doorway struck a match and lit his cigar. The light showed a pale, square-jawed face with keen eyes, and a little white scar near his right eyebrow. His scarfpin was a large diamond, oddly set.

"Twenty years ago to-night," said the man, "I dined here at 'Big

Joe' Brady's with Jimmy Wells, my best chum, and the finest chap in the world. He and I were raised here in New York, just like two brothers, together. I was eighteen and Jimmy was twenty. The next morning I was to start for the West to make my fortune. You couldn't have dragged Jimmy out of New York; he thought it was the only place on earth. Well, we agreed that night that we would meet here again exactly twenty years from that date and time, no matter what our conditions might be or from what distance we might have to come. We figured that in twenty years each of us ought to have our destiny worked out and our fortunes made, whatever they were going to be."

"It sounds pretty interesting," said the policeman. "Rather a long time between meets, though, it seems to me. Haven't you heard from your friend since you left?"

"Well, yes, for a time we corresponded," said the other. "But after a year or two we lost track of each other. You see, the West is a pretty big proposition, and I kept hustling around over it pretty lively. But I know Jimmy will meet me here if he's alive, for he always was the truest, stanchest old chap in the world. He'll never forget. I came a thousand miles to stand in this door to-night, and it's worth it if my old partner turns up."

The waiting man pulled out a handsome watch, the lids of it set with small diamonds.

"Three minutes to ten," he announced. "It was exactly ten o'clock when we parted here at the restaurant door."

"Did pretty well out West, didn't you?" asked the policeman.

"You bet! I hope Jimmy has done half as well. He was a kind of plodder,* though, good fellow as he was. I've had to compete with some of the sharpest wits going to get my pile. A man gets in a groove in New York. It takes the West to put a razor-edge on him."

The policeman twirled his club and took a step or two.

"I'll be on my way. Hope your friend comes around all right. Going to call time on him sharp?"

"I should say not!" said the other. "I'll give him half an hour at least. If Jimmy is alive on earth he'll be here by that time. So long, officer."

---

*A slow person.

"Good-night, sir," said the policeman, passing on along his beat, trying doors as he went.

There was now a fine, cold drizzle falling, and the wind had risen from its uncertain puffs into a steady blow. The few foot passengers astir in that quarter hurried dismally and silently along with coat collars turned high and pocketed hands. And in the door of the hardware store the man who had come a thousand miles to fill an appointment, uncertain almost to absurdity, with the friend of his youth, smoked his cigar and waited.

About twenty minutes he waited, and then a tall man in a long overcoat, with collar turned up to his ears, hurried across from the opposite side of the street. He went directly to the waiting man.

"Is that you, Bob?" he asked, doubtfully.

"Is that you, Jimmy Wells?" cried the man in the door.

"Bless my heart!" exclaimed the new arrival, grasping both the other's hands with his own. "It's Bob, sure as fate. I was certain I'd find you here if you were still in existence. Well, well, well!—twenty years is a long time. The old restaurant's gone, Bob; I wish it had lasted, so we could have had another dinner there. How has the West treated you, old man?"

"Bully;* it has given me everything I asked it for. You've changed lots, Jimmy. I never thought you were so tall by two or three inches."

"Oh, I grew a bit after I was twenty."

"Doing well in New York, Jimmy?"

"Moderately. I have a position in one of the city departments. Come on, Bob; we'll go around to a place I know of, and have a good long talk about old times."

The two men started up the street, arm in arm. The man from the West, his egotism enlarged by success, was beginning to outline the history of his career. The other, submerged in his overcoat, listened with interest.

At the corner stood a drug store, brilliant with electric lights. When they came into this glare each of them turned simultaneously to gaze upon the other's face.

---

*"Great."

The man from the West stopped suddenly and released his arm. "You're not Jimmy Wells," he snapped. "Twenty years is a long time, but not long enough to change a man's nose from a Roman to a pug."

"It sometimes changes a good man into a bad one," said the tall man. "You've been under arrest for ten minutes, 'Silky' Bob. Chicago thinks you may have dropped over our way and wires us she wants to have a chat with you. Going quietly, are you? That's sensible. Now, before we go to the station here's a note I was asked to hand to you. You may read it here at the window. It's from Patrolman Wells."

The man from the West unfolded the little piece of paper handed him. His hand was steady when he began to read, but it trembled a little by the time he had finished. The note was rather short.

BOB: I was at the appointed place on time. When you struck the match to light your cigar I saw it was the face of the man wanted in Chicago. Somehow I couldn't do it myself, so I went around and got a plain clothes man to do the job.

JIMMY

—from *The Four Million* (1906)

THE GREEN DOOR

S uppose you should be walking down Broadway after dinner, with ten minutes allotted to the consummation of your cigar while you are choosing between a diverting tragedy and something serious in the way of vaudeville. Suddenly a hand is laid upon your arm. You turn to look into the thrilling eyes of a beautiful woman, wonderful in diamonds and Russian sables. She thrusts hurriedly into your hand an extremely hot buttered roll, flashes out a tiny pair of scissors, snips off the second button of your overcoat, meaningly ejaculates the one word, "parallelogram!" and swiftly flies down a cross street, looking back fearfully over her shoulder.

That would be pure adventure. Would you accept it? Not you. You would flush with embarrassment; you would sheepishly drop the roll and continue down Broadway, fumbling feebly for the missing button. This you would do unless you are one of the blessed few in whom the pure spirit of adventure is not dead.

True adventurers have never been plentiful. They who are set down in print as such have been mostly business men with newly invented methods. They have been out after the things they wanted—golden fleeces, holy grails, lady loves, treasure, crowns and fame. The true adventurer goes forth aimless and uncalculating to meet and greet unknown fate. A fine example was the Prodigal Son[1]—when he started back home.

Half-adventurers—brave and splendid figures—have been numerous. From the Crusades to the Palisades[2] they have enriched the arts of history and fiction and the trade of historical fiction. But each of them had a prize to win, a goal to kick, an axe to grind, a race to run, a new thrust in tierce to deliver, a name to carve, a crow to pick—so they were not followers of true adventure.

In the big city the twin spirits Romance and Adventure are always abroad seeking worthy wooers. As we roam the streets they slyly peep at us and challenge us in twenty different guises. Without knowing why, we look up suddenly to see in a window a face that seems to belong to our gallery of intimate portraits; in a sleeping thoroughfare we hear a cry of agony and fear coming from an empty and shuttered house; instead of at our familiar curb a cab-driver deposits us before a strange door, which one, with a smile, opens for us and bids us enter; a slip of paper, written upon, flutters down to our feet from the high lattices of Chance; we exchange glances of instantaneous hate, affection, and fear with hurrying strangers in the passing crowds; a sudden souse of rain—and our umbrella may be sheltering the daughter of the Full Moon and first cousin of the Sidereal System;* at every corner handkerchiefs drop, fingers beckon, eyes besiege, and the lost, lonely, the rapturous, the mysterious, the perilous changing clues of adventure are slipped into our fingers. But few of us are willing to hold and follow them. We are grown stiff with the ramrod of convention down our backs. We pass on; and some day we come, at the end of a very dull life, to reflect that our romance has been a pallid thing of a marriage or two, a satin rosette kept in a safe-deposit drawer, and a lifelong feud with a steam radiator.

Rudolf Steiner was a true adventurer. Few were the evenings on which he did not go forth from his hall bedchamber in search of the unexpected and the egregious. The most interesting thing in life seemed to him to be what might lie just around the next corner. Sometimes his willingness to tempt fate led him into strange paths. Twice he had spent the night in a station-house; again and again he had found himself the dupe of ingenious and mercenary tricksters; his watch and money had been the price of one flattering allurement. But with undiminished ardor he picked up every glove cast before him into the merry lists of adventure.

One evening Rudolf was strolling along a cross-town street in the older central part of the city. Two streams of people filled the sidewalks—the home-hurrying, and that restless contingent that abandons home for the specious welcome of the thousand-candle-power *table d'hôte*.

---

*System of stars and constellations.

The young adventurer was of pleasing presence, and moved serenely and watchfully. By daylight he was a salesman in a piano store. He wore his tie drawn through a topaz ring instead of fastened with a stick pin; and once he had written to the editor of a magazine that "Junie's Love Test," by Miss Libbey,[3] had been the book that had most influenced his life.

During his walk a violent chattering of teeth in a glass case on the sidewalk seemed at first to draw his attention (with a qualm) to a restaurant before which it was set; but a second glance revealed the electric letters of a dentist's sign high above the next door. A giant negro, fantastically dressed in a red embroidered coat, yellow trousers and a military cap, discreetly distributed cards to those of the passing crowd who consented to take them.

This mode of dentistic advertising was a common sight to Rudolf. Usually he passed the dispenser of the dentist's cards without reducing his store; but to-night the African slipped one into his hand so deftly that he retained it there smiling a little at the successful feat.

When he had travelled a few yards further he glanced at the card indifferently. Surprised, he turned it over and looked again with interest. One side of the card was blank; on the other was written in ink three words, "The Green Door." And then Rudolf saw, three steps in front of him, a man throw down the card the negro had given him as he passed. Rudolf picked it up. It was printed with the dentist's name and address and the usual schedule of "plate work" and "bridge work" and "crowns," and specious promises of "painless" operations.

The adventurous piano salesman halted at the corner and considered. Then he crossed the street, walked down a block, recrossed and joined the upward current of people again. Without seeming to notice the negro as he passed the second time, he carelessly took the card that was handed him. Ten steps away he inspected it. In the same handwriting that appeared on the first card "The Green Door" was inscribed upon it. Three or four cards were tossed to the pavement by pedestrians both following and leading him. These fell blank side up. Rudolf turned them over. Everyone bore the printed legend of the dental "parlors."

Rarely did the arch sprite Adventure need to beckon twice to

Rudolf Steiner, his true follower. But twice it had been done, and the quest was on.

Rudolf walked slowly back to where the giant negro stood by the case of rattling teeth. This time as he passed he received no card. In spite of his gaudy and ridiculous garb, the Ethiopian displayed a natural barbaric dignity as he stood, offering the cards suavely to some, allowing others to pass unmolested. Every half minute he chanted a harsh, unintelligible phrase akin to the jabber of car conductors and grand opera. And not only did he withhold a card this time but it seemed to Rudolf that he received from the shining and massive black countenance a look of cold, almost contemptuous disdain.

The look stung the adventurer. He read in it a silent accusation that he had been found wanting. Whatever the mysterious written words on the cards might mean, the black had selected him twice from the throng for their recipient; and now seemed to have condemned him as deficient in the wit and spirit to engage the enigma.

Standing aside from the rush, the young man made a rapid estimate of the building in which he conceived that his adventure must lie. Five stories high it rose. A small restaurant occupied the basement.

The first floor, now closed, seemed to house millinery or furs. The second floor, by the winking electric letters, was the dentist's. Above this a polyglot babel of signs struggled to indicate the abodes of palmists, dressmakers, musicians, and doctors. Still higher up draped curtains and milk bottles white on the window sills proclaimed the regions of domesticity.

After concluding his survey Rudolf walked briskly up the high flight of stone steps into the house. Up two flights of the carpeted stairway he continued; and at its top paused. The hallway there was dimly lighted by two pale jets of gas—one far to his right, the other nearer, to his left. He looked toward the nearer light and saw, within its wan halo, a green door. For one moment he hesitated; then he seemed to see the contumelious sneer of the African juggler of cards; and then he walked straight to the green door and knocked against it.

Moments like those that passed before his knock was answered measure the quick breath of true adventure. What might not be

behind those green panels! Gamesters at play; cunning rogues bait-
ing their traps with subtle skill; beauty in love with courage, and
thus planning to be sought by it; danger, death, love, disappoint-
ment, ridicule—any of these might respond to that temerarious*
rap.

A faint rustle was heard inside, and the door slowly opened. A
girl not yet twenty stood there white-faced and tottering. She
loosed the knob and swayed weakly, groping with one hand. Rudolf
caught her and laid her on a faded couch that stood against the
wall. He closed the door and took a swift glance around the room
by the light of a flickering gas jet. Neat, but extreme poverty was
the story that he read.

The girl lay still, as if in a faint. Rudolf looked around the room
excitedly for a barrel. People must be rolled upon a barrel who—
no, no; that was for drowned persons. He began to fan her with
his hat. That was successful, for he struck her nose with the brim
of his derby and she opened her eyes. And then the young man
saw that hers, indeed, was the one missing face from his heart's
gallery of intimate portraits. The frank, gray eyes, the little nose,
turning pertly outward; the chestnut hair, curling like the tendrils
of a pea vine, seemed the right end and reward of all his wonderful
adventures. But the face was woefully thin and pale.

The girl looked at him calmly, and then smiled.

"Fainted, didn't I?" she asked, weakly. "Well, who wouldn't? You
try going without anything to eat for three days and see!"

"Himmel!"† exclaimed Rudolf, jumping up. "Wait till I come
back."

He dashed out the green door and down the stairs. In twenty
minutes he was back again kicking at the door with his toe for her
to open it. With both arms he hugged an array of wares from the
grocery and the restaurant. On the table he laid them—bread and
butter, cold meats, cakes, pies, pickles, oysters, a roasted chicken,
a bottle of milk and one of red-hot tea.

"This is ridiculous," said Rudolf, blusteringly, "to go without
eating. You must quit making election bets of this kind. Supper is

---

*Bold or reckless.
†"Heavens!" (German).

ready." He helped her to a chair at the table and asked: "Is there a cup for the tea?" "On the shelf by the window," she answered. When he turned again with the cup he saw her, with eyes shining rapturously, beginning upon a huge dill pickle that she had rooted out from the paper bags with a woman's unerring instinct. He took it from her, laughingly, and poured the cup full of milk. "Drink that first," he ordered, "and then you shall have some tea, and then a chicken wing. If you are very good you shall have a pickle to-morrow. And now, if you'll allow me to be your guest we'll have supper."

He drew up the other chair. The tea brightened the girl's eyes and brought back some of her color. She began to eat with a sort of dainty ferocity like some starved wild animal. She seemed to regard the young man's presence and the aid he had rendered her as a natural thing—not as though she undervalued the conventions; but as one whose great stress gave her the right to put aside the artificial for the human. But gradually, with the return of strength and comfort, came also a sense of the little conventions that belong; and she began to tell him her little story. It was one of a thousand such as the city yawns at every day—the shop girl's story of insufficient wages, further reduced by "fines" that go to swell the store's profits; of time lost through illness; and then of lost positions, lost hope, and—the knock of the adventurer upon the green door.

But to Rudolf the history sounded as big as the Iliad[4] or the crisis in "Junie's Love Test."

"To think of you going through all that," he exclaimed.

"It was something fierce," said the girl, solemnly.

"And you have no relatives or friends in the city?"

"None whatever."

"I am all alone in the world, too," said Rudolf, after a pause.

"I am glad of that," said the girl, promptly; and somehow it pleased the young man to hear that she approved of his bereft condition.

Very suddenly her eyelids dropped and she sighed deeply.

"I'm awfully sleepy," she said, "and I feel so good."

Rudolf rose and took his hat.

"Then I'll say good-night. A long night's sleep will be fine for you."

He held out his hand, and she took it and said "good-night." But her eyes asked a question so eloquently, so frankly and pathetically that he answered it with words.

"Oh, I'm coming back to-morrow to see how you are getting along. You can't get rid of me so easily."

Then, at the door, as though the way of his coming had been so much less important than the fact that he had come, she asked: "How did you come to knock at my door?"

He looked at her for a moment, remembering the cards, and felt a sudden jealous pain. What if they had fallen into other hands as adventurous as his? Quickly he decided that she must never know the truth. He would never let her know that he was aware of the strange expedient to which she had been driven by her great distress.

"One of our piano tuners lives in this house," he said. "I knocked at your door by mistake."

The last thing he saw in the room before the green door closed was her smile.

At the head of the stairway he paused and looked curiously about him. And then he went along the hallway to its other end; and, coming back, ascended to the floor above and continued his puzzled explorations. Every door that he found in the house was painted green.

Wondering, he descended to the sidewalk. The fantastic African was still there. Rudolf confronted him with his two cards in his hand.

"Will you tell me why you gave me these cards and what they mean?" he asked.

In a broad, good-natured grin the negro exhibited a splendid advertisement of his master's profession.

"Dar it is, boss," he said, pointing down the street. "But I 'spect you is a little late for de fust act."

Looking the way he pointed Rudolf saw above the entrance to a theatre the blazing electric sign of its new play, "The Green Door."

"I'm informed dat it's a fust-rate show, sah," said the negro. "De agent what represents it pussented me with a dollar, sah, to distribute a few of his cards along with de doctah's. May I offer you one of de doctah's cards, suh?"

At the corner of the block in which he lived Rudolf stopped for a glass of beer and a cigar. When he had come out with his lighted weed he buttoned his coat, pushed back his hat and said, stoutly, to the lamp post on the corner:

"All the same, I believe it was the hand of Fate that doped out the way for me to find her."

Which conclusion, under the circumstances, certainly admits Rudolf Steiner to the ranks of the true followers of Romance and Adventure.

—from *The Four Million* (1906)

A LICKPENNY LOVER

There were 3,000 girls in the Biggest Store. Masie was one of them. She was eighteen and a saleslady in the gents' gloves. Here she became versed in two varieties of human beings—the kind of gents who buy their gloves in department stores and the kind of women who buy gloves for unfortunate gents. Besides this wide knowledge of the human species, Masie had acquired other information. She had listened to the promulgated wisdom of the 2,999 other girls and had stored it in a brain that was as secretive and wary as that of a Maltese cat. Perhaps nature, foreseeing that she would lack wise counsellors, had mingled the saving ingredient of shrewdness along with her beauty, as she has endowed the silver fox of the priceless fur above the other animals with cunning.

For Masie was beautiful. She was a deep-tinted blonde, with the calm poise of a lady who cooks butter cakes in a window. She stood behind her counter in the Biggest Store; and as you closed your hand over the tape-line for your glove measure you thought of Hebe;* and as you looked again you wondered how she had come by Minerva's† eyes.

When the floorwalker‡ was not looking Masie chewed tutti frutti§; when he was looking she gazed up as if at the clouds and smiled wistfully.

That is the shopgirl smile, and I enjoin you to shun it unless you are well fortified with callosity‖ of the heart, caramels and a

---

*Greek goddess of youth.
†Roman goddess of wisdom.
‡Floor manager in a department store.
§All fruits (Italian); here, a flavor of chewing gum.
‖Hardness, lack of emotion.

congeniality for the capers of Cupid. This smile belonged to Masie's recreation hours and not to the store; but the floorwalker must have his own. He is the Shylock of the stores. When he comes nosing around the bridge of his nose is a toll-bridge. It is goo-goo eyes or "git" when he looks toward a pretty girl. Of course not all floorwalkers are thus. Only a few days ago the papers printed news of one over eighty years of age.

One day Irving Carter, painter, millionaire, traveller, poet, automobilist, happened to enter the Biggest Store. It is due to him to add that his visit was not voluntary. Filial duty took him by the collar and dragged him inside, while his mother philandered among the bronze and terra-cotta statuettes.

Carter strolled across to the glove counter in order to shoot a few minutes on the wing. His need for gloves was genuine; he had forgotten to bring a pair with him. But his action hardly calls for apology, because he had never heard of glove-counter flirtations.

As he neared the vicinity of his fate he hesitated, suddenly conscious of this unknown phase of Cupid's less worthy profession.

Three or four cheap fellows, sonorously garbed, were leaning over the counters, wrestling with the mediatorial hand-coverings, while giggling girls played vivacious seconds to their lead upon the strident string of coquetry. Carter would have retreated, but he had gone too far. Masie confronted him behind her counter with a questioning look in eyes as coldly, beautifully, warmly blue as the glint of summer sunshine on an iceberg drifting in Southern seas.

And then Irving Carter, painter, millionaire, etc., felt a warm flush rise to his aristocratically pale face. But not from diffidence. The blush was intellectual in origin. He knew in a moment that he stood in the ranks of the ready-made youths who wooed the giggling girls at other counters. Himself leaned against the oaken trysting place of a cockney* Cupid with a desire in his heart for the favor of a glove salesgirl. He was no more than Bill and Jack and Mickey. And then he felt a sudden tolerance for them, and an elating, courageous contempt for the conventions upon which he had fed, and an unhesitating determination to have this perfect creature for his own.

---

*Of or pertaining to a lower-class district of London.

When the gloves were paid for and wrapped Carter lingered for a moment. The dimples at the corners of Masie's damask mouth deepened. All gentlemen who bought gloves lingered in just that way. She curved an arm, showing like Psyche's[1] through her shirt-waist sleeve, and rested an elbow upon the show-case edge.

Carter had never before encountered a situation of which he had not been perfect master. But now he stood far more awkward than Bill or Jack or Mickey. He had no chance of meeting this beautiful girl socially. His mind struggled to recall the nature and habits of shopgirls as he had read or heard of them. Somehow he had received the idea that they sometimes did not insist too strictly upon the regular channels of introduction. His heart beat loudly at the thought of proposing an unconventional meeting with this lovely and virginal being. But the tumult in his heart gave him courage.

After a few friendly and well-received remarks on general subjects, he laid his card by her hand on the counter.

"Will you please pardon me," he said, "if I seem too bold; but I earnestly hope you will allow me the pleasure of seeing you again. There is my name; I assure you that it is with the greatest respect that I ask the favor of becoming one of your fr—acquaintances. May I not hope for the privilege?"

Masie knew men—especially men who buy gloves. Without hesitation she looked him frankly and smilingly in the eyes, and said:

"Sure. I guess you're all right. I don't usually go out with strange gentlemen, though. It ain't quite ladylike. When should you want to see me again?"

"As soon as I may," said Carter. "If you would allow me to call at your home, I——"

Masie laughed musically. "Oh, gee, no!" she said, emphatically. "If you could see our flat once! There's five of us in three rooms. I'd just like to see ma's face if I was to bring a gentleman friend there!"

"Anywhere, then," said the enamored Carter, "that will be convenient to you."

"Say," suggested Masie, with a bright-idea look in her peach-blow face; "I guess Thursday night will about suit me. Suppose you come to the corner of Eighth Avenue and Forty-eighth Street at

7:30. I live right near the corner. But I've got to be back home by eleven. Ma never lets me stay out after eleven."

Carter promised gratefully to keep the tryst, and then hastened to his mother, who was looking about for him to ratify her purchase of a bronze Diana.

A salesgirl, with small eyes and an obtuse nose, strolled near Masie, with a friendly leer.

"Did you make a hit with his nobs,* Mase?" she asked, familiarly.

"The gentleman asked permission to call," answered Masie, with the grand air, as she slipped Carter's card into the bosom of her waist.

"Permission to call!" echoed small eyes, with a snigger. "Did he say anything about dinner in the Waldorf and a spin in his auto afterward?"

"Oh, cheese it!" said Masie, wearily. "You've been used to swell things, I don't think. You've had a swelled head ever since that hose-cart† driver took you out to a chop suey joint. No, he never mentioned the Waldorf; but there's a Fifth Avenue address on his card, and if he buys the supper you can bet your life there won't be no pigtail on the waiter what takes the order."

As Carter glided away from the Biggest Store with his mother in his electric runabout, he bit his lip with a dull pain at his heart. He knew that love had come to him for the first time in all the twenty-nine years of his life. And that the object of it should make so readily an appointment with him at a street corner, though it was a step toward his desires, tortured him with misgivings.

Carter did not know the shopgirl. He did not know that her home is often either a scarcely habitable tiny room or a domicile filled to overflowing with kith and kin. The street-corner is her parlor, the park is her drawing-room; the avenue is her garden walk; yet for the most part she is as inviolate mistress of herself in them as is my lady inside her tapestried chamber.

One evening at dusk, two weeks after their first meeting, Carter and Masie strolled arm-in-arm into a little, dimly-lit park. They found a bench, tree-shadowed and secluded, and sat there.

---

*Slang for a man of wealth and social distinction.
†Cart used to transport a hose to a fire; predecessor of a fire truck.

For the first time his arm stole gently around her. Her golden-bronze head slid restfully against his shoulder.

"Gee!" sighed Masie, thankfully. "Why didn't you ever think of that before?"

"Masie," said Carter, earnestly, "you surely know that I love you. I ask you sincerely to marry me. You know me well enough by this time to have no doubts of me. I want you, and I must have you. I care nothing for the difference in our stations."

"What is the difference?" asked Masie, curiously.

"Well, there isn't any," said Carter, quickly, "except in the minds of foolish people. It is in my power to give you a life of luxury. My social position is beyond dispute, and my means are ample."

"They all say that," remarked Masie. "It's the kid they all give you. I suppose you really work in a delicatessen or follow the races. I ain't as green as I look."

"I can furnish you all the proofs you want," said Carter, gently. "And I want you, Masie. I loved you the first day I saw you."

"They all do," said Masie, with an amused laugh, "to hear 'em talk. If I could meet a man that got stuck on me the third time he'd seen me I think I'd get mashed on him."

"Please don't say such things," pleaded Carter. "Listen to me, dear. Ever since I first looked into your eyes you have been the only woman in the world for me."

"Oh, ain't you the kidder!" smiled Masie. "How many other girls did you ever tell that?"

But Carter persisted. And at length he reached the flimsy, fluttering little soul of the shopgirl that existed somewhere deep down in her lovely bosom. His words penetrated the heart whose very lightness was its safest armor. She looked up at him with eyes that saw. And a warm glow visited her cool cheeks. Tremblingly, awfully, her moth wings closed, and she seemed about to settle upon the flower of love. Some faint glimmer of life and its possibilities on the other side of her glove counter dawned upon her. Carter felt the change and crowded the opportunity.

"Marry me, Masie," he whispered softly, "and we will go away from this ugly city to beautiful ones. We will forget work and business, and life will be one long holiday. I know where I should take you—I have been there often. Just think of a shore where summer is eternal, where the waves are always rippling on the lovely beach and the people are happy and free as children. We will sail to those shores and remain there as long as you please. In one of those far-away cities there are grand and lovely palaces and towers full of beautiful pictures and statues. The streets of the city are water, and one travels about in——"

"I know," said Masie, sitting up suddenly. "Gondolas."

"Yes," smiled Carter.

"I thought so," said Masie.

"And then," continued Carter, "we will travel on and see what-ever we wish in the world. After the European cities we will visit India and the ancient cities there, and ride on elephants and see the wonderful temples of the Hindoos and Brahmins[2] and the Jap-anese gardens and the camel trains and the chariot races in Persia, and all the queer sights of foreign countries. Don't you think you would like it, Masie?"

Masie rose to her feet.

"I think we had better be going home," she said, coolly. "It's getting late."

Carter humored her. He had come to know her varying, thistle-down moods,* and that it was useless to combat them. But he felt a certain happy triumph. He had held for a moment, though but by a silken thread, the soul of his wild Psyche, and hope was stronger within him. Once she had folded her wings and her cool hand had closed about his own.

At the Biggest Store the next day Masie's chum, Lulu, waylaid her in an angle of the counter.

"How are you and your swell friend making it?" she asked.

"Oh, him?" said Masie, patting her side curls. "He ain't in it any more. Say, Lu, what do you think that fellow wanted me to do?"

"Go on the stage?" guessed Lulu, breathlessly.

"Nit; he's too cheap a guy for that. He wanted me to marry him and go down to Coney Island for a wedding tour!"

—from *The Voice of the City* (1908)

---

*Flighty moods; thistle down are wispy tufts atop a thistle plant that catch in the wind and carry the thistle seeds.

LOST ON DRESS PARADE

M r. Towers Chandler was pressing his evening suit in his hall bedroom. One iron was heating on a small gas stove; the other was being pushed vigorously back and forth to make the desirable crease that would be seen later on extending in straight lines from Mr. Chandler's patent leather shoes to the edge of his low-cut vest. So much of the hero's toilet may be intrusted to our confidence. The remainder may be guessed by those whom genteel poverty has driven to ignoble expedient. Our next view of him shall be as he descends the steps of his lodging-house immaculately and correctly clothed; calm, assured, handsome—in appearance the typical New York young clubman setting out, slightly bored, to inaugurate the pleasures of the evening.

Chandler's honorarium was $18 per week. He was employed in the office of an architect. He was twenty-two years old; he considered architecture to be truly an art; and he honestly believed—though he would not have dared to admit it in New York—that the Flatiron Building was inferior in design to the great cathedral in Milan.[1]

Out of each week's earnings Chandler set aside $1. At the end of each ten weeks with the extra capital thus accumulated, he purchased one gentleman's evening from the bargain counter of stingy old Father Time. He arrayed himself in the regalia of millionaires and presidents; he took himself to the quarter where life is brightest and showiest, and there dined with taste and luxury. With ten dollars a man may, for a few hours, play the wealthy idler to perfection. The sum is ample for a well-considered meal, a bottle bearing a respectable label commensurate tips, a smoke, cab fare, and the ordinary etceteras.

This one delectable evening culled from each dull seventy was to Chandler a source of renascent bliss. To the society bud comes but one début; it stands alone sweet in her memory when her hair was whitened; but to Chandler each ten weeks brought a joy as keen, as thrilling, as new as the first had been. To sit among *bon vivants** under palms in the swirl of concealed music, to look upon the *habitués*† of such a paradise and to be looked upon by them—what is a girl's first dance and short-sleeved tulle compared with this?

Up Broadway Chandler moved with the vespertine dress parade. For this evening he was an exhibit as well as a gazer. For the next sixty-nine evenings he would be dining in cheviot and worsted at dubious *table d'hôtes*, at whirlwind lunch counters, on sandwiches and beer in his hall bedroom. He was willing to do that, for he was a true son of the great city of razzle-dazzle, and to him one evening in the limelight made up for many dark ones.

Chandler protracted his walk until the Forties began to intersect the great and glittering primrose way, for the evening was yet young, and when one is of the *beau monde*‡ only one day in seventy, one loves to protract the pleasure. Eyes bright, sinister, curious, admiring, provocative, alluring were bent upon him, for his garb and air proclaimed him a devotee to the hour of solace and pleasure.

At a certain corner he came to a standstill, proposing to himself the question of turning back toward the showy and fashionable restaurant in which he usually dined on the evenings of his especial luxury. Just then a girl scuddled lightly around the corner, slipped on a patch of icy snow and fell plump upon the sidewalk.

Chandler assisted her to her feet with instant and solicitous courtesy. The girl hobbled to the wall of the building, leaned against it, and thanked him demurely.

"I think my ankle is strained," she said. "It twisted when I fell."

"Does it pain you much?" inquired Chandler.

"Only when I rest my weight upon it. I think I will be able to walk in a minute or two."

"If I can be of any further service," suggested the young man, "I will call a cab, or——"

---

*Literally, good livers (French); people who are fond of good living.
†Regular visitors (French).
‡Literally, beautiful world (French); world of high society and fashion.

"Thank you," said the girl, softly but heartily. "I am sure you need not trouble yourself any further. It was so awkward of me. And my shoe heels are horridly commonsense; I can't blame them at all."

Chandler looked at the girl and found her swiftly drawing his interest. She was pretty in a refined way; and her eye was both merry and kind. She was inexpensively clothed in a plain black dress that suggested a sort of uniform such as shop-girls wear. Her glossy dark-brown hair showed its coils beneath a cheap hat of black straw whose only ornament was a velvet ribbon and bow. She could have posed as a model for the self-respecting working girl of the best type.

A sudden idea came into the head of the young architect. He would ask this girl to dine with him. Here was the element that his splendid but solitary periodic feats had lacked. His brief season of elegant luxury would be doubly enjoyable if he could add to it a lady's society. This girl was a lady, he was sure—her manner and speech settled that. And in spite of her extremely plain attire he felt that he would be pleased to sit at table with her.

These thoughts passed swiftly through his mind, and he decided to ask her. It was a breach of etiquette, of course, but oftentimes wage-earning girls waived formalities in matters of this kind. They were generally shrewd judges of men; and thought better of their own judgment than they did of useless conventions. His ten dollars, discreetly expended, would enable the two to dine very well indeed. The dinner would no doubt be a wonderful experience thrown into the dull routine of the girl's life; and her lively appreciation of it would add to his own triumph and pleasure.

"I think," he said to her, with frank gravity, "that your foot needs a longer rest than you suppose. Now, I am going to suggest a way in which you can give it that and at the same time do me a favor. I was on my way to dine all by my lonely self when you came tumbling around the corner. You come with me and we'll have a cozy dinner and a pleasant talk together, and by that time your game ankle will carry you home very nicely, I am sure."

The girl looked quickly up into Chandler's clear, pleasant countenance. Her eyes twinkled once very brightly, and then she smiled ingenuously.

"But we don't know each other—it wouldn't be right, would it?" she said, doubtfully.

"There is nothing wrong about it," said the young man, candidly. "I'll introduce myself—permit me—Mr. Towers Chandler. After our dinner, which I will try to make as pleasant as possible, I will bid you good-evening, or attend you safely to your door, whichever you prefer."

"But, dear me!" said the girl, with a glance at Chandler's faultless attire. "In this old dress and hat!"

"Never mind that," said Chandler, cheerfully. "I'm sure you look more charming in them than any one we shall see in the most elaborate dinner toilette."

"My ankle does hurt yet," admitted the girl, attempting a limping step. "I think I will accept your invitation, Mr. Chandler. You may call me—Miss Marian."*

"Come then, Miss Marian," said the young architect, gaily, but with perfect courtesy; "you will not have far to walk. There is a very respectable and good restaurant in the next block. You will have to lean on my arm—so—and walk slowly. It is lonely dining all by one's self. I'm just a little bit glad that you slipped on the ice."

When the two were established at a well-appointed table, with a promising waiter hovering in attendance, Chandler began to experience the real joy that his regular outing always brought to him.

The restaurant was not so showy or pretentious as the one further down Broadway, which he always preferred, but it was nearly so. The tables were well filled with prosperous-looking diners, there was a good orchestra, playing softly enough to make conversation a possible pleasure, and the cuisine and service were beyond criticism. His companion, even in her cheap hat and dress, held herself with an air that added distinction to the natural beauty of her face and figure. And it is certain that she looked at Chandler, with his animated but self-possessed manner and his kindling and frank blue eyes, with something not far from admiration in her own charming face.

Then it was that the Madness of Manhattan, the Frenzy of Fuss and Feathers, the Bacillus† of Brag, the Provincial Plague of Pose seized upon Towers Chandler. He was on Broadway, surrounded

---

*Maid Marian is the heroine of the legend of Robin Hood.
†Disease-producing bacterium.

by pomp and style, and there were eyes to look at him. On the stage of that comedy he had assumed to play the one-night part of a butterfly of fashion and an idler of means and taste. He was dressed for the part, and all his good angels had not the power to prevent him from acting it.

So he began to prate to Miss Marian of clubs, of teas, of golf and riding and kennels and cotillions and tours abroad and threw out hints of a yacht lying at Larchmont.* He could see that she was vastly impressed by this vague talk, so he endorsed his pose by random insinuations concerning great wealth, and mentioned familiarly a few names that are handled reverently by the proletariat. It was Chandler's short little day, and he was wringing from it the best that could be had, as he saw it. And yet once or twice he saw the pure gold of this girl shine through the mist that his egotism had raised between him and all objects.

"This way of living that you speak of," she said, "sounds so futile and purposeless. Haven't you any work to do in the world that might interest you more?"

"My dear Miss Marian," he exclaimed—"work! Think of dressing every day for dinner, of making half a dozen calls in an afternoon—with a policeman at every corner ready to jump into your auto and take you to the station, if you get up any greater speed than a donkey cart's gait. We do-nothings are the hardest workers in the land."

The dinner was concluded, the waiter generously fed, and the two walked out to the corner where they had met. Miss Marian walked very well now; her limp was scarcely noticeable.

"Thank you for a nice time," she said, frankly. "I must run home now. I liked the dinner very much, Mr. Chandler."

He shook hands with her, smiling cordially, and said something about a game of bridge at his club. He watched her for a moment, walking rather rapidly eastward, and then he found a cab to drive him slowly homeward.

In his chilly bedroom Chandler laid away his evening clothes for a sixty-nine day's rest. He went about it thoughtfully.

"That was a stunning girl," he said to himself. "She's all right,

---

*Town north of New York City, once a fashionable resort.

too, I'd be sworn, even if she does have to work. Perhaps if I'd told her the truth instead of all that razzle-dazzle we might—but, confound it! I had to play up to my clothes."

Thus spoke the brave who was born and reared in the wigwams of the tribe of the Manhattans.

The girl, after leaving her entertainer, sped swiftly cross-town until she arrived at a handsome and sedate mansion two squares to the east, facing on that avenue which is the highway of Mammon* and the auxiliary gods. Here she entered hurriedly and ascended to a room where a handsome young lady in an elaborate house dress was looking anxiously out the window.

"Oh, you madcap!" exclaimed the elder girl, when the other entered. "When will you quit frightening us this way? It's two hours since you ran out in that rag of an old dress and Marie's hat. Mamma has been so alarmed. She sent Louis in the auto to try to find you. You are a bad, thoughtless Puss."

The elder girl touched a button, and a maid came in a moment.

"Marie, tell mamma that Miss Marian has returned."

"Don't scold, Sister. I only ran down to Mme. Theo's to tell her to use mauve insertion instead of pink. My costume and Marie's hat were just what I needed. Every one thought I was a shop-girl, I am sure."

"Dinner is over, dear; you stayed so late."

"I know. I slipped on the sidewalk and turned my ankle. I could not walk, so I hobbled into a restaurant and sat there until I was better. That is why I was so long."

The two girls sat in the window seat, looking out at the lights and the stream of hurrying vehicles in the avenue. The younger one cuddled down with her head in her sister's lap.

"We will have to marry some day," she said, dreamily—"both of us. We have so much money that we will not be allowed to disappoint the public. Do you want me to tell you the kind of a man I could love, Sis?"

"Go on, you scatterbrain," smiled the other.

"I could love a man with dark and kind blue eyes, who is gentle and respectful to poor girls, who is handsome and good and does

---

*Material riches.

not try to flirt. But I could love him only if he had an ambition, an object, some work to do in the world. I would not care how poor he was if I could help him build his way up. But, Sister dear, the kind of man we always meet—the man who lives an idle life between society and his clubs—I could not love a man like that, even if his eyes were blue and he were so kind to poor girls whom he met in the street."

—from *The Four Million* (1906)

TRANSIENTS IN ARCADIA

There is a hotel on Broadway that has escaped discovery by the summer-resort promoters. It is deep and wide and cool. Its rooms are finished in dark oak of a low temperature. Home-made breezes and deep-green shrubbery give it the delights without the inconveniences of the Adirondacks.[1] One can mount its broad staircases or glide dreamily upward in its aërial elevators, attended by guides in brass buttons, with a serene joy that Alpine climbers have never attained. There is a chef in its kitchen who will prepare for you brook trout better than the White Mountains ever served, sea food that would turn Old Point Comfort—"by Gad, sah!"—green with envy,[2] and Maine venison that would melt the official heart of a game warden.

A few have found out this oasis in the July desert of Manhattan. During that month you will see the hotel's reduced array of guests scattered luxuriously about in the cool twilight of its lofty dining-room, gazing at one another across the snowy waste of unoccupied tables, silently congratulatory.

Superfluous, watchful, pneumatically moving waiters hover near, supplying every want before it is expressed. The temperature is perpetual April. The ceiling is painted in water colors to counterfeit a summer sky across which delicate clouds drift and do not vanish as those of nature do to our regret.

The pleasing, distant roar of Broadway is transformed in the imagination of the happy guests to the noise of a waterfall filling the woods with its restful sound. At every strange footstep the guests turn an anxious ear, fearful lest their retreat be discovered and invaded by the restless pleasure-seekers who are forever hounding nature to her deepest lairs.

Thus in the depopulated caravansary the little band of connoisseurs jealously hide themselves during the heated season, enjoying to the uttermost the delights of mountain and seashore that art and skill have gathered and served to them.

In this July came to the hotel one whose card that she sent to the clerk for her name to be registered read "Mme. Héloise D'Arcy Beaumont."

Madame Beaumont was a guest such as the Hotel Lotus[3] loved. She possessed the fine air of the élite, tempered and sweetened by a cordial graciousness that made the hotel employés her slaves. Bell-boys fought for the honor of answering her ring; the clerks, but for the question of ownership, would have deeded to her the hotel and its contents; the other guests regarded her as the final touch of feminine exclusiveness and beauty that rendered the entourage perfect.

This super-excellent guest rarely left the hotel. Her habits were consonant with the customs of the discriminating patrons of the Hotel Lotus. To enjoy that delectable hostelry one must forego the city as though it were leagues away. By night a brief excursion to the nearby roofs is in order; but during the torrid day one remains in the umbrageous* fastnesses of the Lotus as a trout hangs poised in the pellucid sanctuaries of his favorite pool.

Though alone in the Hotel Lotus, Madame Beaumont preserved the state of a queen whose loneliness was of position only. She breakfasted at ten, a cool, sweet, leisurely, delicate being who glowed softly in the dimness like a jasmine flower in the dusk.

But at dinner was Madame's glory at its height. She wore a gown as beautiful and immaterial as the mist from an unseen cataract in a mountain gorge. The nomenclature of this gown is beyond the guess of the scribe. Always pale-red roses reposed against its lace-garnished front. It was a gown that the head-waiter viewed with respect and met at the door. You thought of Paris when you saw it, and maybe of mysterious countesses, and certainly of Versailles[4] and rapiers and Mrs. Fiske[5] and rouge-et-noir.† There was an un-traceable rumor in the Hotel Lotus that Madame was a cosmop-olite, and that she was pulling with her slender white hands certain

---

*Shadowed.

†Card game played on a table marked with black and red diamonds.

strings between the nations in the favor of Russia. Being a citizeness of the world's smoothest roads it was small wonder that she was quick to recognize in the refined purlieus of the Hotel Lotus the most desirable spot in America for a restful sojourn during the heat of midsummer.

On the third day of Madame Beaumont's residence in the hotel a young man entered and registered himself as a guest. His clothing—to speak of his points in approved order—was quietly in the mode; his features good and regular; his expression that of a poised and sophisticated man of the world. He informed the clerk that he would remain three or four days, inquired concerning the sailing of European steamships, and sank into the blissful inanition of the nonpareil hotel with the contented air of a traveller in his favorite inn.

The young man—not to question the veracity of the register— was Harold Farrington. He drifted into the exclusive and calm current of life in the Lotus so tactfully and silently that not a ripple alarmed his fellow-seekers after rest. He ate in the Lotus and of its patronym, and was lulled into blissful peace with the other fortunate mariners. In one day he acquired his table and his waiter and the fear lest the panting chasers after repose that kept Broadway warm should pounce upon and destroy this contiguous but covert haven.

After dinner on the next day after the arrival of Harold Farrington Madame Beaumont dropped her handkerchief in passing out. Mr. Farrington recovered and returned it without the effusiveness of a seeker after acquaintance.

Perhaps there was a mystic freemasonry between the discriminating guests of the Lotus. Perhaps they were drawn one to another by the fact of their common good fortune in discovering the acme of summer resorts in a Broadway hotel. Words delicate in courtesy and tentative in departure from formality passed between the two. And, as if in the expedient atmosphere of a real summer resort, an acquaintance grew, flowered and fructified on the spot as does the mystic plant of the conjuror. For a few moments they stood on a balcony upon which the corridor ended, and tossed the feathery ball of conversation.

"One tires of the old resorts," said Madame Beaumont, with a faint but sweet smile. "What is the use to fly to the mountains or the seashore to escape noise and dust when the very people that make both follow us there?"

"Even on the ocean," remarked Farrington, sadly, "the Philistines* be upon you. The most exclusive steamers are getting to be scarcely more than ferry boats. Heaven help us when the summer resorter discovers that the Lotus is further away from Broadway than Thousand Islands or Mackinac."[6]

"I hope our secret will be safe for a week, anyhow," said Madame, with a sigh and a smile. "I do not know where I would go if they should descend upon the dear Lotus. I know of but one place so delightful in summer, and that is the castle of Count Polinski, in the Ural Mountains."

"I hear that Baden-Baden and Cannes[7] are almost deserted this season," said Farrington. "Year by year the old resorts fall in disrepute. Perhaps many others, like ourselves, are seeking out the quiet nooks that are overlooked by the majority."

"I promise myself three days more of this delicious rest," said Madame Beaumont. "On Monday the *Cedric* sails."

Harold Farrington's eyes proclaimed his regret. "I too must leave on Monday," he said, "but I do not go abroad."

Madame Beaumont shrugged one round shoulder in a foreign gesture.

"One cannot hide here forever, charming though it may be. The château has been in preparation for me longer than a month. Those house parties that one must give—what a nuisance! But I shall never forget my week in the Hotel Lotus."

"Nor shall I," said Farrington in a low voice, "and I shall never *forgive* the *Cedric*."

On Sunday evening, three days afterward, the two sat at a little table on the same balcony. A discreet waiter brought ices and small glasses of claret cup.

Madame Beaumont wore the same beautiful evening gown that she had worn each day at dinner. She seemed thoughtful. Near her hand on the table lay a small chatelaine purse. After she had eaten her ice she opened the purse and took out a one-dollar bill.

---

*Ignorant or uncultured people; name of Old Testament enemies of the Israelites.

"Mr. Farrington," she said, with the smile that had won the Hotel Lotus, "I want to tell you something. I'm going to leave before breakfast in the morning, because I've got to go back to my work. I'm behind the hosiery counter at Casey's Mammoth Store, and my vacation's up at eight o'clock tomorrow. That paper dollar is the last cent I'll see till I draw my eight dollars salary next Saturday night. You're a real gentleman, and you've been good to me, and I wanted to tell you before I went.

"I've been saving up out of my wages for a year just for this vacation. I wanted to spend one week like a lady if I never do another one. I wanted to get up when I please instead of having to crawl out at seven every morning; and I wanted to live on the best and be waited on and ring bells for things just like rich folks do. Now I've done it, and I've had the happiest time I ever expect to have in my life. I'm going back to my work and my little hall bedroom satisfied for another year. I wanted to tell you about it, Mr. Farrington, because I—I thought you kind of liked me, and I—I liked you. But, oh, I couldn't help deceiving you up till now, for it was all just like a fairy tale to me. So I talked about Europe and the things I've read about in other countries and made you think I was a great lady.

"This dress I've got on—it's the only one I have that's fit to wear—I bought from O'Dowd & Levinsky on the instalment plan.

"Seventy-five dollars is the price, and it was made to measure. I paid $10 down, and they're to collect $1 a week till it's paid for. That'll be about all I have to say, Mr. Farrington, except that my name is Mamie Siviter instead of Madame Beaumont, and I thank you for your attentions. This dollar will pay the instalment due on the dress to-morrow. I guess I'll go up to my room now."

Harold Farrington listened to the recital of the Lotus's loveliest guest with an impassive countenance. When she had concluded he drew a small book like a checkbook from his coat pocket. He wrote upon a blank form in this with a stub of pencil, tore out the leaf, tossed it over to his companion and took up the paper dollar.

"I've got to go to work, too, in the morning," he said, "and I might as well begin now. There's a receipt for the dollar instalment. I've been a collector for O'Dowd & Levinsky for three years. Funny, ain't it, that you and me both had the same idea about spending our vacation? I've always wanted to put up at a swell hotel, and I saved up out of my twenty per, and did it. Say, Mame, how about a trip to Coney Saturday night on the boat—what?"

The face of the pseudo Madame Héloise D'Arcy Beaumont beamed.

"Oh, you bet I'll go, Mr. Farrington. The store closes at twelve on Saturdays. I guess Coney'll be all right even if we did spend a week with the swells."

Below the balcony the sweltering city growled and buzzed in the July night. Inside the Hotel Lotus the tempered, cool shadows reigned, and the solicitous waiter single-footed near the low windows, ready at a nod to serve Madame and her escort.

At the door of the elevator Farrington took his leave, and Madame Beaumont made her last ascent. But before they reached the noiseless cage he said: "Just forget that 'Harold Farrington,' will you?—McManus is the name—James McManus. Some call me Jimmy."

"Good-night, Jimmy," said Madame.

—from *The Voice of the City* (1908)

Blinker was displeased. A man of less culture and poise and wealth would have sworn. But Blinker always remembered that he was a gentleman—a thing that no gentleman should do. So he merely looked bored and sardonic while he rode in a hansom to the centre of disturbance, which was the Broadway office of Lawyer Oldport, who was agent for the Blinker estate.

"I don't see," said Blinker, "why I should be always signing confounded papers. I am packed, and was to have left for the North Woods[1] this morning. Now I must wait until to-morrow morning. I hate night trains. My best razors are, of course, at the bottom of some unidentifiable trunk. It is a plot to drive me to bay rum and a monologuing, thumb-handed barber. Give me a pen that doesn't scratch. I hate pens that scratch."

"Sit down," said double-chinned, gray Lawyer Oldport. "The worst has not been told you. Oh, the hardships of the rich! The papers are not yet ready to sign. They will be laid before you to-morrow at eleven. You will miss another day. Twice shall the barber tweak the helpless nose of a Blinker. Be thankful that your sorrows do not embrace a haircut."

"If," said Blinker, rising, "the act did not involve more signing of papers I would take my business out of your hands at once. Give me a cigar, please."

"If," said Lawyer Oldport, "I had cared to see an old friend's son gulped down at one mouthful by sharks I would have ordered you to take it away long ago. Now, let's quit fooling, Alexander. Besides the grinding task of signing your name some thirty times to-morrow, I must impose upon you the consideration of a matter of business—of business, and I may say humanity or right. I spoke to you about this five years ago, but you would not listen—you were in a hurry for a coaching trip, I think. The subject has come up again. The property——"

"Oh, property!" interrupted Blinker. "Dear Mr. Oldport, I think you mentioned to-morrow. Let's have it all at one dose to-morrow—signatures and property and snappy rubber bands and that smelly sealing-wax and all. Have luncheon with me? Well, I'll try to remember to drop in at eleven to-morrow. Morning."

The Blinker wealth was in lands, tenements, and hereditaments, as the legal phrase goes. Lawyer Oldport had once taken Alexander in his little pulmonary gasoline runabout to see the many buildings and rows of buildings that he owned in the city. For Alexander was sole heir. They had amused Blinker very much. The houses looked so incapable of producing the big sums of money that Lawyer Oldport kept piling up in banks for him to spend.

In the evening Blinker went to one of his clubs, intending to dine. Nobody was there except some old fogies playing whist who spoke to him with grave politeness and glared at him with savage contempt. Everybody was out of town. But here he was kept in like a schoolboy to write his name over and over on pieces of paper. His wounds were deep.

Blinker turned his back on the fogies, and said to the club steward who had come forward with some nonsense about cold fresh salmon roe:

"Symons, I'm going to Coney Island." He said it as one might say: "All's off, I'm going to jump into the river."

The joke pleased Symons. He laughed with a sixteenth of a note of the audibility permitted by the laws governing employees.

"Certainly, sir," he tittered. "Of course, sir, I think I can see you at Coney, Mr. Blinker."

Blinker got a paper and looked up the movements of Sunday steamboats. Then he found a cab at the first corner and drove to a North River pier. He stood in line, as democratic as you or I, and bought a ticket, and was trampled upon and shoved forward until, at last, he found himself on the upper deck of the boat staring brazenly at a girl who sat alone upon a camp stool. But Blinker did not intend to be brazen; the girl was so wonderfully good looking that he forgot for one minute that he was the prince incog,* and behaved just as he did in society.

She was looking at him, too, and not severely. A puff of wind threatened Blinker's straw hat. He caught it warily and settled it again. The movement gave the effect of a bow. The girl nodded and smiled, and in another instant he was seated at her side. She was dressed all in white, she was paler than Blinker imagined milkmaids and girls of humble stations to be, but she was as tidy as a cherry blossom, and her steady, supremely frank gray eyes looked out from the intrepid depths of an unshadowed and untroubled soul.

"How dare you raise your hat to me?" she asked, with a smile-redeemed severity.

"I didn't," Blinker said, but he quickly covered the mistake by extending it to "I didn't know how to keep from it after I saw you."

"I do not allow gentlemen to sit by me to whom I have not been introduced," she said with a sudden haughtiness that deceived him. He rose reluctantly, but her clear, teasing laugh brought him down to his chair again.

"I guess you weren't going far," she declared, with beauty's magnificent self-confidence.

"Are you going to Coney Island?" asked Blinker.

"Me?" She turned upon him wide-open eyes full of bantering surprise. "Why, what a question! Can't you see that I'm riding a bicycle in the park?" Her drollery took the form of impertinence.

"And I'm laying bricks on a tall factory chimney," said Blinker. "Mayn't we see Coney together? I'm all alone and I've never been there before."

"It depends," said the girl, "on how nicely you behave. I'll consider your application until we get there."

Blinker took pains to provide against the rejection of his application. He strove to please. To adopt the metaphor of his nonsensical phrase, he laid brick upon brick on the tall chimney of his devoirs† until, at length, the structure was stable and complete. The manners of the best society come around finally to simplicity; and

---

*Incognito (colloquial).
†Duties.

as the girl's way was that naturally, they were on a mutual plane of communication from the beginning.

He learned that she was twenty, and her name was Florence; that she trimmed hats in a millinery shop; that she lived in a furnished room with her best chum Ella, who was cashier in a shoe store; and that a glass of milk from the bottle on the window-sill and an egg that boils itself while you twist up your hair makes a breakfast good enough for any one. Florence laughed when she heard "Blinker."

"Well," she said. "It certainly shows that you have imagination. It gives the 'Smiths' a chance for a little rest, anyhow."

They landed at Coney, and were dashed on the crest of a great human wave of mad pleasure-seekers into the walks and avenues of Fairyland gone into vaudeville.

With a curious eye, a critical mind, and a fairly withheld judgment Blinker considered the temples, pagodas and kiosks of popularized delights. Hoi polloi* trampled, hustled, and crowded him. Basket parties bumped him; sticky children tumbled, howling, under his feet, candying his clothes. Insolent youths strolling among the booths with hard-won canes under one arm and easily won girls on the other, blew defiant smoke from cheap cigars into his face. The publicity gentlemen with megaphones, each before his own stupendous attraction, roared like Niagara in his ears. Music of all kinds that could be tortured from brass, reed, hide, or string, fought in the air to gain space for its vibrations against its competitors. But what held Blinker in awful fascination was the mob, the multitude, the proletariat shrieking, struggling, hurrying, panting, hurling itself in incontinent frenzy, with unabashed abandon, into the ridiculous sham palaces of trumpery and tinsel pleasures. The vulgarity of it, its brutal overriding of all the tenets of repression and taste that were held by his caste, repelled him strongly.

In the midst of his disgust he turned and looked down at Florence by his side. She was ready with her quick smile and upturned, happy eyes, as bright and clear as the water in trout pools. The eyes were saying that they had the right to be shining and happy, for was their owner not with her (for the present) Man, her Gentleman Friend and holder of the keys to the enchanted city of fun.

---

*The masses (Greek).

Blinker did not read her look accurately, but by some miracle he suddenly saw Coney aright.

He no longer saw a mass of vulgarians seeking gross joys. He now looked clearly upon a hundred thousand true idealists. Their offenses were wiped out. Counterfeit and false though the garish joys of these spangled temples were, he perceived that deep under the gilt surface they offered saving and apposite balm and satisfaction to the restless human heart. Here, at least, was the husk of Romance, the empty but shining casque of Chivalry, the breath-catching though safe-guarded dip and flight of Adventure, the magic carpet that transports you to the realms of fairyland, though its journey be through but a few poor yards of space. He no longer saw a rabble, but his brothers seeking the ideal. There was no magic of poesy here or of art; but the glamour of their imagination turned yellow calico into cloth of gold and the megaphone into the silver trumpets of joy's heralds.

Almost humbled, Blinker rolled up the shirt sleeves of his mind and joined the idealists.

"You are the lady doctor," he said to Florence. "How shall we go about doing this jolly conglomeration of fairy tales, incorporated?"

"We will begin there," said the Princess, pointing to a fun pagoda on the edge of the sea, "and we will take them all in, one by one."

They caught the eight o'clock returning boat and sat, filled with pleasant fatigue, against the rail in the bow, listening to the Italians' fiddle and harp. Blinker had thrown off all care. The North Woods seemed to him an uninhabitable wilderness. What a fuss he had made over signing his name—pooh! he could sign it a hundred times. And her name was as pretty as she was—"Florence," he said it to himself a great many times.

As the boat was nearing its pier in the North River a two-funnelled, drab, foreign-looking sea-going steamer was dropping down toward the bay. The boat turned its nose in towards its slip. The steamer veered as if to seek mid-stream, and then yawned, seemed to increase its speed and struck the Coney boat on the side near the stern, cutting into it with a terrifying shock and crash.

While the six hundred passengers on the boat were mostly tumbling about the decks in a shrieking panic the captain was shouting at the steamer that it should not back off and leave the rent exposed for the water to enter. But the steamer tore its way out like a savage sawfish and cleaved its heartless way, full speed ahead.

The boat began to sink at its stern, but moved slowly toward the slip. The passengers were a frantic mob, unpleasant to behold.

Blinker held Florence tightly until the boat had righted itself. She made no sound or sign of fear. He stood on a camp stool, ripped off the slats above his head and pulled down a number of the life preservers. He began to buckle one around Florence. The rotten canvas split and the fraudulent granulated cork came pouring out in a stream. Florence caught a handful of it and laughed gleefully.

"It looks like breakfast food," she said. "Take it off. They're no good."

She unbuckled it and threw it on the deck. She made Blinker sit down and sat by his side and put her hand in his. "What'll you bet we don't reach the pier all right?" she said, and began to hum a song.

And now the captain moved among the passengers and compelled order. The boat would undoubtedly make her slip, he said, and ordered the women and children to the bow, where they could land first. The boat, very low in the water at the stern, tried gallantly to make his promise good.

"Florence," said Blinker, as she held him close by an arm and hand, "I love you."

"That's what they all say," she replied, lightly.

"I am not one of 'they all,' " he persisted. "I never knew any one I could love before. I could pass my life with you and be happy every day. I am rich. I can make things all right for you."

"That's what they all say," said the girl again, weaving the words into her little, reckless song.

"Don't say that again," said Blinker in a tone that made her look at him in frank surprise.

"Why shouldn't I say it?" she asked, calmly. "They all do."

"Who are 'they'?" he asked, jealous for the first time in his existence.

"Why, the fellows I know."

"Do you know so many?"

"Oh, well, I'm not a wall flower," she answered with modest complacency.

"Where do you see these—these men? At your home?"

"Of course not. I meet them just as I did you. Sometimes on the boat, sometimes in the park, sometimes on the street. I'm a pretty good judge of a man. I can tell in a minute if a fellow is one who is likely to get fresh."

"What do you mean by 'fresh'?"

"Who try to kiss you—me, I mean."

"Do any of them try that?" asked Blinker, clenching his teeth.

"Sure. All men do. You know that."

"Do you allow them?"

"Some. Not many. They won't take you out anywhere unless you do."

She turned her head and looked searchingly at Blinker. Her eyes were as innocent as a child's. There was a puzzled look in them, as though she did not understand him.

"What's wrong about my meeting fellows?" she asked, wonderingly.

"Everything," he answered, almost savagely. "Why don't you entertain your company in the house where you live? Is it necessary to pick up Tom, Dick, and Harry on the streets?"

She kept her absolutely ingenuous eyes upon his.

"If you could see the place where I live you wouldn't ask that. I live in Brickdust Row. They call it that because there's red dust from the bricks crumbling over everything. I've lived there for more than four years. There's no place to receive company. You can't have anybody come to your room. What else is there to do? A girl has got to meet the men, hasn't she?"

"Yes," he said hoarsely. "A girl has got to meet a—has got to meet the men."

"The first time one spoke to me on the street," she continued, "I ran home and cried all night. But you get used to it. I meet a good many nice fellows at church. I go on rainy days and stand in the vestibule until one comes up with an umbrella. I wish there was a parlor, so I could ask you to call, Mr. Blinker—are you really sure it isn't 'Smith,' now?"

The boat landed safely. Blinker had a confused impression of walking with the girl through quiet crosstown streets until she stopped at a corner and held out her hand.

"I live just one more block over," she said. "Thank you for a very pleasant afternoon."

Blinker muttered something and plunged northward till he found a cab. A big, gray church loomed slowly at his right. Blinker shook his fist at it through the window.

"I gave you a thousand dollars last week," he cried under his breath, "and she meets them in your very doors. There is something wrong; there is something wrong."

At eleven the next day Blinker signed his name thirty times with a new pen provided by Lawyer Oldport.

"Now let me get to the woods," he said, surlily.

"You are not looking well," said Lawyer Oldport. "The trip will do you good. But listen, if you will, to that little matter of business of which I spoke to you yesterday, and also five years ago. There are some buildings, fifteen in number, of which there are new five-year leases to be signed. Your father contemplated a change in the lease provisions, but never made it. He intended that the parlors of these houses should not be sublet, but that the tenants should be allowed to use them for reception rooms. These houses are in the shopping districts, and are mainly tenanted by young working girls. As it is they are forced to seek companionship outside. This row of red brick—"

Blinker interrupted him with a loud, discordant laugh.

"Brickdust Row for an even hundred," he cried. "And I own it. Have I guessed right?"

"The tenants have some such name for it," said Lawyer Oldport.

Blinker arose and jammed his hat down to his eyes.

"Do what you please with it," he said, harshly. "Remodel it, burn it, raze it to the ground. But, man, it's too late, I tell you. It's too late. It's too late. It's too late."

—from *The Trimmed Lamp* (1907)

THE FURNISHED ROOM

Restless, shifting, fugacious as time itself is a certain vast bulk
of the population of the red brick district of the lower West
Side. Homeless, they have a hundred homes. They flit from
furnished room to furnished room, transients forever—transients
in abode, transients in heart and mind. They sing "Home, Sweet
Home" in ragtime;[1] they carry their *lares et penates** in a bandbox;[†]
their vine is entwined about a picture hat; a rubber plant is their
fig tree.

Hence the houses of this district, having had a thousand dwellers, should have a thousand tales to tell, mostly dull ones, no doubt;
but it would be strange if there could not be found a ghost or two
in the wake of all these vagrant guests.

One evening after dark a young man prowled among these
crumbling red mansions, ringing their bells. At the twelfth he
rested his lean hand-baggage upon the step and wiped the dust
from his hatband and forehead. The bell sounded faint and far away
in some remote, hollow depths.

To the door of this, the twelfth house whose bell he had rung,
came a housekeeper who made him think of an unwholesome, sur-
feited worm that had eaten its nut to a hollow shell and now sought
to fill the vacancy with edible lodgers.

He asked if there was a room to let.

"Come in," said the housekeeper. Her voice came from her
throat; her throat seemed lined with fur. "I have the third-floor
back, vacant since a week back. Should you wish to look at it?"

---

*Personal or household belongings; in ancient Rome, *lares* were household deities,
and *penates* were guardian deities of the home.
†Small box used to carry small articles of clothing.

The young man followed her up the stairs. A faint light from no particular source mitigated the shadows of the halls. They trod noiselessly upon a stair carpet that its own loom would have forsworn. It seemed to have become vegetable; to have degenerated in that rank, sunless air to lush lichen or spreading moss that grew in patches to the stair-case and was viscid under the foot like organic matter. At each turn of the stairs were vacant niches in the wall. Perhaps plants had once been set within them. If so they had died in that foul and tainted air. It may be that statues of the saints had stood there, but it was not difficult to conceive that imps and devils had dragged them forth in the darkness and down to the unholy depths of some furnished pit below.

"This is the room," said the housekeeper, from her furry throat. "It's a nice room. It ain't often vacant. I had some most elegant people in it last summer—no trouble at all, and paid in advance to the minute. The water's at the end of the hall. Sprowls and Mooney kept it three months. They done a vaudeville sketch. Miss B'retta Sprowls—you may have heard of her—Oh, that was just the stage names—right there over the dresser is where the marriage certificate hung, framed. The gas is here, and you see there is plenty of closet room. It's a room everybody likes. It never stays idle long."

"Do you have many theatrical people rooming here?" asked the young man.

"They comes and goes. A good proportion of my lodgers is connected with the theatres. Yes, sir, this is the theatrical district. Actor people never stays long anywhere. I get my share. Yes, they comes and they goes."

He engaged the room, paying for a week in advance. He was tired, he said, and would take possession at once. He counted out the money. The room had been made ready, she said, even to towels and water. As the housekeeper moved away he put, for the thousandth time, the question that he carried at the end of his tongue.

"A young girl—Miss Vashner—Miss Eloise Vashner—do you remember such a one among your lodgers? She would be singing on the stage, most likely. A fair girl, of medium height and slender, with reddish, gold hair and dark mole near her left eyebrow."

"No, I don't remember the name. Them stage people has names

they change as often as their rooms. They comes and they goes. No, I don't call that one to mind."

No. Always no. Five months of ceaseless interrogation and the inevitable negative. So much time spent by day in questioning managers, agents, schools and choruses; by night among the audiences of theatres from all-star casts down to music halls so low that he dreaded to find what he most hoped for. He who had loved her best had tried to find her. He was sure that since her disappearance from home this great, water-girt city held her somewhere, but it was like a monstrous quicksand, shifting its particles constantly, with no foundation, its upper granules of to-day buried to-morrow in ooze and slime.

The furnished room received its latest guest with a first glow of pseudo-hospitality, a hectic, haggard, perfunctory welcome like the specious smile of a demirep.* The sophistical† comfort came in reflected gleams from the decayed furniture, the ragged brocade upholstery of a couch and two chairs, a foot-wide cheap pier glass between the two windows, from one or two gilt picture frames and a brass bedstead in a corner.

The guest reclined, inert, upon a chair, while the room, confused in speech as though it were an apartment in Babel,² tried to discourse to him of its divers tenantry.

A polychromatic rug like some brilliant-flowered, rectangular, tropical islet lay surrounded by a billowy sea of soiled matting. Upon the gay-papered wall were those pictures that pursue the homeless one from house to house—The Huguenot Lovers, The First Quarrel, The Wedding Breakfast, Psyche at the Fountain. The mantel's chastely severe outline was ingloriously veiled behind some pert drapery drawn rakishly askew like the sashes of the Amazonian ballet. Upon it was some desolate flotsam cast aside by the room's marooned when a lucky sail had borne them to a fresh port—a trifling vase or two, pictures of actresses, a medicine bottle, some stray cards out of a deck.

One by one, as the characters of a cryptograph‡ became explicit,

---

*Loose woman; literally, "half a reprobate."
†Deceptive.
‡Coded message.

the little signs left by the furnished rooms' procession of guests developed a significance. The threadbare space in the rug in front of the dresser told that lovely woman had marched in the throng. The tiny fingerprints on the wall spoke of little prisoners trying to feel their way to sun and air. A splattered stain, raying like the shadow of a bursting bomb, witnessed where a hurled glass or bottle had splintered with its contents against the wall. Across the pier glass had been scrawled with a diamond in staggering letters the name "Marie." It seemed that the succession of dwellers in the furnished room had turned in fury—perhaps tempted beyond forbearance by its garish coldness—and wreaked upon it their passions. The furniture was chipped and bruised; the couch, distorted by bursting springs, seemed a horrible monster that had been slain during the stress of some grotesque convulsion. Some more potent upheaval had cloven a great slice from the marble mantel. Each plank in the floor owned its particular cant and shriek as from a separate and individual agony. It seemed incredible that all this malice and injury had been wrought upon the room by those who had called it for a time their home; and yet it may have been the cheated home instinct surviving blindly, the resentful rage at false household gods that had kindled their wrath. A hut that is our own we can sweep and adorn and cherish.

The young tenant in the chair allowed these thoughts to file, soft-shod, through his mind, while there drifted into the room furnished sounds and furnished scents. He heard in one room a tittering and incontinent, slack laughter; in others the monologue of a scold, the rattling of dice, a lullaby, and one crying dully; above him a banjo tinkled with spirit. Doors banged somewhere; the elevated trains roared intermittently; a cat yowled miserably upon a back fence. And he breathed the breath of the house—a dank savor rather than a smell—a cold, musty effluvium as from underground vaults mingled with the reeking exhalations of linoleum and mildewed and rotten woodwork.

Then suddenly, as he rested there, the room was filled with the strong, sweet odor of mignonette.* It came as upon a single buffet

---

*Plant with fragrant blossoms.

of wind with such sureness and fragrance and emphasis that it almost seemed a living visitant. And the man cried aloud: "What, dear?" as if he had been called, and sprang up and faced about. The rich odor clung to him and wrapped him around. He reached out his arms for it, all his senses for the time confused and commingled. How could one be peremptorily called by an odor? Surely it must have been a sound. But, was it not the sound that had touched, that had caressed him?

"She has been in this room," he cried, and he sprang to wrest from it a token, for he knew he would recognize the smallest thing that had belonged to her or that she had touched. This enveloping scent of mignonette, the odor that she had loved and made her own—whence came it?

The room had been but carelessly set in order. Scattered upon the flimsy dresser scarf were half a dozen hairpins—those discreet, indistinguishable friends of womankind, feminine of gender, infinite of mood and uncommunicative of tense. These he ignored, conscious of their triumphant lack of identity. Ransacking the drawers of the dresser he came upon a discarded, tiny, ragged handkerchief. He pressed it to his face. It was racy and insolent with heliotrope; he hurled it to the floor. In another drawer he found odd buttons, a theatre programme, a pawnbroker's card, two lost marshmallows, a book on the divination of dreams. In the last was a woman's black satin hair bow, which halted him, poised between ice and fire. But the black satin bow also is femininity's demure, impersonal common ornament and tells no tales.

And then he traversed the room like a hound on the scent, skimming the walls, considering the corners of the bulging matting on his hands and knees, rummaging mantel and tables, the curtains and hangings, the drunken cabinet in the corner, for a visible sign, unable to perceive that she was there beside, around, against, within, above him, clinging to him, wooing him, calling him so poignantly through the finer senses that even his grosser ones became cognizant of the call. Once again he answered loudly: "Yes, dear!" and turned, wild-eyed, to gaze on vacancy, for he could not yet discern form and color and love and outstretched arms in the odor of mignonette. Oh, God! whence that odor, and since when have odors had a voice to call? Thus he groped.

He burrowed in crevices and corners, and found corks and cigarettes. These he passed in passive contempt. But once he found in a fold of the matting a half-smoked cigar, and this he ground beneath his heel with a green and trenchant oath. He sifted the room from end to end. He found dreary and ignoble small records of many a peripatetic tenant; but of her whom he sought, and who may have lodged there, and whose spirit seemed to hover there, he found no trace.

And then he thought of the housekeeper.

He ran from the haunted room downstairs and to a door that showed a crack of light. She came out to his knock. He smothered his excitement as best he could.

"Will you tell me, madam," he besought her, "who occupied the room I have before I came?"

"Yes, sir. I can tell you again. 'Twas Sprowls and Mooney, as I said. Miss B'retta Sprowls it was in the theatres, but Missis Mooney she was. My house is well known for respectability. The marriage certificate hung, framed, on a nail over—"

"What kind of a lady was Miss Sprowls—in looks, I mean?"

"Why, black-haired, sir, short, and stout, with a comical face. They left a week ago Tuesday."

"And before they occupied it?"

"Why, there was a single gentleman connected with the draying business. He left owing me a week. Before him was Missis Crowder and her two children, that stayed four months; and back of them was old Mr. Doyle, whose sons paid for him. He kept the room six months. That goes back a year, sir, and further I do not remember."

He thanked her and crept back to his room. The room was dead. The essence that had vivified it was gone. The perfume of mignonette had departed. In its place was the old, stale odor of mouldy house furniture, of atmosphere in storage.

The ebbing of his hope drained his faith. He sat staring at the yellow, singing gaslight. Soon he walked to the bed and began to tear the sheets into strips. With the blade of his knife he drove them tightly into every crevice around windows and door. When all was snug and taut he turned out the light, turned the gas full on again and laid himself gratefully upon the bed.

*   *   *

It was Mrs. McCool's night to go with the can for beer. So she fetched it and sat with Mrs. Purdy in one of those subterranean retreats where housekeepers foregather and the worm dieth seldom.

"I rented out my third-floor-back this evening," said Mrs. Purdy, across a fine circle of foam. "A young man took it. He went up to bed two hours ago."

"Now, did ye, Mrs. Purdy, ma'am?" said Mrs. McCool, with intense admiration. "You do be a wonder for rentin' rooms of that kind. And did ye tell him, then?" she concluded in a husky whisper laden with mystery.

"Rooms," said Mrs. Purdy, in her furriest tones, "are furnished for to rent. I did not tell him, Mrs. McCool."

" 'Tis right ye are, ma'am; 'tis by renting rooms we kape alive. Ye have the rale sense for business, ma'am. There be many people will rayjict* the rentin' of a room if they be tould a suicide has been after dyin' in the bed of it."

"As you say, we has our living to be making," remarked Mrs. Purdy.

"Yis, ma'am; 'tis true. 'Tis just one wake ago this day I helped ye lay out the third-floor-back. A pretty slip of a colleen† she was to be killin' herself wid the gas—a swate little face she had, Mrs. Purdy, ma'am."

"She'd a-been called handsome, as you say," said Mrs. Purdy, assenting but critical, "but for that mole she had a-growin' by her left eyebrow. Do fill up your glass again, Mrs. McCool."

—from The Four Million (1906)

---

*Meaning "reject."
†Young Irish girl.

SCHOOLS AND SCHOOLS

Old Jerome Warren lived in a hundred-thousand-dollar house at 35 East Fifty-Soforth Street. He was a downtown broker, so rich that he could afford to walk—for his health—a few blocks in the direction of his office every morning and then call a cab.

He had an adopted son, the son of an old friend named Gilbert—Cyril Scott could play him nicely[1]—who was becoming a successful painter as fast as he could squeeze the paint out of his tubes. Another member of the household was Barbara Ross, a stepniece. Man is born to trouble; so, as old Jerome had no family of his own, he took up the burdens of others.

Gilbert and Barbara got along swimmingly. There was a tacit and tactical understanding all round that the two would stand up under a floral bell some high noon, and promise the minister to keep old Jerome's money in a state of high commotion. But at this point complications must be introduced.

Thirty years before, when old Jerome was young Jerome, there was a brother of his named Dick. Dick went West to seek his or somebody else's fortune. Nothing was heard of him until one day old Jerome had a letter from his brother. It was badly written on ruled paper that smelled of salt bacon and coffee-grounds. The writing was asthmatic and the spelling St. Vitusy.[2]

It appeared that instead of Dick having forced Fortune to stand and deliver, he had been held up himself, and made to give hostages to the enemy. That is, as his letter disclosed, he was on the point of pegging out with a complication of disorders that even whiskey had failed to check. All that his thirty years of prospecting had netted him was one daughter, nineteen years old, as per invoice, whom he was shipping East, charges prepaid, for Jerome to clothe, feed, educate, comfort, and cherish for the rest of her natural life or until matrimony should them part.

Old Jerome was a board-walk. Everybody knows that the world is supported by the shoulders of Atlas; and that Atlas stands on a rail-fence; and that the rail-fence is built on a turtle's back. Now, the turtle has to stand on something; and that is a board-walk made of men like old Jerome.

I do not know whether immortality shall accrue to man; but if not so, I would like to know when men like old Jerome get what is due them?

They met Nevada Warren at the station. She was a little girl, deeply sunburned and wholesomely good-looking, with a manner that was frankly unsophisticated, yet one that not even a cigar-drummer would intrude upon without thinking twice. Looking at her, somehow you would expect to see her in a short skirt and leather leggings, shooting glass balls or taming mustangs. But in her plain white waist and black skirt she sent you guessing again. With an easy exhibition of strength she swung along a heavy valise, which the uniformed porters tried in vain to wrest from her.

"I am sure we shall be the best of friends," said Barbara, pecking at the firm, sunburned cheek.

"I hope so," said Nevada.

"Dear little niece," said old Jerome, "you are as welcome to my house as if it were your father's own."

"Thanks," said Nevada.

"And I am going to call you 'cousin,'" said Gilbert, with his charming smile.

"Take the valise, please," said Nevada. "It weighs a million pounds. It's got samples from six of dad's old mines in it," she explained to Barbara. "I calculate they'd assay about nine cents to the thousand tons, but I promised him to bring them along."

II

It is a common custom to refer to the usual complications between one man and two ladies, or one lady and two men, or a lady and a man and a nobleman, or—well, any of these problems—as the triangle. But they are never unqualified triangles. They are always isosceles—never equilateral. So, upon the coming of Nevada Warren, she and Gilbert and Barbara Ross lined up into such a figurative triangle; and of that triangle Barbara formed the hypotenuse.

One morning old Jerome was lingering long after breakfast over the dullest morning paper in the city before setting forth to his downtown fly-trap. He had become quite fond of Nevada, finding in her much of his dead brother's quiet independence and unsuspicious frankness.

A maid brought in a note for Miss Nevada Warren.

"A messenger-boy delivered it at the door, please," she said. "He's waiting for an answer."

Nevada, who was whistling a Spanish waltz between her teeth, and watching the carriages and autos roll by in the street, took the envelope. She knew it was from Gilbert, before she opened it, by the little gold palette in the upper left-hand corner.

After tearing it open she pored over the contents for a while, absorbedly. Then, with a serious face, she went and stood at her uncle's elbow.

"Uncle Jerome, Gilbert is a nice boy, isn't he?"

"Why, bless the child!" said old Jerome, crackling his paper loudly; "of course he is. I raised him myself."

"He wouldn't write anything to anybody that wasn't exactly—I mean that everybody couldn't know and read, would he?"

"I'd just like to see him try it," said uncle, tearing a handful from his newspaper. "Why, what—"

"Read this note he just sent me, uncle, and see if you think it's all right and proper. You see, I don't know much about city people and their ways."

Old Jerome threw his paper down and set both his feet upon it. He took Gilbert's note and fiercely perused it twice, and then a third time.

"Why, child," said he, "you had me almost excited, although I was sure of that boy. He's a duplicate of his father, and he was a gilt-edged diamond. He only asks if you and Barbara will be ready at four o'clock this afternoon for an automobile drive over to Long Island. I don't see anything to criticize in it except the stationery. I always did hate that shade of blue."

"Would it be all right to go?" asked Nevada, eagerly.

"Yes, yes, yes, child, of course. Why not? Still, it pleases me to see you so careful and candid. Go, by all means."

"I don't know," said Nevada, demurely. "I thought I'd ask you. Couldn't you go with us, uncle?"

"I? No, no, no, no! I've ridden once in a car that boy was driving. Never again! But it's entirely proper for you and Barbara to go. Yes, yes. But I will not. No, no, no, no!"

Nevada flew to the door, and said to the maid:

"You bet we'll go. I'll answer for Miss Barbara. Tell the boy to say to Mr. Warren, 'You bet we'll go.'"

"Nevada," called old Jerome, "pardon me, my dear, but wouldn't it be as well to send him a note in reply? Just a line would do."

"No, I won't bother about that," said Nevada, gayly. "Gilbert will understand—he always does. I never rode in an automobile in my life; but I've paddled a canoe down Little Devil River through the Lost Horse Cañon, and if it's any livelier than that I'd like to know!"

III

Two months are supposed to have elapsed.

Barbara sat in the study of the hundred-thousand-dollar house. It was a good place for her. Many places are provided in the world where men and women may repair for the purpose of extricating themselves from divers difficulties. There are cloisters, wailing-places, watering-places, confessionals, hermitages, lawyers' offices, beauty-parlors, air-ships, and studies; and the greatest of these are studies.

It usually takes a hypotenuse a long time to discover that it is the longest side of a triangle. But it's a long line that has no turning.

Barbara was alone. Uncle Jerome and Nevada had gone to the theatre. Barbara had not cared to go. She wanted to stay at home and study in the study. If you, miss, were a stunning New York girl, and saw every day that a brown, ingenuous Western witch was getting hobbles and a lasso on the young man you wanted for yourself, you, too, would lose taste for the oxidized silver setting of a musical comedy.

Barbara sat by the quartered-oak library table. Her right arm rested upon the table, and her dextral fingers nervously manipulated a sealed letter. The letter was addressed to Nevada Warren; and in the upper left-hand corner of the envelope was Gilbert's little gold palette. It had been delivered at nine o'clock, after Nevada had left.

Barbara would have given her pearl necklace to know what that letter contained; but she could not open and read it by the aid of steam, or a pen-handle, or a hair-pin, or any of the generally approved methods, because her position in society forbade such an act. She had tried to read some of the lines of the letter by holding the envelope up to a strong light and pressing it hard against the paper, but Gilbert had too good a taste in stationery to make that possible.

At eleven-thirty the theatre-goers returned. It was a delicious winter night. Even so far as from the cab to the door they were powdered thickly with the big flakes downpouring diagonally from the east. Old Jerome growled good-naturedly about villainous cab service and blockaded streets. Nevada, colored like a rose, with sapphire eyes, babbled of the stormy nights in the mountains around dad's cabin. During all these wintry apostrophes, Barbara, cold at heart, sawed wood*—the only appropriate thing she could think of to do.

Old Jerome went immediately upstairs to hot-water-bottles and quinine. Nevada fluttered into the study, the only cheerfully lighted room, subsided into an armchair, and, while at the interminable task of unbuttoning her elbow gloves, gave oral testimony as to the demerits of the "show."

"Yes, I think Mr. Fields[3] is really amusing—sometimes," said Barbara. "Here is a letter for you, dear, that came by special delivery just after you had gone."

"Who is it from?" asked Nevada, tugging at a button.

"Well, really," said Barbara, with a smile, "I can only guess. The envelope has that queer little thing in one corner that Gilbert calls a palette, but which looks to me rather like a gilt heart on a school-girl's valentine."

"I wonder what he's writing to me about," remarked Nevada, listlessly.

---

*In turn-of-the-century slang, to saw wood means to work while others talk; the phrase could also mean to take a nap. O. Henry's meaning here is not clear.

"We're all alike," said Barbara; "all women. We try to find out what is in a letter by studying the postmark. As a last resort we use scissors, and read it from the bottom upward. Here it is."

She made a motion as if to toss the letter across the table to Nevada.

"Great catamounts!"* exclaimed Nevada. "These centre-fire buttons are a nuisance. I'd rather wear buckskins. Oh, Barbara, please shuck the hide off that letter and read it. It'll be midnight before I get these gloves off!"

"Why, dear, you don't want me to open Gilbert's letter to you? It's for you, and you wouldn't wish any one else to read it, of course!"

Nevada raised her steady, calm, sapphire eyes from her gloves.

"Nobody writes me anything that everybody mightn't read," she said. "Go on, Barbara. Maybe Gilbert wants us to go out in his car again tomorrow."

Curiosity can do more things than kill a cat; and if emotions, well recognized as feminine, are inimical to feline life, then jealousy would soon leave the whole world catless. Barbara opened the letter, with an indulgent, slightly bored air.

"Well, dear," she said, "I'll read it if you want me to."

She slit the envelope, and read the missive with swift-travelling eyes; read it again, and cast a quick, shrewd glance at Nevada, who, for the time, seemed to consider gloves as the world of her interest, and letters from rising artists as no more than messages from Mars.

For a quarter of a minute Barbara looked at Nevada with a strange steadfastness; and then a smile so small that it widened her mouth only the sixteenth part of an inch, and narrowed her eyes no more than a twentieth flashed like an inspired thought across her face.

Since the beginning no woman has been a mystery to another woman. Swift as light travels, each penetrates the heart and mind of another, sifts her sister's words of their cunningest disguises, reads her most hidden desires, and plucks the sophistry from her wiliest talk like hairs from a comb, twiddling them sardonically between her thumb and fingers before letting them float away on

---

*Wild cats, such as pumas or cougars.

the breezes of fundamental doubt. Long ago Eve's son rang the door-bell of the family residence in Paradise Park, bearing a strange lady on his arm, whom he introduced. Eve took her daughter-in-law aside and lifted a classic eyebrow.

"The Land of Nod," said the bride, languidly flirting the leaf of a palm. "I suppose you've been there, of course?"

"Not lately," said Eve, absolutely unstaggered. "Don't you think the applesauce they serve over there is execrable? I rather like that mulberry-leaf tunic effect, dear; but, of course, the real fig goods are not to be had over there. Come over behind this lilac-bush while the gentlemen split a celery tonic. I think the caterpillar-holes have made your dress open a little in the back."

So, then and there—according to the records—was the alliance formed by the only two who's-who ladies in the world. Then it was agreed that women should forever remain as clear as a pane of glass—though glass was yet to be discovered—to other women, and that she should palm herself off on a man as a mystery.

Barbara seemed to hesitate.

"Really, Nevada," she said, with a little show of embarrassment, "you shouldn't have insisted on my opening this. I—I'm sure it wasn't meant for any one else to know."

Nevada forgot her gloves for a moment.

"Then read it aloud," she said. "Since you've already read it, what's the difference? If Mr. Warren has written to me something that any one else oughtn't to know, that is all the more reason why everybody should know it."

"Well," said Barbara, "this is what is says: 'Dearest Nevada—Come to my studio at twelve o'clock to-night. Do not fail.' " Barbara rose and dropped the note in Nevada's lap. "I'm awfully sorry," she said, "that I knew. It isn't like Gilbert. There must be some mistake. Just consider that I am ignorant of it, will you, dear? I must go upstairs now, I have such a headache. I'm sure I don't understand the note. Perhaps Gilbert has been dining too well, and will explain. Good night!"

IV

Nevada tiptoed to the hall, and heard Barbara's door close upstairs. The bronze clock in the study told the hour of twelve was fifteen minutes away. She ran swiftly to the front door, and let herself out into the snowstorm. Gilbert Warren's studio was six squares away.

By aërial ferry the white, silent forces of the storm attacked the city from beyond the sullen East River. Already the snow lay a foot deep on the pavements, the drifts heaping themselves like scaling-ladders against the walls of the besieged town. The Avenue was as quiet as a street in Pompeii.[4] Cabs now and then skimmed past like white-winged gulls over a moonlit ocean; and less frequent motor-cars—sustaining the comparison—hissed through the foaming waves like submarine boats on their jocund, perilous journeys.

Nevada plunged like a wind-driven storm-petrel on her way. She looked up at the ragged sierras of cloud-capped buildings[5] that rose above the streets, shaded by the night lights and the congealed vapors to gray, drab, ashen, lavender, dun, and cerulean tints. They were so like the wintry mountains of her Western home that she felt a satisfaction such as the hundred-thousand-dollar house had seldom brought her.

A policeman caused her to waver on a corner, just by his eye and weight.

"Hello, Mabel!" said he. "Kind of late for you to be out, ain't it?"

"I—I am just going to the drug store," said Nevada, hurrying past him.

The excuse serves as a passport for the most sophisticated. Does it prove that woman never progresses, or that she sprang from Adam's rib,[6] full-fledged in intellect and wiles?

Turning eastward, the direct blast cut down Nevada's speed one half. She made zigzag tracks in the snow; but she was as tough as a piñon sapling, and bowed to it as gracefully. Suddenly the studio-building loomed before her, a familiar landmark, like a cliff above some well-remembered cañon. The haunt of business and its hostile neighbor, art, was darkened and silent. The elevator stopped at ten.

Up eight flights of Stygian* stairs Nevada climbed, and rapped firmly at the door numbered "89." She had been there many times before, with Barbara and Uncle Jerome.

---

*Meaning hellish and dark; from Styx, the principal river of the underworld in Greek mythology.

Gilbert opened the door. He had a crayon pencil in one hand, a green shade over his eyes, and a pipe in his mouth. The pipe dropped to the floor.

"Am I late?" asked Nevada. "I came as quick as I could. Uncle and me were at the theatre this evening. Here I am, Gilbert!"

Gilbert did a Pygmalion-and-Galatea act. He changed from a statue of stupefaction to a young man with a problem to tackle.[7] He admitted Nevada, got a whiskbroom, and began to brush the snow from her clothes. A great lamp, with a green shade, hung over an easel, where the artist had been sketching in crayon.

"You wanted me," said Nevada, simply, "and I came. You said so in your letter. What did you send for me for?"

"You read my letter?" inquired Gilbert, sparring for wind.

"Barbara read it to me. I saw it afterward. It said: 'Come to my studio at twelve to-night, and do not fail.' I thought you were sick, of course, but you don't seem to be."

"Aha!" said Gilbert, irrelevantly. "I'll tell you why I asked you to come, Nevada. I want you to marry me immediately—to-night. What's a little snowstorm? Will you do it?"

"You might have noticed that I would, long ago," said Nevada. "And I'm rather stuck on the snowstorm idea, myself. I surely would hate one of those flowery church noon-weddings. Gilbert, I didn't know you had grit enough to propose in this way. Let's shock 'em— it's our funeral, ain't it?"

"You bet!" said Gilbert. "Where did I hear that expression?" he added to himself. "Wait a minute, Nevada; I want to do a little 'phoning."

He shut himself up in a little dressing-room, and called upon the lightnings of the heavens—condensed into unromantic numbers and districts.

"That you, Jack? You confounded sleepy-head! Yes, wake up; this is me—or I—oh, bother the difference in grammar! I'm going to be married right away. Yes! Wake up your sister—don't answer me back; bring her along, too—you *must*. Remind Agnes of the time I saved her from drowning in Lake Ronkonkoma[8]—I know it's caddish to refer to it, but she *must* come with you. Yes! Nevada is here, waiting. We've been engaged quite a while. Some opposition among the relatives, you know, and we have to pull it off this way. We're waiting here for you. Don't let Agnes out-talk you—bring her! You will? Good old boy! I'll order a carriage to call for you, double-quick time. Confound you, Jack, you're all right!"

Gilbert returned to the room where Nevada waited.

"My old friend, Jack Peyton, and his sister were to have been here at a quarter to twelve," he explained; "but Jack is so confoundedly slow. I've just 'phoned them to hurry. They'll be here in a few minutes. I'm the happiest man in the world, Nevada! What did you do with the letter I sent you to-day?"

"I've got it cinched here," said Nevada, pulling it out from beneath her opera-cloak.

Gilbert drew the letter from the envelope and looked it over carefully. Then he looked at Nevada thoughtfully.

"Didn't you think it rather queer that I should ask you to come to my studio at midnight?" he asked.

"Why, no," said Nevada, rounding her eyes. "Not if you needed me. Out West, when a pal sends you a hurry call—ain't that what you say here?—we get there first and talk about it after the row is over. And it's usually snowing there, too, when things happen. So I didn't mind."

Gilbert rushed into another room, and came back burdened with overcoats warranted to turn wind, rain, or snow.

"Put this raincoat on," he said, holding it for her. "We have a quarter of a mile to go. Old Jack and his sister will be here in a few minutes." He began to struggle into a heavy coat. "Oh, Nevada," he said, "just look at the headlines on the front page of that evening paper on the table, will you? It's about your section of the West, and I know it will interest you."

He waited a full minute, pretending to find trouble in the getting on of his overcoat, and then turned. Nevada had not moved. She was looking at him with strange and pensive directness. Her cheeks had a flush on them beyond the color that had been contributed by the wind and snow; but her eyes were steady.

"I was going to tell you," she said, "anyhow, before you—before we—before—well, before anything. Dad never gave me a day of schooling. I never learned to read or write a darned word. Now if—"

Pounding their uncertain way upstairs, the feet of Jack, the somnolent, and Agnes, the grateful, were heard.

V

When Mr. and Mrs. Gilbert Warren were spinning softly homeward in a closed carriage, after the ceremony, Gilbert said:

"Nevada, would you really like to know what I wrote you in the letter that you received to-night?"

"Fire away!" said his bride.

"Word for word," said Gilbert, "it was this: 'My dear Miss Warren—You were right about the flower. It was a hydrangea, and not a lilac.'"

"All right," said Nevada. "But let's forget it. The joke's on Barbara, anyway!"

—from *Options* (1909)

THE DEFEAT OF THE CITY

Robert Walmsley's descent upon the city resulted in a Kilkenny struggle. He came out of the fight victor by a fortune and a reputation. On the other hand, he was swallowed up by the city. The city gave him what he demanded and then branded him with its brand. It remodelled, cut, trimmed and stamped him to the pattern it approves. It opened its social gates to him and shut him in on a close-cropped, formal lawn with the select herd of ruminants. In dress, habits, manners, provincialism, routine and narrowness he acquired that charming insolence, that irritating completeness, that sophisticated crassness, that overbalanced poise that makes the Manhattan gentleman so delightfully small in his greatness.

One of the up-state rural counties pointed with pride to the successful young metropolitan lawyer as a product of its soil. Six years earlier this county had removed the wheat straw from between its huckleberry-stained teeth and emitted a derisive and bucolic laugh as old man Walmsley's freckle-faced "Bob" abandoned the certain three-per-diem meals of the one-horse farm for the discontinuous quick lunch counters of the three-ringed metropolis. At the end of the six years no murder trial, coaching party, automobile accident or cotillion was complete in which the name of Robert Walmsley did not figure. Tailors waylaid him in the street to get a new wrinkle from the cut of his unwrinkled trousers. Hyphenated fellows in the clubs and members of the oldest subpoenaed families were glad to clap him on the back and allow him three letters of his name.

But the Matterhorn of Robert Walmsley's success was not scaled until he married Alicia Van Der Pool. I cite the Matterhorn, for just so high and cool and white and inaccessible was this daughter of the old burghers.* The social Alps that ranged about her—over whose bleak passes a thousand climbers struggled—reached only to her knees. She towered in her own atmosphere, serene, chaste, prideful, wading in no fountains, dining no monkeys, breeding no dogs for bench shows. She was a Van Der Pool. Fountains were made to play for her; monkeys were made for other people's ancestors; dogs, she understood, were created to be companions of blind persons and objectionable characters who smoked pipes.

This was the Matterhorn that Robert Walmsley accomplished. If he found, with the good poet with the game foot and artificially curled hair,[1] that he who ascends to mountain tops will find the loftiest peaks most wrapped in clouds and snow, he concealed his chilblains† beneath a brave and smiling exterior. He was a lucky man and knew it, even though he were imitating the Spartan boy‡ with an ice-cream freezer beneath his doublet frappéeing§ the region of his heart.

After a brief wedding tour abroad, the couple returned to create a decided ripple in the calm cistern (so placid and cool and sunless it is) of the best society. They entertained at their red brick mausoleum of ancient greatness in an old square that is a cemetery of crumbled glory. And Robert Walmsley was proud of his wife; although while one of his hands shook his guests' the other held tightly to his alpenstock and thermometer.

One day Alicia found a letter written to Robert by his mother. It was an unerudite letter, full of crops and motherly love and farm notes. It chronicled the health of the pig and the recent red calf, and asked concerning Robert's in return. It was a letter direct from the soil, straight from home, full of biographies of bees, tales of turnips, pæans of new-laid eggs, neglected parents and the slump in dried apples.

"Why have I not been shown your mother's letters?" asked Alicia. There was always something in her voice that made you think

---

*Good and prosperous middle-class citizens.
†Sores or inflammation caused by excessive exposure to cold.
‡Referring to the Spartan legend of a boy who concealed a stolen fox under his shirt and stoically showed no expression as it chewed into his stomach.
§Freezing (from the French word *frappée*, for iced).

of lorgnettes,* of accounts at Tiffany's, of sledges smoothly gliding on the trail from Dawson to Forty Mile,[2] of the tinkling of pendant prisms on your grandmothers' chandeliers, of snow lying on a convent roof; of a police sergeant refusing bail. "Your mother," continued Alicia, "invites us to make a visit to the farm. I have never seen a farm. We will go there for a week or two, Robert."

"We will," said Robert, with the grand air of an associate Supreme Justice concurring in an opinion. "I did not lay the invitation before you because I thought you would not care to go. I am much pleased at your decision."

"I will write to her myself," answered Alicia, with a faint foreshadowing of enthusiasm. "Félice shall pack my trunks at once. Seven, I think, will be enough. I do not suppose that your mother entertains a great deal. Does she give many house parties?"

Robert arose, and as attorney for rural places filed a demurrer against six of the seven trunks. He endeavored to define, picture, elucidate, set forth and describe a farm. His own words sounded strange in his ears. He had not realized how thoroughly urbsidized† he had become.

A week passed and found them landed at the little country station five hours out from the city. A grinning, stentorian, sarcastic youth driving a mule to a spring wagon hailed Robert savagely.

"Hallo, Mr. Walmsley. Found your way back at last, have you? Sorry I couldn't bring in the automobile for you, but dad's bulltonguing‡ the ten-acre clover patch with it to-day. Guess you'll excuse my not wearing a dress suit over to meet you—it ain't six o'clock yet, you know."

"I'm glad to see you, Tom," said Robert, grasping his brother's hand. "Yes, I've found my way at last. You've a right to say 'at last.' It's been over two years since the last time. But it will be oftener after this, my boy."

Alicia, cool in the summer heat as an Arctic wraith, white as a Norse snow maiden in her flimsy muslin and fluttering lace parasol, came round the corner of the station; and Tom was stripped of his

---

*Opera glasses or eyeglasses held to the face by a long handle.
†A play on the word "urbanized."
‡Plowing; a bull tongue is the wide blade on a plow.

assurance. He became chiefly eyesight clothed in blue jeans, and on the homeward drive to the mule alone did he confide in language the inwardness of his thoughts.

They drove homeward. The low sun dropped a spendthrift flood of gold upon the fortunate fields of wheat. The cities were far away. The road lay curling around wood and dale and hill like a ribbon lost from the robe of careless summer. The wind followed like a whinnying colt in the track of Phœbus's steeds.[3]

By and by the farmhouse peeped gray out of its faithful grove; they saw the long lane with its convoy of walnut trees running from the road to the house; they smelled the wild rose and the breath of cool, damp willows in the creek's bed. And then in unison all the voices of the soil began a chant addressed to the soul of Robert Walmsley. Out of the tilted aisles of the dim wood they came hollowly; they chirped and buzzed from the parched grass; they trilled from the ripples of the creek ford; they floated up in clear Pan's pipe notes[4] from the dimming meadows; the whippoorwills joined in as they pursued midges in the upper air; slow-going cow-bells struck out a homely accompaniment—and this was what each one said: "You've found your way back at last, have you?"

The old voices of the soil spoke to him. Leaf and bud and blossom conversed with him in the old vocabulary of his careless youth—the inanimate things, the familiar stones and rails, the gates and furrows and roofs and turns of the road had an eloquence, too, and a power in the transformation. The country had smiled and he had felt the breath of it, and his heart was drawn as if in a moment back to his old love. The city was far away.

This rural atavism,* then, seized Robert Walmsley and possessed him. A queer thing he noticed in connection with it was that Alicia, sitting at his side, suddenly seemed to him a stranger. She did not belong to this recurrent phase. Never before had she seemed so remote, so colorless and high—so intangible and unreal. And yet he had never admired her more than when she sat there by him in the rickety spring wagon, chiming no more with his mood and with

---

*Reappearance of a characteristic after generations of dormancy; usually refers to a genetic trait.

her environment than the Matterhorn chimes with a peasant's cabbage garden.

That night when the greetings and the supper were over, the
entire family, including Buff, the yellow dog, bestrewed itself upon
the front porch. Alicia, not haughty but silent, sat in the shadow
dressed in an exquisite pale-gray tea gown. Robert's mother dis-
coursed to her happily concerning marmalade and lumbago.* Tom
sat on the top step; Sisters Millie and Pam on the lowest step to
catch the lightning bugs. Mother had the willow rocker. Father sat
in the big armchair with one of its arms gone. Buff sprawled in the
middle of the porch in everybody's way. The twilight pixies and
pucks stole forth unseen and plunged other poignant shafts of
memory into the heart of Robert. A rural madness entered his soul.
The city was far away.

Father sat without his pipe, writhing in his heavy boots, a sac-
rifice to rigid courtesy. Robert shouted: "No, you don't!" He fetched
the pipe and lit it; he seized the old gentleman's boots and tore
them off. The last one slipped suddenly, and Mr. Robert Walmsley,
of Washington Square, tumbled off the porch backward with Buff
on top of him, howling fearfully. Tom laughed sarcastically.

Robert tore off his coat and vest and hurled them into a lilac
bush.

"Come out here, you landlubber," he cried to Tom, "and I'll put
grass seed on your back. I think you called me a 'dude'† a while
ago. Come along and cut your capers."

Tom understood the invitation and accepted it with delight.
Three times they wrestled on the grass, "side holds," even as the
giants of the mat. And twice was Tom forced to bite grass at the
hands of the distinguished lawyer. Dishevelled, panting, each still
boasting of his own prowess, they stumbled back to the porch.
Millie cast a pert reflection upon the qualities of a city brother. In
an instant Robert had secured a horrid katydid in his fingers and
bore down upon her. Screaming wildly, she fled up the lane, pursued by the avenging glass of form. A quarter of a mile and they

---

*Lower-back pain.
†Dandy; a fastidiously dressed city dweller unfamiliar with country life.

returned, she full of apology to the victorious "dude." The rustic mania possessed him unabatedly.

"I can do up a cowpenful of you slow hayseeds," he proclaimed, vaingloriously. "Bring on your bull-dogs, your hired men and your log-rollers."

He turned handsprings on the grass that prodded Tom to envious sarcasm. And then, with a whoop, he clattered to the rear and brought back Uncle Ike, a battered colored retainer of the family, with his banjo, and strewed sand on the porch and danced "Chicken in the Bread Tray"* and did buck-and-wing† wonders for half an hour longer. Incredibly wild and boisterous things he did. He sang, he told stories that set all but one shrieking, he played the yokel,‡ the humorous clodhopper; he was mad, mad with the revival of the old life in his blood.

He became so extravagant that once his mother sought gently to reprove him. Then Alicia moved as though she were about to speak, but she did not. Through it all she sat immovable, a slim, white spirit in the dusk that no man might question or read.

By and by she asked permission to ascend to her room, saying that she was tired. On her way she passed Robert. He was standing in the door, the figure of vulgar comedy, with ruffled hair, reddened face and unpardonable confusion of attire—no trace there of the immaculate Robert Walmsley, the courted clubman and ornament of select circles. He was doing a conjuring trick with some household utensils, and the family, now won over to him without exception, was beholding him with worshipful admiration.

As Alicia passed in Robert started suddenly. He had forgotten for the moment that she was present. Without a glance at him she went on upstairs.

After that the fun grew quiet. An hour passed in talk, and then Robert went up himself.

She was standing by the window when he entered their room. She was still clothed as when they were on the porch. Outside and crowding against the window was a giant apple tree, full blossomed.

---

*Title of a folk song traditionally played on a fiddle.
†Type of tap dance popular in the nineteenth century popularized by the African-American minstrel shows.
‡Country fool.

Robert sighed and went near the window. He was ready to meet his fate. A confessed vulgarian, he foresaw the verdict of justice in the shape of that still, whiteclad form. He knew the rigid lines that a Van Der Pool would draw. He was a peasant gambolling indecorously in the valley, and the pure, cold, white, unthawed summit of the Matterhorn could not but frown on him. He had been unmasked by his own actions. All the polish, the poise, the form that the city had given him had fallen from him like an ill-fitting mantle at the first breath of a country breeze. Dully he awaited the approaching condemnation.

"Robert," said the calm, cool voice of his judge, "I thought I married a gentleman."

Yes, it was coming. And yet, in the face of it, Robert Walmsley was eagerly regarding a certain branch of the apple tree upon which he used to climb out of that very window. He believed he could do it now. He wondered how many blossoms there were on the tree—ten millions? But here was some one speaking again:

"I thought I married a gentleman," the voice went on, "but——"

Why had she come and was standing so close by his side?

"But I find that I have married"—was this Alicia talking?— "something better—a man—Bob, dear, kiss me, won't you?"

The city was far away.

—from *The Voice of the City* (1908)

MADAME BO-PEEP,
OF THE RANCHES

A unt Ellen," said Octavia, cheerfully, as she threw her black kid gloves carefully at the dignified Persian cat on the window-seat, "I'm a pauper."

"You are so extreme in your statements, Octavia, dear," said Aunt Ellen, mildly, looking up from her paper. "If you find yourself temporarily in need of some small change for bonbons, you will find my purse in the drawer of the writing desk."

Octavia Beaupree removed her hat and seated herself on a footstool near her aunt's chair, clasping her hands about her knees. Her slim and flexible figure, clad in a modish mourning costume, accommodated itself easily and gracefully to the trying position. Her bright and youthful face, with its pair of sparkling, life-enamoured eyes, tried to compose itself to the seriousness that the occasion seemed to demand.

"You good auntie, it isn't a case of bonbons; it is abject, staring, unpicturesque poverty, with ready-made clothes, gasolined gloves, and probably one o'clock dinners all waiting with the traditional wolf at the door. I've just come from my lawyer, auntie, and, 'Please, ma'am, I ain't got nothink 't all. Flowers, lady? Buttonhole, gentleman? Pencils, sir, three for five, to help a poor widow?' Do I do it nicely, auntie, or, as a bread-winner accomplishment, were my lessons in elocution entirely wasted?"

"Do be serious, my dear," said Aunt Ellen, letting her paper fall to the floor, "long enough to tell me what you mean. Colonel Beaupree's estate——"

"Colonel Beaupree's estate," interrupted Octavia, emphasizing her words with appropriate dramatic gestures, "is of Spanish castellar architecture.* Colonel Beaupree's resources are—wind. Colonel Beaupree's stocks are—water. Colonel Beaupree's income is—all in. The statement lacks the legal technicalities to which I have been listening for an hour, but that is what it means when translated."

"Octavia!" Aunt Ellen was now visibly possessed by consternation. "I can hardly believe it. And it was the impression that he was worth a million. And the De Peysters themselves introduced him!"

Octavia rippled out a laugh, and then became properly grave.

"*De mortuis nil*,† auntie—not even the rest of it. The dear old colonel—what a gold brick he was, after all! I paid for my bargain fairly—I'm all here, am I not?—items: eyes, fingers, toes, youth, old family, unquestionable position in society as called for in the contract—no wild-cat stock here." Octavia picked up the morning paper from the floor. "But I'm not going to 'squeal'—isn't that what they call it when you rail at Fortune because you've lost the game?" She turned the pages of the paper calmly. " 'Stock market'—no use for that. 'Society's doings'—that's done. Here is my page—the wish column. A Van Dresser could not be said to 'want' for anything, of course. 'Chambermaids, cooks, canvassers, stenographers——' "

"Dear," said Aunt Ellen, with a little tremor in her voice, "please do not talk in that way. Even if your affairs are in so unfortunate a condition, there is my three thousand——"

Octavia sprang up lithely, and deposited a smart kiss on the delicate cheek of the prim little elderly maid.

"Blessed auntie, your three thousand is just sufficient to insure your Hyson‡ to be free from willow leaves and keep the Persian in sterilized cream. I know I'd be welcome, but I prefer to strike bottom like Beelzebub rather than hang around like the Peri[1] listening to the music from the side entrance. I'm going to earn my own living. There's nothing else to do. I'm a—Oh, oh, oh!—I had forgotten. There's one thing saved from the wreck. It's a corral—no, a ranch in—let me see—Texas: an asset, dear old Mr. Bannister

---

*Castle-like structures.

†Part of the Latin phrase *De mortuis nil nisi bonum*, meaning "of the dead speak kindly or not at all."

‡Type of green tea.

called it. How pleased he was to show me something he could describe as unencumbered! I've a description of it among those stupid papers he made me bring away with me from his office. I'll try to find it."

Octavia found her shopping-bag, and drew from it a long envelope filled with typewritten documents.

"A ranch in Texas," sighed Aunt Ellen. "It sounds to me more like a liability than an asset. Those are the places where the centipedes are found, and cowboys, and fandangos."*

" 'The Rancho de las Sombras,' "† read Octavia from a sheet of violently purple typewriting, " 'is situated one hundred and ten miles southeast of San Antonio, and thirty-eight miles from its nearest railroad station, Nopal, on the I. and G.N. Ranch, consists of 7,680 acres of well-watered land, with title conferred by State patents, and twenty-two sections, or 14,080 acres, partly under yearly running lease and partly bought under State's twenty-year-purchase act. Eight thousand graded merino sheep, with the necessary equipment of horses, vehicles and general ranch paraphernalia. Ranch-house built of brick, with six rooms comfortably furnished according to the requirements of the climate. All within a strong barbed-wire fence.

" 'The present ranch manager seems to be competent and reliable, and is rapidly placing upon a paying basis a business that, in other hands, had been allowed to suffer from neglect and misconduct.

" 'This property was secured by Colonel Beaupree in a deal with a Western irrigation syndicate, and the title to it seems to be perfect. With careful management and the natural increase of land values, it ought to be made the foundation for a comfortable fortune for its owner.' "

When Octavia ceased reading, Aunt Ellen uttered something as near a sniff as her breeding permitted.

"The prospectus," she said, with uncompromising metropolitan suspicion, "doesn't mention the centipedes, or the Indians. And you

---

*Lively Spanish-American dances.
†Ranch of the Shadows (Spanish).

never did like mutton, Octavia. I don't see what advantage you can derive from this—desert."

But Octavia was in a trance. Her eyes were steadily regarding something quite beyond their focus. Her lips were parted, and her face was lighted by the kindling furor of the explorer, the ardent, stirring disquiet of the adventurer. Suddenly she clasped her hands together exultantly.

"The problem solves itself, auntie," she cried. "I'm going to that ranch. I'm going to live on it. I'm going to learn to like mutton, and even concede the good qualities of centipedes—at a respectful distance. It's just what I need. It's a new life that comes when my old one is just ending. It's a release, auntie; it isn't a narrowing. Think of the gallops over those leagues of prairies, with the wind tugging at the roots of your hair, the coming close to the earth and learning over again the stories of the growing grass and the little wild flowers without names! Glorious is what it will be. Shall I be a shepherdess with a Watteau hat,[2] and a crook to keep the bad wolves from the lambs, or a typical Western ranch girl, with short hair, like the pictures of her in the Sunday papers? I think the latter. And they'll have my picture, too, with the wild-cats I've slain, single-handed, hanging from my saddle horn. 'From the Four Hundred to the Flocks' is the way they'll headline it, and they'll print photographs of the old Van Dresser mansion and the church where I was married. They won't have my picture, but they'll get an artist to draw it. I'll be wild and woolly, and I'll grow my own wool."

"Octavia!" Aunt Ellen condensed into the one word all the protests she was unable to utter.

"Don't say a word, auntie. I'm going. I'll see the sky at night fit down on the world like a big butter-dish cover, and I'll make friends again with the stars that I haven't had a chat with since I was a wee child. I wish to go. I'm tired of all this. I'm glad I haven't any money. I could bless Colonel Beaupree for that ranch, and forgive him for all his bubbles. What if the life will be rough and lonely! I—I deserve it. I shut my heart to everything except that miserable ambition. I—oh, I wish to go away, and forget—forget!"

Octavia swerved suddenly to her knees, laid her flushed face in her aunt's lap, and shook with turbulent sobs.

Aunt Ellen bent over her, and smoothed the coppery-brown hair.

"I didn't know," she said, gently; "I didn't know—that. Who was it, dear?"

When Mrs. Octavia Beaupree, née Van Dresser, stepped from the train at Nopal, her manner lost, for the moment, some of that easy certitude which had always marked her movements. The town was of recent establishment, and seemed to have been hastily constructed of undressed lumber and flapping canvas. The element that had congregated about the station, though not offensively demonstrative, was clearly composed of citizens accustomed to and prepared for rude alarms.

Octavia stood on the platform, against the telegraph office, and attempted to choose by intuition from the swaggering, straggling string of loungers, the manager of the Rancho de las Sombras, who had been instructed by Mr. Bannister to meet her there. That tall, serious-looking, elderly man in the blue flannel shirt and white tie she thought must be he. But, no; he passed by, removing his gaze from the lady as hers rested on him, according to the Southern custom. The manager, she thought, with some impatience at being kept waiting, should have no difficulty in selecting her. Young women wearing the most recent thing in ash-coloured travelling suits were not so plentiful in Nopal!

Thus keeping a speculative watch on all persons of possible managerial aspect, Octavia, with a catching breath and a start of surprise, suddenly became aware of Teddy Westlake hurrying along the platform in the direction of the train—of Teddy Westlake or his sun-browned ghost in cheviot,* boots and leather-girdled hat—Theodore Westlake, Jr., amateur polo (almost) champion, all-round butterfly and cumberer of the soil; but a broader, surer, more emphasized and determined Teddy than the one she had known a year ago when last she saw him.

He perceived Octavia at almost the same time, deflected his course, and steered for her in his old, straightforward way. Some-

---

*Wool.

thing like awe came upon her as the strangeness of his meta-
morphosis was brought into closer range; the rich, red-brown of
his complexion brought out so vividly his straw-coloured mustache
and steel-gray eyes. He seemed more grown-up, and, somehow,
farther away. But, when he spoke, the old, boyish Teddy came back
again. They had been friends from childhood.

"Why, 'Tave!" he exclaimed, unable to reduce his perplexity to
coherence. "How—what—when—where?"

"Train," said Octavia; "necessity; ten minutes ago; home. Your
complexion's gone, Teddy. Now, how—what—when—where?"

"I'm working down here," said Teddy. He cast side glances about
the station as one does who tries to combine politeness with duty.

"You didn't notice on the train," he asked, "an old lady with gray
curls and a poodle, who occupied two seats with her bundles and
quarrelled with the conductor, and you?"

"I think not," answered Octavia, reflecting. "And you haven't,
by any chance, noticed a big, gray-mustached man in a blue shirt
and six-shooters, with little flakes of merino wool sticking in his
hair, have you?"

"Lots of 'em," said Teddy, with symptoms of mental delirium
under the strain. "Do you happen to know any such individual?"

"No; the description is imaginary. Is your interest in the old lady
whom you describe a personal one?"

"Never saw her in my life. She's painted entirely from fancy. She
owns the little piece of property where I earn my bread and butter—
the Rancho de las Sombras. I drove up to meet her according to
arrangement with her lawyer."

Octavia leaned against the wall of the telegraph office. Was this
possible? And didn't he know?

"Are you the manager of that ranch?" she asked weakly.

"I am," said Teddy, with pride.

"I am Mrs. Beaupree," said Octavia faintly; "but my hair never
would curl, and I was polite to the conductor."

For a moment that strange, grown-up look came back, and removed Teddy miles away from her.

"I hope you'll excuse me," he said, rather awkwardly. "You see,
I've been down here in the chaparral a year. I hadn't heard. Give
me your checks, please, and I'll have your traps loaded into the

wagon. José will follow with them. We travel ahead in the buckboard."

Seated by Teddy in a feather-weight buckboard, behind a pair of wild, cream-coloured Spanish ponies, Octavia abandoned all thought for the exhilaration of the present. They swept out of the little town and down the level road toward the south. Soon the road dwindled and disappeared, and they struck across a world carpeted with an endless reach of curly mesquite grass. The wheels made no sound. The tireless ponies bounded ahead at an unbroken gallop. The temperate wind, made fragrant by thousands of acres of blue and yellow wild flowers, roared gloriously in their ears. The motion was aërial, ecstatic, with a thrilling sense of perpetuity in its effect. Octavia sat silent, possessed by a feeling of elemental, sensual bliss. Teddy seemed to be wrestling with some internal problem.

"I'm going to call you madama," he announced as the result of his labours. "That is what the Mexicans will call you—they're nearly all Mexicans on the ranch, you know. That seems to me about the proper thing."

"Very well, Mr. Westlake," said Octavia, primly.

"Oh, now," said Teddy, in some consternation, "that's carrying the thing too far, isn't it?"

"Don't worry me with your beastly etiquette. I'm just beginning to live. Don't remind me of anything artificial. If only this air could be bottled! This much alone is worth coming for. Oh, look! there goes a deer!"

"Jack-rabbit," said Teddy, without turning his head.

"Could I—might I drive?" suggested Octavia, panting, with rose-tinted cheeks and the eye of an eager child.

"On one condition. Could I—might I smoke?"

"Forever!" cried Octavia, taking the lines with solemn joy. "How shall I know which way to drive?"

"Keep her sou' by sou'east, and all sail set. You see that black speck on the horizon under that lowermost Gulf cloud? That's a group of live-oaks and a landmark. Steer halfway between that and the little hill to the left. I'll recite you the whole code of driving rules for the Texas prairies: keep the reins from under the horses' feet, and swear at 'em frequent."

"I'm too happy to swear, Ted. Oh, why do people buy yachts or travel in palace-cars, when a buckboard and a pair of plugs and a spring morning like this can satisfy all desire?"

"Now, I'll ask you," protested Teddy, who was futilely striking match after match on the dashboard, "not to call those denizens of the air plugs. They can kick out a hundred miles between daylight and dark." At last he succeeded in snatching a light for his cigar from the flame held in the hollow of his hands.

"Room!" said Octavia, intensely. "That's what produces the effect. I know now what I've wanted—scope—range—room!"

"Smoking-room," said Teddy, unsentimentally. "I love to smoke in a buckboard. The wind blows the smoke into you and out again. It saves exertion."

The two fell so naturally into their old-time goodfellowship that it was only by degrees that a sense of the strangeness of the new relations between them came to be felt.

"Madama," said Teddy, wonderingly, "however did you get it into your head to cut the crowd and come down here? Is it a fad now among the upper classes to trot off to sheep ranches instead of to Newport?"

"I was broke, Teddy," said Octavia, sweetly, with her interest centred upon steering safely between a Spanish dagger plant and a clump of chaparral; "I haven't a thing in the world but this ranch—not even any other home to go to."

"Come, now," said Teddy, anxiously but incredulously, "you don't mean it?"

"When my husband," said Octavia, with a shy slurring of the word, "died three months ago I thought I had a reasonable amount of the world's goods. His lawyer exploded that theory in a sixty-minute fully illustrated lecture. I took to the sheep as a last resort. Do you happen to know of any fashionable caprice among the gilded youth of Manhattan that induces them to abandon polo and club windows to become managers of sheep ranches?"

"It's easily explained in my case," responded Teddy, promptly. "I had to go to work. I couldn't have earned my board in New York, so I chummed a while with old Sandford, one of the syndicate that owned the ranch before Colonel Beaupree bought it, and got a place down here. I wasn't manager at first. I jogged around on ponies and studied the business in detail, until I got all the points in my head. I saw where it was losing and what the remedies were, and then Sandford put me in charge. I get a hundred dollars a month, and I earn it."

"Poor Teddy!" said Octavia, with a smile.

"You needn't. I like it. I save half my wages, and I'm as hard as a water plug. It beats polo."

"Will it furnish bread and tea and jam for another outcast from civilization?"

"The spring shearing," said the manager, "just cleaned up a deficit in last year's business. Wastefulness and inattention have been the rule heretofore. The autumn clip will leave a small profit over all expenses. Next year there will be jam."

When, about four o'clock in the afternoon, the ponies rounded a gentle, brush-covered hill, and then swooped, like a double cream-coloured cyclone, upon the Rancho de las Sombras, Octavia gave a little cry of delight. A lordly grove of magnificent live-oaks cast an area of grateful, cool shade, whence the ranch had drawn its name, "de las Sombras"—of the shadows. The house, of red brick, one story, ran low and long beneath the trees. Through its middle, dividing its six rooms in half, extended a broad, arched passageway, picturesque with flowering cactus and hanging red earthern jars. A "gallery," low and broad, encircled the building. Vines climbed about it, and the adjacent ground was, for a space, covered with transplanted grass and shrubs. A little lake, long and narrow, glimmered in the sun at the rear. Further away stood the shacks of the Mexican workers, the corrals, wool sheds and shearing pens. To the right lay the low hills, splattered with dark patches of chaparral; to the left the unbounded green prairie blending against the blue heavens.

"It's a home, Teddy," said Octavia, breathlessly; "that's what it is—it's a home."

"Not so bad for a sheep ranch," admitted Teddy, with excusable pride. "I've been tinkering on it at odd times."

A Mexican youth sprang from somewhere in the grass, and took charge of the creams. The mistress and the manager entered the house.

"Here's Mrs. MacIntyre," said Teddy, as a placid, neat, elderly lady came out upon the gallery to meet them. "Mrs. Mac, here's the boss. Very likely she will be wanting a hunk of bacon and a dish of beans after her drive."

Mrs. MacIntyre, the housekeeper, as much a fixture on the place as the lake or the live-oaks, received the imputation of the ranch's resources of refreshment with mild indignation, and was about to give it utterance when Octavia spoke.

"Oh, Mrs. MacIntyre, don't apologize for Teddy. Yes, I call him Teddy. So does every one whom he hasn't duped into taking him seriously. You see, we used to cut paper dolls and play jackstraws together ages ago. No one minds what he says."

"No," said Teddy, "no one minds what he says, just so he doesn't do it again."

Octavia cast one of those subtle, sidelong glances toward him from beneath her lowered eyelids—a glance that Teddy used to describe as an upper-cut. But there was nothing in his ingenuous, weather-tanned face to warrant a suspicion that he was making an allusion—nothing. Beyond a doubt, thought Octavia, he had forgotten.

"Mr. Westlake likes his fun," said Mrs. MacIntyre, as she conducted Octavia to her rooms. "But," she added, loyally, "people around here usually pay attention to what he says when he talks in earnest. I don't know what would have become of this place without him."

Two rooms at the east end of the house had been arranged for the occupancy of the ranch's mistress. When she entered them a slight dismay seized her at their bare appearance and the scantiness of their furniture; but she quickly reflected that the climate was a semi-tropical one, and was moved to appreciation of the well-conceived efforts to conform to it. The sashes had already been removed from the big windows, and white curtains waved in the Gulf breeze that streamed through the wide jalousies.* The bare floor was amply strewn with cool rugs; the chairs were inviting, deep, dreamy willows; the walls were papered with a light, cheerful olive. One whole side of her sitting room was covered with books on smooth, unpainted pine shelves. She flew to these at once. Be-

---

*Windows made of glass louvers.

fore her was a well-selected library. She caught glimpses of titles of volumes of fiction and travel not yet seasoned from the dampness of the press.

Presently, recollecting that she was now in a wilderness given over to mutton, centipedes and privations, the incongruity of these luxuries struck her, and, with intuitive feminine suspicion, she began turning to the fly-leaves of volume after volume. Upon each one was inscribed in fluent characters the name of Theodore Westlake, Jr.

Octavia, fatigued by her long journey, retired early that night. Lying upon her white, cool bed, she rested deliciously, but sleep coquetted long with her. She listened to faint noises whose strangeness kept her faculties on the alert—the fractious yelping of the coyotes, the ceaseless, low symphony of the wind, the distant booming of the frogs about the lake, the lamentation of a concertina* in the Mexicans' quarters. There were many conflicting feelings in her heart—thankfulness and rebellion, peace and disquietude, loneliness and a sense of protecting care, happiness and an old, haunting pain.

She did what any other woman would have done—sought relief in a wholesome tide of unreasonable tears, and her last words, murmured to herself before slumber, capitulating, came softly to woo her, were, "He has forgotten."

The manager of the Rancho de las Sombras was no dilettante. He was a "hustler."† He was generally up, mounted, and away of mornings before the rest of the household were awake, making the rounds of the flocks and camps. This was the duty of the major-domo,‡ a stately old Mexican with a princely air and manner, but Teddy seemed to have a great deal of confidence in his own eyesight. Except in the busy seasons, he nearly always returned to the ranch to breakfast at eight o'clock, with Octavia and Mrs. MacIntyre, at the little table set in the central hallway, bringing with him a tonic and breezy cheerfulness full of the health and flavour of the prairies.

---

*Small, portable instrument, similar to an accordion.
†Hard worker.
‡Head servant.

A few days after Octavia's arrival he made her get out one of her riding skirts, and curtail it to a shortness demanded by the chaparral brakes.

With some misgivings she donned this and the pair of buckskin leggings he prescribed in addition, and, mounted upon a dancing pony, rode with him to view her possessions. He showed her every-thing—the flocks of ewes, muttons and grazing lambs, the dipping vats, the shearing pens, the uncouth merino rams in their little pasture, the water-tanks prepared against the summer drought—giving account of his stewardship with a boyish enthusiasm that never flagged.

Where was the old Teddy that she knew so well? This side of him was the same, and it was a side that pleased her; but this was all she ever saw of him now. Where was his sentimentality—those old, varying moods of impetuous love-making, of fanciful, quixotic devotion, of heart-breaking gloom, of alternating, absurd tender-ness and haughty dignity? His nature had been a sensitive one, his temperament bordering closely on the artistic. She knew that, be-sides being a follower of fashion and its fads and sports, he had cultivated tastes of a finer nature. He had written things, he had tampered with colours, he was something of a student in certain branches of art, and once she had been admitted to all his aspira-tions and thoughts. But now—and she could not avoid the con-clusion—Teddy had barricaded against her every side of himself except one—the side that showed the manager of the Rancho de las Sombras and a jolly chum who had forgiven and forgotten. Queerly enough the words of Mr. Bannister's description of her property came into her mind—"all inclosed within a strong barbed-wire fence."

"Teddy's fenced, too," said Octavia to herself.

It was not difficult for her to reason out the cause of his forti-fications. It had originated one night at the Hammersmiths' ball. It occurred at a time soon after she had decided to accept Colonel Beaupree and his million, which was no more than her looks and the entrée she held to the inner circles were worth. Teddy had proposed with all his impetuosity and fire, and she looked him straight in the eyes, and said, coldly and finally: "Never let me hear any such silly nonsense from you again." "You won't," said Teddy, with a new expression around his mouth, and—now Teddy was inclosed within a strong barbed-wire fence.

It was on this first ride of inspection that Teddy was seized by the inspiration that suggested the name of Mother Goose's heroine, and he at once bestowed it upon Octavia. The idea, supported by both a similarity of names and identity of occupations, seemed to strike him as a peculiarly happy one, and he never tired of using it. The Mexicans on the ranch also took up the name, adding another syllable to accommodate their lingual incapacity for the final "p," gravely referring to her as "La Madama Bo-Peepy." Eventually it spread, and "Madame Bo-Peep's ranch" was as often mentioned as the "Rancho de las Sombras."

Came the long, hot season from May to September, when work is scarce on the ranches. Octavia passed the days in a kind of lotus-eater's* dream. Books, hammocks, correspondence with a few intimate friends, a renewed interest in her old water-colour box and easel—these disposed of the sultry hours of daylight. The evenings were always sure to bring enjoyment. Best of all were the rapturous horseback rides with Teddy, when the moon gave light over the wind-swept leagues, chaperoned by the wheeling night-hawk and the startled owl. Often the Mexicans would come up from their shacks with their guitars and sing the weirdest of heart-breaking songs. There were long, cosy chats on the breezy gallery, and an interminable warfare of wits between Teddy and Mrs. MacIntyre, whose abundant Scotch shrewdness often more than overmatched the lighter humour in which she was lacking.

And the nights came, one after another, and were filed away by weeks and months—nights soft and languorous and fragrant, that should have driven Strephon to Chloe[3] over wires however barbed, that might have drawn Cupid himself to hunt, lasso in hand, among those amorous pastures—but Teddy kept his fences up.

One July night Madame Bo-Peep and her ranch manager were sitting on the east gallery. Teddy had been exhausting the science of prognostication as to the probabilities of a price of twenty-four

---

*In Greek mythology, lotus-eaters subsisted on the lotus flower, causing them to forget their past and live in a dream-like state (see endnote 3 for "Transients in Arcadia").

cents for the autumn clip, and had then subsided into an anæsthetic cloud of Havana smoke. Only as incompetent a judge as a woman would have failed to note long ago that at least a third of his salary must have gone up in the fumes of those imported Regalias.

"Teddy," said Octavia, suddenly, and rather sharply, "what are you working down here on a ranch for?"

"One hundred per," said Teddy, glibly, "and found."

"I've a good mind to discharge you."

"Can't do it," said Teddy, with a grin.

"Why not?" demanded Octavia, with argumentative heat.

"Under contract. Terms of sale respect all unexpired contracts. Mine runs until 12 P.M., December thirty-first. You might get up at midnight on that date and fire me. If you try it sooner I'll be in a position to bring legal proceedings."

Octavia seemed to be considering the prospects of litigation.

"But," continued Teddy cheerfully, "I've been thinking of resigning anyway."

Octavia's rocking-chair ceased its motion. There were centipedes in this country, she felt sure; and Indians; and vast, lonely, desolate, empty wastes; all within strong barbed-wire fence. There was a Van Dresser pride, but there was also a Van Dresser heart. She must know for certain whether or not he had forgotten.

"Ah, well, Teddy," she said, with a fine assumption of polite interest, "it's lonely down here; you're longing to get back to the old life—to polo and lobsters and theatres and balls."

"Never cared much for balls," said Teddy virtuously.

"You're getting old, Teddy. Your memory is failing. Nobody ever knew you to miss a dance, unless it occurred on the same night with another one which you attended. And you showed such shocking bad taste, too, in dancing too often with the same partner. Let me see, what was that Forbes girl's name—the one with wall eyes—Mabel, wasn't it?"

"No; Adéle. Mabel was the one with the bony elbows. That wasn't wall in Adéle's eyes. It was soul. We used to talk sonnets together, and Verlaine.[4] Just then I was trying to run a pipe from the Pierian spring."*

---

*In Greek mythology, a spring in Pieria, a region of ancient Macedonia where the Muses were born; considered a source of inspiration.

"You were on the floor with her," said Octavia, undeflected, "five times at the Hammersmiths'."

"Hammersmiths' what?" questioned Teddy, vacuously.

"Ball—ball," said Octavia, viciously. "What were we talking of?"

"Eyes, I thought," said Teddy, after some reflection; "and elbows."

"Those Hammersmiths," went on Octavia, in her sweetest society prattle, after subduing an intense desire to yank a handful of sunburnt, sandy hair from the head lying back contentedly against the canvas of the steamer chair, "had too much money. Mines, wasn't it? It was something that paid something to the ton. You couldn't get a glass of plain water in their house. Everything at that ball was dreadfully overdone."

"It was," said Teddy.

"Such a crowd there was!" Octavia continued, conscious that she was talking the rapid drivel of a school-girl describing her first dance. "The balconies were as warm as the rooms. I—lost—something at that ball." The last sentence was uttered in a tone calculated to remove the barbs from miles of wire.

"So did I," confessed Teddy, in a lower voice.

"A glove," said Octavia, falling back as the enemy approached her ditches.

"Caste," said Teddy, halting his firing line without loss. "I hobnobbed, half the evening with one of Hammersmith's miners, a fellow who kept his hands in his pockets, and talked like an archangel about reduction plants and drifts and levels and sluice-boxes."

"A pearl-gray glove, nearly new," sighed Octavia, mournfully.

"A bang-up chap, that McArdle," maintained Teddy approvingly. "A man who hated olives and elevators; a man who handled mountains as croquettes, and built tunnels in the air; a man who never uttered a word of silly nonsense in his life. Did you sign those lease-renewal applications yet, madama? They've got to be on file in the land office by the thirty-first."

Teddy turned his head lazily. Octavia's chair was vacant.

A certain centipede, crawling along the lines marked out by fate, expounded the situation. It was early one morning while Octavia and Mrs. MacIntyre were trimming the honeysuckle on the west gallery. Teddy had risen and departed hastily before daylight in response to word that a flock of ewes had been scattered from their bedding ground during the night by a thunder-storm.

The centipede, driven by destiny, showed himself on the floor of the gallery, and then, the screeches of the two women giving him his cue, he scuttled with all his yellow legs through the open door into the furthermost west room, which was Teddy's. Arming themselves with domestic utensils selected with regard to their length, Octavia and Mrs. MacIntyre, with much clutching of skirts and skirmishing for the position of rear guard in the attacking force, followed.

Once outside, the centipede seemed to have disappeared, and his prospective murderers began a thorough but cautious search for their victim.

Even in the midst of such a dangerous and absorbing adventure Octavia was conscious of an awed curiosity on finding herself in Teddy's sanctum. In that room he sat alone, silently communing with those secret thoughts that he now shared with no one, dreamed there whatever dreams he now called on no one to interpret.

It was the room of a Spartan or a soldier. In one corner stood a wide, canvas-covered cot; in another, a small bookcase; in another, a grim stand of Winchesters and shotguns. An immense table, strewn with letters, papers and documents and surmounted by a set of pigeonholes, occupied one side.

The centipede showed genius in concealing himself in such bare quarters. Mrs. MacIntyre was poking a broom-handle behind the bookcase. Octavia approached Teddy's cot. The room was just as the manager had left it in his hurry. The Mexican maid had not yet given it her attention. There was his big pillow with the imprint of his head still in the centre. She thought the horrid beast might have climbed the cot and hidden itself to bite Teddy. Centipedes were thus cruel and vindictive toward managers.

She cautiously overturned the pillow, and then parted her lips to give the signal for reinforcements at sight of a long, slender, dark object lying there. But, repressing it in time, she caught up a glove, a pearl-gray glove, flattened—it might be conceived—by many, many months of nightly pressure beneath the pillow of the man who had forgotten the Hammersmiths' ball. Teddy must have left so hurriedly that morning that he had, for once, forgotten to transfer it to its resting-place by day. Even managers, who are notoriously wily and cunning, are sometimes caught up with.

Octavia slid the gray glove into the bosom of her summery morning gown. It was hers. Men who put themselves within a strong barbed-wire fence, and remember Hammersmith balls only by the talk of miners about sluice-boxes, should not be allowed to possess such articles.

After all, what a paradise this prairie country was! How it blossomed like the rose when you found things that were thought to be lost! How delicious was that morning breeze coming in the windows, fresh and sweet with the breath of the yellow ratama blooms! Might one not stand, for a minute, with shining, far-gazing eyes, and dream that mistakes might be corrected?

Why was Mrs. MacIntyre poking about so absurdly with a broom?

"I've found it," said Mrs. MacIntyre, banging the door. "Here it is."

"Did you lose something?" asked Octavia, with sweetly polite non-interest.

"The little devil!" said Mrs. MacIntyre, driven to violence. "Ye've no forgotten him alretty?"

Between them they slew the centipede. Thus was he rewarded for his agency toward the recovery of things lost at the Hammersmiths' ball.

It seems that Teddy, in due course, remembered the glove, and when he returned to the house at sunset made a secret but exhaustive search for it. Not until evening, upon the moonlit eastern gallery, did he find it. It was upon the hand that he had thought lost to him forever, and so he was moved to repeat certain nonsense that he had been commanded never, never to utter again. Teddy's fences were down.

This time there was no ambition to stand in the way, and the wooing was as natural and successful as should be between ardent shepherd and gentle shepherdess.

The prairies changed to a garden. The Rancho de las Sombras became the Ranch of Light.

A few days later Octavia received a letter from Mr. Bannister, in reply to one she had written to him asking some questions about her business. A portion of the letter ran as follows:

"I am at a loss to account for your references to the sheep ranch. Two months after your departure to take up your residence upon it, it was discovered that Colonel Beaupree's title was worthless. A deed came to light showing that he disposed of the property before his death. The matter was reported to your manager, Mr. Westlake, who at once repurchased the property. It is entirely beyond my powers of conjecture to imagine how you have remained in ignorance of this fact. I beg that you will at once confer with that gentleman, who will, at least, corroborate my statement."

Octavia sought Teddy, with battle in her eye.

"What are you working on this ranch for?" she asked once more.

"One hundred—" he began to repeat, but saw in her face that she knew. She held Mr. Bannister's letter in her hand. He knew that the game was up.

"It's my ranch," said Teddy, like a schoolboy detected in evil. "It's a mighty poor manager that isn't able to absorb the boss's business if you give him time."

"Why were you working down here?" pursued Octavia, still struggling after the key to the riddle of Teddy.

"To tell the truth,'Tave," said Teddy, with quiet candour, "it wasn't for the salary. That about kept me in cigars and sunburn lotions. I was sent south by my doctor. 'Twas that right lung that was going to the bad on account of over-exercise and strain at polo and gymnastics. I needed climate and ozone and rest and things of that sort."

In an instant Octavia was close against the vicinity of the affected organ. Mr. Bannister's letter fluttered to the floor.

"It's—it's well now, isn't it, Teddy?"

"Sound as a mesquite chunk. I deceived you in one thing. I paid fifty thousand for your ranch as soon as I found you had no title. I had just about that much income accumulated at my banker's while I've been herding sheep down here, so it was almost like picking the thing up on a bargain-counter for a penny. There's another little surplus of unearned increment piling up there,'Tave. I've been thinking of a wedding trip in a yacht with white ribbons tied to the mast, through the Mediterranean, and then up among the Hebrides and down Norway to the Zuyder Zee."

"And I was thinking," said Octavia, softly, "of a wedding gallop with my manager among the flocks of sheep and back to a wedding breakfast with Mrs. MacIntyre on the gallery, with, maybe, a sprig of orange blossom fastened to the red jar above the table."

Teddy laughed, and began to chant:

> "Little Bo-Peep has lost her sheep,
> And doesn't know where to find 'em.
> Let 'em alone, and they'll come home,
> And——"[5]

Octavia drew his head down, and whispered in his ear.

But that is one of the tales they brought behind them.

—from *Whirligigs* (1910)

FROM EACH ACCORDING
TO HIS ABILITY

Vuyning left his club, cursing it softly, without any particular anger. From ten in the morning until eleven it had bored him immeasurably. Kirk with his fish story, Brooks with his Porto Rico cigars, old Morrison with his anecdote about the widow, Hepburn with his invariable luck at billiards—all these afflictions had been repeated without change of bill or scenery. Besides these morning evils Miss Allison had refused him again on the night before. But that was a chronic trouble. Five times she had laughed at his offer to make her Mrs. Vuyning. He intended to ask her again the next Wednesday evening.

Vuyning walked along Forty-fourth Street to Broadway, and then drifted down the great sluice that washes out the dust of the gold-mines of Gotham. He wore a morning suit of light gray, low, dull kid shoes, a plain, finely woven straw hat, and his visible linen was the most delicate possible shade of heliotrope. His necktie was the blue-gray of a November sky, and its knot was plainly the outcome of a lordly carelessness combined with an accurate conception of the most recent dictum of fashion.

Now, to write of a man's haberdashery is a worse thing than to write a historical novel "around" Paul Jones,[1] or to pen a testimonial to a hay-fever cure.

Therefore, let it be known that the description of Vuyning's apparel is germane to the movements of the story, and not to make room for the new fall stock of goods.

Even Broadway that morning was a discord in Vuyning's ears; and in his eyes it paralleled for a few dreamy, dreary minutes a certain howling, scorching, seething, malodorous slice of street that he remembered in Morocco. He saw the struggling mass of dogs, beggars, fakirs,* slave-drivers and veiled women in carts without horses,† the sun blazing brightly among the bazaars, the piles of rubbish from ruined temples in the street—and then a lady, passing, jabbed the ferrule of a parasol in his side and brought him back to Broadway.

Five minutes of his stroll brought him to a certain corner, where a number of silent, pale-faced men are accustomed to stand, immovably, for hours, busy with the file blades of their penknives, with their hat brims on a level with their eyelids. Wall Street speculators, driving home in their carriages, love to point out these men to their visiting friends and tell them of this rather famous lounging-place of the "crooks." On Wall Street the speculators never use the file blades of their knives.

Vuyning was delighted when one of this company stepped forth and addressed him as he was passing. He was hungry for something out of the ordinary, and to be accosted by this smooth-faced, keen-eyed, low-voiced, athletic member of the under world, with his grim, yet pleasant smile, had all the taste of an adventure to the convention-weary Vuyning.

"Excuse me, friend," said he. "Could I have a few minutes' talk with you—on the level?"

"Certainly," said Vuyning, with a smile. "But, suppose we step aside to a quieter place. There is a divan—a café over here that will do. Schrumm will give us a private corner."

Schrumm established them under a growing palm, with two seidls between them. Vuyning made a pleasant reference to meteorological conditions, thus forming a hinge upon which might be swung the door leading from the thought repository of the other.

"In the first place," said his companion, with the air of one who presents his credentials, "I want you to understand that I am a crook. Out West I am known as Rowdy the Dude. Pickpocket, supper man, second-story man, yeggman, boxman, all-round burglar, card-sharp and slickest con man west of the Twenty-third Street ferry landing—that's my history. That's to show I'm on the square—with you. My name's Emerson."

---

*Religious beggars or mendicants.
†In Morocco, taxi carts pulled by men.

"Confound old Kirk with his fish stories," said Vuyning to himself, with silent glee as he went through his pockets for a card. "It's pronounced 'Vining,' " he said, as he tossed it over to the other. "And I'll be as frank with you. I'm just a kind of a loafer, I guess, living on my daddy's money. At the club they call me 'Left-at-the-Post.'* I never did a day's work in my life; and I haven't the heart to run over a chicken when I'm motoring. It's a pretty shabby record, altogether."

"There's one thing you can do," said Emerson, admiringly; "you can carry duds. I've watched you several times pass on Broadway. You look the best dressed man I've seen. And I'll bet you a gold mine I've got $50 worth more gent's furnishings on my frame than you have. That's what I wanted to see you about. I can't do the trick. Take a look at me. What's wrong?"

"Stand up," said Vuyning.

Emerson arose, and slowly revolved.

"You've been 'outfitted,' " declared the clubman. "Some Broadway window-dresser has misused you. That's an expensive suit, though, Emerson."

"A hundred dollars," said Emerson.

"Twenty too much," said Vuyning. "Six months old in cut, one inch too long, and half an inch too much lapel. Your hat is plainly dated one year ago, although there's only a sixteenth of an inch lacking in the brim to tell the story. That English poke in your collar is too short by the distance between Troy and London. A plain gold link cuff-button would take all the shine out of those pearl ones with diamond settings. Those tan shoes would be exactly the articles to work into the heart of a Brooklyn school-ma'am on a two weeks' visit to Lake Ronkonkoma. I think I caught a glimpse of a blue silk sock embroidered with russet lilies of the valley when you—improperly—drew up your trousers as you sat down. There are always plain ones to be had in the stores. Have I hurt your feelings, Emerson?"

"Double the ante!" cried the criticised one, greedily. "Give me more of it. There's a way to tote the haberdashery, and I want to

---

*An idiom meaning "failed to complete"; refers to a race-horse stalling at the starting post.

get wise to it. Say, you're the right kind of a swell. Anything else to the queer about me?"

"Your tie," said Vuyning, "is tied with absolute precision and correctness."

"Thanks," gratefully—"I spent over half an hour at it before I——"

"Thereby," interrupted Vuyning, "completing your resemblance to a dummy in a Broadway store window."

"Yours truly," said Emerson, sitting down again. "It's bully* of you to put me wise. I knew there was something wrong, but I couldn't just put my finger on it. I guess it comes by nature to know how to wear clothes."

"Oh, I suppose," said Vuyning, with a laugh, "that my ancestors picked up the knack while they were peddling clothes from house to house a couple of hundred years ago. I'm told they did that."

"And mine," said Emerson, cheerfully, "were making their visits at night, I guess, and didn't have a chance to catch on to the correct styles."

"I tell you what," said Vuyning, whose ennui had taken wings, "I'll take you to my tailor. He'll eliminate the mark of the beast from your exterior. That is, if you care to go any further in the way of expense."

"Play 'em to the ceiling," said Emerson, with a boyish smile of joy. "I've got a roll as big around as a barrel of black-eyed peas and as loose as the wrapper of a two-for-fiver. I don't mind telling you that I was not touring among the Antipodes† when the burglar-proof safe of the Farmers' National Bank of Butterville, Ia., flew open some moonless nights ago to the tune of $16,000."

"Aren't you afraid," asked Vuyning, "that I'll call a cop and hand you over?"

"You tell me," said Emerson, coolly, "why I didn't keep them."

He laid Vuyning's pocketbook and watch—the Vuyning 100-year-old family watch—on the table.

"Man," said Vuyning, revelling, "did you ever hear the tale Kirk tells about the six-pound trout and the old fisherman?"

---

*Great.
†Colloquial term for Australia and New Zealand.

"Seems not," said Emerson, politely. "I'd like to."

"But you won't," said Vuyning. "I've heard it scores of times. That's why I won't tell you. I was just thinking how much better this is than a club. Now, shall we go to my tailor?"

"Boys, and elderly gents," said Vuyning, five days later at his club, standing up against the window where his coterie was gathered, and keeping out the breeze, "a friend of mine from the West will dine at our table this evening."

"Will he ask if we have heard the latest from Denver?" said a member, squirming in his chair.

"Will he mention the new twenty-three-story Masonic Temple, in Quincy, Ill.?" inquired another, dropping his nose-glasses.

"Will he spring one of those Western Mississippi River catfish stories, in which they use yearling calves for bait?" demanded Kirk, fiercely.

"Be comforted," said Vuyning. "He has none of the little vices. He is a burglar and safe-blower, and a pal of mine."

"Oh, Mary Ann!" said they. "Must you always adorn every statement with your alleged humor?"

It came to pass that at eight in the evening a calm, smooth, brilliant, affable man sat at Vuyning's right hand during dinner. And when the ones who pass their lives in city streets spoke of skyscrapers or of the little Czar on his far, frozen throne, or of insignificant fish from inconsequential streams, this big, deep-chested man, faultlessly clothed, and eyed like an Emperor, disposed of their Lilliputian chatter[2] with a wink of his eyelash.

And then he painted for them with hard, broad strokes a marvellous lingual panorama of the West. He stacked snow-topped mountains on the table, freezing the hot dishes of the waiting diners. With a wave of his hand he swept the clubhouse into a pine-crowned gorge, turning the waiters into a grim posse, and each listener into a blood-stained fugitive, climbing with torn fingers upon the ensanguined* rocks. He touched the table and spake, and the five panted as they gazed on barren lava beds, and each man

---

*Blood-stained.

took his tongue between his teeth and felt his mouth bake at the tale of a land empty of water and food. As simply as Homer sang,[3] while he dug a tine of his fork leisurely into the tablecloth, he opened a new world to their view, as does one who tells a child of the Looking-Glass Country.[4]

As one of his listeners might have spoken of tea too strong at a Madison Square "afternoon," so he depicted the ravages of "red-eye"* in a border town when the caballeros† of the lariat and "forty-five"‡ reduced ennui to a minimum.

And then, with a sweep of his white, unringed hands, he dismissed Melpomene, and forthwith Diana and Amaryllis[5] footed it before the mind's eyes of the clubmen.

The savannas of the continent spread before them. The wind, humming through a hundred leagues of sage brush and mesquite, closed their ears to the city's staccato noises. He told them of camps, of ranches marooned in a sea of fragrant prairie blossoms, of gallops in the stilly night that Apollo§ would have forsaken his daytime steeds to enjoy; he read them the great, rough epic of the cattle and the hills that have not been spoiled by the hand of man, the mason. His words were a telescope to the city men, whose eyes had looked upon Youngstown, O., and whose tongues had called it "West."

In fact, Emerson had them "going."

The next morning at ten he met Vuyning, by appointment, at a Forty-second Street café.

Emerson was to leave for the West that day. He wore a suit of dark cheviot that looked to have been draped upon him by an ancient Grecian tailor who was a few thousand years ahead of the styles.

"Mr. Vuyning," said he, with the clear, ingenuous smile of the successful "crook," "it's up to me to go the limit for you any time I can do so. You're the real thing; and if I can ever return the favor, you bet your life I'll do it."

---

*Cheap whiskey.
†Horsemen (Spanish).
‡Type of handgun.
§In some versions of Greek mythology, Apollo drove the chariot of the sun across the heavens each day.

"What was that cow-puncher's name?" asked Vuyning, "who used to catch a mustang by the nose and mane, and throw him till he put the bridle on?"

"Bates," said Emerson.

"Thanks," said Vuyning. "I thought it was Yates. Oh, about that toggery business—I'd forgotten that."

"I've been looking for some guy to put me on the right track for years," said Emerson. "You're the goods, duty free, and half-way to the warehouse in a red wagon."

"Bacon, toasted on a green willow switch over red coals, ought to put broiled lobsters out of business," said Vuyning. "And you say a horse at the end of a thirty-foot rope can't pull a ten-inch stake out of wet prairie? Well, good-bye, old man, if you must be off."

At one o'clock Vuyning had luncheon with Miss Allison by previous arrangement.

For thirty minutes he babbled to her, unaccountably, of ranches, horses, cañons, cyclones, round-ups, Rocky Mountains and beans and bacon. She looked at him with wondering and half-terrified eyes.

"I was going to propose again to-day," said Vuyning, cheerily, "but I won't. I've worried you often enough. You know dad has a ranch in Colorado. What's the good of staying here? Jumping jonquils! but it's great out there. I'm going to start next Tuesday."

"No, you won't," said Miss Allison.

"What?" said Vuyning.

"Not alone," said Miss Allison, dropping a tear upon her salad. "What do you think?"

"Betty!" exclaimed Vuyning, "what do you mean?"

"I'll go too," said Miss Allison, forcibly.

Vuyning filled her glass with Apollinaris.*

"Here's to Rowdy the Dude!" he gave—a toast mysterious.

"Don't know him," said Miss Allison; "but if he's your friend, Jimmy—here goes!"

—from *The Voice of the City* (1908)

---

*Brand of sparkling mineral water.

THE CABALLERO'S WAY

The Cisco Kid had killed six men in more or less fair scrimmages, had murdered twice as many (mostly Mexicans), and had winged a larger number whom he modestly forbore to count. Therefore a woman loved him.

The Kid was twenty-five, looked twenty; and a careful insurance company would have estimated the probable time of his demise at, say, twenty-six. His habitat was anywhere between the Frio* and the Rio Grande. He killed for the love of it—because he was quick-tempered—to avoid arrest—for his own amusement—any reason that came to his mind would suffice. He had escaped capture because he could shoot five-sixths of a second sooner than any sheriff or ranger in the service, and because he rode a speckled roan horse that knew every cow-path in the mesquite and pear thickets from San Antonio to Matamoras.

Tonia Perez, the girl who loved the Cisco Kid, was half Carmen, half Madonna,[1] and the rest—oh, yes, a woman who is half Carmen and half Madonna can always be something more—the rest, let us say, was humming-bird. She lived in a grass-roofed *jacal*† near a little Mexican settlement at the Lone Wolf Crossing of the Frio. With her lived a father or grandfather, a lineal Aztec, somewhat less than a thousand years old, who herded a hundred goats and lived in a continuous drunken dream from drinking *mescal*.‡ Back of the *jacal* a tremendous forest of bristling pear, twenty feet high at its worst, crowded almost to its door. It was along the bewildering maze of this spinous thicket that the speckled roan would bring

---

*River in Texas, some 150 miles from the Rio Grande.
†Hut (Spanish).
‡Powerful Mexican liquor.

the Kid to see his girl. And once, clinging like a lizard to the ridge-pole, high up under the peaked grass roof, he had heard Tonia, with her Madonna face and Carmen beauty and humming-bird soul, parley with the sheriff's posse, denying knowledge of her man in her soft *mélange** of Spanish and English.

One day the adjutant-general of the State, who is *ex officio*,[†] commander of the ranger forces, wrote some sarcastic lines to Captain Duval of Company X, stationed at Laredo, relative to the serene and undisturbed existence led by murderers and desperadoes in the said captain's territory.

The captain turned the colour of brick dust under his tan, and forwarded the letter, after adding a few comments, per ranger Private Bill Adamson, to ranger Lieutenant Sandridge, camped at a water hole on the Nueces with a squad of five men in preservation of law and order.

Lieutenant Sandridge turned a beautiful *couleur de rose* through his ordinary strawberry complexion, tucked the letter in his hip pocket, and chewed off the ends of his gamboge moustache.

The next morning he saddled his horse and rode alone to the Mexican settlement at the Lone Wolf Crossing of the Frio, twenty miles away.

Six feet two, blond as a Viking, quiet as a deacon, dangerous as a machine gun, Sandridge moved among the *Jacales*, patiently seeking news of the Cisco Kid.

Far more than the law, the Mexicans dreaded the cold and certain vengeance of the lone rider that the ranger sought. It had been one of the Kid's pastimes to shoot Mexicans "to see them kick": if he demanded from them moribund Terpsichorean[‡] feats, simply that he might be entertained, what terrible and extreme penalties would be certain to follow should they anger him! One and all they lounged with upturned palms and shrugging shoulders, filling the air with "*quien sabes*"[§] and denials of the Kid's acquaintance.

But there was a man named Fink who kept a store at the

---

*Mixture (French).
†By virtue of the office (Latin).
‡Relating to dancing; in Greek mythology, Terpsichore is the Muse of the dance.
§"Who knows" (Spanish).

Crossing—a man of many nationalities, tongues, interests, and ways of thinking.

"No use to ask them Mexicans," he said to Sandridge. "They're afraid to tell. This *hombre** they call the Kid—Goodall is his name, ain't it?—he's been in my store once or twice. I have an idea you might run across him at—but I guess I don't keer to say, myself. I'm two seconds later in pulling a gun than I used to be, and the difference is worth thinking about. But this Kid's got a half-Mexican girl at the Crossing that he comes to see. She lives in that *jacal* a hundred yards down the arroyo at the edge of the pear. Maybe she—no, I don't suppose she would, but that *jacal* would be a good place to watch, anyway."

Sandridge rode down to the *jacal* of Perez. The sun was low, and the broad shade of the great pear thicket already covered the grass-thatched hut. The goats were enclosed for the night in a brush corral near by. A few kids walked the top of it, nibbling the chaparral leaves. The old Mexican lay upon a blanket on the grass, already in a stupor from his mescal, and dreaming, perhaps, of the nights when he and Pizarro touched glasses to their New World fortunes[2]—so old his wrinkled face seemed to proclaim him to be. And in the door of the *jacal* stood Tonia. And Lieutenant Sandridge sat in his saddle staring at her like a gannet† agape at a sailorman.

The Cisco Kid was a vain person, as all eminent and successful assassins are, and his bosom would have been ruffled had he known that at a simple exchange of glances two persons, in whose minds he had been looming large, suddenly abandoned (at least for the time) all thought of him.

Never before had Tonia seen such a man as this. He seemed to be made of sunshine and blood-red tissue and clear weather. He seemed to illuminate the shadow of the pear when he smiled, as though the sun were rising again. The men she had known had been small and dark. Even the Kid, in spite of his achievements, was a stripling no larger than herself, with black, straight hair and a cold, marble face that chilled the noonday.

---

*Man (Spanish).
†Large seabird.

As for Tonia, though she sends description to the poorhouse, let her make a millionaire of your fancy. Her blue-black hair, smoothly divided in the middle and bound close to her head, and her large eyes full of the Latin melancholy, gave her the Madonna touch. Her motions and air spoke of the concealed fire and the desire to charm that she had inherited from the *gitanas** of the Basque province.[3] As for the humming-bird part of her, that dwelt in her heart; you could not perceive it unless her bright red skirt and dark blue blouse gave you a symbolic hint of the vagarious bird.

The newly lighted sun-god asked for a drink of water. Tonia brought it from the red jar hanging under the brush shelter. Sandridge considered it necessary to dismount so as to lessen the trouble of her ministrations.

I play no spy; nor do I assume to master the thoughts of any human heart; but I assert, by the chronicler's right, that before a quarter of an hour had sped, Sandridge was teaching her how to plait a six-strand rawhide stake-rope, and Tonia had explained to him that were it not for her little English book that the peripatetic *padre*[†] had given her and the little crippled *chivo*,[‡] that she fed from a bottle, she would be very, very lonely indeed.

Which leads to a suspicion that the Kid's fences needed repairing, and that the adjutant-general's sarcasm had fallen upon unproductive soil.

In his camp by the water hole Lieutenant Sandridge announced and reiterated his intention of either causing the Cisco Kid to nibble the black loam of the Frio country prairies or of haling him before a judge and jury. That sounded business-like. Twice a week he rode over to the Lone Wolf Crossing of the Frio, and directed Tonia's slim, slightly lemon-tinted fingers among the intricacies of the slowly growing lariata.[§] A six-strand plait is hard to learn and easy to teach.

The ranger knew that he might find the Kid there at any visit. He kept his armament ready, and had a frequent eye for the pear

---

*Female gypsies (Spanish).
†Itinerant priest (Spanish).
‡Billy goat (Spanish).
§Type of braided rope, used like a lasso.

thicket at the rear of the *jacal*. Thus he might bring down the kite and the humming-bird with one stone.

While the sunny-haired ornithologist was pursuing his studies the Cisco Kid was also attending to his professional duties. He moodily shot up a saloon in a small cow village on Quintana Creek, killed the town marshal (plugging him neatly in the centre of his tin badge), and then rode away, morose and unsatisfied. No true artist is uplifted by shooting an aged man carrying an old-style .38 bulldog.

On his way the Kid suddenly experienced the yearning that all men feel when wrong-doing loses its keen edge of delight. He yearned for the woman he loved to reassure him that she was his in spite of it. He wanted her to call his bloodthirstiness bravery and his cruelty devotion. He wanted Tonia to bring him water from the red jar under the brush shelter, and tell him how the *chivo* was thriving on the bottle.

The Kid turned the speckled roan's head up the ten-mile pear flat that stretches along the Arroyo Hondo until it ends at the Lone Wolf Crossing of the Frio. The roan whickered; for he had a sense of locality and direction equal to that of a belt-line street-car horse; and he knew he would soon be nibbling the rich mesquite grass at the end of a forty-foot stake-rope while Ulysses rested his head in Circe's straw-footed hut.[4]

More weird and lonesome than the journey of an Amazonian explorer is the ride of one through a Texas pear flat. With dismal monotony and startling variety the uncanny and multiform shapes of the cacti lift their twisted trunks, and fat, bristly hands to encumber the way. The demon plant, appearing to live without soil or rain, seems to taunt the parched traveller with its lush grey greenness. It warps itself a thousand times about what look to be open and inviting paths, only to lure the rider into blind and impassable spine-defended "bottoms of the bag," leaving him to retreat, if he can, with the points of the compass whirling in his head.

To be lost in the pear is to die almost the death of the thief on the cross, pierced by nails and with grotesque shapes of all the fiends hovering about.

But it was not so with the Kid and his mount. Winding, twisting, circling, tracing the most fantastic and bewildering trail ever

picked out, the good roan lessened the distance to the Lone Wolf
Crossing with every coil and turn that he made.

While they fared the Kid sang. He knew but one tune and sang
it, as he knew but one code and lived it, and but one girl and loved
her. He was a single-minded man of conventional ideas. He had a
voice like a coyote with bronchitis, but whenever he chose to sing
his song he sang it. It was a conventional song of the camps and
trail, running at its beginning as near as may be to these words:

> Don't you monkey with my Lulu girl
> Or I'll tell you what I'll do—

and so on.[5] The roan was inured to it, and did not mind.

But even the poorest singer will, after a certain time, gain his
own consent to refrain from contributing to the world's noises. So
the Kid, by the time he was within a mile or two of Tonia's *jacal*,
had reluctantly allowed his song to die away—not because his vocal
performance had become less charming to his own ears, but because
his laryngeal muscles were aweary.

As though he were in a circus ring the speckled roan wheeled
and danced through the labyrinth of pear until at length his rider
knew by certain landmarks that the Lone Wolf Crossing was close
at hand. Then, where the pear was thinner, he caught sight of the
grass roof of the *jacal* and the hackberry tree on the edge of the
arroyo. A few yards farther the Kid stopped the roan and gazed
intently through the prickly openings. Then he dismounted,
dropped the roan's reins, and proceeded on foot, stooping and silent, like an Indian. The roan, knowing his part, stood still, making
no sound.

The Kid crept noiselessly to the very edge of the pear thicket
and reconnoitered between the leaves of a clump of cactus.

Ten yards from his hiding-place, in the shade of the *jacal*, sat
his Tonia calmly plaiting a rawhide lariat. So far she might surely
escape condemnation; women have been known, from time to time,
to engage in more mischievous occupations. But if all must be told,
there is to be added that her head reposed against the broad and
comfortable chest of a tall red-and-yellow man, and that his arm

was about her, guiding her nimble small fingers that required so many lessons at the intricate six-strand plait.

Sandridge glanced quickly at the dark mass of pear when he heard a slight squeaking sound that was not altogether unfamiliar. A gun-scabbard will make that sound when one grasps the handle of a six-shooter suddenly. But the sound was not repeated; and Tonia's fingers needed close attention.

And then, in the shadow of death, they began to talk to their love; and in the still July afternoon every word they uttered reached the ears of the Kid.

"Remember, then," said Tonia, "you must not come again until I send for you. Soon he will be here. A *vaquero** at the *tienda*† said to-day he saw him on the Guadalupe three days ago. When he is that near he always comes. If he comes and finds you here he will kill you. So, for my sake, you must come no more until I send you the word."

"All right," said the ranger. "And then what?"

"And then," said the girl, "you must bring your men here and kill him. If not, he will kill you."

"He ain't a man to surrender, that's sure," said Sandridge. "It's kill or be killed for the officer that goes up against Mr. Cisco Kid."

"He must die," said the girl. "Otherwise there will not be any peace in the world for thee and me. He has killed many. Let him so die. Bring your men, and give him no chance to escape."

"You used to think right much of him," said Sandridge.

Tonia dropped the lariat, twisted herself around, and curved a lemon-tinted arm over the ranger's shoulder.

"But then," she murmured in liquid Spanish, "I had not beheld thee, thou great, red mountain of a man! And thou art kind and good, as well as strong. Could one choose him, knowing thee? Let him die; for then I will not be filled with fear by day and night lest he hurt thee or me."

"How can I know when he comes?" asked Sandridge.

"When he comes," said Tonia, "he remains two days, sometimes

---

*Cowboy (Spanish).
†Store (Spanish).

three. Gregorio, the small son of old Luisa, the *lavandera*,* has a swift pony. I will write a letter to thee and send it by him, saying how it will be best to come upon him. By Gregorio will the letter come. And bring many men with thee, and have much care, oh, dear red one, for the rattlesnake is not quicker to strike than is '*El Chivato*,'† as they call him, to send a ball from his *pistola*."

"The Kid's handy with his gun, sure enough," admitted Sandridge, "but when I come for him I shall come alone. I'll get him by myself or not at all. The Cap wrote one or two things to me that make me want to do the trick without any help. You let me know when Mr. Kid arrives, and I'll do the rest."

"I will send you the message by the boy Gregorio," said the girl. "I knew you were braver than that small slayer of men who never smiles. How could I ever have thought I cared for him?"

It was time for the ranger to ride back to his camp on the water hole. Before he mounted his horse he raised the slight form of Tonia with one arm high from the earth for a parting salute. The drowsy stillness of the torpid summer air still lay thick upon the dreaming afternoon. The smoke from the fire in the *jacal*, where the *frijoles*‡ blubbered in the iron pot, rose straight as a plumb-line above the clay-daubed chimney. No sound or movement disturbed the serenity of the dense pear thicket ten yards away.

When the form of Sandridge had disappeared, loping his big dun down the steep banks of the Frio crossing, the Kid crept back to his own horse, mounted him, and rode back along the tortuous trail he had come.

But not far. He stopped and waited in the silent depths of the pear until half an hour had passed. And then Tonia heard the high, untrue notes of his unmusical singing coming nearer and nearer; and she ran to the edge of the pear to meet him.

The Kid seldom smiled; but he smiled and waved his hat when he saw her. He dismounted, and his girl sprang into his arms. The Kid looked at her fondly. His thick, black hair clung to his head like a wrinkled mat. The meeting brought a slight ripple of some

---

*Washerwoman (Spanish).
†Big shot (Spanish slang).
‡Beans (Spanish).

undercurrent of feeling to his smooth, dark face that was usually as motionless as a clay mask.

"How's my girl?" he asked, holding her close.

"Sick of waiting so long for you, dear one," she answered. "My eyes are dim with always gazing into that devil's pincushion through which you come. And I can see into it such a little way, too. But you are here, beloved one, and I will not scold. *Que mal muchacho!* not to come to see your *alma** more often. Go in and rest, and let me water your horse and stake him with the long rope. There is cool water in the jar for you."

The Kid kissed her affectionately.

"Not if the court knows itself do I let a lady stake my horse for me," said he. "But if you'll run in, *chica,*† and throw a pot of coffee together while I attend to the *caballo,*‡ I'll be a good deal obliged."

Besides his marksmanship the Kid had another attribute for which he admired himself greatly. He was *muy caballero*, as the Mexicans express it, where the ladies were concerned. For them he had always gentle words and consideration. He could not have spoken a harsh word to a woman. He might ruthlessly slay their husbands and brothers, but he could not have laid the weight of a finger in anger upon a woman. Wherefore many of that interesting division of humanity who had come under the spell of his politeness declared their disbelief in the stories circulated about Mr. Kid. One shouldn't believe everything one heard, they said. When confronted by their indignant men folk with proof of the *caballero's* deeds of infamy, they said maybe he had been driven to it, and that he knew how to treat a lady, anyhow.

Considering this extremely courteous idiosyncrasy of the Kid and the pride that he took in it, one can perceive that the solution of the problem that was presented to him by what he saw and heard from his hiding-place in the pear that afternoon (at least as to one of the actors) must have been obscured by difficulties. And yet one could not think of the Kid overlooking little matters of that kind.

At the end of the short twilight they gathered around a supper

---

*"What a bad boy, not to come see your sweetheart more often" (Spanish).
†Girl (Spanish).
‡Horse (Spanish).

of *frijoles*, goat steaks, canned peaches, and coffee, by the light of a lantern in the *jacal*. Afterward, the ancestor, his flock corralled, smoked a cigarette and became a mummy in a grey blanket. Tonia washed the few dishes while the Kid dried them with the flour-sacking towel. Her eyes shone; she chatted volubly of the inconsequent happenings of her small world since the Kid's last visit; it was as all his other home-comings had been.

Then outside Tonia swung in a grass hammock with her guitar and sang sad *canciones de amor.**

"Do you love me just the same, old girl?" asked the Kid, hunting for his cigarette papers.

"Always the same, little one," said Tonia, her dark eyes lingering upon him.

"I must go over to Fink's," said the Kid, rising, "for some tobacco. I thought I had another sack in my coat. I'll be back in a quarter of an hour."

"Hasten," said Tonia, "and tell me—how long shall I call you my own this time? Will you be gone again to-morrow, leaving me to grieve, or will you be longer with your Tonia?"

"Oh, I might stay two or three days this trip," said the Kid, yawning. "I've been on the dodge for a month, and I'd like to rest up."

He was gone half an hour for his tobacco. When he returned Tonia was still lying in the hammock.

"It's funny," said the Kid, "how I feel. I feel like there was somebody lying behind every bush and tree waiting to shoot me. I never had mullygrubs like them before. Maybe it's one of them presumptions. I've got half a notion to light out in the morning before day. The Guadalupe country is burning up about that old Dutchman I plugged down there."

"You are not afraid—no one could make my brave little one fear."

"Well, I haven't been usually regarded as a jack-rabbit when it comes to scrapping; but I don't want a posse smoking me out when I'm in your *jacal*. Somebody might get hurt that oughtn't to."

---

*Love songs (Spanish).

"Remain with your Tonia; no one will find you here."

The Kid looked keenly into the shadows up and down the arroyo and toward the dim lights of the Mexican village.

"I'll see how it looks later on," was his decision.

At midnight a horseman rode into the rangers' camp, blazing his way by noisy "halloes" to indicate a pacific mission. Sandridge and one or two others turned out to investigate the row. The rider announced himself to be Domingo Sales, from the Lone Wolf Crossing. He bore a letter for Señor Sandridge. Old Luisa, the *lavandera*, had persuaded him to bring it, he said, her son Gregorio being too ill of a fever to ride.

Sandridge lighted the camp lantern and read the letter. These were its words:

DEAR ONE: He has come. Hardly had you ridden away when he came out of the pear. When he first talked he said he would stay three days or more. Then as it grew later he was like a wolf or a fox, and walked about without rest, looking and listening. Soon he said he must leave before daylight when it is dark and stillest. And then he seemed to suspect that I be not true to him. He looked at me so strange that I am frightened. I swear to him that I love him, his own Tonia. Last of all he said I must prove to him I am true. He thinks that even now men are waiting to kill him as he rides from my house. To escape he says he will dress in my clothes, my red skirt and the blue waist I wear and the brown mantilla over the head, and thus ride away. But before that he says that I must put on his clothes, his *pantalones* and *camisa** and hat, and ride away on his horse from the jacal as far as the big road beyond the crossing and back again. This before he goes, so he can tell if I am true and if men are hidden to shoot him. It is a terrible thing. An hour before daybreak this is to be. Come, my dear one, and kill this man and take me for your Tonia. Do not try to take hold of him alive, but kill him quickly. Knowing all, you should do that. You must come long before the time and hide yourself in the little shed near the

---

*Pants and shirt (Spanish).

jacal where the wagon and saddles are kept. It is dark in there. He will wear my red skirt and blue waist and brown mantilla. I send you a hundred kisses. Come surely and shoot quickly and straight.

THINE OWN TONIA.

Sandridge quickly explained to his men the official part of the missive. The rangers protested against his going alone.

"I'll get him easy enough," said the lieutenant. "The girl's got him trapped. And don't even think he'll get the drop on me."

Sandridge saddled his horse and rode to the Lone Wolf Crossing. He tied his big dun in a clump of brush on the arroyo, took his Winchester from its scabbard, and carefully approached the Perez *jacal*. There was only the half of a high moon drifted over by ragged, milk-white gulf clouds.

The wagon-shed was an excellent place for ambush; and the ranger got inside it safely. In the black shadow of the brush shelter in front of the *jacal* he could see a horse tied and hear him impatiently pawing the hard-trodden earth.

He waited almost an hour before two figures came out of the *jacal*. One, in man's clothes, quickly mounted the horse and galloped past the wagon-shed toward the crossing and village. And then the other figure, in skirt, waist, and mantilla over its head, stepped out into the faint moonlight, gazing after the rider. Sandridge thought he would take his chance then before Tonia rode back. He fancied she might not care to see it.

"Throw up your hands," he ordered loudly, stepping out of the wagon-shed with his Winchester at his shoulder.

There was a quick turn of the figure, but no movement to obey, so the ranger pumped in the bullets—one—two—three—and then twice more; for you never could be too sure of bringing down the Cisco Kid. There was no danger of missing at ten paces even in that half moonlight.

The old ancestor, asleep on his blanket, was awakened by the shots. Listening further, he heard a great cry from some man in mortal distress or anguish, and rose up grumbling at the disturbing ways of moderns.

The tall, red ghost of a man burst into the *facal*, reaching one hand, shaking like a *tule* reed, for the lantern hanging on its nail. The other spread a letter on the table.

"Look at this letter, Perez," cried the man. "Who wrote it?"

"*Ah, Dios!** it is Señor Sandridge," mumbled the old man, approaching. "*Pues, señor,*† that letter was written by '*El Chivato*,' as he is called—by the man of Tonia. They say he is a bad man; I do not know. While Tonia slept he wrote the letter and sent it by this old hand of mine to Domingo Sales to be brought to you. Is there anything wrong in the letter? I am very old; and I did not know. *Valgame Dios!*‡ it is a very foolish world; and there is nothing in the house to drink—nothing to drink."

Just then all that Sandridge could think of to do was to go outside and throw himself face downward in the dust by the side of his humming-bird, of whom not a feather fluttered. He was not a *caballero* by instinct, and he could not understand the niceties of revenge.

A mile away the rider who had ridden past the wagon-shed struck up a harsh, untuneful song, the words of which began:

> Don't you monkey with my Lulu girl
> Or I'll tell you what I'll do—

—from *The Heart of the West* (1907)

---

*"Oh, God!" (Spanish).
†"But, mister" (Spanish).
‡"Good God!" (Spanish).

HYGEIA AT THE SOLITO

If you are knowing in the chronicles of the ring you will recall to mind an event in the early 'nineties when, for a minute and sundry odd seconds, a champion and a "would-be" faced each other on the alien side of an international river. So brief a conflict had rarely imposed upon the fair promise of true sport. The reporters made what they could of it, but, divested of padding, the action was sadly fugacious. The champion merely smote his victim, turned his back upon him, remarking, "I know what I done to dat stiff," and extended an arm like a ship's mast for his glove to be removed.

Which accounts for a trainload of extremely disgusted gentlemen in an uproar of fancy vests and neck-wear being spilled from their Pullmans in San Antonio in the early morning following the fight. Which also partly accounts for the unhappy predicament in which "Cricket" McGuire found himself as he tumbled from his car and sat upon the depot platform, torn by a spasm of that hollow, racking cough so familiar to San Antonian ears.[1] At that time, in the uncertain light of dawn, that way passed Curtis Raidler, the Nueces County cattleman—may his shadow never measure under six feet two.

The cattleman, out this early to catch the southbound for his ranch station, stopped at the side of the distressed patron of sport, and spoke in the kindly drawl of his ilk and region, "Got it pretty bad, bud?"

"Cricket" McGuire, ex-feather-weight prizefighter, tout, jockey, follower of the "ponies," all-round sport, and manipulator of the gum balls and walnut shells, looked up pugnaciously at the imputation cast by "bud."

"G'wan," he rasped, "telegraph pole. I didn't ring for yer."

216

Another paroxysm wrung him, and he leaned limply against a convenient baggage truck. Raidler waited patiently, glancing around at the white hats, short overcoats, and big cigars thronging the platform. "You're from the No'th, ain't you, bud?" he asked when the other was partially recovered. "Come down to see the fight?"

"Fight!" snapped McGuire. "Puss-in-the-corner!* 'Twas a hypodermic injection. Handed him just one like a squirt of dope, and he's asleep, and no tanbark needed in front of his residence. Fight!" He rattled a bit, coughed, and went on, hardly addressing the cattleman, but rather for the relief of voicing his troubles. "No more dead sure t'ings for me. But Rus Sage himself would have snatched at it.[2] Five to one dat de boy from Cork† wouldn't stay t'ree rounds is what I invested in. Put my last cent on, and could already smell the sawdust in dat all-night joint of Jimmy Delaney's on T'irty-seventh Street I was goin' to buy. And den—say, telegraph pole, what a gazaboo a guy is to put his whole roll on one turn of the gaboozlum!"

"You're plenty right," said the big cattleman; "more 'specially when you lose. Son, you get up and light out for a hotel. You got a mighty bad cough. Had it long?"

"Lungs," said McGuire comprehensively. "I got it. The croaker says I'll come to time for six months longer—maybe a year if I hold my gait. I wanted to settle down and take care of myself. Dat's why I speculated on dat five to one perhaps. I had a t'ousand iron dollars saved up. If I winned I was goin' to buy Delaney's café. Who'd a t'ought dat stiff would take a nap in de foist round—say?"

"It's a hard deal," commented Raidler, looking down at the diminutive form of McGuire crumpled against the truck. "But you go to a hotel and rest. There's the Menger and the Maverick, and—"

"And the Fi'th Av'noo, and the Waldorf-Astoria," mimicked McGuire. "Told you I went broke. I'm on de bum proper. I've got one dime left. Maybe a trip to Europe or a sail in me private yacht would fix me up—pa-per!"

---

*A children's game.
†County of Ireland.

He flung his dime at a newsboy, got his *Express*, propped his back against the truck, and was at once rapt in the account of his Waterloo,[3] as expanded by the ingenious press.

Curtis Raidler interrogated an enormous gold watch, and laid his hand on McGuire's shoulder.

"Come on, bud," he said. "We got three minutes to catch the train."

Sarcasm seemed to be McGuire's vein.

"You ain't seen me cash in any chips or call a turn since I told you I was broke, a minute ago, have you? Friend, chase yourself away."

"You're going down to my ranch," said the cattleman, "and stay till you get well. Six months 'll fix you good as new." He lifted McGuire with one hand, and half-dragged him in the direction of the train.

"What about the money?" said McGuire, struggling weakly to escape.

"Money for what?" asked Raidler, puzzled. They eyed each other, not understanding, for they touched only as at the gear of bevelled cog-wheels—at right angles, and moving upon different axes.

Passengers on the south-bound saw them seated together, and wondered at the conflux of two such antipodes. McGuire was five feet one, with a countenance belonging to either Yokohama or Dublin. Bright-beady of eye, bony of cheek and jaw, scarred, toughened, broken and reknit, indestructible, grisly, gladiatorial as a hornet, he was a type neither new nor unfamiliar. Raidler was the product of a different soil. Six feet two in height, miles broad, and no deeper than a crystal brook, he represented the union of the West and South. Few accurate pictures of his kind have been made, for art galleries are so small and the mutoscope* is as yet unknown in Texas. After all, the only possible medium of portrayal of Raidler's kind would be the fresco—something high and simple and cool and unframed.

They were rolling southward on the International. The timber

---

*Photographic device used to record an object in motion.

was huddling into little, dense green motts at rare distances before the inundation of the downright, vert prairies. This was the land of the ranches; the domain of the kings of the kine.*

McGuire sat, collapsed into his corner of the seat, receiving with acid suspicion the conversation of the cattleman. What was the "game" of this big "geezer" who was carrying him off? Altruism would have been McGuire's last guess. "He ain't no farmer," thought the captive, "and he ain't no con man, for sure. W'at's his lay? You trail in, Cricket, and see how many cards he draws. You're up against it, anyhow. You got a nickel and gallopin' consumption, and you better lay low. Lay low and see w'at's his game."

At Rincon, a hundred miles from San Antonio, they left the train for a buckboard which was waiting there for Raidler. In this they travelled the thirty miles between the station and their destination. If anything could, this drive should have stirred the acrimonious McGuire to a sense of his ransom. They sped upon velvety wheels across an exhilarant savanna. The pair of Spanish ponies struck a nimble, tireless trot, which gait they occasionally relieved by a wild, untrammelled gallop. The air was wine and seltzer, perfumed, as they absorbed it, with the delicate redolence of prairie flowers. The road perished, and the buckboard swam the uncharted billows of the grass itself, steered by the practised hand of Raidler, to whom each tiny distant mott of trees was a signboard, each convolution of the low hills a voucher of course and distance. But McGuire reclined upon his spine, seeing nothing but a desert, and receiving the cattleman's advances with sullen distrust. "W'at's he up to?" was the burden of his thoughts; "w'at kind of a gold brick has the big guy got to sell?" McGuire was only applying the measure of the streets he had walked to a range bounded by the horizon and the fourth dimension.

A week before, while riding the prairies, Raidler had come upon a sick and weakling calf deserted and bawling. Without dismounting he had reached and slung the distressed bossy across his saddle, and dropped it at the ranch for the boys to attend to. It was impossible for McGuire to know or comprehend that, in the eyes of

_____

*The plural for cow.

the cattleman, his case and that of the calf were identical in interest
and demand upon his assistance. A creature was ill and helpless;
he had the power to render aid—these were the only postulates
required for the cattleman to act. They formed his system of logic
and the most of his creed. McGuire was the seventh invalid whom
Raidler had picked up thus casually in San Antonio, where so many
thousand go for the ozone that is said to linger about its contracted
streets. Five of them had been guests of Solito Ranch until they
had been able to leave, cured or better, and exhausting the vocabulary of tearful gratitude. One came too late, but rested very comfortably, at last, under a ratama tree in the garden.

So, then, it was no surprise to the ranchhold when the buckboard
spun to the door, and Raidler took up his debile *protégé** like a
handful of rags and set him down upon the gallery.

McGuire looked upon things strange to him. The ranch-house
was the best in the country. It was built of brick hauled one hundred
miles by wagon, but it was of but one story, and its four rooms
were completely encircled by a mud floor "gallery." The miscella-
neous setting of horses, dogs, saddles, wagons, guns, and cow-
punchers' paraphernalia oppressed the metropolitan eye of the
wrecked sportsman.

"Well, here we are at home," said Raidler, cheeringly.

"It's a h—l† of a looking place," said McGuire promptly, as he
rolled upon the gallery floor in a fit of coughing.

"We'll try to make it comfortable for you, buddy," said the cattleman gently. "It ain't fine inside; but it's the outdoors, anyway,
that'll do you the most good. This'll be your room, in here. Anything we got, you ask for it."

He led McGuire into the east room. The floor was bare and
clean. White curtains waved in the gulf breeze through the open
windows. A big willow rocker, two straight chairs, a long table
covered with newspapers, pipes, tobacco, spurs, and cartridges
stood in the centre. Some well-mounted heads of deer and one of

---

*Refers to the sick calf; *débile* is "weak" in Spanish, and *protégé* is French for protected or dependent.
†Hell.

an enormous black javeli* projected from the walls. A wide, cool cot-bed stood in a corner. Nueces County people regarded this guest chamber as fit for a prince. McGuire showed his eyeteeth at it. He took out his nickel and spun it up to the ceiling.

"T'ought I was lyin' about the money, did ye? Well, you can frisk me if you wanter. Dat's the last simoleon in the treasury.[4] Who's goin' to pay?"

The cattleman's clear grey eyes looked steadily from under his grizzly brows into the huckleberry optics of his guest. After a little he said simply, and not ungraciously, "I'll be much obliged to you, son, if you won't mention money any more. Once was quite a plenty. Folks I ask to my ranch don't have to pay anything, and they very scarcely ever offers it. Supper'll be ready in half an hour. There's water in the pitcher, and some, cooler, to drink, in that red jar hanging on the gallery.

"Where's the bell?" asked McGuire, looking about.

"Bell for what?"

"Bell to ring for things. I can't—see here," he exploded in a sudden, weak fury, "I never asked you to bring me here. I never held you up for a cent. I never gave you a hard-luck story till you asked me. Here I am fifty miles from a bellboy or a cocktail. I'm sick. I can't hustle. Gee! but I'm up against it!" McGuire fell upon the cot and sobbed shiveringly.

Raidler went to the door and called. A slender, bright-complexioned Mexican youth about twenty came quickly. Raidler spoke to him in Spanish.

"Ylario, it is in my mind that I promised you the position of *vaquero* on the San Carlos range at the fall *rodea*."

"*Si, señor*, such was your goodness."

"Listen. This *señorito* is my friend. He is very sick. Place yourself at his side. Attend to his wants at all times. Have much patience and care with him. And when he is well, or—and when he is well, instead of *vaquero* I will make you *mayordomo* of the Rancho de las Piedras. *Esta bueno?*"

"*Si, si—mil gracias,*[†] *señor.*" Ylario tried to kneel upon the floor

---

*Meaning javelina, a pig-like mammal found in southwestern deserts.

†*Vaquero*: cowboy; *rodea*: possibly rodeo; *senorito*: little man; *mayordomo*: head servant; *esta bueno?*: is it good?; *mil gracias*: a thousand thanks (Spanish).

in his gratitude, but the cattleman kicked at him benevolently, growling, "None of your opery-house antics, now."

Ten minutes later Ylario came from McGuire's room and stood before Raidler.

"The little *señor*," he announced, "presents his compliments" (Raidler credited Ylario with the preliminary) "and desires some pounded ice, one hot bath, one gin feez-z, that the windows be all closed, toast, one shave, one 'Newyorkheral',* cigarettes, and to send one telegram."

Raidler took a quart bottle of whisky from his medicine cabinet. "Here, take him this," he said.

Thus was instituted the reign of terror at the Solito Ranch. For a few weeks McGuire blustered and boasted and swaggered before the cow-punchers who rode in for miles around to see this latest importation of Raidler's. He was an absolutely new experience to them. He explained to them all the intricate points of sparring and the tricks of training and defence. He opened to their minds' view all the indecorous life of a tagger after professional sports. His jargon of slang was a continuous joy and surprise to them. His gestures, his strange poses, his frank ribaldry of tongue and principle fascinated them. He was like a being from a new world.

Strange to say, this new world he had entered did not exist to him. He was an utter egoist of bricks and mortar. He had dropped out, he felt, into open space for a time, and all it contained was an audience for his reminiscences. Neither the limitless freedom of the prairie days nor the grand hush of the close-drawn, spangled nights touched him. All the hues of Aurora could not win him from the pink pages of a sporting journal. "Get something for nothing," was his mission in life; "T'irty-seventh" Street was his goal.

Nearly two months after his arrival he began to complain that he felt worse. It was then that he became the ranch's incubus, its harpy, its Old Man of the Sea. He shut himself in his room like some venomous kobold† or flibbertigibbet, whining, complaining, cursing, accusing. The keynote of his plaint was that he had been

---

*The *New York Herald* newspaper.
†Haunting spirit, in German folklore.

inveigled into a gehenna* against his will; that he was dying of neglect and lack of comforts. With all his dire protestations of increasing illness, to the eye of others he remained unchanged. His currant-like eyes were as bright and diabolic as ever; his voice was as rasping; his callous face, with the skin drawn tense as a drumhead, had no flesh to lose. A flush on his prominent cheek bones each afternoon hinted that a clinical thermometer might have revealed a symptom, and percussion might have established the fact that McGuire was breathing with only one lung, but his appearance remained the same.

In constant attendance upon him was Ylario, whom the coming reward of the *mayordomo*ship must have greatly stimulated, for McGuire chained him to a bitter existence. The air—the man's only chance for life—he commanded to be kept out by closed windows and drawn curtains. The room was always blue and foul with cigarette smoke; whosoever entered it must sit, suffocating, and listen to the imp's interminable gasconade,† concerning his scandalous career.

The oddest thing of all was the relation existing between McGuire and his benefactor. The attitude of the invalid toward the cattleman was something like that of a peevish, perverse child toward an indulgent parent. When Raidler would leave the ranch McGuire would fall into a fit of malevolent, silent sullenness. When he returned, he would be met by a string of violent and stinging reproaches. Raidler's attitude toward his charge was quite inexplicable in its way. The cattleman seemed actually to assume and feel the character assigned him by McGuire's intemperate accusations— the character of tyrant and guilty oppressor. He seemed to have adopted the responsibility of the fellow's condition, and he always met his tirades with a pacific, patient, and even remorseful kindness that never altered.

One day Raidler said to him, "Try more air, son. You can have the buckboard and a driver every day if you'll go. Try a week or two in one of the cow camps. I'll fix you up plum comfortable. The ground, and the air next to it—them's the things to cure you. I

---

*Place of torture, hell.
†Boasting.

knowed a man from Philadelphy, sicker than you are, got lost on the Guadalupe, and slept on the bare grass in sheep camps for two weeks. Well, sir, it started him getting well, which he done. Close to the ground—that's where the medicine in the air stays. Try a little hossback riding now. There's a gentle pony—"

"What've I done to yer?" screamed McGuire. "Did I ever double-cross yer? Did I ask you to bring me here? Drive me out to your camps if you wanter; or stick a knife in me and save trouble. Ride! I can't lift my feet. I couldn't sidestep a jab from a five-year-old kid. That's what your d—d* ranch has done for me. There's nothing to eat, nothing to see, and nobody to talk to but a lot of Reubens† who don't know a punching bag from a lobster salad."

"It's a lonesome place, for certain," apologised Raidler abashedly. "We got plenty, but it's rough enough. Anything you think of you want, the boys'll ride up and fetch it down for you."

It was Chad Murchison, a cow-puncher from the Circle Bar outfit, who first suggested that McGuire's illness was fraudulent. Chad had brought a basket of grapes for him thirty miles, and four out of his way, tied to his saddle-horn. After remaining in the smoke-tainted room for a while, he emerged and bluntly confided his suspicions to Raidler.

"His arm," said Chad, "is harder'n a diamond. He interduced me to what he called a shore-perplexus punch, and 'twas like being kicked twice by a mustang. He's playin' it low down on you, Curt. He ain't no sicker'n I am. I hate to say it, but the runt's workin' you for range and shelter."

The cattleman's ingenuous mind refused to entertain Chad's view of the case, and when, later, he came to apply the test, doubt entered not into his motives.

One day, about noon, two men drove up to the ranch, alighted, hitched, and came in to dinner; standing and general invitations being the custom of the country. One of them was a great San Antonio doctor, whose costly services had been engaged by a wealthy cowman who had been laid low by an accidental bullet. He was now being driven to the station to take the train back to town.

---

*Damned.
†Rubes, meaning farmers or rustics; Reub or Rube is a nickname for Reuben.

After dinner Raidler took him aside, pushed a twenty-dollar bill against his hand, and said:

"Doc, there's a young chap in that room I guess has got a bad case of consumption. I'd like for you to look him over and see just how bad he is, and if we can do anything for him."

"How much was that dinner I just ate, Mr. Raidler?" said the doctor bluffly, looking over his spectacles. Raidler returned the money to his pocket. The doctor immediately entered McGuire's room, and the cattleman seated himself upon a heap of saddles on the gallery, ready to reproach himself in the event the verdict should be unfavourable.

In ten minutes the doctor came briskly out. "Your man," he said promptly, "is as sound as a new dollar. His lungs are better than mine. Respiration, temperature, and pulse normal. Chest expansion four inches. Not a sign of weakness anywhere. Of course I didn't examine for the bacillus, but it isn't there. You can put my name to the diagnosis. Even cigarettes and a vilely close room haven't hurt him. Coughs, does he? Well, you tell him it isn't necessary. You asked if there is anything we could do for him. Well, I advise you to set him digging post-holes or breaking mustangs. There's our team ready. Good-day, sir." And like a puff of wholesome, blustery wind the doctor was off.

Raidler reached out and plucked a leaf from a mesquite bush by the railing, and began chewing it thoughtfully.

The branding season was at hand, and the next morning Ross Hargis, foreman of the outfit, was mustering his force of some twenty-five men at the ranch, ready to start for the San Carlos range, where the work was to begin. By six o'clock the horses were all saddled, the grub wagon ready, and the cow-punchers were swinging themselves upon their mounts, when Raidler bade them wait. A boy was bringing up an extra pony, bridled and saddled, to the gate. Raidler walked to McGuire's room and threw open the door. McGuire was lying on his cot, not yet dressed, smoking.

"Get up," said the cattleman, and his voice was clear and brassy, like a bugle.

"How's that?" asked McGuire, a little startled.

"Get up and dress. I can stand a rattlesnake, but I hate a liar.

Do I have to tell you again?" He caught McGuire by the neck and stood him on the floor.

"Say, friend," cried McGuire wildly, "are you bug-house? I'm sick—see? I'll croak if I got to hustle. What've I done to yer?"— he began his chronic whine—"I never asked yer to—"

"Put on your clothes," called Raidler in a rising tone.

Swearing, stumbling, shivering, keeping his amazed, shiny eyes upon the now menacing form of the aroused cattleman, McGuire managed to tumble into his clothes. Then Raidler took him by the collar and shoved him out and across the yard to the extra pony hitched at the gate. The cow-punchers lolled in their saddles, open-mouthed.

"Take this man," said Raidler to Ross Hargis, "and put him to work. Make him work hard, sleep hard, and eat hard. You boys know I done what I could for him, and he was welcome. Yesterday the best doctor in San Antone examined him, and says he's got the lungs of a burro and the constitution of a steer. You know what to do with him, Ross."

Ross Hargis only smiled grimly.

"Aw," said McGuire, looking intently at Raidler, with a peculiar expression upon his face, "the croaker said I was all right, did he? Said I was fakin', did he? You put him onto me. You t'ought I wasn't sick. You said I was a liar. Say, friend, I talked rough, I know, but I didn't mean most of it. If you felt like I did—aw! I forgot—I ain't sick, the croaker says. Well, friend, now I'll go work for yer. Here's where you play even."

He sprang into the saddle easily as a bird, got the quirt from the horn, and gave his pony a slash with it. "Cricket," who once brought in Good Boy by a neck at Hawthorne—and a 10 to 1 shot—had his foot in the stirrups again.

McGuire led the cavalcade as they dashed away for San Carlos, and the cow-punchers gave a yell of applause as they closed in behind his dust.

But in less than a mile he had lagged to the rear, and was last man when they struck the patch of high chaparral below the horse pens. Behind a clump of this he drew rein, and held a handkerchief to his mouth. He took it away drenched with bright, arterial blood, and threw it carefully into a clump of prickly pear. Then he slashed with his quirt again, gasped "G'wan" to his astonished pony, and galloped after the gang.

That night Raidler received a message from his old home in Alabama. There had been a death in the family; an estate was to divide, and they called for him to come. Daylight found him in the buckboard, skimming the prairies for the station. It was two months before he returned. When he arrived at the ranch house he found it well-nigh deserted save for Ylario, who acted as a kind of steward during his absence. Little by little the youth made him acquainted with the work done while he was away. The branding camp, he was informed, was still doing business. On account of many severe storms the cattle had been badly scattered, and the branding had been accomplished but slowly. The camp was now in the valley of the Guadalupe, twenty miles away.

"By the way," said Raidler, suddenly remembering, "that fellow I sent along with them—McGuire—is he working yet?"

"I do not know," said Ylario. "Mans from the camp come verree few times to the ranch. So plentee work with the leetle calves. They no say. Oh, I think that fellow McGuire he dead much time ago."

"Dead!" said Raidler. "What you talking about?"

"Verree sick fellow, McGuire," replied Ylario, with a shrug of his shoulder. "I theenk he no live one, two month when he go away."

"Shucks!" said Raidler. "He humbugged you, too, did he? The doctor examined him and said he was sound as a mesquite knot."

"That doctor," said Ylario, smiling, "he tell you so? That doctor no see McGuire."

"Talk up," ordered Raidler. "What the devil do you mean?"

"McGuire," continued the boy tranquilly, "he getting drink water outside when that doctor come in room. That doctor take me and pound me all over here with his fingers"—putting his hand to his chest—"I not know for what. He put his ear here and here and here, and listen—I not know for what. He put little glass stick in my mouth. He feel my arm here. He make me count like whisper—so—twenty, *treinta, cuarenta.** Who knows," concluded Ylario,

---

*Thirty, forty (Spanish).

with a deprecating spread of his hands, "for what that doctor do those verree droll and such-like things?"

"What horses are up?" asked Raidler shortly.

"Paisano is grazing but behind the little corral, *señor.*"

"Saddle him for me at once."

Within a very few minutes the cattleman was mounted and away. Paisano, well named after that ungainly but swift-running bird, struck into his long lope that ate up the road like a strip of macaroni. In two hours and a quarter Raidler, from a gentle swell, saw the branding camp by a water hole in the Guadalupe. Sick with expectancy of the news he feared, he rode up, dismounted, and dropped Paisano's reins. So gentle was his heart that at that moment he would have pleaded guilty to the murder of McGuire.

The only being in the camp was the cook, who was just arranging the hunks of barbecued beef, and distributing the tin coffee cups for supper. Raidler evaded a direct question concerning the one subject in his mind.

"Everything all right in camp, Pete?" he managed to inquire.

"So, so," said Pete conservatively. "Grub give out twice. Wind scattered the cattle, and we've had to rake the brush for forty mile. I need a new coffee-pot. And the mosquitos is some more hellish than common."

"The boys—all well?"

Pete was no optimist. Besides, inquiries concerning the health of cow-punchers were not only superfluous, but bordered on flaccidity. It was not like the boss to make them.

"What's left of 'em don't miss no calls to grub," the cook conceded.

"What's left of 'em?" repeated Raidler in a husky voice. Mechanically he began to look around for McGuire's grave. He had in his mind a white slab such as he had seen in the Alabama churchyard. But immediately he knew that was foolish.

"Sure," said Pete; "what's left. Cow camps change in two months. Some's gone."

Raidler nerved himself.

"That—chap—I sent along—McGuire—did—he—"

"Say," interrupted Pete, rising with a chunk of corn bread in each hand, "that was a dirty shame, sending that poor, sick kid to a cow camp. A doctor that couldn't tell he was graveyard meat ought to be skinned with a cinch buckle. Game as he was, too— it's a scandal among snakes—lemme tell you what he done. First night in camp the boys started to initiate him in the leather breeches degree. Ross Hargis busted him one swipe with his chaparreras,* and what do you reckon the poor child did? Got up, the little skeeter, and licked Ross. Licked Ross Hargis. Licked him good. Hit him plenty and everywhere and hard. Ross'd just get up and pick out a fresh place to lay down on agin.

"Then that McGuire goes off there and lays down with his head in the grass and bleeds. A hem'ridge they calls it. He lays there eighteen hours by the watch, and they can't budge him. Then Ross Hargis, who loves any man who can lick him, goes to work and damns the doctors from Greenland to Poland Chiny; and him and Green Branch Johnson they gets McGuire in a tent, and spells each other feedin' him chopped raw meat and whisky.

"But it looks like the kid ain't got no appetite to git well, for they misses him from the tent in the night and finds him rootin' in the grass, and likewise a drizzle fallin'. 'Gwan,' he says, 'lemme go and die like I wanter. He said I was a liar and a fake and I was playin' sick. Lemme alone.'

"Two weeks," went on the cook, "he laid around, not noticin' nobody, and then—"

A sudden thunder filled the air, and a score of galloping centaurs crashed through the brush into camp.

"Illustrious rattlesnakes!" exclaimed Pete, springing all ways at once; "here's the boys come, and I'm an assassinated man if supper ain't ready in three minutes."

But Raidler saw only one thing. A little, brown-faced, grinning chap, springing from his saddle in the full light of the fire. McGuire was not like that, and yet—

In another instant the cattleman was holding him by the hand and shoulder.

"Son, son, how goes it?" was all he found to say.

"Close to the ground, says you," shouted McGuire, crunching

---

*Chaps (Spanish); leather leggings worn over trousers.

Raidler's fingers in a grip of steel; "and dat's where I found it—healt' and strengt', and tumbled to what a cheap skate I been actin'. T'anks fer kickin' me out, old man. And—say! de joke's on dat croaker, ain't it? I looked t'rough the window and see him playin' tag on dat Dago kid's⁵ solar plexus."

"You son of a tinker," growled the cattleman "whyn't you talk up and say the doctor never examined you?"

"Aw—g'wan!" said McGuire, with a flash of his old asperity, "nobody can't bluff me. You never ast me. You made your spiel, and you t'rowed me out, and I let it go at dat. And, say, friend, dis chasin' cows is outer sight. Dis is de whitest bunch of sports I ever travelled with. You'll let me stay, won't yer, old man?"

Raidler looked wonderingly toward Ross Hargis.

"That cussed little runt," remarked Ross tenderly, "is the Jodartin'est hustler—and the hardest hitter in anybody's cow camp."

—from *The Heart of the West* (1907)

THE HIGHER ABDICATION

Curly the tramp sidled toward the free-lunch counter. He caught a fleeting glance from the bartender's eye, and stood still, trying to look like a business man who had just dined at the Menger[1] and was waiting for a friend who had promised to pick him up in his motor car. Curly's histrionic powers were equal to the impersonation; but his make-up was wanting.

The bartender rounded the bar in a casual way, looking up at the ceiling as though he was pondering some intricate problem of kalsomining,* and then fell upon Curly so suddenly that the roadster had no excuses ready. Irresistibly, but so composedly that it seemed almost absentmindedness on his part, the dispenser of drinks pushed Curly to the swinging doors and kicked him out, with a nonchalance that almost amounted to sadness. That was the way of the Southwest.

Curly arose from the gutter leisurely. He felt no anger or resentment toward his ejector. Fifteen years of tramphood spent out of the twenty-two years of his life had hardened the fibres of his spirit. The slings and arrows of outrageous fortune[2] fell blunted from the buckler of his armoured pride. With especial resignation did he suffer contumely and injury at the hands of bartenders. Naturally, they were his enemies; and unnaturally, they were often his friends. He had to take his chances with them. But he had not yet learned to estimate these cool, languid, Southwestern knights of the bungstarter,† who had the manners of an Earl of Pawtucket, and who, when they disapproved of your presence, moved you with the silence and despatch of a chess automaton advancing a pawn.

---

*Painting with kalsomine, an inexpensive wash for walls and ceilings.
†Meaning bartenders; a bung is a pouring hole in a cask.

Curly stood for a few moments in the narrow, mesquite-paved street. San Antonio puzzled and disturbed him. Three days he had been a non-paying guest of the town, having dropped off there from a box car of an I. & G. N. freight, because Greaser Johnny had told him in Des Moines that the Alamo City was manna fallen, gathered, cooked, and served free with cream and sugar. Curly had found the tip partly a good one. There was hospitality in plenty of a careless, liberal, irregular sort. But the town itself was a weight upon his spirits after his experience with the rushing, business-like, systematised cities of the North and East. Here he was often flung a dollar, but too frequently a good-natured kick would follow it. Once a band of hilarious cowboys had roped him on Military Plaza and dragged him across the black soil until no respectable rag-bag would have stood sponsor for his clothes. The winding, doubling streets, leading nowhere, bewildered him. And then there was a little river, crooked as a pot-hook, that crawled through the middle of the town, crossed by a hundred little bridges so nearly alike that they got on Curly's nerves. And the last bartender wore a number nine shoe.

The saloon stood on a corner. The hour was eight o'clock. Homefarers and outgoers jostled Curly on the narrow stone side-walk. Between the buildings to his left he looked down a cleft that proclaimed itself another thoroughfare. The alley was dark except for one patch of light. Where there was light there were sure to be human beings. Where there were human beings after nightfall in San Antonio there might be food, and there was sure to be drink. So Curly headed for the light.

The illumination came from Schwegel's Café. On the sidewalk in front of it Curly picked up an old envelope. It might have contained a check for a million. It was empty; but the wanderer read the address, "Mr. Otto Schwegel," and the name of the town and State. The postmark was Detroit.

Curly entered the saloon. And now in the light it could be perceived that he bore the stamp of many years of vagabondage. He had none of the tidiness of the calculating and shrewd professional tramp. His wardrobe represented the cast-off specimens of half a dozen fashions and eras. Two factories had combined their efforts in providing shoes for his feet. As you gazed at him there passed through your mind vague impressions of mummies, wax figures, Russian exiles, and men lost on desert islands. His face was covered almost to his eyes with a curly brown beard that he kept trimmed short with a pocket-knife, and that had furnished him with his *nom de route*.* Light-blue eyes, full of sullenness, fear, cunning, impudence, and fawning, witnessed the stress that had been laid upon his soul.

The saloon was small, and in its atmosphere the odours of meat and drink struggled for the ascendency. The pig and the cabbage wrestled with hydrogen and oxygen. Behind the bar Schwegel laboured with an assistant whose epidermal pores showed no signs of being obstructed. Hot wienerwurst and sauerkraut were being served to purchasers of beer. Curly shuffled to the end of the bar, coughed hollowly, and told Schwegel that he was a Detroit cabinet-maker out of a job.

It followed as the night the day that he got his schooner and lunch.

"Was you acquainted maybe mit Heinrich Strauss in Detroit?" asked Schwegel.

"Did I know Heinrich Strauss?" repeated Curly, affectionately. "Why, say,' Bo, I wish I had a dollar for every game of pinocle† me and Heine has played on Sunday afternoons."

More beer and a second plate of steaming food was set before the diplomat. And then Curly, knowing to a fluid-drachm how far a "con" game would go, shuffled out into the unpromising street.

And now he began to perceive the inconveniences of this stony Southern town. There was none of the outdoor gaiety and brilliancy and music that provided distraction even to the poorest in the cities of the North. Here, even so early, the gloomy, rock-walled houses were closed and barred against the murky dampness of the night. The streets were mere fissures through which flowed grey wreaths of river mist. As he walked he heard laughter and the chink of coin and chips behind darkened windows, and music coming from every chink of wood and stone. But the diversions were selfish; the day of popular pastimes had not yet come to San Antonio.

---

*Name of the road (French).
†A card game.

But at length Curly, as he strayed, turned the sharp angle of another lost street and came upon a rollicking band of stockmen from the outlying ranches celebrating in the open in front of an ancient wooden hotel. One great roisterer from the sheep country who had just instigated a movement toward the bar, swept Curly in like a stray goat with the rest of his flock. The princes of kine* and wool hailed him as a new zoological discovery, and uproariously strove to preserve him in the diluted alcohol of their compliments and regards.

An hour afterward Curly staggered from the hotel barroom dismissed by his fickle friends, whose interest in him had subsided as quickly as it had risen. Full—stoked with alcoholic fuel and cargoed with food, the only question remaining to disturb him was that of shelter and bed.

A drizzling, cold Texas rain had begun to fall—an endless, lazy, unintermittent downfall that lowered the spirits of men and raised a reluctant steam from the warm stones of the streets and houses. Thus comes the "norther" dousing gentle spring and amiable autumn with the chilling salutes and adieux of coming and departing winter.

Curly followed his nose down the first tortuous street into which his irresponsible feet conducted him. At the lower end of it, on the bank of the serpentine stream, he perceived an open gate in a cemented rock wall. Inside he saw camp fires and a row of low wooden sheds built against three sides of the enclosing wall. He entered the enclosure. Under the sheds many horses were champing at their oats and corn. Many wagons and buckboards stood about with their teams' harness thrown carelessly upon the shafts and doubletrees. Curly recognised the place as a wagon-yard, such as is provided by merchants for their out-of-town friends and customers. No one was in sight. No doubt the drivers of those wagons were scattered about the town "seeing the elephant and hearing the owl." In their haste to become patrons of the town's dispensaries of mirth and good cheer the last ones to depart must have left the great wooden gate swinging open.

---

*The plural for cow.

Curly had satisfied the hunger of an anaconda and the thirst of a camel, so he was neither in the mood nor the condition of an explorer. He zigzagged his way to the first wagon that his eyesight distinguished in the semi-darkness under the shed. It was a two-horse wagon with a top of white canvas. The wagon was half filled with loose piles of wool sacks, two or three great bundles of grey blankets, and a number of bales, bundles, and boxes. A reasoning eye would have estimated the load at once as ranch supplies, bound on the morrow for some outlying hacienda. But to the drowsy intelligence of Curly they represented only warmth and softness and protection against the cold humidity of the night. After several unlucky efforts, at last he conquered gravity so far as to climb over a wheel and pitch forward upon the best and warmest bed he had fallen upon in many a day. Then he became instinctively a burrowing animal, and dug his way like a prairie-dog down among the sacks and blankets, hiding himself from the cold air as snug and safe as a bear in his den. For three nights sleep had visited Curly only in broken and shivering doses. So now, when Morpheus* condescended to pay him a call, Curly got such a strangle hold on the mythological old gentleman that it was a wonder that anyone else in the whole world got a wink of sleep that night.

Six cowpunchers of the Cibolo Ranch were waiting around the door of the ranch store. Their ponies cropped grass near by, tied in the Texas fashion—which is not tied at all. Their bridle reins had been dropped to the earth, which is a more effectual way of securing them (such is the power of habit and imagination) than you could devise out of a half-inch rope and a live-oak tree.

These guardians of the cow lounged about, each with a brown cigarette paper in his hand, and gently but unceasingly cursed Sam Revell, the storekeeper. Sam stood in the door, snapping the red elastic bands on his pink madras shirtsleeves and looking down affectionately at the only pair of tan shoes within a forty-mile radius. His offence had been serious, and he was divided between humble apology and admiration for the beauty of his raiment. He had allowed the ranch stock of "smoking" to become exhausted.

---

*Greek god of dreams.

"I thought sure there was another case of it under the counter, boys," he explained. "But it happened to be catterdges."

"You've sure got a case of happenedicitis," said Poky Rodgers, fence rider of the Largo Verde *potrero*.* "Somebody ought to happen to give you a knock on the head with the butt end of a quirt.† I've rode in nine miles for some tobacco; and it don't appear natural and seemly that you ought to be allowed to live."

"The boys was smokin' cut plug and dried mesquite leaves mixed when I left," sighed Mustang Taylor, horse wrangler of the Three Elm camp. "They'll be lookin' for me back by nine. They'll be settin' up, with their papers ready to roll a whiff of the real thing before bedtime. And I've got to tell 'em that this pink-eyed, sheep-headed, sulphur-footed, shirt-waisted son of a calico broncho, Sam Revell, hasn't got no tobacco on hand."

Gregorio Falcon, Mexican vaquero‡ and best thrower of the rope on the Cibolo, pushed his heavy, silver-embroidered straw sombrero back upon his thicket of jet black curls, and scraped the bottoms of his pockets for a few crumbs of the precious weed.

"Ah, Don Samuel," he said, reproachfully, but with his touch of Castilian§ manners, "escuse me. Dthey say dthe jackrabbeet and dthe sheep have dthe most leetle *sesos*—how you call dthem—brain-es? Ah don' believe dthat, Don Samuel—escuse me. Ah dthink people w'at don' keep esmokin' tobacco, dthey‖—bot you weel escuse me, Don Samuel."

"Now, what's the use of chewin' the rag, boys," said the untroubled Sam, stooping over to rub the toes of his shoes with a red-and-yellow handkerchief. "Ranse took the order for some more smokin' to San Antone with him Tuesday. Pancho rode Ranse's hoss back yesterday; and Ranse is goin' to drive the wagon back himself. There wa'n't much of a load—just some woolsacks and blankets and nails and canned peaches and a few things we was out of. I look for Ranse to roll in to-day sure. He's an early starter and

*Grassland, or pasture (Spanish); Poky Rodgers mends fences on the *potrero*.
†Riding whip.
‡Cowboy (Spanish).
§Spanish, but with a sense of the "proper" Spanish.
‖"I think people who don't keep smoking tobacco, they—"

a hell-to-split driver, and he ought to be here not far from sundown."

"What plugs is he drivin'?" asked Mustang Taylor, with a smack of hope in his tones.

"The buckboard greys," said Sam.

"I'll wait a spell, then," said the wrangler. "Them plugs eat up a trail like a road-runner swallowin' a whip snake. And you may bust me open a can of green-gage plums, Sam, while I'm waitin' for somethin' better."

"Open me some yellow clings," ordered Poky Rodgers. "I'll wait, too."

The tobaccoless punchers arranged themselves comfortably on the steps of the store. Inside Sam chopped open with a hatchet the tops of the cans of fruit.

The store, a big, white wooden building like a barn, stood fifty yards from the ranch-house. Beyond it were the horse corrals; and still farther the wool sheds and the brush-topped shearing pens— for the Rancho Cibolo raised both cattle and sheep. Behind the store, at a little distance, were the grass-thatched *jacals* of the Mexicans who bestowed their allegiance upon the Cibolo.

The ranch-house was composed of four large rooms, with plastered adobe walls, and a two-room wooden ell. A twenty-feet-wide "gallery" circumvented the structure. It was set in a grove of immense live-oaks and water-elms near a lake—a long, not very wide, and tremendously deep lake in which at nightfall, great gars leaped to the surface and plunged with the noise of hippopotamuses frolicking at their bath. From the trees hung garlands and massive pendants of the melancholy grey moss of the South. Indeed, the Cibolo ranch-house seemed more of the South than of the West. It looked as if old "Kiowa" Truesdell[3] might have brought it with him from the lowlands of Mississippi when he came to Texas with his rifle in the hollow of his arm in '55.

But, though he did not bring the family mansion, Truesdell did bring something in the way of a family inheritance that was more lasting than brick or stone. He brought one end of the Truesdell-Curtis family feud. And when a Curtis bought the Rancho de los Olmos, sixteen miles from the Cibolo, there were lively times on the pear flats and in the chaparral thickets off the Southwest. In those days Truesdell cleaned the brush of many a wolf and tiger cat and Mexican lion; and one or two Curtises fell heirs to notches on his rifle stock. Also he buried a brother with a Curtis bullet in him on the bank of the lake at Cibolo. And then the Kiowa Indians made their last raid upon the ranches between the Frio and the Rio Grande, and Truesdell at the head of his rangers rid the earth of them to the last brave, earning his sobriquet. Then came prosperity in the form of waxing herds and broadening lands. And then old age and bitterness, when he sat, with his great mane of hair as white as the Spanish-dagger blossoms and his fierce, pale-blue eyes, on the shaded gallery at Cibolo, growling like the pumas that he had slain. He snapped his fingers at old age; the bitter taste to life did not come from that. The cup that stuck at his lips was that his only son Ransom wanted to marry a Curtis, the last youthful survivor of the other end of the feud.

For a while the only sounds to be heard at the store were the rattling of the tin spoons and the gurgling intake of the juicy fruits by the cowpunchers, the stamping of the grazing ponies, and the singing of a doleful song by Sam as he contentedly brushed his stiff auburn hair for the twentieth time that day before a crinkly mirror.

From the door of the store could be seen the irregular, sloping stretch of prairie to the south, with its reaches of light-green, billowy mesquite flats in the lower places, and its rises crowned with nearly black masses of short chaparral. Through the mesquite flat wound the ranch road that, five miles away, flowed into the old government trail to San Antonio. The sun was so low that the gentlest elevation cast its grey shadow miles into the green-gold sea of sunshine.

That evening ears were quicker than eyes.

The Mexican held up a tawny finger to still the scraping of tin against tin.

"One waggeen," said he, "cross dthe Arroyo Hondo. Ah hear dthe wheel. Verree rockee place, dthe Hondo."

"You've got good ears, Gregorio," said Mustang Taylor. "I never heard nothin' but the song-bird in the bush and the zephyr skallyhootin' across the peaceful dell."

In ten minutes Taylor remarked: "I see the dust of a wagon risin' right above the fur end of the flat."

"You have verree good eyes, señor," said Gregorio, smiling.

Two miles away they saw a faint cloud dimming the green ripples of the mesquites. In twenty minutes they heard the clatter of the horses' hoofs: in five minutes more the grey plugs dashed out of the thicket, whickering for oats and drawing the light wagon behind them like a toy.

From the *jacals**** came a cry of: "*El Amo!† El Amo!*" Four Mexican youths raced to unharness the greys. The cowpunchers gave a yell of greeting and delight.

Ranse Truesdell, driving, threw the reins to the ground and laughed.

"It's under the wagon sheet, boys," he said. "I know what you're waiting for. If Sam lets it run out again we'll use them yellow shoes of his for a target. There's two cases. Pull 'em out and light up. I know you all want a smoke."

After striking dry country Ranse had removed the wagon sheet from the bows and thrown it over the goods in the wagon. Six pair of hasty hands dragged it off and grabbled beneath the sacks and blankets for the cases of tobacco.

Long Collins, tobacco messenger from the San Gabriel outfit, who rode with the longest stirrups west of the Mississippi, delved with an arm like the tongue of a wagon. He caught something harder than a blanket and pulled out a fearful thing—a shapeless, muddy bunch of leather tied together with wire and twine. From its ragged end, like the head and claws of a disturbed turtle, protruded human toes.

"Who-ee!" yelled Long Collins. "Ranse, are you a-packin' around of corpuses? Here's a—howlin' grasshoppers!"

Up from his long slumber popped Curly, like some vile worm from its burrow. He clawed his way out and sat blinking like a disreputable, drunken owl. His face was as bluish-red and puffed and seamed and cross-lined as the cheapest round steak of the butcher. His eyes were swollen slits; his nose a pickled beet; his

---

*Huts (Spanish).

†"The Master!" (Spanish).

hair would have made the wildest thatch of a Jack-in-the-box look like the satin poll of a Cléo de Mérode.[4] The rest of him was scarecrow done to the life.

Ranse jumped down from his seat and looked at his strange cargo with wide-open eyes.

"Here, you maverick, what are you doing in my wagon? How did you get in there?"

The punchers gathered around in delight. For the time they had forgotten tobacco.

Curly looked around him slowly in every direction. He snarled like a Scotch terrier through his ragged beard.

"Where is this?" he rasped through his parched throat. "It's a damn farm in an old field. What'd you bring me here for—say? Did I say I wanted to come here? What are you Reubs rubberin' at—hey? G'wan or I'll punch some of yer faces."

"Drag him out, Collins," said Ranse.

Curly took a slide and felt the ground rise up and collide with his shoulder blades. He got up and sat on the steps of the store shivering from outraged nerves, hugging his knees and sneering. Taylor lifted out a case of tobacco and wrenched off its top. Six cigarettes began to glow, bringing peace and forgiveness to Sam.

"How'd you come in my wagon?" repeated Ranse, this time in a voice that drew a reply.

Curly recognised the tone. He had heard it used by freight brakemen and large persons in blue carrying clubs.

"Me?" he growled. "Oh, was you talkin' to me? Why, I was on my way to the Menger, but my valet had forgot to pack my pajamas. So I crawled into that wagon in the wagon-yard—see? I never told you to bring me out to this bloomin' farm—see?"

"What is it, Mustang?" asked Poky Rodgers, almost forgetting to smoke in his ecstasy. "What do it live on?"

"It's a galliwampus, Poky," said Mustang. "It's the thing that hollers 'willi-walloo' up in ellum trees in the low grounds of nights. I don't know if it bites."

"No, it ain't, Mustang," volunteered Long Collins. "Them galliwampuses has fins on their backs, and eighteen toes. This here is a hicklesnifter. It lives under the ground and eats cherries. Don't stand so close to it. It wipes out villages with one stroke of its prehensile tail."

Sam, the cosmopolite, who called bartenders in San Antone by their first name, stood in the door. He was a better zoologist.

"Well, ain't that a Willie for your whiskers?" he commented. "Where'd you dig up the hobo, Ranse? Goin' to make an auditorium for inbreviates out of the ranch?"

"Say," said Curly, from whose panoplied breast all shafts of wit fell blunted. "Any of you kiddin' guys got a drink on you? Have your fun. Say, I've been hittin' the stuff till I don't know straight up."

He turned to Ranse. "Say, you shanghaied me on your d—d old prairie schooner—did I tell you to drive me to a farm? I want a drink. I'm goin' all to little pieces. What's doin'?"

Ranse saw that the tramp's nerves were racking him. He despatched one of the Mexican boys to the ranch-house for a glass of whisky. Curly gulped it down; and into his eyes came a brief, grateful glow—as human as the expression in the eye of a faithful setter dog.

"Thanky, boss," he said, quietly.

"You're thirty miles from a railroad, and forty miles from a saloon," said Ranse.

Curly fell back weakly against the steps.

"Since you are here," continued the ranchman, "come along with me. We can't turn you out on the prairie. A rabbit might tear you to pieces."

He conducted Curly to a large shed where the ranch vehicles were kept. There he spread out a canvas cot and brought blankets.

"I don't suppose you can sleep," said Ranse, "since you've been pounding your ear for twenty-four hours. But you can camp here till morning. I'll have Pedro fetch you up some grub."

"Sleep!" said Curly. "I can sleep a week. Say, sport, have you got a coffin nail* on you?"

Fifty miles had Ransom Truesdell driven that day. And yet this is what he did.

---

*Meaning he can sleep a sleep as deep as death.

Old "Kiowa" Truesdell sat in his great wicker chair reading by the light of an immense oil lamp. Ranse laid a bundle of newspapers fresh from town at his elbow.

"Back, Ranse?" said the old man, looking up.

"Son," old "Kiowa" continued, "I've been thinking all day about a certain matter that we have talked about. I want you to tell me again. I've lived for you. I've fought wolves and Indians and worse white men to protect you. You never had any mother that you can remember. I've taught you to shoot straight, ride hard, and live clean. Later on I've worked to pile up dollars that'll be yours. You'll be a rich man, Ranse, when my chunk goes out. I've made you. I've licked you into shape like a leopard cat licks its cubs. You don't belong to yourself—you've got to be a Truesdell first. Now, is there to be any more nonsense about this Curtis girl?"

"I'll tell you once more," said Ranse, slowly. "As I am a Truesdell and as you are my father, I'll never marry a Curtis."

"Good boy," said old "Kiowa." "You'd better go get some supper."

Ranse went to the kitchen at the rear of the house. Pedro, the Mexican cook, sprang up to bring the food he was keeping warm in the stove.

"Just a cup of coffee, Pedro," he said, and drank it standing. And then:

"There's a tramp on a cot in the wagon-shed. Take him something to eat. Better make it enough for two."

Ranse walked out toward the *jacals*. A boy came running.

"Manuel, can you catch Vaminos,* in the little pasture, for me?"

"Why not, señor? I saw him near the *puerta*† but two hours past. He bears a drag-rope."

"Get him and saddle him as quick as you can."

"*Prontito,*‡ *señor.*"

Soon, mounted on Vaminos, Ranse leaned in the saddle, pressed with his knees, and galloped eastward past the store, where sat Sam trying his guitar in the moonlight.

---

*Let's go (Spanish).
†Gate (Spanish).
‡"Right away, sir" (Spanish).

Vaminos shall have a word—Vaminos the good dun horse. The Mexicans, who have a hundred names for the colours of a horse, called him *gruyo*.* He was a mouse-coloured, slate-coloured, flea-bitten roan-dun, if you can conceive it. Down his back from his mane to his tail went a line of black. He would live forever; and surveyors have not laid off as many miles in the world as he could travel in a day.

Eight miles east of the Cibolo ranch-house Ranse loosened the pressure of his knees, and Vaminos stopped under a big ratama tree. The yellow ratama blossoms showered fragrance that would have undone the roses of France. The moon made the earth a great concave bowl with a crystal sky for a lid. In a glade five jack-rabbits leaped and played together like kittens. Eight miles farther east shone a faint star that appeared to have dropped below the horizon. Night riders, who often steered their course by it, knew it to be the light in the Rancho de los Olmos.

In ten minutes Yenna Curtis galloped to the tree on her sorrel pony Dancer. The two leaned and clasped hands heartily.

"I ought to have ridden nearer your home," said Ranse. "But you never will let me."

Yenna laughed. And in the soft light you could see her strong white teeth and fearless eyes. No sentimentality there, in spite of the moonlight, the odour of the ratamas, and the admirable figure of Ranse Truesdell, the lover. But she was there, eight miles from her home, to meet him.

"How often have I told you, Ranse," she said, "that I am your half-way girl? Always half-way."

"Well?" said Ranse, with a question in his tones.

"I did," said Yenna, with almost a sigh. "I told him after dinner when I thought he would be in a good humour. Did you ever wake up a lion, Ranse, with the mistaken idea that he would be a kitten? He almost tore the ranch to pieces. It's all up. I love my daddy, Ranse, and I'm afraid—I'm afraid of him, too. He ordered me to promise that I'd never marry a Truesdell. I promised. That's all. What luck did you have?"

Grullo means "gray horse" (Spanish).

"The same," said Ranse, slowly. "I promised him that his son would never marry a Curtis. Somehow I couldn't go against him. He's mighty old. I'm sorry, Yenna."

The girl leaned in her saddle and laid one hand on Ranse's, on the horn of his saddle.

"I never thought I'd like you better for giving me up," she said ardently, "but I do. I must ride back now, Ranse. I slipped out of the house and saddled Dancer myself. Good-night, neighbour."

"Good-night," said Ranse. "Ride carefully over them badger holes."

They wheeled and rode away in opposite directions. Yenna turned in her saddle and called clearly:

"Don't forget I'm your half-way girl, Ranse."

"Damn all family feuds and inherited scraps," muttered Ranse vindictively to the breeze as he rode back to the Cibolo.

Ranse turned his horse into the small pasture and went to his own room. He opened the lowest drawer of an old bureau to get out the packet of letters that Yenna had written him one summer when she had gone to Mississippi for a visit. The drawer stuck, and he yanked at it savagely—as a man will. It came out of the bureau, and bruised both his shins—as a drawer will. An old, folded yellow letter without an envelope fell from somewhere—probably from where it had lodged in one of the upper drawers. Ranse took it to the lamp and read it curiously.

Then he took his hat and walked to one of the Mexican *jacals*.

"Tia* Juana," he said, "I would like to talk with you a while."

An old, old Mexican woman, white-haired and wonderfully wrinkled, rose from a stool.

"Sit down," said Ranse, removing his hat and taking the one chair in the *jacal*. "Who am I, Tia Juana?" he asked, speaking Spanish.

"Don Ransom, our good friend and employer. Why do you ask?" answered the old woman wonderingly.

"Tia Juana, who am I?" he repeated, with his stern eyes looking into hers.

---

*Aunt (Spanish).

A frightened look came in the old woman's face. She fumbled with her black shawl.

"Who am I, Tia Juana?" said Ranse once more.

"Thirty-two years I have lived on the Rancho Cibolo," said Tia Juana. "I thought to be buried under the coma mott* beyond the garden before these things should be known. Close the door, Don Ransom, and I will speak. I see in your face that you know."

An hour Ranse spent behind Tia Juana's closed door. As he was on his way back to the house Curly called to him from the wagon-shed.

The tramp sat on his cot, swinging his feet and smoking.

"Say, sport," he grumbled. "This is no way to treat a man after kidnappin' him. I went up to the store and borrowed a razor from that fresh guy and had a shave. But that ain't all a man needs. Say—can't you loosen up for about three fingers more of that booze? I never asked you to bring me to your d—d† farm."

"Stand up out here in the light," said Ranse, looking at him closely.

Curly got up sullenly and took a step or two.

His face, now shaven smooth, seemed transformed. His hair had been combed, and it fell back from the right side of his forehead with a peculiar wave. The moonlight charitably softened the ravages of drink; and his aquiline, well-shaped nose and small, square cleft chin almost gave distinction to his looks.

Ranse sat on the foot of the cot and looked at him curiously.

"Where did you come from—have you got any home or folks anywhere?"

"Me? Why, I'm a dook,"‡ said Curly. "I'm Sir Reginald—oh, cheese it. No; I don't know anything about my ancestors. I've been a tramp ever since I can remember. Say, old pal, are you going to set 'em up again to-night or not?"

"You answer my questions and maybe I will. How did you come to be a tramp?"

"Me?" answered Curly. "Why, I adopted that profession when I

---

*Possibly, a grassy hill.
†Damned.
‡Duke.

was an infant. Case of had to. First thing I can remember, I belonged to a big, lazy hobo called Beefsteak Charley. He sent me
around to houses to beg. I wasn't hardly big enough to reach the
latch of a gate."

"Did he ever tell you how he got you?" asked Ranse.

"Once when he was sober he said he bought me for an old six-
shooter and six bits from a band of drunken Mexican sheep-
shearers. But what's the diff? That's all I know."

"All right," said Ranse. "I reckon you're a maverick for certain.
I'm going to put the Rancho Cibolo brand on you. I'll start you to
work in one of the camps to-morrow."

"Work!" sniffed Curly, disdainfully. "What do you take me for?
Do you think I'd chase cows, and hop-skip-and-jump around after
crazy sheep like that pink and yellow guy at the store says these
Reubs* do? Forget it."

"Oh, you'll like it when you get used to it," said Ranse. "Yes, I'll
send you up one more drink by Pedro. I think you'll make a first-
class cowpuncher before I get through with you."

"Me?" said Curly. "I pity the cows you set me to chaperon. They
can go chase themselves. Don't forget my nightcap, please, boss."

Ranse paid a visit to the store before going to the house. Sam
Revell was taking off his tan shoes regretfully and preparing for
bed.

"Any of the boys from the San Gabriel camp riding in early in
the morning?" asked Ranse.

"Long Collins," said Sam briefly. "For the mail."

"Tell him," said Ranse, "to take that tramp out to camp with
him and keep him till I get there."

Curly was sitting on his blankets in the San Gabriel camp cursing talentedly when Ranse Truesdell rode up and dismounted on
the next afternoon. The cow-punchers were ignoring the stray. He
was grimy with dust and black dirt. His clothes were making their
last stand in favour of the conventions.

Ranse went up to Buck Rabb, the camp boss, and spoke briefly.

"He's a plumb buzzard," said Buck. "He won't work, and he's

---

*Country bumpkins; reub or rube (from Reuben) is a generic term for a farmer or
rustic.

the low-downest passel of inhumanity I ever see. I didn't know what you wanted done with him, Ranse, so I just let him set. That seems to suit him. He's been condemned to death by the boys a dozen times, but I told 'em maybe you was savin' him for torture."

Ranse took off his coat.

"I've got a hard job before me, Buck, I reckon, but it has to be done. I've got to make a man out of that thing. That's what I've come to camp for."

He went up to Curly.

"Brother," he said, "don't you think if you had a bath it would allow you to take a seat in the company of your fellow-man with less injustice to the atmosphere."

"Run away, farmer," said Curly, sardonically. "Willie will send for nursey when he feels like having his tub."

The *charco*, or water hole, was twelve yards away. Ranse took one of Curly's ankles and dragged him like a sack of potatoes to the brink. Then with the strength and sleight of a hammer-thrower he hurled the offending member of society far into the lake.

Curly crawled out and up the bank spluttering like a porpoise.

Ranse met him with a piece of soap and a coarse towel in his hands.

"Go to the other end of the lake and use this," he said. "Buck will give you some dry clothes at the wagon."

The tramp obeyed without protest. By the time supper was ready he had returned to camp. He was hardly to be recognised in his new blue shirt and brown duck clothes. Ranse observed him out of the corner of his eye.

"Lordy, I hope he ain't a coward," he was saying to himself. "I hope he won't turn out to be a coward."

His doubts were soon allayed. Curly walked straight to where he stood. His light-blue eyes were blazing.

"Now I'm clean," he said meaningly, "maybe you'll talk to me. Think you've got a picnic here, do you? You clodhoppers think you can run over a man because you know he can't get away. All right. Now, what do you think of that?"

Curly planted a stinging slap against Ranse's left cheek. The print of his hand stood out a dull red against the tan.

Ranse smiled happily.

The cowpunchers talk to this day of the battle that followed.

Somewhere in his restless tour of the cities Curly had acquired the art of self-defence. The ranchman was equipped only with the splendid strength and equilibrium of perfect health and the endurance conferred by decent living. The two attributes nearly matched. There were no formal rounds. At last the fibre of the clean liver prevailed. The last time Curly went down from one of the ranchman's awkward but powerful blows he remained on the grass, but looking up with an unquenched eye.

Ranse went to the water barrel and washed the red from a cut on his chin in the stream from the faucet.

On his face was a grin of satisfaction.

Much benefit might accrue to educators and moralists if they could know the details of the curriculum of reclamation through which Ranse put his waif during the month that he spent in the San Gabriel camp. The ranchman had no fine theories to work out—perhaps his whole stock of pedagogy embraced only a knowledge of horse-breaking and a belief in heredity.

The cowpunchers saw that their boss was trying to make a man out of the strange animal that he had sent among them; and they tacitly organised themselves into a faculty of assistants. But their system was their own.

Curly's first lesson stuck. He became on friendly and then on intimate terms with soap and water. And the thing that pleased Ranse most was that his "subject" held his ground at each successive higher step. But the steps were sometimes far apart.

Once he got at the quart bottle of whisky kept sacredly in the grub tent for rattlesnake bites, and spent sixteen hours on the grass, magnificently drunk. But when he staggered to his feet his first move was to find his soap and towel and start for the *charco*. And once, when a treat came from the ranch in the form of a basket of fresh tomatoes and young onions, Curly devoured the entire consignment before the punchers reached the camp at supper time.

And then the punchers punished him in their own way. For three days they did not speak to him, except to reply to his own questions or remarks. And they spoke with absolute and unfailing politeness. They played tricks on one another; they pounded one another hurtfully and affectionately; they heaped upon one another's heads friendly curses and obloquy; but they were polite to Curly. He saw it, and it stung him as much as Ranse hoped it would.

Then came a night that brought a cold, wet norther. Wilson, the youngest of the outfit, had lain in camp two days, ill with a fever. When Joe got up at daylight to begin breakfast he found Curly sitting asleep against a wheel of the grub wagon with only a saddle blanket around him, while Curly's blankets were stretched over Wilson to protect him from the rain and wind.

Three nights after that Curly rolled himself in his blanket and went to sleep. Then the other punchers rose up softly and began to make preparations. Ranse saw Long Collins tie a rope to the horn of a saddle. Others were getting out their six-shooters.

"Boys," said Ranse, "I'm much obliged. I was hoping you would. But I didn't like to ask."

Half a dozen six-shooters began to pop—awful yells rent the air—Long Collins galloped wildly across Curly's bed, dragging the saddle after him. That was merely their way of gently awaking their victim. Then they hazed him for an hour, carefully and ridiculously, after the code of cow camps. Whenever he uttered protest they held him stretched over a roll of blankets and thrashed him woefully with a pair of leather leggings.

And all this meant that Curly had won his spurs, that he was receiving the puncher's accolade. Nevermore would they be polite to him. But he would be their "pardner" and stirrup-brother, foot to foot.

When the fooling was ended all hands made a raid on Joe's big coffee-pot by the fire for a Java nightcap. Ranse watched the new knight carefully to see if he understood and was worthy. Curly limped with his cup of coffee to a log and sat upon it. Long Collins followed and sat by his side. Buck Rabb went and sat at the other. Curly—grinned.

And then Ranse furnished Curly with mounts and saddle and equipment, and turned him over to Buck Rabb, instructing him to finish the job.

Three weeks later Ranse rode from the ranch into Rabb's camp, which was then in Snake Valley. The boys were saddling for the day's ride. He sought out Long Collins among them.

"How about that bronco?" he asked.

Long Collins grinned.

"Reach out your hand, Ranse Truesdell," he said, and you'll touch him. And you can shake his'n, too, if you like, for he's plumb white and there's none better in no camp."

Ranse looked again at the clear-faced, bronzed, smiling cow-puncher who stood at Collins's side. Could that be Curly? He held out his hand, and Curly grasped it with the muscles of a bronco-buster.

"I want you at the ranch," said Ranse.

"All right, sport," said Curly, heartily. "But I want to come back again. Say, pal, this is a dandy farm. And I don't want any better fun than hustlin' cows with this bunch of guys. They're all to the merry-merry."

At the Cibolo ranch-house they dismounted. Ranse bade Curly wait at the door of the living room. He walked inside. Old "Kiowa" Truesdell was reading at a table.

"Good-morning, Mr. Truesdell," said Ranse.

The old man turned his white head quickly.

"How is this?" he began. "Why do you call me 'Mr.—'?"

When he looked at Ranse's face he stopped, and the hand that held his newspaper shook slightly.

"Boy," he said slowly, "how did you find it out?"

"It's all right," said Ranse, with a smile. "I made Tia Juana tell me. It was kind of by accident, but it's all right."

"You've been like a son to me," said old "Kiowa," trembling.

"Tia Juana told me all about it," said Ranse. "She told me how you adopted me when I was knee-high to a puddle duck out of a wagon train of prospectors that was bound West. And she told me how the kid—your own kid, you know—got lost or was run away with. And she said it was the same day that the sheep-shearers got on a bender and left the ranch."

"Our boy strayed from the house when he was two years old," said the old man. "And then along came these emigrant wagons with a youngster they didn't want; and we took you. I never in-tended you to know, Ranse. We never heard of our boy again."

"He's right outside, unless I'm mighty mistaken," said Ranse, opening the door and beckoning.

Curly walked in.

No one could have doubted. The old man and the young had the same sweep of hair, the same nose, chin, line of face, and prominent light-blue eyes.

Old "Kiowa" rose eagerly.

Curly looked about the room curiously. A puzzled expression came over his face. He pointed to the wall opposite.

"Where's the tick-tock?" he asked, absent-mindedly.

"The clock," cried old "Kiowa" loudly. "The eight-day clock used to stand there. Why—"

He turned to Ranse, but Ranse was not there.

Already a hundred yards away, Vaminos, the good flea-bitten dun, was bearing him eastward like a racer through dust and chaparral towards the Rancho de los Olmos.

—from *The Heart of the West* (1907)

A DOUBLE-DYED DECEIVER

The trouble began in Laredo. It was the Llano* Kid's fault, for he should have confined his habit of manslaughter to Mexicans. But the Kid was past twenty; and to have only Mexicans to one's credit at twenty is to blush unseen on the Rio Grande border.

It happened in old Justo Valdos's gambling house. There was a poker game at which sat players who were not all friends, as happens often where men ride in from afar to shoot Folly as she gallops. There was a row over so small a matter as a pair of queens; and when the smoke had cleared away it was found that the Kid had committed an indiscretion, and his adversary had been guilty of a blunder. For, the unfortunate combatant, instead of being a Greaser,† was a high-blooded youth from the cow ranches, of about the Kid's own age and possessed of friends and champions. His blunder in missing the Kid's right ear only a sixteenth of an inch when he pulled his gun did not lessen the indiscretion of the better marksman.

The Kid, not being equipped with a retinue, nor bountifully supplied with personal admirers and supporters—on account of a rather umbrageous reputation, even for the border—considered it not incompatible with his indisputable gameness to perform that judicious tractional act known as "pulling his freight."

Quickly the avengers gathered and sought him. Three of them overtook him within a rod of the station. The Kid turned and showed his teeth in that brilliant but mirthless smile that usually

---

*Treeless plain, like the Great Plains of the Southwest; the Kid's moniker would refer to his territory.
†Slang for a Mexican; also, a cowboy whose job it is to grease sheep.

preceded his deeds of insolence and violence, and his pursuers fell back without making it necessary for him even to reach for his weapon.

But in this affair the Kid had not felt the grim thirst for encounter that usually urged him on to battle. It had been a purely chance row, born of the cards and certain epithets impossible for a gentleman to brook that had passed between the two. The Kid had rather liked the slim, haughty, brown-faced young chap whom his bullet had cut off in the first pride of manhood. And now he wanted no more blood. He wanted to get away and have a good long sleep somewhere in the sun on the mesquit grass with his handkerchief over his face. Even a Mexican might have crossed his path in safety while he was in this mood.

The Kid openly boarded the north-bound passenger train that departed five minutes later. But at Webb, a few miles out, where it was flagged to take on a traveller, he abandoned that manner of escape. There were telegraph stations ahead; and the Kid looked askance at electricity and steam. Saddle and spur were his rocks of safety.

The man whom he had shot was a stranger to him. But the Kid knew that he was of the Coralitos outfit from Hidalgo; and that the punchers from that ranch were more relentless and vengeful than Kentucky feudists when wrong or harm was done to one of them. So, with the wisdom that has characterized many great fighters, the Kid decided to pile up as many leagues as possible of chaparral and pear between himself and the retaliation of the Coralitos bunch.

Near the station was a store; and near the store, scattered among the mesquits and elms, stood the saddled horses of the customers. Most of them waited, half asleep, with sagging limbs and drooping heads. But one, a long-legged roan with a curved neck, snorted and pawed the turf. Him the Kid mounted, gripped with his knees, and slapped gently with the owner's own quirt.*

If the slaying of the temerarious card-player had cast a cloud over the Kid's standing as a good and true citizen, this last act of

---

*Riding whip.

his veiled his figure in the darkest shadows of disrepute. On the Rio Grande border if you take a man's life you sometimes take trash; but if you take his horse, you take a thing the loss of which renders him poor, indeed, and which enriches you not—if you are caught. For the Kid there was no turning back now.

With the springing roan under him he felt little care or uneasiness. After a five-mile gallop he drew in to the plainsman's jogging trot, and rode northeastward toward the Nueces River bottoms. He knew the country well—its most tortuous and obscure trails through the great wilderness of brush and pear, and its camps and lonesome ranches where one might find safe entertainment. Always he bore to the east; for the Kid had never seen the ocean, and he had a fancy to lay his hand upon the mane of the great Gulf,* the gamesome colt of the greater waters.

So after three days he stood on the shore at Corpus Christi, and looked out across the gentle ripples of a quiet sea.

Captain Boone, of the schooner *Flyaway*, stood near his skiff, which one of his crew was guarding in the surf. When ready to sail he had discovered that one of the necessaries of life, in the parallelogrammatic shape of plug tobacco, had been forgotten. A sailor had been dispatched for the missing cargo. Meanwhile the captain paced the sands, chewing profanely at his pocket store.

A slim, wiry youth in high-heeled boots came down to the water's edge. His face was boyish, but with a premature severity that hinted at a man's experience. His complexion was naturally dark; and the sun and wind of an outdoor life had burned it to a coffee brown. His hair was as black and straight as an Indian's; his face had not yet been upturned to the humiliation of a razor; his eyes were a cold and steady blue. He carried his left arm somewhat away from his body, for pearl-handled .45s are frowned upon by town marshals, and are a little bulky when packed in the left armhole of one's vest. He looked beyond Captain Boone at the gulf with the impersonal and expressionless dignity of a Chinese emperor.

"Thinkin' of buyin' that'ar gulf, buddy?" asked the captain, made sarcastic by his narrow escape from a tobaccoless voyage.

---

*Gulf of Mexico.

"Why, no," said the Kid gently, "I reckon not. I never saw it before. I was just looking at it. Not thinking of selling it, are you?"

"Not this trip," said the captain. "I'll send it to you C. O. D. when I get back to Buenas Tierras.* Here comes that capstan-footed lubber with the chewin'. I ought to've weighed anchor an hour ago."

"Is that your ship out there?" asked the Kid.

"Why, yes," answered the captain, "if you want to call a schooner a ship, and I don't mind lyin'. But you better say Miller and Gonzales, owners, and ordinary plain, Billy-be-damned old Samuel K. Boone, skipper."

"Where are you going to?" asked the refugee.

"Buenas Tierras, coast of South America—I forgot what they called the country the last time I was there. Cargo—lumber, corrugated iron, and machetes."

"What kind of a country is it?" asked the Kid—"hot or cold?"

"Warmish, buddy," said the captain. "But a regular Paradise Lost[1] for elegance of scenery and be-yooty of geography. Ye're wakened every morning by the sweet singin' of red birds with seven purple tails, and the sighin' of breezes in the posies and roses. And the inhabitants never work, for they can reach out and pick steamer baskets of the choicest hothouse fruit without gettin' out of bed. And there's no Sunday and no ice and no rent and no troubles and no use and no nothin'. It's a great country for a man to go to sleep with, and wait for somethin' to turn up. The bananys and oranges and hurricanes and pineapples that ye eat comes from there."

"That sounds to me!" said the Kid, at last betraying interest. "What'll the expressage be to take me out there with you?"

"Twenty-four dollars," said Captain Boone; "grub and transportation. Second cabin. I haven't got a first cabin."

"You've got my company," said the Kid, pulling out a buckskin bag.

With three hundred dollars he had gone to Laredo for his regular "blowout." The duel in Valdos's had cut short his season of hilarity, but it had left him with nearly $200 for aid in the fight that it had made necessary.

---

*Good Lands (Spanish).

"All right, buddy," said the captain. "I hope your ma won't blame me for this little childish escapade of yours." He beckoned to one of the boat's crew "Let Sanchez lift you out to the skiff so you won't get your feet wet."

Thacker, the United States consul at Buenas Tierras, was not yet drunk. It was only eleven o'clock; and he never arrived at his desired state of beatitude—a state wherein he sang ancient maudlin vaudeville songs and pelted his screaming parrot with banana peels—until the middle of the afternoon. So, when he looked up from his hammock at the sound of a slight cough, and saw the Kid standing in the door of the consulate, he was still in a condition to extend the hospitality and courtesy due from the representative of a great nation. "Don't disturb yourself," said the Kid easily. "I just dropped in. They told me it was customary to light at your camp before starting in to round up the town. I just came in on a ship from Texas."

"Glad to see you, Mr.——," said the consul.

The Kid laughed.

"Sprague Dalton," he said. "It sounds funny to me to hear it. I'm called the Llano Kid in the Rio Grande country."

"I'm Thacker," said the consul. "Take that cane-bottom chair. Now if you've come to invest, you want somebody to advise you. These dingies will cheat you out of the gold in your teeth if you don't understand their ways. Try a cigar?"

"Much obliged," said the Kid, "but if it wasn't for my corn shucks and the little bag in my back pocket I couldn't live a minute." He took out his "makings," and rolled a cigarette.

"They speak Spanish here," said the consul. "You'll need an interpreter. If there's anything I can do, why, I'd be delighted. If you're buying fruit lands or looking for a concession of any sort, you'll want somebody who knows the ropes to look out for you."

"I speak Spanish," said the Kid, "about nine times better than I do English. Everybody speaks it on the range where I come from. And I'm not in the market for anything."

"You speak Spanish?" said Thacker thoughtfully. He regarded the Kid absorbedly.

"You look like a Spaniard, too," he continued. "And you're from

A Double-Dyed Deceiver 257

Texas. And you can't be more than twenty or twenty-one. I wonder if you've got any nerve."

"You got a deal of some kind to put through?" asked the Texan, with unexpected shrewdness.

"Are you open to a proposition?" said Thacker.

"What's the use to deny it?" said the Kid. "I got into a little gun frolic down in Laredo and plugged a white man. There wasn't any Mexican handy. And I come down to your parrot-and-monkey range just for to smell the morning-glories and marigolds. Now, do you *sabe*?"*

Thacker got up and closed the door.

"Let me see your hand," he said.

He took the Kid's left hand, and examined the back of it closely.

"I can do it," he said excitedly. "Your flesh is as hard as wood and as healthy as a baby's. It will heal in a week."

"If it's a fist fight you want to back me for," said the Kid, "don't put your money up yet. Make it gun work, and I'll keep you company. But no barehanded scrapping, like ladies at a tea-party, for me."

"It's easier than that," said Thacker. "Just step here, will you?"

Through the window he pointed to a two-story white-stuccoed house with wide galleries rising amid the deep-green tropical foliage on a wooded hill that sloped gently from the sea.

"In that house," said Thacker, "a fine old Castilian gentleman and his wife are yearning to gather you into their arms and fill your pockets with money. Old Santos Urique lives there. He owns half the gold-mines in the country."

"You haven't been eating loco† weed, have you?" asked the Kid.

"Sit down again," said Thacker, "and I'll tell you. Twelve years ago they lost a kid. No, he didn't die—although most of 'em here do from drinking the surface water. He was a wild little devil, even if he wasn't but eight years old. Everybody knows about it. Some Americans who were through here prospecting for gold had letters to Señor Urique, and the boy was a favourite with them. They filled his head with big stories about the States; and about a month after

*Know, understand (Spanish).
†Crazy (Spanish).

they left, the kid disappeared, too. He was supposed to have stowed himself away among the banana bunches on a fruit steamer, and gone to New Orleans. He was seen once afterward in Texas, it was thought, but they never heard anything more of him. Old Urique has spent thousands of dollars having him looked for. The madam was broken up worst of all. The kid was her life. She wears mourning yet. But they say she believes he'll come back to her some day, and never gives up hope. On the back of the boy's left hand was tattooed a flying eagle carrying a spear in his claws. That's old Urique's coat of arms or something that he inherited in Spain."

The Kid raised his left hand slowly and gazed at it curiously.

"That's it," said Thacker, reaching behind the official desk for his bottle of smuggled brandy. "You're not so slow. I can do it. What was I consul at Sandakan for?[2] I never knew till now. In a week I'll have the eagle bird with the frog-sticker blended in so you'd think you were born with it. I brought a set of the needles and ink just because I was sure you'd drop in some day, Mr. Dalton."

"Oh, hell," said the Kid. "I thought I told you my name!"

"All right, 'Kid,' then. It won't be that long. How does Señorito Urique sound, for a change?"

"I never played son any that I remember of," said the Kid. "If I had any parents to mention they went over the divide about the time I gave my first bleat. What is the plan of your round-up?"

Thacker leaned back against the wall and held his glass up to the light.

"We've come now," said he, "to the question of how far you're willing to go in a little matter of the sort."

"I told you why I came down here," said the Kid simply.

"A good answer," said the consul. "But you won't have to go that far. Here's the scheme. After I get the trademark tattooed on your hand I'll notify old Urique. In the meantime I'll furnish you with all of the family history I can find out, so you can be studying up points to talk about. You've got the looks, you speak the Spanish, you know the facts, you can tell about Texas, you've got the tattoo mark. When I notify them that the rightful heir has returned and is waiting to know whether he will be received and pardoned, what will happen? They'll simply rush down here and fall on your neck, and the curtain goes down for refreshments and a stroll in the lobby."

"I'm waiting," said the Kid. "I haven't had my saddle off in your camp long, pardner, and I never met you before; but if you intend to let it go at a parental blessing, why, I'm mistaken in my man, that's all."

"Thanks," said the consul. "I haven't met anybody in a long time that keeps up with an argument as well as you do. The rest of it is simple. If they take you in only for a while it's long enough. Don't give 'em time to hunt up the strawberry mark on your left shoulder. Old Urique keeps anywhere from $50,000 to $100,000 in his house all the time in a little safe that you could open with a shoe buttoner. Get it. My skill as a tattooer is worth half the boodle. We go halves and catch a tramp steamer for Rio Janeiro.[3] Let the United States go to pieces if it can't get along without my services. *Que dice, senor?*"*

"It sounds to me!" said the Kid, nodding his head. "I'm out for the dust."

"All right, then," said Thacker. "You'll have to keep close until we get the bird on you. You can live in the back room here. I do my own cooking, and I'll make you as comfortable as a parsimonious Government will allow me."

Thacker had set the time at a week, but it was two weeks before the design that he patiently tattooed upon the Kid's hand was to his notion. And then Thacker called a *muchacho,*† and dispatched this note to the intended victim:

EL SENOR DON SANTOS URIQUE,
LA CASA BLANCA,

MY DEAR SIR:

I beg permission to inform you that there is in my house as a temporary guest a young man who arrived in Buenas Tierras from the United States some days ago. Without wishing to excite any hopes that may not be realized, I think there is a possibility of his being your long-absent son. It might be well for you to

---

*"What'da you say, mister?" (Spanish).
†Boy (Spanish).

call and see him. If he is, it is my opinion that his intention was to return to his home, but upon arriving here, his courage failed him from doubts as to how he would be received.

YOUR TRUE SERVANT,

THOMPSON THACKER.

Half an hour afterward—quick time for Buenas Tierras—Señor Urique's ancient landau drove to the consul's door, with the barefooted coachman beating and shouting at the team of fat, awkward horses.

A tall man with a white moustache alighted, and assisted to the ground a lady who was dressed and veiled in unrelieved black.

The two hastened inside, and were met by Thacker with his best diplomatic bow. By his desk stood a slender young man with clearcut, sun-browned features and smoothly brushed black hair.

Señora Urique threw back her heavy veil with a quick gesture. She was past middle age, and her hair was beginning to silver, but her full, proud figure and clear olive skin retained traces of the beauty peculiar to the *Basque* province.[4] But once you had seen her eyes, and comprehended the great sadness that was revealed in their deep shadows and hopeless expression, you saw that the woman lived only in some memory.

She bent upon the young man a long look of the most agonized questioning. Then her great black eyes turned, and her gaze rested upon his left hand. And then with a sob, not loud, but seeming to shake the room, she cried *"Hijo mio!"** and caught the Llano Kid to her heart.

A month afterward the Kid came to the consulate in response to a message sent by Thacker.

He looked the young Spanish *caballero*. His clothes were imported, and the wiles of the jewellers had not been spent upon him in vain. A more than respectable diamond shone on his finger as he rolled a shuck cigarette.[†]

"What's doing?" asked Thacker.

"Nothing much," said the Kid calmly. "I eat my first iguana steak

---

*"My son!" (Spanish).

†Tobacco rolled in a corn husk.

to-day. They're them big lizards, you *sabe*? I reckon, though, that frijoles and side bacon would do me about as well. Do you care for iguanas, Thacker?"

"No, nor for some other kinds of reptiles," said Thacker.

It was three in the afternoon, and in another hour he would be in his state of beatitude.

"It's time you were making good, sonny," he went on, with an ugly look on his reddened face. "You're not playing up to me square. You've been the prodigal son for four weeks now, and you could have had veal for every meal on a gold dish if you'd wanted it. Now, Mr. Kid, do you think it's right to leave me out so long on a husk diet? What's the trouble? Don't you get your filial eyes on anything that looks like cash in the Casa Blanca? Don't tell me you don't. Everybody knows where old Urique keeps his stuff. It's U. S. currency, too; he don't accept anything else. What's doing? Don't say 'nothing' this time."

"Why, sure," said the Kid, admiring his diamond, "there's plenty of money up there. I'm no judge of collateral in bunches, but I will undertake for to say that I've seen the rise of $50,000 at a time in that tin grub box that my adopted father calls his safe. And he lets me carry the key sometimes just to show me that he knows I'm the real little Francisco that strayed from the herd a long time ago."

"Well, what are you waiting for?" asked Thacker angrily. "Don't you forget that I can upset your apple-cart any day I want to. If old Urique knew you were an impostor, what sort of things would happen to you? Oh, you don't know this country, Mr. Texas Kid. The laws here have got mustard spread between 'em. These people here'd stretch you out like a frog that had been stepped on, and give you about fifty sticks at every corner of the plaza. And they'd wear every stick out, too. What was left of you they'd feed to alligators."

"I might as well tell you now, pardner," said the Kid, sliding down low on his steamer chair, "that things are going to stay just as they are. They're about right now."

"What do you mean?" asked Thacker, rattling the bottom of his glass on his desk.

"The scheme's off," said the Kid. "And whenever you have the pleasure of speaking to me address me as Don Francisco Urique.

I'll guarantee I'll answer to it. We'll let Colonel Urique keep his money. His little tin safe is as good as the time-locker in the First National Bank of Laredo as far as you and me are concerned."

"You're going to throw me down, then, are you?" said the consul.

"Sure," said the Kid cheerfully. "Throw you down. That's it. And now I'll tell you why. The first night I was up at the colonel's house they introduced me to a bedroom. No blankets on the floor—a real room, with a bed and things in it. And before I was asleep, in comes this artificial mother of mine and tucks in the covers. 'Panchito,'* she says, 'my little lost one, God has brought you back to me. I bless His name forever.' It was that, or some truck like that, she said. And down comes a drop or two of rain and hits me on the nose. And all that stuck by me, Mr. Thacker. And it's been that way ever since. And it's got to stay that way. Don't you think that it's for what's in it for me, either, that I say so. If you have any such ideas, keep 'em to yourself. I haven't had much truck with women in my life, and no mothers to speak of, but here's a lady that we've got to keep fooled. Once she stood it; twice she won't. I'm a low-down wolf, and the devil may have sent me on this trail instead of God, but I'll travel it to the end. And now, don't forget that I'm Don Francisco Urique whenever you happen to mention my name."

"I'll expose you to-day, you—you double-dyed traitor," stammered Thacker.

The Kid arose and, without violence, took Thacker by the throat with a hand of steel, and shoved him slowly into a corner. Then he drew from under his left arm his pearl-handled .45 and poked the cold muzzle of it against the consul's mouth.

"I told you why I come here," he said, with his old freezing smile. "If I leave here, you'll be the reason. Never forget it, pardner. Now, what is my name?"

"Er—Don Francisco Urique," gasped Thacker.

From outside came a sound of wheels, and the shouting of some one, and the sharp thwacks of a wooden whipstock upon the backs of fat horses.

The Kid put up his gun, and walked toward the door. But he

---

*In Spanish, adding "ito" to the end of a name indicates affection.

turned again and came back to the trembling Thacker, and held up his left hand with its back toward the consul.

"There's one more reason," he said slowly, "why things have got to stand as they are. The fellow I killed in Laredo had one of them same pictures on his left hand."

Outside, the ancient landau of Don Santos Urique rattled to the door. The coachman ceased his bellowing. Señora Urique, in a voluminous gay gown of white lace and flying ribbons, leaned forward with a happy look in her great soft eyes.

"Are you within, dear son?" she called, in the rippling Castilian.*

"*Madre mia, yo vengo* [mother, I come]," answered the young Don Francisco Urique.

—from *The Roads of Destiny* (1909)

---

*Upper-class Spanish; Castilian, the dialect of the Spanish region of Castile, is the official and literary language of Spain.

FRIENDS IN SAN ROSARIO

The west-bound stopped at San Rosario on time at 8.20 A.M. A man with a thick black-leather wallet under his arm left the train and walked rapidly up the main street of the town. There were other passengers who also got off at San Rosario, but they either slouched limberly over to the railroad eating-house or the Silver Dollar saloon, or joined the groups of idlers about the station.

Indecision had no part in the movements of the man with the wallet. He was short in stature, but strongly built, with very light, closely-trimmed hair, smooth, determined face, and aggressive, gold-rimmed nose glasses. He was well dressed in the prevailing Eastern style. His air denoted a quiet but conscious reserve force, if not actual authority.

After walking a distance of three squares he came to the centre of the town's business area. Here another street of importance crossed the main one, forming the hub of San Rosario's life and commerce. Upon one corner stood the post-office. Upon another Rubensky's Clothing Emporium. The other two diagonally opposing corners were occupied by the town's two banks, the First National and the Stockmen's National. Into the First National Bank of San Rosario the newcomer walked, never slowing his brisk step until he stood at the cashier's window. The bank opened for business at nine, and the working force was already assembled, each member preparing his department for the day's business. The cashier was examining the mail when he noticed the stranger standing at his window.

"Bank doesn't open 'til nine," he remarked, curtly, but without feeling. He had had to make that statement so often to early birds since San Rosario adopted city banking hours.

"I am well aware of that," said the other man, in cool, brittle tones. "Will you kindly receive my card?"

The cashier drew the small, spotless parallelogram inside the bars of his wicket, and read:

```
J. F. C. NETTLEWICK

National Bank Examiner
```

"Oh—er—will you walk around inside, Mr.—er—Nettlewick. Your first visit—didn't know your business, of course. Walk right around, please."

The examiner was quickly inside the sacred precincts of the bank, where he was ponderously introduced to each employee in turn by Mr. Edlinger, the cashier—a middle-aged gentleman of deliberation, discretion, and method.

"I was kind of expecting Sam Turner round again, pretty soon," said Mr. Edlinger. "Sam's been examining us now, for about four years. I guess you'll find us all right, though, considering the tightness in business. Not overly much money on hand, but able to stand the storms, sir, stand the storms."

"Mr. Turner and I have been ordered by the Comptroller to exchange districts," said the examiner, in his decisive, formal tones. "He is covering my old territory in Southern Illinois and Indiana. I will take the cash first, please."

Perry Dorsey, the teller, was already arranging his cash on the counter for the examiner's inspection. He knew it was right to a cent, and he had nothing to fear, but he was nervous and flustered. So was every man in the bank. There was something so icy and swift, so impersonal and uncompromising about this man that his very presence seemed an accusation. He looked to be a man who would never make nor overlook an error.

Mr. Nettlewick first seized the currency, and with a rapid, almost juggling motion, counted it by packages. Then he spun the sponge cup toward him and verified the count by bills. His thin, white fingers flew like some expert musician's upon the keys of a piano. He dumped the gold upon the counter with a crash, and the coins whined and sang as they skimmed across the marble slab from the tips of his nimble digits. The air was full of fractional currency when he came to the halves and quarters. He counted the last nickle and dime. He had the scales brought, and he weighed every sack of silver in the vault. He questioned Dorsey concerning each of the cash memoranda—certain checks, charge slips, etc., carried over from the previous day's work—with unimpeachable courtesy, yet with something so mysteriously momentous in his frigid manner, that the teller was reduced to pink cheeks and a stammering tongue.

This newly-imported examiner was so different from Sam Turner. It had been Sam's way to enter the bank with a shout, pass the cigars, and tell the latest stories he had picked up on his rounds. His customary greeting to Dorsey had been, "Hello, Perry! Haven't skipped out with the boodle yet, I see." Turner's way of counting the cash had been different, too. He would finger the packages of bills in a tired kind of way, and then go into the vault and kick over a few sacks of silver, and the thing was done. Halves and quarters and dimes? Not for Sam Turner. "No chicken feed for me," he would say when they were set before him. "I'm not in the agricultural department." But, then, Turner was a Texan, an old friend of the bank's president, and had known Dorsey since he was a baby.

While the examiner was counting the cash, Major Thomas B. Kingman—known to every one as "Major Tom"—the president of the First National, drove up to the side door with his old dun horse and buggy, and came inside. He saw the examiner busy with the money, and, going into the little "pony corral," as he called it, in which his desk was railed off, he began to look over his letters.

Earlier, a little incident had occurred that even the sharp eyes of the examiner had failed to notice. When he had begun his work at the cash counter, Mr. Edlinger had winked significantly at Roy Wilson, the youthful bank messenger, and nodded his head slightly toward the front door. Roy understood, got his hat and walked leisurely out, with his collector's book under his arm. Once outside, he made a beeline for the Stockmen's National. That bank was also getting ready to open. No customers had, as yet, presented themselves.

"Say, you people!" cried Roy, with the familiarity of youth and long acquaintance, "you want to get a move on you. There's a new bank examiner over at the First, and he's a stem-winder. He's counting nickles on Perry, and he's got the whole outfit bluffed. Mr. Edlinger gave me the tip to let you know."

Mr. Buckley, president of the Stockmen's National—a stout, elderly man, looking like a farmer dressed for Sunday—heard Roy from his private office at the rear and called him.

"Has Major Kingman come down to the bank yet?" he asked of the boy.

"Yes, sir, he was just driving up as I left," said Roy.

"I want you to take him a note. Put it into his own hands as soon as you get back."

Mr. Buckley sat down and began to write.

Roy returned and handed to Major Kingman the envelope containing the note. The major read it, folded it, and slipped it into his vest pocket. He leaned back in his chair for a few moments as if he were meditating deeply, and then rose and went into the vault. He came out with the bulky, old-fashioned leather note case stamped on the back in gilt letters, "Bills Discounted." In this were the notes due the bank with their attached securities, and the major, in his rough way, dumped the lot upon his desk and began to sort them over.

By this time Nettlewick had finished his count of the cash. His pencil fluttered like a swallow over the sheet of paper on which he had set his figures. He opened his black wallet, which seemed to be also a kind of secret memorandum book, made a few rapid figures in it, wheeled and transfixed Dorsey with the glare of his spectacles. That look seemed to say: "You're safe this time, but—"

"Cash all correct," snapped the examiner. He made a dash for the individual bookkeeper, and, for a few minutes there was a fluttering of ledger leaves and a sailing of balance sheets through the air.

"How often do you balance your pass-books?" he demanded, suddenly.

"Er—once a month," faltered the individual bookkeeper, wondering how many years they would give him.

"All right," said the examiner, turning and charging upon the general bookkeeper, who had the statements of his foreign banks and their reconcilement memoranda ready. Everything there was found to be all right. Then the stub book of the certificates of deposit. Flutter—flutter—zip—zip—check! All right. List of over-drafts, please. Thanks. H'm-m. Unsigned bills of the bank, next. All right.

Then came the cashier's turn, and easy-going Mr. Edlinger rubbed his nose and polished his glasses nervously under the quick fire of questions concerning the circulation, undivided profits, bank real estate, and stock ownership.

Presently Nettlewick was aware of a big man towering above him at his elbow—a man sixty years of age, rugged and hale, with a rough, grizzled beard, a mass of gray hair, and a pair of pene-trating blue eyes that confronted the formidable glasses of the ex-aminer without a flicker.

"Er—Major Kingman, our president—er—Mr. Nettlewick," said the cashier.

Two men of very different types shook hands. One was a fin-ished product of the world of straight lines, conventional methods, and formal affairs. The other was something freer, wider and nearer to nature. Tom Kingman had not been cut to any pattern. He had been mule-driver, cowboy, ranger, soldier, sheriff, prospector, and cattleman. Now, when he was bank president, his old comrades from the prairies, of the saddle, tent, and trail found no change in him. He had made his fortune when Texas cattle were at the high tide of value, and had organized the First National Bank of San Rosario. In spite of his largeness of heart and sometimes unwise generosity toward his old friends, the bank had prospered, for Ma-jor Tom Kingman knew men as well as he knew cattle. Of late years the cattle business had known a depression,[1] and the major's bank was one of the few whose losses had not been great.

"And now," said the examiner, briskly, pulling out his watch, "the last thing is the loans. We will take them up now, if you please."

He had gone through the First National at almost record-breaking speed—but thoroughly, as he did everything. The running order of the bank was smooth and clean, and that had facilitated his work. There was but one other bank in the town. He received from the Government a fee of twenty-five dollars for each bank that he examined. He should be able to go over those loans and discounts in half an hour. If so, he could examine the other bank immediately afterward, and catch the 11.45, the only other train that day in the direction he was working. Otherwise, he would have to spend the night and Sunday in this uninteresting Western town. That was why Mr. Nettlewick was rushing matters.

"Come with me, sir," said Major Kingman, in his deep voice, that united the Southern drawl with the rhythmic twang of the West; "We will go over them together. Nobody in the bank knows those notes as I do. Some of 'em are a little wobbly on their legs, and some are mavericks without extra many brands on their backs, but they'll most all pay out at the round-up."

The two sat down at the president's desk. First, the examiner went through the notes at lightning speed, and added up their total, finding it to agree with the amount of loans carried on the book of daily balances. Next, he took up the larger loans, inquiring scrupulously into the condition of their indorsers or securities. The new examiner's mind seemed to course and turn and make unexpected dashes hither and thither like a bloodhound seeking a trail. Finally he pushed aside all the notes except a few, which he arranged in a neat pile before him, and began a dry, formal little speech.

"I find, sir, the condition of your bank to be very good, considering the poor crops and the depression in the cattle interests of your state. The clerical work seems to be done accurately and punctually. Your past-due paper is moderate in amount, and promises only a small loss. I would recommend the calling in of your large loans, and the making of only sixty and ninety day or call loans until general business revives. And now, there is one thing more, and I will have finished with the bank. Here are six notes aggregating something like $40,000. They are secured, according to their faces, by various stocks, bonds, shares, etc. to the value of $70,000. Those securities are missing from the notes to which they should be attached. I suppose you have them in the safe or vault. You will permit me to examine them."

Major Tom's light-blue eyes turned unflinchingly toward the examiner.

"No, sir," he said, in a low but steady tone; "those securities are neither in the safe nor the vault. I have taken them. You may hold me personally responsible for their absence."

Nettlewick felt a slight thrill. He had not expected this. He had struck a momentous trail when the hunt was drawing to a close.

"Ah!" said the examiner. He waited a moment, and then continued: "May I ask you to explain more definitely?"

"The securities were taken by me," repeated the major. "It was not for my own use, but to save an old friend in trouble. Come in here, sir, and we'll talk it over."

He led the examiner into the bank's private office at the rear, and closed the door. There was a desk, and a table, and half-a-dozen leather-covered chairs. On the wall was the mounted head of a Texas steer with horns five feet from tip to tip. Opposite hung the major's old cavalry saber that he had carried at Shiloh and Fort Pillow.

Placing a chair for Nettlewick, the major seated himself by the window, from which he could see the post-office and the carved limestone front of the Stockman's National. He did not speak at once, and Nettlewick felt, perhaps, that the ice should be broken by something so near its own temperature as the voice of official warning.

"Your statement," he began, "since you have failed to modify it, amounts, as you must know, to a very serious thing. You are aware, also, of what my duty must compel me to do. I shall have to go before the United States Commissioner and make—"

"I know, I know," said Major Tom, with a wave of his hand. "You don't suppose I'd run a bank without being posted on national banking laws and the revised statutes! Do your duty. I'm not asking any favours. But, I spoke of my friend. I did want you to hear me tell you about Bob."

Nettlewick settled himself in his chair. There would be no leaving San Rosario for him that day. He would have to telegraph to the Comptroller of the Currency; he would have to swear out a warrant before the United States Commissioner for the arrest of Major Kingman; perhaps he would be ordered to close the bank on account of the loss of the securities. It was not the first crime the examiner had unearthed. Once or twice the terrible upheaval of human emotions that his investigations had loosed had almost caused a ripple in his official calm. He had seen bank men kneel and plead and cry like women for a chance—an hour's time—the overlooking of a single error. One cashier had shot himself at his desk before him. None of them had taken it with the dignity and coolness of this stern old Westerner. Nettlewick felt that he owed it to him at least to listen if he wished to talk. With his elbow on the arm of his chair, and his square chin resting upon the fingers of his right hand, the bank examiner waited to hear the confession of the president of the First National Bank of San Rosario.

"When a man's your friend," began Major Tom, somewhat didactically, "for forty years, and tried by water, fire, earth, and cyclones, when you can do him a little favour you feel like doing it."

("Embezzle for him $70,000 worth of securities," thought the examiner.)

"We were cowboys together, Bob and I," continued the major, speaking slowly, and deliberately, and musingly, as if his thoughts were rather with the past than the critical present, "and we prospected together for gold and silver over Arizona, New Mexico, and a good part of California. We were both in the war of 'sixty-one,* but in different commands. We've fought Indians and horse thieves side by side; we've starved for weeks in a cabin in the Arizona mountains, buried twenty feet deep in snow; we've ridden herd together when the wind blew so hard the lightning couldn't strike— well, Bob and I have been through some rough spells since the first time we met in the branding camp of the old Anchor-Bar ranch. And during that time we've found it necessary more than once to help each other out of tight places. In those days it was expected of a man to stick to his friend, and he didn't ask any credit for it. Probably next day you'd need him to get at your back and help stand off a band of Apaches, or put a tourniquet on your leg above a rattlesnake bite and ride for whisky. So, after all, it was give and take, and if you didn't stand square with your pardner, why, you might be shy one when you needed him. But Bob was a man who was willing to go further than that. He never played a limit.

"Twenty years ago I was sheriff of this county, and I made Bob my chief deputy. That was before the boom in cattle when we both made our stake. I was sheriff and collector, and it was a big thing

---

*The American Civil War began in 1861 and ended in 1865.

for me then. I was married, and we had a boy and a girl—a four and a six year old. There was a comfortable house next to the court-house, furnished by the county, rent free, and I was saving some money. Bob did most of the office work. Both of us had seen rough times and plenty of rustling and danger, and I tell you it was great to hear the rain and the sleet dashing against the windows of nights, and be warm and safe and comfortable, and know you could get up in the morning and be shaved and have folks call you 'mister.' And then, I had the finest wife and kids that ever struck the range, and my old friend with me enjoying the first fruits of prosperity and white shirts, and I guess I was happy. Yes, I was happy about that time."

The major sighed and glanced casually out of the window. The bank examiner changed his position, and leaned his chin upon his other hand.

"One winter," continued the major, "the money for the county taxes came pouring in so fast that I didn't have time to take the stuff to the bank for a week. I just shoved the checks into a cigar box and the money into a sack, and locked them in the big safe that belonged in the sheriff's office.

"I had been overworked that week, and was about sick, anyway. My nerves were out of order, and my sleep at night didn't seem to rest me. The doctor had some scientific name for it, and I was taking medicine. And so, added to the rest, I went to bed at night with that money on my mind. Not that there was much need of being worried, for the safe was a good one, and nobody but Bob and I knew the combination. On Friday night there was about $6,500 in cash in the bag. On Saturday morning I went to the office as usual. The safe was locked, and Bob was writing at his desk. I opened the safe, and the money was gone. I called Bob, and roused everybody in the court-house to announce the robbery. It struck me that Bob took it pretty quiet, considering how much it reflected upon both him and me.

"Two days went by and we never got a clew. It couldn't have been burglars, for the safe had been opened by the combination in the proper way. People must have begun to talk, for one afternoon in comes Alice—that's my wife—and the boy and girl, and Alice stamps her foot, and her eyes flash, and she cries out, 'The lying wretches—Tom, Tom!' and I catch her in a faint, and bring her 'round little by little, and she lays her head down and cries and cries for the first time since she took Tom Kingman's name and fortunes. And Jack and Zilla—the youngsters—they were always wild as tiger cubs to rush at Bob and climb all over him whenever they were allowed to come to the court-house—they stood and kicked their little shoes, and herded together like scared partridges. They were having their first trip down into the shadows of life. Bob was working at his desk, and he got up and went out without a word. The grand jury was in session then, and the next morning Bob went before them and confessed that he stole the money. He said he lost it in a poker game. In fifteen minutes they had found a true bill and sent me the warrant to arrest the man with whom I'd been closer than a thousand brothers for many a year.

"I did it, and then I said to Bob, pointing: 'There's my house, and here's my office, and up there's Maine, and out that way is California, and over there is Florida—and that's your range 'til court meets. You're in my charge, and I take the responsibility. You be here when you're wanted.'

" 'Thanks, Tom,' he said, kind of carelessly; 'I was sort of hoping you wouldn't lock me up. Court meets next Monday, so, if you don't object, I'll just loaf around the office until then. I've got one favour to ask, if it isn't too much. If you'd let the kids come out in the yard once in a while and have a romp I'd like it.'

" 'Why not?' I answered him. 'They're welcome, and so are you. And come to my house, the same as ever.' You see, Mr. Nettlewick, you can't make a friend of a thief, but neither can you make a thief of a friend, all at once."

The examiner made no answer. At that moment was heard the shrill whistle of a locomotive pulling into the depot. That was the train on the little, narrow-gauge road that struck into San Rosario from the south. The major cocked his ear and listened for a moment, and looked at his watch. The narrow-gauge was in on time—10.35. The major continued:

"So Bob hung around the office, reading the papers and smoking. I put another deputy to work in his place, and, after a while, the first excitement of the case wore off.

"One day when we were alone in the office Bob came over to

where I was sitting. He was looking sort of grim and blue—the same look he used to get when he'd been up watching for Indians all night or herd-riding.

" 'Tom,' says he, 'it's harder than standing off redskins; it's harder than lying in the lava desert forty miles from water; but I'm going to stick it out to the end. You know that's been my style. But if you'd tip me the smallest kind of a sign—if you'd just say, "Bob I understand," why, it would make it lots easier.'

"I was surprised. 'I don't know what you mean, Bob,' I said. 'Of course, you know that I'd do anything under the sun to help you that I could. But you've got me guessing.'

" 'All right, Tom,' was all he said, and he went back to his newspaper and lit another cigar.

"It was the night before court met when I found out what he meant. I went to bed that night with that same old, light-headed, nervous feeling come back upon me. I dropped off to sleep about midnight. When I awoke I was standing half dressed in one of the court-house corridors. Bob was holding one of my arms, our family doctor the other, and Alice was shaking me and half crying. She had sent for the doctor without my knowing it, and when he came they had found me out of bed and missing, and had begun a search.

" 'Sleep-walking,' said the doctor.

"All of us went back to the house, and the doctor told us some remarkable stories about the strange things people had done while in that condition. I was feeling rather chilly after my trip out, and, as my wife was out of the room at the time, I pulled open the door of an old wardrobe that stood in the room and dragged out a big quilt I had seen in there. With it tumbled out the bag of money for stealing which Bob was to be tried—and convicted—in the morning.

" 'How the jumping rattlesnakes did that get there?' I yelled, and all hands must have seen how surprised I was. Bob knew in a flash.

" 'You darned old snoozer,' he said, with the old-time look on his face, 'I saw you put it there. I watched you open the safe and take it out, and I followed you. I looked through the window and saw you hide it in that wardrobe.'

" 'Then, you blankety-blank, flop-eared, sheep-headed coyote, what did you say you took it, for?'

" 'Because,' said Bob, simply, 'I didn't know you were asleep.'

"I saw him glance toward the door of the room where Jack and Zilla were, and I knew then what it meant to be a man's friend from Bob's point of view."

Major Tom paused, and again directed his glance out of the window. He saw some one in the Stockmen's National Bank reach and draw a yellow shade down the whole length of its plate-glass, big front window, although the position of the sun did not seem to warrant such a defensive movement against its rays.

Nettlewick sat up straight in his chair. He had listened patiently, but without consuming interest, to the major's story. It had impressed him as irrelevant to the situation, and it could certainly have no effect upon the consequences. Those Western people, he thought, had an exaggerated sentimentality. They were not business-like. They needed to be protected from their friends. Evidently the major had concluded. And what he had said amounted to nothing.

"May I ask," said the examiner, "if you have anything further to say that bears directly upon the question of those abstracted securities?"

"Abstracted securities, sir!" Major Tom turned suddenly in his chair, his blue eyes flashing upon the examiner. "What do you mean, sir?"

He drew from his coat pocket a batch of folded papers held together by a rubber band, tossed them into Nettlewick's hands, and rose to his feet.

"You'll find those securities there, sir, every stock, bond, and share of 'em. I took them from the notes while you were counting the cash. Examine and compare them for yourself."

The major led the way back into the banking room. The examiner, astounded, perplexed, nettled, at sea, followed. He felt that he had been made the victim of something that was not exactly a hoax, but that left him in the shoes of one who had been played upon, used, and then discarded, without even an inkling of the game. Perhaps, also, his official position had been irreverently juggled with. But there was nothing he could take hold of. An official report of the matter would be an absurdity. And, somehow, he felt that he would never know anything more about the matter than he did then.

Frigidly, mechanically, Nettlewick examined the securities, found them to tally with the notes, gathered his black wallet, and rose to depart.

"I will say," he protested, turning the indignant glare of his glasses upon Major Kingman, "that your statements—your misleading statements, which you have not condescended to explain—do not appear to be quite the thing, regarded either as business or humour. I do not understand such motives or actions."

Major Tom looked down at him serenely and not unkindly.

"Son," he said, "there are plenty of things in the chaparral, and on the prairies, and up the cañons that you don't understand. But I want to thank you for listening to a garrulous old man's prosy story. We old Texans love to talk about our adventures and our old comrades, and the home folks have long ago learned to run when we begin with 'Once upon a time,' so we have to spin our yarns to the stranger within our gates."

The major smiled, but the examiner only bowed coldly, and abruptly quitted the bank. They saw him travel diagonally across the street in a straight line and enter the Stockmen's National Bank.

Major Tom sat down at his desk, and drew from his vest pocket the note Roy had given him. He had read it once, but hurriedly, and now, with something like a twinkle in his eyes, he read it again. These were the words he read:

DEAR TOM:

I hear there's one of Uncle Sam's grayhound's going through you, and that means that we'll catch him inside of a couple of hours, maybe. Now, I want you to do something for me. We've got just $2,200 in the bank, and the law requires that we have $20,000. I let Ross and Fisher have $18,000 late yesterday afternoon to buy up that Gibson bunch of cattle. They'll realize $40,000 in less than thirty days on the transaction, but that won't make my cash on hand look any prettier to that bank examiner. Now, I can't show him those notes, for they're just plain notes of hand without any security in sight, but you know very well that Pink Ross and Jim Fisher are two of the finest white men God ever made, and they'll do the square thing. You remember Jim Fisher—he was the one who shot that faro dealer in El Paso. I wired Sam Bradshaw's bank to send me $20,000, and it will get in on the narrow-gauge at 10.35. You can't let a bank examiner in to count $2,200 and close your doors. Tom, you hold that examiner. Hold him. Hold him if you have to rope him and sit on his head. Watch our front window after the narrow-gauge gets in, and when we've got the cash inside we'll pull down the shade for a signal. Don't turn him loose till then. I'm counting on you, Tom.

YOUR OLD PARD,

BOB BUCKLEY,

Prest. Stockmen's National.

The major began to tear the note into small pieces and throw them into his waste basket. He gave a satisfied little chuckle as he did so.

"Confounded old reckless cowpuncher!" he growled, contentedly, "that pays him some on account for what he tried to do for me in the sheriff's office twenty years ago."

—from *The Roads of Destiny* (1909)

THE HIDING OF BLACK BILL

Alank, strong, red-faced man with a Wellington beak and small, fiery eyes tempered by flaxen lashes, sat on the station platform at Los Pinos swinging his legs to and fro. At his side sat another man, fat, melancholy, and seedy, who seemed to be his friend. They had the appearance of men to whom life had appeared as a reversible coat—seamy on both sides.

"Ain't seen you in about four years, Ham," said the seedy man. "Which way you been travelling?"

"Texas," said the red-faced man. "It was too cold in Alaska for me. And I found it warm in Texas. I'll tell you about one hot spell I went through there.

"One morning I steps off the International at a water-tank and lets it go on without me. 'Twas a ranch country, and fuller of spite-houses than New York City. Only out there they build 'em twenty miles away so you can't smell what they've got for dinner, instead of running 'em up two inches from their neighbors' windows.

"There wasn't any roads in sight, so I footed it 'cross country. The grass was shoe-top deep, and the mesquite timber looked just like a peach orchard. It was so much like a gentleman's private estate that every minute you expected a kennelful of bulldogs to run out and bite you. But I must have walked twenty miles before I came in sight of a ranch-house. It was a little one, about as big as an elevated railroad station.

"There was a little man in a white shirt and brown overalls and pink handkerchief around his neck rolling cigarettes under a tree in front of the door.

" 'Greetings,' says I. 'Any refreshments, welcome, emoluments, or even work for a comparative stranger?'

" 'Oh, come in,' says he, in a refined tone. 'Sit down on that stool, please. I didn't hear your horse coming.'

" 'He isn't near enough yet,' says I. 'I walked. I don't want to be a burden, but I wonder if you have three or four gallons of water handy.'

" 'You do look pretty dusty,' says he; 'but our bathing arrangements—'

" 'It's a drink I want,' says I. 'Never mind the dust that's on the outside.'

"He gets me a dipper of water out of a red jar hanging up, and then goes on:

" 'Do you want work?'

" 'For a time,' says I. 'This is a rather quiet section of the country, isn't it?'

" 'It is,' says he. 'Sometimes—so I have been told—one sees no human being pass for weeks at a time. I've been here only a month. I bought the ranch from an old settler who wanted to move farther west.'

" 'It suits me,' says I. 'Quiet and retirement are good for a man sometimes. And I need a job. I can tend bar, salt mines, lecture, float stock, do a little middle-weight slugging, and play the piano.'

" 'Can you herd sheep?' asks the little ranchman.

" 'Do you mean *have* I heard sheep?' says I.

" 'Can you herd 'em—take charge of a flock of 'em?' says he.

" 'Oh,' says I, 'now I understand. You mean chase 'em around and bark at 'em like collie dogs. Well, I might,' says I. 'I've never exactly done any sheep-herding, but I've often seen 'em from car windows masticating daisies, and they don't look dangerous.'

" 'I'm short a herder,' says the ranchman. 'You never can depend on the Mexicans. I've only got two flocks. You may take out my bunch of muttons—there are only eight hundred of 'em—in the morning, if you like. The pay is twelve dollars a month and your rations furnished. You camp in a tent on the prairie with your sheep. You do your own cooking, but wood and water are brought to your camp. It's an easy job.'

" 'I'm on,' says I. 'I'll take the job even if I have to garland my brow and hold on to a crook and wear a loose effect and play on a pipe like the shepherds do in pictures.'

"So the next morning the little ranchman helps me drive the flock of muttons from the corral to about two miles out and let 'em

graze on a little hillside on the prairie. He gives me a lot of instructions about not letting bunches of them stray off from the herd,
and driving 'em down to a water-hole to drink at noon.

" 'I'll bring out your tent and camping outfit and rations in the
buckboard before night,' says he.

" 'Fine,' says I. 'And don't forget the rations. Nor the camping
outfit. And be sure to bring the tent. Your name's Zollicoffer, ain't
it?'

" 'My name,' said he, 'is Henry Ogden.'

" 'All right, Mr. Ogden,' says I. 'Mine is Mr. Percival Saint
Clair.'

"I herded sheep for five days on the Rancho Chiquito; and then
the wool entered my soul. That getting next to Nature certainly got
next to me. I was lonesomer than Crusoe's goat.[1] I've seen a lot of
persons more entertaining as companions than those sheep were.
I'd drive 'em to the corral and pen 'em every evening, and then cook
my corn-bread and mutton and coffee, and lie down in a tent the
size of a tablecloth, and listen to the coyotes and whip-poor-wills
singing around the camp.

"The fifth evening, after I had corralled my costly but uncon-
genial muttons, I walked over to the ranch-house and stepped in
the door.

" 'Mr. Ogden,' says I, 'you and me have got to get sociable. Sheep
are all very well to dot the landscape and furnish eight-dollar cotton
suitings for man, but for table-talk and fireside companions they
rank along with five-o'clock teazers. If you've got a deck of cards,
or a parcheesi outfit, or a game of authors, get 'em out, and let's
get on a mental basis. I've got to do something in an intellectual
line, if it's only to knock somebody's brains out.'

"This Henry Ogden was a peculiar kind of ranchman. He wore
finger-rings and a big gold watch and careful neckties. And his face
was calm, and his nose-spectacles was kept very shiny. I saw once,
in Muscogee, an outlaw hung for murdering six men, who was a
dead ringer for him. But I knew a preacher in Arkansas that you
would have taken to be his brother. I didn't care much for him
either way; what I wanted was some fellowship and communion
with holy saints or lost sinners—anything sheepless would do.

" 'Well, Saint Clair,' says he, laying down the book he was reading, 'I guess it must be pretty lonesome for you at first. And I don't deny that it's monotonous for me. Are you sure you corralled your sheep so they won't stray out?'

" 'They're shut up as tight as the jury of a millionaire murderer,' says I. 'And I'll be back with them long before they'll need their trained nurse.

"So Ogden digs up a deck of cards, and we play casino. After five days and nights of my sheep-camp it was like a toot on Broadway. When I caught big casino I felt as excited as if I had made a million in Trinity. And when H. O. loosened up a little and told the story about the lady in the Pullman car I laughed for five minutes.

"That showed what a comparative thing life is. A man may see so much that he'd be bored to turn his head to look at a $3,000,000 fire for Joe Weber[2] or the Adriatic Sea.[3] But let him herd sheep for a spell, and you'll see him splitting his ribs laughing at 'Curfew Shall Not Ring To-night,'[4] or really enjoying himself playing cards with ladies.

"By-and-by Ogden gets out a decanter of Bourbon, and there is a total eclipse of sheep.

" 'Do you remember reading in the papers about a month ago,' says he, 'about a train hold-up on the M. K. & T.? The express agent was shot through the shoulder and about $15,000 in currency taken. And it's said that only one man did the job.'

" 'Seems to me I do,' says I. 'But such things happen so often they don't linger long in the human Texas mind. Did they overtake, overhaul, seize, or lay hands upon the despoiler?'

" 'He escaped,' says Ogden. 'And I was just reading in a paper to-day that the officers have tracked him down into this part of the country. It seems the bills the robbers got were all the first issue of currency to the Second National Bank of Espinosa City. And so they've followed the trail where they've been spent, and it leads this way.'

"Ogden pours out some more Bourbon, and shoves me the bottle.

" 'Imagine,' says I, after ingurgitating another modicum of the royal booze, 'that it wouldn't be at all a disingenuous idea for a train-robber to run down into this part of the country to hide for a spell. A sheep-ranch, now,' says I, 'would be the finest kind of a place. Who'd ever expect to find such a desperate character among these song-birds and muttons and wild flowers? And, by the way,' says I, kind of looking H. Ogden over, 'was there any description mentioned to this single-handed terror? Was his lineaments or height and thickness or teeth fillings or style of habiliments set forth in print?'

" 'Why, no,' says Ogden; 'because they say nobody got a good sight of him because he wore a mask. But they know it was a train-robber called Black Bill, because he always works alone and because he dropped a handkerchief in the express-car that had his name on it.'

" 'All right,' says I. 'I approve of Black Bill's retreat to the sheep-ranges. I guess they won't find him.'

" 'There's one thousand dollars reward for his capture,' says Ogden.

" 'I don't need that kind of money,' says I, looking Mr. Sheep-man straight in the eye. 'The twelve dollars a month you pay me is enough. I need a rest, and I can save up until I get enough to pay my fare to Texarkana, where my widowed mother lives. If Black Bill,' I goes on, looking significantly at Ogden, 'was to have come down this way—say, a month ago—and bought a little sheep-ranch and—'

" 'Stop,' says Ogden, getting out of his chair and looking pretty vicious. 'Do you mean to insinuate—'

" 'Nothing,' says I; 'no insinuations. I'm stating a hypodermical case. I say, if Black Bill had come down here and bought a sheep-ranch and hired me to Little-Boy-Blue 'em⁵ and treated me square and friendly, as you've done, he'd never have anything to fear from me. A man is a man, regardless of any complications he may have with sheep or railroad trains. Now you know where I stand.'

"Ogden looks black as camp-coffee for nine seconds, and then he laughs, amused.

" 'You'll do, Saint Clair,' says he. 'If I *was* Black Bill I wouldn't be afraid to trust you. Let's have a game or two of seven-up to-night. That is, if you don't mind playing with a train-robber.'

" 'I've told you,' says I, 'my oral sentiments, and there's no strings to 'em.'

."While I was shuffling after the first hand, I asked Ogden, as if the idea was a kind of a casualty, where he was from.

" 'Oh,' says he, 'from the Mississippi Valley.'

" 'That's a nice little place,' says I. 'I've often stopped over there. But didn't you find the sheets a little damp and the food poor? Now, I hail,' says I, 'from the Pacific Slope. Ever put up there?'

" 'Too draughty,' says Ogden. 'But if you're ever in the Middle West just mention my name, and you'll get foot-warmers and dripped coffee.'

" 'Well,' says I, 'I wasn't exactly fishing for your private telephone number and the middle name of your aunt that carried off that Cumberland Presbyterian minister. It don't matter. I just want you to know you are safe in the hands of your shepherd. Now, don't play hearts on spades, and don't get nervous.'

" 'Still harping,' says Ogden, laughing again. 'Don't you suppose that if I was Black Bill and thought you suspected me, I'd put a Winchester bullet into you and stop my nervousness if I had any?'

" 'Not any,' says I. 'A man who's got the nerve to hold up a train single-handed wouldn't do a trick like that. I've knocked about enough to know that them are the kind of men who put a value on a friend. Not that I can claim being a friend of yours, Mr. Ogden,' says I, 'being only your sheep-herder; but under more expeditious circumstances we might have been.'

" 'Forget the sheep temporarily, I beg,' says Ogden, 'and cut for deal.'

"About four days afterwards, while my muttons was nooning on the water-hole and I deep in the interstices of making a pot of coffee, up rides softly on the grass a mysterious person in the garb of the being he wished to represent. He was dressed somewhere between a Kansas City detective, Buffalo Bill, and the town dog-catcher of Baton Rouge. His chin and eye wasn't moulded on fighting lines, so I knew he was only a scout.

" 'Herdin' sheep?' he asks me.

" 'Well,' says I, 'to a man of your evident gumptional endowments, I wouldn't have the nerve to state that I am engaged in decorating old bronzes or oiling bicycle sprockets.'

" 'You don't talk or look like a sheep-herder to me,' says he.

" 'But you talk like what you look like to me,' says I.

"And then he asks me who I was working for, and I shows him Rancho Chiquito, two miles away, in the shadow of a low hill, and he tells me he's a deputy sheriff.

" 'There's a train-robber called Black Bill supposed to be somewhere in these parts,' says the scout. 'He's been traced as far as San Antonio, and may be farther. Have you seen or heard of any strangers around here during the past month?'

" 'I have not,' says I, 'except a report of one over at the Mexican quarters of Loomis' ranch, on the Frio.'

" 'What do you know about him?' asks the deputy.

" 'He's three days old,' says I.

" 'What kind of a looking man is the man you work for?' he asks. 'Does old George Ramey own this place yet? He's run sheep here for the last ten years, but never had no success.'

" 'The old man had sold out and gone West,' I tells him. 'Another sheep-fancier bought him out about a month ago.'

" 'What kind of a looking man is he?' asks the deputy again.

" 'Oh,' says I, 'a big, fat kind of a Dutchman with long whiskers and blue specs. I don't think he knows a sheep from a ground-squirrel. I guess old George soaked him pretty well on the deal,' says I.

"After indulging himself in a lot more non-communicative information and two thirds of my dinner, the deputy rides away.

"That night I mentions the matter to Ogden.

" 'They're drawing the tendrils of the octopus around Black Bill,' says I. And then I told him about the deputy sheriff, and how I'd described him to the deputy, and what the deputy said about the matter.

" 'Oh, well,' says Ogden, 'let's don't borrow any of Black Bill's troubles. We've a few of our own. Get the Bourbon out of the cupboard and we'll drink to his health—unless,' says he, with his little cackling laugh, 'you're prejudiced against train-robbers.'

" 'I'll drink,' says I, 'to any man who's a friend to a friend. And I believe that Black Bill,' I goes on, 'would be that. So here's to Black Bill, and may he have good luck.'

"And both of us drank.

"About two weeks later comes shearing-time. The sheep had to be driven up to the ranch, and a lot of frowzy-headed Mexicans would snip the fur off them with back-action scissors. So the afternoon before the barbers were to come I hustled my underdone muttons over the hill, across the dell, down by the winding brook, and up to the ranch-house, when I penned 'em in a corral and bade 'em my nightly adieus.

"I went from there to the ranch-house. I find H. Ogden, Esquire, lying asleep on his little cot bed. I guess he had been overcome by anti-insomnia or diswakefulness or some of the diseases peculiar to the sheep business. His mouth and vest were open, and he breathed like a second-hand bicycle pump. I looked at him and gave vent to just a few musings. 'Imperial Caesar,' says I, 'asleep in such a way, might shut his mouth and keep the wind away.'

"A man asleep is certainly a sight to make angels weep. What good is all his brain, muscle, backing, nerve, influence, and family connections? He's at the mercy of his enemies, and more so of his friends. And he's about as beautiful as a cab-horse leaning against the Metropolitan Opera House at 12:30 A.M. dreaming of the plains of Arabia. Now, a woman asleep you regard as different. No matter how she looks, you know it's better for all hands for her to be that way.

"Well, I took a drink of Bourbon and one for Ogden, and started in to be comfortable while he was taking his nap. He had some books on his table on indigenous subjects, such as Japan and drainage and physical culture—and some tobacco, which seemed more to the point.

"After I'd smoked a few, and listened to the sartorial breathing of H. O., I happened to look out the window toward the shearing-pens, where there was a kind of a road coming up from a kind of a road across a kind of a creek farther away.

"I saw five men riding up to the house. All of 'em carried guns across their saddles, and among 'em was the deputy that had talked to me at my camp.

"They rode up careful, in open formation, with their guns ready. I set apart with my eye the one I opinionated to be the boss muckraker of this law-and-order cavalry.

" 'Good-evening, gents,' says I. 'Won't you 'light and tie your horses?'

"The boss rides up close, and swings his gun over till the opening in it seems to cover my whole front elevation.

" 'Don't you move your hands none,' says he, 'till you and me indulge in a adequate amount of necessary conversation.'

" 'I will not,' says I. 'I am no deaf-mute, and therefore will not have to disobey your injunctions in replying.'

" 'We are on the lookout,' says he, 'for Black Bill, the man that held up the Katy for $15,000 in May. We are searching the ranches and everybody on 'em. What is your name, and what do you do on this ranch?'

" 'Captain,' says I, 'Percival Saint Clair is my occupation, and my name is sheep-herder. I've got my flock of veals—no, muttons—penned here to-night. The searchers are coming to-morrow to give them a haircut—with baa-a-rum, I suppose.'

" 'Where's the boss of this ranch?' the captain of the gang asks me.

" 'Wait just a minute, cap'n,' says I. 'Wasn't there a kind of a reward offered for the capture of this desperate character you have referred to in your preamble?'

" 'There's a thousand dollars reward offered,' says the captain, 'but it's for his capture and conviction. There don't seem to be no provision made for an informer.'

" 'It looks like it might rain in a day or so,' says I, in a tired way, looking up at the cerulean blue sky.

" 'If you know anything about the locality, disposition, or secretiveness of this here Black Bill,' says he, in a severe dialect, 'you are amiable to the law in not reporting it.'

" 'I heard a fence-rider say,' says I, in a desultory kind of voice, 'that a Mexican told a cowboy named Jake over at Pidgin's store on the Nueces that he heard that Black Bill had been seen in Matamoras by a sheepman's cousin two weeks ago.'

" 'Tell you what I'll do, Tight Mouth,' says the captain, after looking me over for bargains. 'If you put us on so we can scoop Black Bill, I'll pay you a hundred dollars out of my own—out of our own—pockets. That's liberal,' says he. 'You ain't entitled to anything. Now, what do you say?'

" 'Cash down now?' I ask.

"The captain has a sort of discussion with his helpmates, and they all produce the contents of their pockets for analysis. Out of the general results they figured up $102.30 in cash and $31 worth of plug tobacco.

" 'Come nearer, captain meeo,'* says I, 'and listen.' He so did.

" 'I am mighty poor and low down in the world,' says I. 'I am working for twelve dollars a month trying to keep a lot of animals together whose only thought seems to be to get asunder. Although,' says I, 'I regard myself as some better than the State of South Dakota, it's a come-down to a man who has heretofore regarded sheep only in the form of chops. I'm pretty far reduced in the world on account of foiled ambitions and rum and a kind of cocktail they make along the P. R. R. all the way from Scranton to Cincinnati— dry gin, French vermouth, one squeeze of a lime, and a good dash of orange bitters. If you're ever up that way, don't fail to let one try you. And, again,' says I, 'I have never yet went back on a friend. I've stayed by 'em when they had plenty, and when adversity's over-taken me I've never forsook 'em.

" 'But,' I goes on, 'this is not exactly the case of a friend. Twelve dollars a month is only bowing-acquaintance money. And I do not consider brown beans and cornbread the food of friendship. I am a poor man,' says I, 'and I have a widowed mother in Texarkana. You will find Black Bill,' says I, 'lying asleep in this house on a cot in the room to your right. He's the man you want, as I know from his words and conversation. He was in a way a friend,' I explains, 'and if I was the man I once was the entire product of the mines of Gondola would not have tempted me to betray him. But,' says I, 'every week half of the beans was wormy, and not nigh enough wood in camp.'

" 'Better go in careful, gentlemen,' says I. 'He seems impatient at times, and when you think of his late professional pursuits one would look for abrupt actions if he was come upon sudden.'

"So the whole posse unmounts and ties their horses, and unlimbers their ammunition and equipments, and tiptoes into the house. And I follows, like Delilah when she set the Philip Steins on to Samson.[6]

---

*My captain (*mio* is Spanish for "mine").

"The leader of the posse shakes Ogden and wakes him up. And then he jumps up and two more of the reward-hunters grab him. Ogden was mighty tough with all his slimness, and gives 'em as neat a single-footed tussle against odds as I ever see.

" 'What does this mean?' he says, after they had him down.

" 'You're scooped in, Mr. Black Bill,' says the captain. 'That's all.'

" 'It's an outrage,' says H. Ogden, madder yet.

" 'It was,' says the peace-and-good-will man. 'The Katy wasn't bothering you, and there's a law against monkeying with express packages.'

"And he sits on H. Ogden's stomach and goes through his pockets symptomatically and careful.

" 'I'll make you perspire for this,' says Ogden, perspiring some himself. 'I can prove who I am.'

" 'So can I,' says the captain, as he draws from H. Ogden's inside coat-pocket a handful of new bills of the Second National Bank of Espinosa City. 'Your regular engraved Tuesdays-and-Fridays visiting-card wouldn't have a louder voice in proclaiming your indemnity than this here currency. You can get up now and prepare to go with us and expatriate your sins.'

"H. Ogden gets up and fixes his necktie. He says no more after they have taken the money off of him.

" 'A well-greased idea,' says the sheriff captain, admiring, 'to slip off down here and buy a little sheep-ranch where the hand of man is seldom heard. It was the slickest hide-out I ever see,' says the captain.

"So one of the men goes to the shearing-pen and hunts up the other herder, a Mexican they call John Sallies, and he saddles Ogden's horse, and the sheriffs all ride up close around him with their guns in hand, ready to take their prisoner to town.

"Before starting, Ogden puts the ranch in John Sallies' hands and gives him orders about the shearing and where to graze the sheep, just as if he intended to be back in a few days. And a couple of hours afterward one Percival Saint Clair, an ex-sheep-herder of the Rancho Chiquito, might have been seen, with a hundred and nine dollars—wages and blood money—in his pocket, riding south on another horse belonging to said ranch."

The red-faced man paused and listened. The whistle of a coming freight-train sounded far away among the low hills.

The fat, seedy man at his side sniffed, and shook his frowzy head slowly and disparagingly.

"What is it, Snipy?" asked the other. "Got the blues again?"

"No, I ain't," said the seedy one, sniffing again. "But I don't like your talk. You and me have been friends, off and on, for fifteen year; and I never yet knew or heard of you giving anybody up to the law—not no one. And here was a man whose saleratus you had et and at whose table you had played games of cards—if casino can be so called. And yet you inform him to the law and take money for it. It never was like you, I say."

"This H. Ogden," resumed the red-faced man, "through a lawyer, proved himself free by alibis and other legal terminalities, as I so heard afterward. He never suffered no harm. He did me favors, and I hated to hand him over."

"How about the bills they found in his pocket?" asked the seedy man.

"I put 'em there," said the red-faced man, "while he was asleep, when I saw the posse riding up. I was Black Bill. Look out, Snipy, here she comes! We'll board her on the bumpers when she takes water."

—from *Options* (1909)

JEFF PETERS AS
A PERSONAL MAGNET

J eff Peters has been engaged in as many schemes for making
money as there are recipes for cooking rice in Charleston, S. C.

Best of all I like to hear him tell of his earlier days when he
sold liniments and cough cures on street corners, living hand to
mouth, heart to heart with the people, throwing heads or tails with
fortune for his last coin.

"I struck Fisher Hill, Arkansaw," said he, "in a buckskin suit,
moccasins, long hair and a thirty-carat diamond ring that I got from
an actor in Texarkana. I don't know what he ever did with the
pocket knife I swapped him for it.

"I was Dr. Waugh-hoo, the celebrated Indian medicine man. I
carried only one best bet just then, and that was Resurrection Bitters. It was made of life-giving plants and herbs accidentally discovered by Ta-qua-la, the beautiful wife of the chief of the Choctaw
Nation,[1] while gathering truck to garnish a platter of boiled dog
for the annual corn dance.

"Business hadn't been good at the last town, so I only had five
dollars. I went to the Fisher Hill druggist and he credited me for
half a gross of eight-ounce bottles and corks. I had the labels and
ingredients in my valise, left over from the last town. Life began to
look rosy again after I got in my hotel room with the water running
from the tap, and the Resurrection Bitters lining up on the table
by the dozen.

"Fake? No, sir. There was two dollars' worth of fluid extract of
cinchona* and a dime's worth of aniline† in that half-gross of bitters.

---

*The dried bark of the cinchona tree, found in South America, was once used to
treat malaria.
†Chemical base used to produce dyes.

I've gone through towns years afterwards and had folks ask for 'em again.

"I hired a wagon that night and commenced selling the bitters on Main Street. Fisher Hill was a low, malarial town; and a compound hypothetical pneumo-cardiac anti-scorbutic tonic was just what I diagnosed the crowd as needing. The bitters started off like sweetbreads-on-toast at a vegetarian dinner. I had sold two dozen at fifty cents apiece when I felt somebody pull my coat tail. I knew what that meant; so I climbed down and sneaked a five dollar bill into the hand of a man with a German silver star on his lapel.

" 'Constable,' says I, 'it's a fine night.'

" 'Have you got a city license,' he asks, 'to sell this illegitimate essence of spooju* that you flatter by the name of medicine?'

" 'I have not,' says I. 'I didn't know you had a city. If I can find it to-morrow I'll take one out if it's necessary.'

" 'I'll have to close you up till you do,' says the constable.

"I quit selling and went back to the hotel. I was talking to the landlord about it.

" 'Oh, you won't stand no show in Fisher Hill,' says he. 'Dr. Hoskins, the only doctor here, is a brother-in-law of the Mayor, and they won't allow no fake doctor to practice in town.'

" 'I don't practice medicine,' says I, 'I've got a State peddler's license, and I take out a city one wherever they demand it.'

"I went to the Mayor's office the next morning and they told me he hadn't showed up yet. They didn't know when he'd be down. So Doc Waugh-hoo hunches down again in a hotel chair and lights a jimpson-weed regalia, and waits.

"By and by a young man in a blue necktie slips into the chair next to me and asks the time.

" 'Half-past ten,' says I, 'and you are Andy Tucker. I've seen you work. Wasn't it you that put up the Great Cupid Combination package on the Southern States? Let's see, it was a Chilian diamond engagement ring, a wedding ring, a potato masher, a bottle of soothing syrup and Dorothy Vernon²—all for fifty cents.'

"Andy was pleased to hear that I remembered him. He was a

---

*Possibly O. Henry's creative takeoff on "spoof," which means hoax.

"I commenced selling the bitters on Main Street."

good street man; and he was more than that—he respected his profession, and he was satisfied with 300 per cent. profit. He had plenty of offers to go into the illegitimate drug and garden seed business; but he was never to be tempted off of the straight path.

"I wanted a partner, so Andy and me agreed to go out together. I told him about the situation in Fisher Hill and how finances was low on account of the local mixture of politics and jalap.* Andy had just got in on the train that morning. He was pretty low himself, and was going to canvass the town for a few dollars to build a new battleship by popular subscription at Eureka Springs. So we went out and sat on the porch and talked it over.

---

*A purgative drug cultivated from the root of a Mexican climbing plant.

"The next morning at eleven o'clock when I was sitting there alone, an Uncle Tom shuffles into the hotel and asked for the doctor to come and see Judge Banks, who, it seems, was the mayor and a mighty sick man.

" 'I'm no doctor,' says I. 'Why don't you go and get the doctor?'

" 'Boss,' says he, 'Doc Hoskins am done gone twenty miles in de country to see some sick persons. He's de only doctor in de town, and Massa Banks am powerful bad off. He sent me to ax you to please, suh, come.'

" 'As man to man,' says I, 'I'll go and look him over.' So I put a bottle of Resurrection Bitters in my pocket and goes up on the hill to the mayor's mansion, the finest house in town, with a mansard roof and two cast iron dogs on the lawn.

"This Mayor Banks was in bed all but his whiskers and feet. He was making internal noises that would have had everybody in San Francisco hiking for the parks. A young man was standing by the bed holding a cup of water.

" 'Doc,' says the Mayor, 'I'm awful sick. I'm about to die. Can't you do nothing for me?'

" 'Mr. Mayor,' says I, 'I'm not a regular preordained disciple of S. Q. Lapius. I never took a course in a medical college,'[3] says I. 'I've just come as a fellow man to see if I could be of assistance.'

" 'I'm deeply obliged,' says he. 'Doc Waugh-hoo, this is my nephew, Mr. Biddle. He has tried to alleviate my distress, but without success. Oh, Lordy! Ow-ow-ow! !' he sings out.

"I nods at Mr. Biddle and sets down by the bed and feels the mayor's pulse. 'Let me see your liver—your tongue, I mean,' says I. Then I turns up the lids of his eyes and looks close at the pupils of 'em.

" 'How long have you been sick?' I asked.

" 'I was taken down—ow-ouch—last night,' says the Mayor. 'Gimme something for it, doc, won't you?'

" 'Mr. Fiddle,' says I, 'raise the window shade a bit, will you?'

" 'Biddle,' says the young man. 'Do you feel like you could eat some ham and eggs, Uncle James?'

" 'Mr. Mayor,' says I, after laying my ear to his right shoulder blade and listening, 'you've got a bad attack of super-inflammation of the right clavicle of the harpsichord!'

" 'Good Lord!' says he, with a groan, 'Can't you rub something on it, or set it or anything?'

"I picks up my hat and starts for the door.

" 'You ain't going, doc?' says the Mayor with a howl. 'You ain't going away and leave me to die with this—superfluity of the clap-boards, are you?'

" 'Common humanity, Dr. Whoa-ha,' says Mr. Biddle, 'ought to prevent your deserting a fellow-human in distress.'

" 'Dr. Waugh-hoo, when you get through plowing,' says I. And then I walks back to the bed and throws back my long hair.

" 'Mr. Mayor,' says I, 'there is only one hope for you. Drugs will do you no good. But there is another power higher yet, although drugs are high enough,' says I.

" 'And what is that?' says he.

" 'Scientific demonstrations,' says I. 'The triumph of mind over sarsaparilla. The belief that there is no pain and sickness except what is produced when we ain't feeling well. Declare yourself in arrears. Demonstrate.'

" 'What is this paraphernalia you speak of, Doc?' says the Mayor. 'You ain't a Socialist, are you?'

" 'I am speaking,' says I, 'of the great doctrine of psychic finan-ciering—of the enlightened school of long-distance, sub-conscientious treatment of fallacies and meningitis—of that wonderful in-door sport known as personal magnetism.'

" 'Can you work it, doc?' asks the Mayor.

" 'I'm one of the Sole Sanhedrims[4] and Ostensible Hooplas of the Inner Pulpit,' says I. 'The lame talk and the blind rubber* when-ever I make a pass at 'em. I am a medium, a coloratura hypnotist and a spirituous control. It was only through me at the recent se-ances at Ann Arbor that the late president of the Vinegar Bitters Company could revisit the earth to communicate with his sister Jane. You see me peddling medicine on the streets,' says I, 'to the poor. I don't practice personal magnetism on them. I do not drag it in the dust,' says I, 'because they haven't got the dust.'

" 'Will you treat my case?' asks the Mayor.

---

*Onlooker; from "rubberneck."

" 'Listen,' says I. 'I've had a good deal of trouble with medical societies everywhere I've been. I don't practice medicine. But, to save your life, I'll give you the psychic treatment if you'll agree as mayor not to push the license question.'

" 'Of course I will,' says he. 'And now get to work, doc, for them pains are coming on again.'

" 'My fee will be $250.00, cure guaranteed in two treatments,' says I.

" 'All right,' says the Mayor. 'I'll pay it. I guess my life's worth that much.'

"I sat down by the bed and looked him straight in the eye.

" 'Now,' says I, 'get your mind off the disease. You ain't sick. You haven't got a heart or a clavicle or a funny bone or brains or anything. You haven't got any pain. Declare error. Now you feel the pain that you didn't have leaving, don't you?'

" 'I do feel some little better, doc,' says the Mayor, 'darned if I don't. Now state a few lies about my not having this swelling in my left side, and I think I could be propped up and have some sausage and buckwheat cakes.'

"I made a few passes with my hands.

" 'Now,' says I, 'the inflammation's gone. The right lobe of the perihelion has subsided. You're getting sleepy. You can't hold your eyes open any longer. For the present the disease is checked. Now, you are asleep.'

"The Mayor shut his eyes slowly and began to snore.

" 'You observe, Mr. Tiddle,' says I, 'the wonders of modern science.'

" 'Biddle,' says he, 'When will you give uncle the rest of the treatment, Dr. Pooh-pooh?'

" 'Waugh-hoo,' says I. 'I'll come back at eleven to-morrow. When he wakes up give him eight drops of turpentine and three pounds of steak. Good morning.'

"The next morning I went back on time. 'Well, Mr. Riddle,' says I, when he opened the bedroom door, 'and how is uncle this morning?'

" 'He seems much better,' says the young man.

"The mayor's color and pulse was fine. I gave him another treatment, and he said the last of the pain left him.

" 'Now,' says I, 'you'd better stay in bed for a day or two, and you'll be all right. It's a good thing I happened to be in Fisher Hill, Mr. Mayor,' says I, 'for all the remedies in the cornucopia that the regular schools of medicine use couldn't have saved you. And now that error has flew and pain proved a perjurer, let's allude to a cheerfuller subject—say the fee of $250. No checks, please, I hate to write my name on the back of a check almost as bad as I do on the front.'

" 'I've got the cash here,' says the mayor, pulling a pocket book from under his pillow.

"He counts out five fifty-dollar notes and holds 'em in his hand.

" 'Bring the receipt,' he says to Biddle.

"I signed the receipt and the mayor handed me the money. I put it in my inside pocket careful.

" 'Now do your duty officer,' says the mayor grinning much unlike a sick man.

"Mr. Biddle lays his hand on my arm.

" 'You're under arrest, Dr. Waugh-hoo, alias Peters,' says he, 'for practising medicine without authority under the State law.'

" 'Who are you?' I asks.

" 'I'll tell you who he is,' says Mr. Mayor, sitting up in bed. 'He's a detective employed by the State Medical Society. He's been following you over five counties. He came to me yesterday and we fixed up this scheme to catch you. I guess you won't do any more doctoring around these parts, Mr. Fakir.* What was it you said I had, doc?' the mayor laughs, 'compound—well it wasn't softening of the brain, I guess, anyway.'

" 'A detective,' says I.

" 'Correct,' says Biddle. 'I'll have to turn you over to the sheriff.'

" 'Let's see you do it,' says I, and I grabs Biddle by the throat and half throws him out the window, but he pulls a gun and sticks it under my chin, and I stand still. Then he puts handcuffs on me, and takes the money out of my pocket.

" 'I witness,' says he, 'that they're the same bills that you and I marked, Judge Banks. I'll turn them over to the sheriff when we

*O. Henry is using the word "fakir" here to mean swindler or imposter.

get to his office, and he'll send you a receipt. They'll have to be used as evidence in the case.'

" 'All right, Mr. Biddle,' says the mayor. 'And now, Doc Waugh-hoo,' he goes on, 'why don't you demonstrate? Can't you pull the cork out of your magnetism with your teeth and hocus-pocus them handcuffs off?'

" 'Come on, officer,' says I, dignified. 'I may as well make the best of it.' And then I turns to old Banks and rattles my chains.

" 'Mr. Mayor,' says I, 'the time will come soon when you'll believe that personal magnetism is a success. And you'll be sure that it succeeded in this case, too.'

"And I guess it did.

"When we got nearly to the gate, I says: 'We might meet somebody now, Andy. I reckon you better take 'em off, and—' Hey? Why, of course it was Andy Tucker. That was his scheme; and that's how we got the capital to go into business together."

—from *The Gentle Grafter* (1908)

THE MAN HIGHER UP

Across our two dishes of spaghetti, in a corner of Provenzano's restaurant, Jeff Peters was explaining to me the three kinds of graft.

Every winter Jeff comes to New York to eat spaghetti, to watch the shipping in East River from the depths of his chinchilla overcoat, and to lay in a supply of Chicago-made clothing at one of the Fulton street stores. During the other three seasons he may be found further west—his range is from Spokane to Tampa. In his profession he takes a pride which he supports and defends with a serious and unique philosophy of ethics. His profession is no new one. He is an incorporated, uncapitalized, unlimited asylum for the reception of the restless and unwise dollars of his fellowmen.

In the wilderness of stone in which Jeff seeks his annual lonely holiday he is glad to palaver* of his many adventures, as a boy will whistle after sundown in a wood. Wherefore, I mark on my calendar the time of his coming, and open a question of privilege at Provenzano's concerning the little wine-stained table in the corner between the rakish rubber plant and the framed palazzio della something on the wall.

"There are two kinds of grafts," said Jeff, "that ought to be wiped out by law. I mean Wall Street speculation, and burglary."

"Nearly everybody will agree with you as to one of them," said I, with a laugh.

"Well, burglary ought to be wiped out, too," said Jeff; and I wondered whether the laugh had been redundant.

"About three months ago," said Jeff, "it was my privilege to become familiar with a sample of each of the aforesaid branches of

---

*Jabber away, talk profusely.

illegitimate art. I was *sine qua grata* with a member of the house-breakers' union and one of the John D. Napoleons of finance[1] at the same time."

"Interesting combination," said I, with a yawn. "Did I tell you I bagged a duck and a ground-squirrel at one shot last week over in the Ramapos?" I knew well how to draw Jeff's stories.

"Let me tell you first about these barnacles that clog the wheels of society by poisoning the springs of rectitude with their upas-like* eye," said Jeff, with the pure gleam of the muck-raker in his own.

"As I said, three months ago I got into bad company. There are two times in a man's life when he does this—when he's dead broke, and when he's rich.

"Now and then the most legitimate business runs out of luck. It was out in Arkansas I made the wrong turn at a cross-road, and drives into this town of Peavine by mistake. It seems I had already assaulted and disfigured Peavine the spring of the year before. I had sold $600 worth of young fruit trees there—plums, cherries, peaches and pears. The Peaviners were keeping an eye on the country road and hoping I might pass that way again. I drove down Main street as far as the Crystal Palace drugstore before I realized I had committed ambush upon myself and my white horse Bill.

"The Peaviners took me by surprise and Bill by the bridle and began a conversation that wasn't entirely disassociated with the subject of fruit trees. A committee of 'em ran some trace-chains through the armholes of my vest, and escorted me through their gardens and orchards.

"Their fruit trees hadn't lived up to their labels. Most of 'em had turned out to be persimmons and dogwoods, with a grove or two of blackjacks and poplars. The only one that showed any signs of bearing anything was a fine young cottonwood that had put forth a hornet's nest and half of an old corset-cover.

"The Peaviners protracted our fruitless stroll to the edge of town. They took my watch and money on account; and they kept Bill and the wagon as hostages. They said the first time one of them dogwood trees put forth an Amsden's June peach I might come back

---

*The upas is a highly poisonous tree found in Asia; the word is synonymous with anything vile, poisonous, or evil.

and get my things. Then they took off the trace-chains and jerked their thumbs in the direction of the Rocky Mountains; and I struck a Lewis and Clark lope for the swollen rivers and impenetrable forests.[2]

"When I regained intellectualness I found myself walking into an unidentified town on the A., T. & S. F. railroad. The Peaviners hadn't left anything in my pockets except a plug of chewing—they wasn't after my life—and that saved it. I bit off a chunk and sits down on a pile of ties by the track to recogitate my sensations of thought and perspicacity.

"And then along comes a fast freight which slows up a little at the town; and off of it drops a black bundle that rolls for twenty yards in a cloud of dust and then gets up and begins to spit soft coal and interjections. I see it is a young man broad across the face, dressed more for Pullmans than freights, and with a cheerful kind of smile in spite of it all that made Phoebe Snow's* job look like a chimney-sweep's.

" 'Fall off?' says I.

" 'Nunk,' says he. 'Got off. Arrived at my destination. What town is this?'

" 'Haven't looked it up on the map yet,' says I. 'I got in about five minutes before you did. How does it strike you?'

" 'Hard,' says he, twisting one of his arms around. 'I believe that shoulder—no, it's all right.'

"He stoops over to brush the dust off his clothes, when out of his pocket drops a fine, nine-inch burglar's steel jimmy. He picks it up and looks at me sharp, and then grins and holds out his hand.

" 'Brother,' says he, 'greetings. Didn't I see you in Southern Missouri last summer selling colored sand at half-a-dollar a teaspoonful to put into lamps to keep the oil from exploding?'

" 'Oil,' says I, 'never explodes. It's the gas that forms that explodes.' But I shakes hands with him, anyway.

" 'My name's Bill Bassett,' says he to me, 'and if you'll call it professional pride instead of conceit, I'll inform you that you have

---

*Phoebe Snow was an image of a woman in a white dress, used in early twentieth-century railroad advertisements to show that railroad travel was clean.

the pleasure of meeting the best burglar that ever set a gum-shoe on ground drained by the Mississippi River.'

"Well, me and this Bill Bassett sits on the ties and exchanges brags as artists in kindred lines will do. It seems he didn't have a cent, either, and we went into close caucus. He explained why an able burglar sometimes had to travel on freights by telling me that a servant girl had played him false in Little Rock, and he was making a quick get-away.

" 'It's part of my business,' says Bill Bassett, 'to play up to the ruffles* when I want to make a riffle as Raffles. 'Tis loves that makes the bit go 'round. Show me a house with the swag in it and a pretty parlor-maid, and you might as well call the silver melted down and sold, and me spilling truffles and that Château stuff on the napkin under my chin, while the police are calling it an inside job just because the old lady's nephew teaches a Bible class. I first make an impression on the girl,' says Bill, 'and when she lets me inside I make an impression on the locks. But this one in Little Rock done me,' says he. 'She saw me taking a trolley ride with another girl, and when I came 'round on the night she was to leave the door open for me it was fast. And I had keys made for the doors upstairs. But, no sir. She had sure cut off my locks. She was a Delilah,'³ says Bill Bassett.

"It seems that Bill tried to break in anyhow with his jimmy, but the girl emitted a succession of bravura noises like the top-riders of a tally-ho,† and Bill had to take all the hurdles between there and the depot. As he had no baggage they tried hard to check his departure, but he made a train that was just pulling out.

" 'Well,' says Bill Bassett, when we had exchanged memoirs of our dead lives, 'I could eat. This town don't look like it was kept under a Yale lock. Suppose we commit some mild atrocity that will bring in temporary expense money. I don't suppose you've brought along any hair tonic or rolled gold watch-chains, or similar law-defying swindles that you could sell on the plaza to the pikers of the paretic populace, have you?'

" 'No,' says I, 'I left an elegant line of Patagonian diamond ear-

---

*Women's skirts; meaning play up to the women.
†In deer or fox hunting, the cry raised upon sighting the prey.

rings and rainy-day sunbursts in my valise at Peavine. But they're to stay there till some of them black-gum trees begin to glut the market with yellow clings and Japanese plums. I reckon we can't count on them unless we take Luther Burbank in for a partner.'[4]

" 'Very well,' says Bassett, 'we'll do the best we can. Maybe after dark I'll borrow a hairpin from some lady, and open the Farmers and Drovers Marine Bank with it.'

"While we were talking, up pulls a passenger train to the depot near by. A person in a high hat gets off on the wrong side of the train and comes tripping down the track towards us. He was a little, fat man with a big nose and rat's eyes, but dressed expensive, and carrying a hand-satchel careful, as if it had eggs or railroad bonds in it. He passes by us and keeps on down the track, not appearing to notice the town.

" 'Come on,' says Bill Bassett to me, starting after him.

" 'Where?' I asks.

" 'Lordy!' says Bill, 'had you forgot you was in the desert? Didn't you see Colonel Manna drop down right before your eyes? Don't you hear the rustling of General Raven's wings? I'm surprised at you, Elijah.'[5]

"We overtook the stranger in the edge of some woods, and, as it was after sun-down and in a quiet place, nobody saw us stop him. Bill takes the silk hat off the man's head and brushes it with his sleeve and puts it back.

" 'What does this mean, sir?' says the man.

" 'When I wore one of these,' says Bill, 'and felt embarrassed, I always done that. Not having one now I had to use yours. I hardly know how to begin, sir, in explaining our business with you, but I guess we'll try your pockets first.'

"Bill Bassett felt in all of them, and looked disgusted.

" 'Not even a watch,' he says. 'Ain't you ashamed of yourself, you whited sculpture? Going about dressed like a head-waiter, and financed like a Count! You haven't even got carfare. What did you do with your transfer?'

"The man speaks up and says he has no assets or valuables of any sort. But Bassett takes his hand-satchel and opens it. Out comes some collars and socks and a half a page of a newspaper clipped out. Bill reads the clipping careful, and holds out his hand to the held-up party.

" 'Brother,' says he, 'greetings! Accept the apologies of friends. I am Bill Bassett, the burglar. Mr. Peters, you must make the acquaintance of Mr. Alfred E. Ricks. Shake hands. Mr. Peters,' says Bill, 'stands about halfway between me and you, Mr. Ricks, in the line of havoc and corruption. He always gives something for the money he gets. I'm glad to meet you, Mr. Ricks—you and Mr. Peters. This is the first time I ever attended a full gathering of the National Synod of Sharks—housebreaking, swindling, and financiering all represented. Please examine Mr. Rick's credentials, Mr. Peters.'

"The piece of newspaper that Bill Bassett handed me had a good picture of this Ricks on it. It was a Chicago paper, and it had obloquies of Ricks in every paragraph. By reading it over I harvested the intelligence that said alleged Ricks had laid off all that portion of the State of Florida that lies under water into town lots and sold 'em to alleged innocent investors from his magnificently furnished offices in Chicago. After he had taken in a hundred thousand or so dollars one of these fussy purchasers that are always making trouble (I've had 'em actually try gold watches I've sold 'em with acid)* took a cheap excursion down to the land where it is always just before supper to look at his lot and see if it didn't need a new paling or two on the fence, and market a few lemons in time for the Christmas present trade. He hires a surveyor to find his lot for him. They run the line out and find the flourishing town of Paradise Hollow, so advertised, to be about 40 rods and 16 poles S., 27° E. of the middle of Lake Okeechobee.[6] This man's lot was under thirty-six feet of water, and, besides, had been preëmpted so long by the alligators and gars that his title looked fishy.

"Naturally, the man goes back to Chicago and makes it as hot for Alfred E. Ricks as the morning after a prediction of snow by the weather bureau. Ricks defied the allegation, but he couldn't deny the alligators. One morning the papers came out with a column about it, and Ricks come out by the fire-escape. It seems the

---

*An acid test to determine if the gold is real.

alleged authorities had beat him to the safe-deposit box where he kept his winnings, and Ricks has to westward ho! with only feet-wear and a dozen 15^1/$_2$ English pokes* in his shopping bag. He happened to have some mileage left in his book, and that took him as far as the town in the wilderness where he was spilled out on me and Bill Bassett as Elijah III. with not a raven in sight for any of us.

"Then this Alfred E. Ricks lets out a squeak that he is hungry, too, and denies the hypothesis that he is good for the value, let alone the price, of a meal. And so, there was the three of us, representing, if we had a mind to draw syllogisms and parabolas, labor and trade and capital. Now, when trade has no capital there isn't a dicker to be made. And when capital has no money there's a stagnation in steak and onions. That put it up to the man with the jimmy.

" 'Brother bushrangers,' says Bill Bassett, 'never yet, in trouble, did I desert a pal. Hard by, in yon wood, I seem to see unfurnished lodgings. Let us go there and wait till dark.'

"There was an old, deserted cabin in the grove, and we three took possession of it. After dark Bill Bassett tells us to wait, and goes out for half an hour. He comes back with a armful of bread and spareribs and pies.

" 'Panhandled 'em at a farmhouse on Washita Avenue,' says he. 'Eat, drink and be leary.'

"The full moon was coming up bright, so we sat on the floor of the cabin and ate in the light of it. And this Bill Bassett begins to brag.

" 'Sometimes,' says he, with his mouth full of country produce, 'I lose all patience with you people that think you are higher up in the profession than I am. Now, what could either of you have done in the present emergency to set us on our feet again? Could you do it, Ricksy?'

" 'I must confess, Mr. Bassett,' says Ricks, speaking nearly inaudible out of a slice of pie, 'that at this immediate juncture I could not, perhaps, promote an enterprise to relieve the situation. Large

---

*A "poke" is a projecting brim on a woman's bonnet; O. Henry could be using the word to refer to collars.

operations, such as I direct, naturally require careful preparation in advance. I—'

" 'I know, Ricksy,' breaks in Bill Bassett. 'You needn't finish. You need $500 to make the first payment on a blond typewriter, and four roomsful of quartered oak furniture. And you need $500 more for advertising contracts. And you need two weeks' time for the fish to begin to bite. Your line of relief would be about as useful in an emergency as advocating municipal ownership to cure a man suffocated by eighty-cent gas. And your graft ain't much swifter, Brother Peters,' he winds up.

" 'Oh,' says I, 'I haven't seen you turn anything into gold with your wand yet, Mr. Good Fairy. 'Most anybody could rub the magic ring for a little left-over victuals.'

" 'That was only getting the pumpkin ready,' says Bassett, braggy and cheerful. 'The coach and six'll drive up to the door before you know it, Miss Cinderella. Maybe you've got some scheme under your sleeve-holders that will give us a start.'

" 'Son,' says I, 'I'm fifteen years older than you are, and young enough yet to take out an endowment policy. I've been broke before. We can see the lights of that town not half a mile away. I learned under Montague Silver, the greatest street man that ever spoke from a wagon. There are hundreds of men walking those streets this moment with grease spots on their clothes. Give me a gasoline lamp, a dry-goods box, and a two-dollar bar of white castile soap, cut into little—'

" 'Where's your two dollars?' snickered Bill Bassett into my discourse. There was no use arguing with that burglar.

" 'No,' he goes on; 'you're both babes-in-the-wood. Finance has closed the mahogany desk, and trade has put the shutters up. Both of you look to labor to start the wheels going. All right. You admit it. To-night I'll show you what Bill Bassett can do.'

"Bassett tells me and Ricks not to leave the cabin till he comes back, even if it's daylight, and then he starts off toward town, whistling gay.

"This Alfred E. Ricks pulls off his shoes and his coat, lays a silk handkerchief over his hat, and lays down on the floor.

" 'I think I will endeavor to secure a little slumber,' he squeaks. 'The day has been fatiguing. Good-night, my dear Mr. Peters.'

" 'My regards to Morpheus,' says I. 'I think I'll sit up a while.'

"About two o'clock, as near as I could guess by my watch in Peavine, home comes our laboring man and kicks up Ricks, and calls us to the streak of bright moonlight shining in the cabin door. Then he spreads out five packages of one thousand dollars each on the floor, and begins to cackle over the nest-egg like a hen.

" 'I'll tell you a few things about that town,' says he. 'It's named Rocky Springs, and they're building a Masonic temple,[7] and it looks like the Democratic candidate for mayor is going to get soaked by a Pop,* and Judge Tucker's wife, who has been down with pleurisy, is some better. I had a talk on these liliputian[†] thesises before I could get a siphon in the fountain of knowledge that I was after. And there's a bank there called the Lumberman's Fidelity and Plowman's Savings Institution. It closed for business yesterday with $23,000 cash on hand. It will open this morning with $18,000— all silver—that's the reason I didn't bring more. There you are, trade and capital. Now, will you be bad?'

" 'My young friend,' says Alfred E. Ricks, holding up his hands, 'have you robbed this bank? Dear me, dear me!'

" 'You couldn't call it that,' says Bassett. ' "Robbing" sounds harsh. All I had to do was to find out what street it was on. That town is so quiet that I could stand on the corner and hear the tumblers clicking in that safe lock—"right to 45; left twice to 80; right once to 60; left to 15"—as plain as the Yale captain giving orders in the football dialect. Now, boys,' says Bassett, 'this is an early rising town. They tell me the citizens are all up and stirring before daylight. I asked what for, and they said because breakfast was ready at that time. And what of merry Robin Hood? It must be Yoicks! and away with the tinkers' chorus. I'll stake you. How much do you want? Speak up. Capital.'

" 'My dear young friend,' says this ground squirrel of a Ricks, standing on his hind legs and juggling nuts in his paws, 'I have friends in Denver who would assist me. If I had a hundred dollars I—'

---

*Member of the Populist Party, founded in America in 1892.

†Small; the word refers to the race of six-inch-tall pygmies in Jonathan Swift's satirical work *Gulliver's Travels* (1726).

"Bassett unpins a package of the currency and throws five twenties to Ricks.

" 'Trade, how much?' he says to me.

" 'Put your money up, Labor,' says I. 'I never yet drew upon honest toil for its hard-earned pittance. The dollars I get are surplus ones that are burning the pockets of damfools and greenhorns.* When I stand on a street corner and sell a solid gold diamond ring to a yap for $3.00, I make just $2.60. And I know he's going to give it to a girl in return for all the benefits accruing from a $125.00 ring. His profits are $122.00. Which of us is the biggest fakir?'†

" 'And when you sell a poor woman a pinch of sand for fifty cents to keep her lamp from exploding,' says Bassett, 'what do you figure her gross earnings to be, with sand at forty cents a ton?'

" 'Listen,' says I. 'I instruct her to keep her lamp clean and well filled. If she does that it can't burst. And with the sand in it she knows it can't, and she don't worry. It's a kind of Industrial Christian Science. She pays fifty cents, and gets both Rockefeller and Mrs. Eddy on the job.[8] It ain't everybody that can let the gold-dust twins do their work.'

"Alfred E. Ricks all but licks the dust off of Bill Bassett's shoes.

" 'My dear young friend,' says he, 'I will never forget your generosity. Heaven will reward you. But let me implore you to turn from your ways of violence and crime.'

" 'Mousie,' says Bill, 'the hole in the wainscoting‡ for yours. Your dogmas and inculcations sound to me like the last words of a bicycle pump. What has your high moral, elevator-service system of pillage brought you to? Penuriousness and want. Even Brother Peters, who insists upon contaminating the art of robbery with theories of commerce and trade, admitted he was on the lift. Both of you live by the gilded rule. Brother Peters,' says Bill, 'you'd better choose a slice of this embalmed currency. You're welcome.'

"I told Bill Bassett once more to put his money in his pocket. I never had the respect for burglary that some people have. I always

---

*Inexperienced people, ignoramuses.
†Swindler; also, a poor man.
‡Wood paneling on a wall.

gave something for the money I took, even if it was only some little trifle for a souvenir to remind 'em not to get caught again.

"And then Alfred E. Ricks grovels at Bill's feet again, and bids us adieu. He says he will have a team at a farmhouse, and drive to the station below, and take the train for Denver. It salubrified the atmosphere when that lamentable boll-worm took his departure. He was a disgrace to every non-industrial profession in the country. With all his big schemes and fine offices he had wound up unable even to get an honest meal except by the kindness of a strange and maybe unscrupulous burglar. I was glad to see him go, though I felt a little sorry for him, now that he was ruined forever. What could such a man do without a big capital to work with? Why, Alfred E. Ricks, as we left him, was as helpless as a turtle on its back. He couldn't have worked a scheme to beat a little girl out of a penny slate-pencil.

"When me and Bill Bassett was left alone I did a little sleight-of mind turn in my head with a trade secret at the end of it. Thinks I, I'll show this Mr. Burglar Man the difference between business and labor. He had hurt some of my professional self-adulation by casting his Persians upon commerce and trade.

" 'I won't take any of your money as a gift, Mr. Bassett,' says I to him, 'but if you'll pay my expenses as a traveling companion until we get out of the danger zone of the immoral deficit you have caused in this town's finances to-night, I'll be obliged.'

"Bill Bassett agreed to that, and we hiked westward as soon as we could catch a safe train.

"When we got to a town in Arizona called Los Perros I suggested that we once more try our luck on terra-cotta. That was the home of Montague Silver, my old instructor, now retired from business. I knew Monty would stake me to web money if I could show him a fly buzzing 'round in the locality. Bill Bassett said all towns looked alike to him as he worked mainly in the dark. So we got off the train in Los Perros, a fine little town in the silver region.

"I had an elegant little sure thing in the way of a commercial slungshot that I intended to hit Bassett behind the ear with. I wasn't going to take his money while he was asleep, but I was going to leave him with a lottery ticket that would represent in experience to him $4,755—I think that was the amount he had when we got off the train. But the first time I hinted to him about an investment, he turns on me and disencumbers himself of the following terms and expressions.

" 'Brother Peters,' says he, 'it ain't a bad idea to go into an enterprise of some kind, as you suggest. I think I will. But if I do it will be such a cold proposition that nobody but Robert E. Peary and Charlie Fairbanks will be able to sit on the board of directors.'⁹

" 'I thought you might want to turn your money over,' says I.

" 'I do,' says he, 'frequently. I can't sleep on one side all night. I'll tell you, Brother Peters,' says he, 'I'm going to start a poker room. I don't seem to care for the humdrum in swindling, such as peddling egg-beaters and working off breakfast food on Barnum and Bailey for sawdust to strew in their circus rings. But the gambling business,' says he, 'from the profitable side of the table is a good compromise between swiping silver spoons and selling penwipers at a Waldorf-Astoria* charity bazar.'

" 'Then,' says I, 'Mr. Bassett, you don't care to talk over my little business proposition?'

" 'Why,' says he, 'do you know, you can't get a Pasteur institute to start up within fifty miles of where I live.¹⁰ I bite so seldom.'

"So, Bassett rents a room over a saloon and looks around for some furniture and chromos. The same night I went to Monty Silver's house, and he let me have $200 on my prospects. Then I went to the only store in Los Perros that sold playing cards and bought every deck in the house. The next morning when the store opened I was there bringing all the cards back with me. I said that my partner that was going to back me in the game had changed his mind; and I wanted to sell the cards back again. The storekeeper took 'em at half price.

"Yes, I was seventy-five dollars loser up to that time. But while I had the cards that night I marked every one in every deck. That was labor. And then trade and commerce had their innings, and the bread I had cast upon the waters began to come back in the form of cottage pudding with wine sauce.

"Of course I was among the first to buy chips at Bill Bassett's

---

*Expensive hotel in Manhattan.

game. He had bought the only cards there was to be had in town; and I knew the back of every one of them better than I know the back of my head when the barber shows me my haircut in the two mirrors.

"When the game closed I had the five thousand and a few odd dollars, and all Bill Bassett had was the wanderlust and a black cat he had bought for a mascot. Bill shook hands with me when I left.

" 'Brother Peters,' says he, 'I have no business being in business. I was preordained to labor. When a No. 1 burglar tries to make a James out of his jimmy* he perpetrates an improfundity. You have a well-oiled and efficacious system of luck at cards,' says he. 'Peace go with you.' And I never afterward sees Bill Bassett again."

"Well, Jeff," said I, when the Autolycan adventurer[11] seemed to have divulged the gist of his tale, "I hope you took care of the money. That would be a respecta—that is a considerable working capital if you should choose some day to settle down to some sort of regular business."

"Me?" said Jeff, virtuously. "You can bet I've taken care of that five thousand."

He tapped his coat over the region of his chest exultantly.

"Gold mining stock," he explained, "every cent of it. Shares par value one dollar. Bound to go up 500 per cent. within a year. Non-assessable. The Blue Gopher Mine. Just discovered a month ago. Better get in yourself if you've any spare dollars on hand."

"Sometimes," said I, "these mines are not—"

"Oh, this one's solid as an old goose," said Jeff. "Fifty thousand dollars' worth of ore in sight, and 10 per cent monthly earnings guaranteed."

He drew a long envelope from his pocket and cast it on the table.

"Always carry it with me," said he. "So the burglar can't corrupt or the capitalist break in and water it."

I looked at the beautifully engraved certificate of stock.

"In Colorado, I see," said I. "And, by the way, Jeff, what was

---

*Besides a nickname for James, a jimmy is a crowbar used by burglars; Mr. Bassett is saying it is not possible for a burglar such as himself to become respectable.

the name of the little man who went to Denver—the one you and Bill met at the station?"

"Alfred E. Ricks," said Jeff, "was the toad's designation."

"I see," said I, "the president of this mining company signs himself A. L. Fredericks. I was wondering—"

"Let me see that stock," said Jeff quickly, almost snatching it from me.

To mitigate, even though slightly, the embarrassment I summoned the waiter and ordered another bottle of the Barbera.* I thought it was the least I could do.

—from *The Gentle Grafter* (1908)

---

*A red wine.

THE HANDBOOK OF HYMEN

'T is the opinion of myself, Sanderson Pratt, who sets this down, that the educational system of the United States should be in the hands of the weather bureau. I can give you good reasons for it; and you can't tell me why our college professors shouldn't be transferred to the meteorological department. They have been learned to read; and they could very easily glance at the morning papers and then wire in to the main office what kind of weather to expect. But there's the other side of the proposition. I am going on to tell you how the weather furnished me and Idaho Green with an elegant education.

We was up in the Bitter Root Mountains over the Montana line prospecting for gold. A chin-whiskered man in Walla-Walla,[1] carrying a line of hope as excess baggage, had grubstaked* us; and there we was in the foothills pecking away, with enough grub on hand to last an army through a peace conference.

Along one day comes a mail-rider over the mountains from Carlos, and stops to eat three cans of green-gages, and leave us a newspaper of modern date. This paper prints a system of premonitions of the weather, and the card it dealt Bitter Root Mountains from the bottom of the deck was "warmer and fair, with light westerly breezes."

That evening it began to snow, with the wind strong in the cast. Me and Idaho moved camp into an old empty cabin higher up the mountain, thinking it was only a November flurry. But after falling three foot on a level it went to work in earnest; and we knew we was snowed in. We got in plenty of firewood before it got deep,

---

*Provided materials or funds in return for a share of profits; this word was coined during the Gold Rush; later in the paragraph "grub" is used as a slang word for food.

and we had grub enough for two months, so we let the elements rage and cut up all they thought proper.

If you want to instigate the art of manslaughter just shut two men up in a eighteen by twenty-foot cabin for a month. Human nature won't stand it.

When the first snowflakes fell me and Idaho Green laughed at each other's jokes and praised the stuff we turned out of a skillet and called bread. At the end of three weeks Idaho makes this kind of a edict to me. Says he:

"I never exactly heard sour milk dropping out of a balloon on the bottom of a tin pan, but I have an idea it would be music of the spears compared to this attenuated stream of asphyxiated thought that emanates out of your organs of conversation. The kind of half-masticated noises that you emit every day puts me in mind of a cow's cud, only she's lady enough to keep hers to herself, and you ain't."

"Mr. Green," says I, "you having been a friend of mine once, I have some hesitations in confessing to you that if I had my choice for society between you and a common yellow, three-legged cur pup, one of the inmates of this here cabin would be wagging a tail just at present."

This way we goes on for two or three days, and then we quits speaking to one another. We divides up the cooking implements, and Idaho cooks his grub on one side of the fireplace, and me on the other. The snow is up to the windows, and we have to keep a fire all day.

You see me and Idaho never had any education beyond reading and doing "if John had three apples and James five" on a slate. We never felt any special need for a university degree, though we had acquired a species of intrinsic intelligence in knocking around the world that we could use in emergencies. But, snowbound in that cabin in the Bitter Roots, we felt for the first time that if we had studied Homer[2] or Greek and fractions and the higher branches of information, we'd have had some resources in the line of meditation and private thought. I've seen them Eastern college fellows working in camps all through the West, and I never noticed but what education was less of a drawback to 'em than you would think. Why, once over on Snake River, when Andrew McWilliams' saddle horse

got the botts* he sent a buckboard ten miles for one of these strangers that claimed to be a botanist. But that horse died.

One morning Idaho was poking around with a stick on top of
a little shelf that was too high to reach. Two books fell down to
the floor. I started toward 'em, but caught Idaho's eye. He speaks
for the first time in a week.

"Don't burn your fingers," says he. "In spite of the fact that you're
only fit to be the companion of a sleeping mud-turtle, I'll give you
a square deal. And that's more than your parents did when they
turned you loose in the world with the sociability of a rattlesnake
and the bedside manner of a frozen turnip. I'll play you a game of
seven-up, the winner to pick up his choice of the book, the loser
to take the other."

We played; and Idaho won. He picked up his book; and I took
mine. Then each of us got on his side of the house and went to
reading.

I never was as glad to see a ten-ounce nugget as I was that book.
And Idaho looked at his like a kid looks at a stick of candy.

Mine was a little book about five by six inches called "Herkimer's
Handbook of Indispensable Information."† I may be wrong, but I
think that was the greatest book that ever was written. I've got it
to-day; and I can stump you or any man fifty times in five minutes
with the information in it. Talk about Solomon[3] or the New York
Tribune! Herkimer had cases on both of 'em. That man must have
put in fifty years and travelled a million miles to find out all that
stuff. There was the population of all cities in it, and the way to
tell a girl's age, and the number of teeth a camel has. It told you
the longest tunnel in the world, the number of the stars, how long
it takes for chicken pox to break out, what a lady's neck ought to
measure, the veto powers of Governors, the dates of the Roman
aqueducts, how many pounds of rice going without three beers a
day would buy, the average annual temperature of Augusta, Maine,
the quantity of seed required to plant an acre of carrots in drills,
antidotes for poisons, the number of hairs on a blond lady's head,
how to preserve eggs, the height of all the mountains in the world,

---

*Parasitic worms or maggots.
†No such book exists.

and the dates of all wars and battles, and how to restore drowned persons, and sunstroke, and the number of tacks in a pound, and how to make dynamite and flowers and beds, and what to do before the doctor comes—and a hundred times as many things besides. If there was anything Herkimer didn't know I didn't miss it out of the book.

I sat and read that book for four hours. All the wonders of education was compressed in it. I forgot the snow, and I forgot that me and old Idaho was on the outs. He was sitting still on a stool reading away with a kind of partly soft and partly mysterious look shining through his tan-bark whiskers.

"Idaho," says I, "what kind of a book is yours?"

Idaho must have forgot, too, for he answered moderate, without any slander or malignity.

"Why," says he, "this here seems to be a volume by Homer K. M."[4]

"Homer K. M. what?" I asks.

"Why, just Homer K. M.," says he.

"You're a liar," says I, a little riled that Idaho should try to put me up a tree. "No man is going 'round signing books with his initials. If it's Homer K. M. Spoopendyke, or Homer K. M. McSweeney, or Homer K. M. Jones, why don't you say so like a man instead of biting off the end of it like a calf chewing off the tail of a shirt on a clothes-line?"

"I put it to you straight, Sandy," says Idaho, quiet. "It's a poem book," says he, "by Homer K. M. I couldn't get colour out of it at first, but there's a vein if you follow it up. I wouldn't have missed this book for a pair of red blankets."

"You're welcome to it," says I. "What I want is a disinterested statement of facts for the mind to work on, and that's what I seem to find in the book I've drawn."

"What you've got," says Idaho, "is statistics, the lowest grade of information that exists. They'll poison your mind. Give me old K. M.'s system of surmises. He seems to be a kind of a wine agent. His regular toast is 'nothing doing,' and he seems to have a grouch, but he keeps it so well lubricated with booze that his worst kicks sound like an invitation to split a quart. But it's poetry," says Idaho, "and I have sensations of scorn for that truck of yours that tries to convey sense in feet and inches. When it comes to explaining the instinct of philosophy through the art of nature, old K. M. has got your man beat by drills, rows, paragraphs, chest measurement, and average annual rainfall."

So that's the way me and Idaho had it. Day and night all the excitement we got was studying our books. That snowstorm sure fixed us with a fine lot of attainments apiece. By the time the snow melted, if you had stepped up to me suddenly and said: "Sanderson Pratt, what would it cost per square foot to lay a roof with twenty by twenty-eight tin at nine dollars and fifty cents per box?" I'd have told you as quick as light could travel the length of a spade handle at the rate of one hundred and ninety-two thousand miles per second. How many can do it? You wake up 'most any man you know in the middle of the night, and ask him quick to tell you the number of bones in the human skeleton exclusive of the teeth, or what percentage of the vote of the Nebraska Legislature overrules a veto. Will he tell you? Try him and see.

About what benefit Idaho got out of his poetry book I didn't exactly know. Idaho boosted the wine-agent every time he opened his mouth; but I wasn't so sure.

This Homer K. M., from what leaked out of his libretto through Idaho, seemed to me to be a kind of a dog who looked at life like it was a tin can tied to his tail. After running himself half to death, he sits down, hangs his tongue out, and looks at the can and says:

"Oh, well, since we can't shake the growler, let's get it filled at the corner, and all have a drink on me."

Besides that, it seems he was a Persian; and I never hear of Persia producing anything worth mentioning unless it was Turkish rugs and Maltese cats.

That spring me and Idaho struck pay ore. It was a habit of ours to sell out quick and keep moving. We unloaded on our grubstaker for eight thousand dollars apiece; and then we drifted down to this little town of Rosa, on the Salmon River, to rest up, and get some human grub, and have our whiskers harvested.

Rosa was no mining-camp. It laid in the valley, and was as free of uproar and pestilence as one of them rural towns in the country. There was a three-mile trolley line champing its bit in the environs; and me and Idaho spent a week riding on one of the cars, dropping off of nights at the Sunset View Hotel. Being now well read as well as travelled, we was soon *pro re nata** with the best society in Rosa, and was invited out to the most dressed-up and high-toned entertainments. It was at a piano recital and quail-eating contest in the city hall, for the benefit of the fire company, that me and Idaho first met Mrs. De Ormond Sampson, the queen of Rosa society.

Mrs. Sampson was a widow, and owned the only two-story house in town. It was painted yellow, and whichever way you looked from you could see it as plain as egg on the chin of an O'Grady on a Friday. Twenty-two men in Rosa besides me and Idaho was trying to stake a claim on that yellow house.

There was a dance after the song books and quail bones had been raked out of the Hall. Twenty-three of the bunch galloped over to Mrs. Sampson and asked for a dance. I side-stepped the two-step, and asked permission to escort her home. That's where I made a hit.

On the way home says she:

"Ain't the stars lovely and bright to-night, Mr. Pratt?"

"For the chance they've got," says I, "they're humping[†] themselves in a mighty creditable way. That big one you see is sixty-six billions of miles distant. It took thirty-six years for its light to reach us. With an eighteen-foot telescope you can see forty-three millions of 'em, including them of the thirteenth magnitude, which, if one was to go out now, you would keep on seeing it for twenty-seven hundred years."

"My!" says Mrs. Sampson. "I never knew that before. How warm it is! I'm as damp as I can be from dancing so much."

"That's easy to account for," says I, "when you happen to know that you've got two million sweat-glands working all at once. If every one of your perspiratory ducts, which are a quarter of an inch long, was placed end to end, they would reach a distance of seven miles."

"Lawsy!" says Mrs. Sampson. "It sounds like an irrigation ditch

---

*For an occasion that has arisen; as needed (Latin); but this is probably not the meaning Mr. Pratt is trying to convey; O. Henry is playing with the similar-sounding Latin phrase *persona grata*, which means "a welcome person."
†Carrying.

you was describing, Mr. Pratt. How do you get all this knowledge of information?"

"From observation, Mrs. Sampson," I tells her. "I keep my eyes open when I go about the world."

"Mr. Pratt," says she, "I always did admire a man of education. There are so few scholars among the sap-headed plug-uglies of this town that it is a real pleasure to converse with a gentleman of culture. I'd be gratified to have you call at my house whenever you feel so inclined."

And that was the way I got the goodwill of the lady in the yellow house. Every Tuesday and Friday evenings I used to go there and tell her about the wonders of the universe as discovered, tabulated, and compiled from nature by Herkimer. Idaho and the other gay Lutherans of the town got every minute of the rest of the week that they could.

I never imagined that Idaho was trying to work on Mrs. Sampson with old K. M.'s rules of courtship till one afternoon when I was on my way over to take her a basket of wild hog-plums. I met the lady coming down the lane that led to her house. Her eyes was snapping, and her hat made a dangerous dip over one eye.

"Mr. Pratt," she opens up, "this Mr. Green is a friend of yours, I believe."

"For nine years," says I.

"Cut him out," says she. "He's no gentleman!"

"Why ma'am," says I, "he's a plain incumbent of the mountains, with asperities and the usual failings of a spendthrift and a liar, but I never on the most momentous occasion had the heart to deny that he was a gentleman. It may be that in haberdashery and the sense of arrogance and display Idaho offends the eye, but inside, ma'am, I've found him impervious to the lower grades of crime and obesity. After nine years of Idaho's society, Mrs. Sampson," I winds up, "I should hate to impute him, and I should hate to see him imputed."

"It's right plausible of you, Mr. Pratt," says Mrs. Sampson, "to take up the curmudgeons in your friend's behalf; but it don't alter the fact that he has made proposals to me sufficiently obnoxious to ruffle the ignominy of any lady."

"Why, now, now, now!" says I. "Old Idaho do that! I could

believe it of myself sooner. I never knew but one thing to deride in him; and a blizzard was responsible for that. Once while we was snowbound in the mountains he became a prey to a kind of spurious and uneven poetry, which may have corrupted his demeanour."

"It has," says Mrs. Sampson. "Ever since I knew him he has been reciting to me a lot of irreligious rhymes by some person he calls Ruby Ott,* and who is no better than she should be, if you judge by her poetry."

"Then Idaho has struck a new book," says I, "for the one he had was by a man who writes under the *nom de plume*† of K. M."

"He'd better have stuck to it," says Mrs. Sampson, "whatever it was. And to-day he caps the vortex. I get a bunch of flowers from him, and on 'em is pinned a note. Now, Mr. Pratt, you know a lady when you see her; and you know how I stand in Rosa society. Do you think for a moment that I'd skip out to the woods with a man along with a jug of wine and a loaf of bread, and go singing and cavorting up and down under the trees with him? I take a little claret with my meals, but I'm not in the habit of packing a jug of it into the brush and raising Cain⁵ in any such style as that. And of course he'd bring his book of verses along, too. He said so. Let him go on his scandalous picnics alone! Or let him take his Ruby Ott with him. I reckon she wouldn't kick unless it was on account of there being too much bread along. And what do you think of your gentleman friend now, Mr. Pratt?"

"Well, 'm," says I, "it may be that Idaho's invitation was a kind of poetry, and meant no harm. May be it belonged to the class of rhymes they call figurative. They offend law and order, but they get sent through the mails on the grounds that they mean something that they don't say. I'd be glad on Idaho's account if you'd overlook it," says I, "and let us extricate our minds from the low regions of poetry to the higher planes of fact and fancy. On a beautiful afternoon like this, Mrs. Sampson," I goes on, "we should let our thoughts dwell accordingly. Though it is warm here, we should remember that at the equator the line of perpetual frost is at an

---

*Phonetic writing of *Rubaiyat*, the collection of poems by Omar Khayyám (see endnote 4 for this story).
†Pen name (French).

altitude of fifteen thousand feet. Between the latitudes of forty degrees and forty-nine degrees it is from four thousand to nine thousand feet."

"Oh, Mr. Pratt," says Mrs. Sampson, "it's such a comfort to hear
you say them beautiful facts after getting such a jar from that minx
of a Ruby's poetry!"

"Let us sit on this log at the roadside," says I, "and forget the
inhumanity and ribaldry of the poets. It is in the glorious columns
of ascertained facts and legalised measures that beauty is to be
found. In this very log we sit upon, Mrs. Sampson," says I, "is
statistics more wonderful than any poem. The rings show it was
sixty years old. At the depth of two thousand feet it would become
coal in three thousand years. The deepest coal mine in the world
is at Killingworth, near Newcastle. A box four feet long, three feet
wide, and two feet eight inches deep will hold one ton of coal. If
an artery is cut, compress it above the wound. A man's leg contains
thirty bones. The Tower of London was burned in 1841."

"Go on, Mr. Pratt," says Mrs. Sampson. "Them ideas is so original and soothing. I think statistics are just as lovely as they can be."

But it wasn't till two weeks later that I got all that was coming
to me out of Herkimer.

One night I was waked up by folks hollering "Fire!" all around.
I jumped up and dressed and went out of the hotel to enjoy the
scene. When I seen it was Mrs. Sampson's house, I gave forth a
kind of yell, and I was there in two minutes.

The whole lower story of the yellow house was in flames, and
every masculine, feminine, and canine in Rosa was there, screeching
and barking and getting in the way of the firemen. I saw Idaho
trying to get away from six firemen who were holding him. They
was telling him the whole place was on fire down-stairs, and no
man could go in it and come out alive.

"Where's Mrs. Sampson?" I asks.

"She hasn't been seen," says one of the firemen. "She sleeps upstairs. We've tried to get in, but we can't, and our company hasn't
got any ladders yet."

I runs around to the light of the big blaze, and pulls the Handbook out of my inside pocket. I kind of laughed when I felt it in

my hands—I reckon I was some daffy with the sensation of excitement.

"Herky, old boy," I says to it, as I flipped over the pages, "you ain't ever lied to me yet, and you ain't ever throwed me down at a scratch yet. Tell me what, old boy, tell me what!" says I.

I turned to "What to do in Case of Accidents," on page 117. I run my finger down the page, and struck it. Good old Herkimer, he never overlooked anything! It said:

SUFFOCATION FROM INHALING SMOKE OR GAS.—There is nothing better than flaxseed. Place a few seed in the outer corner of the eye.

I shoved the Handbook back in my pocket, and grabbed a boy that was running by.

"Here," says I, giving him some money, "run to the drug store and bring a dollar's worth of flaxseed. Hurry, and you'll get another one for yourself. Now," I sings out to the crowd, "we'll have Mrs. Sampson!" And I throws away my coat and hat.

Four of the firemen and citizens grabs hold of me. It's sure death, they say, to go in the house, for the floors was beginning to fall through.

"How in blazes," I sings out, kind of laughing yet, but not feeling like it, "do you expect me to put flaxseed in a eye without the eye?"

I jabbed each elbow in a fireman's face, kicked the bark off of one citizen's shin, and tripped the other one with a side hold. And then I busted into the house. If I die first I'll write you a letter and tell you if it's any worse down there than the inside of that yellow house was; but don't believe it yet. I was a heap more cooked than the hurry-up orders of broiled chicken that you get in restaurants. The fire and smoke had me down on the floor twice, and was about to shame Herkimer, but the firemen helped me with their little stream of water, and I got to Mrs. Sampson's room. She'd lost conscientiousness from the smoke, so I wrapped her in the bed clothes and got her on my shoulder. Well, the floors wasn't as bad as they said, or I never could have done it—not by no means.

I carried her out fifty yards from the house and laid her on the grass. Then, of course, every one of them other twenty-two plain-

tiffs to the lady's hand crowded around with tin dippers of water
ready to save her. And up runs the boy with the flaxseed.

I unwrapped the covers from Mrs. Sampson's head. She opened
her eyes and says:

"Is that you, Mr. Pratt?"

"S-s-sh," says I. "Don't talk till you've had the remedy."

I runs my arm around her neck and raises her head, gentle, and
breaks the bag of flaxseed with the other hand; and as easy as I
could I bends over and slips three or four of the seeds in the outer
corner of her eye.

Up gallops the village doc by this time, and snorts around, and
grabs at Mrs. Sampson's pulse, and wants to know what I mean by
any such sandblasted nonsense.

"Well, old Jalap* and Jerusalem oakseed," says I, "I'm no regular
practitioner, but I'll show you my authority, anyway."

They fetched my coat, and I gets out the Handbook.

"Look on page 117," says I, "at the remedy for suffocation by
smoke or gas. Flaxseed in the outer corner of the eye, it says. I don't
know whether it works as a smoke consumer or whether it hikes
the compound gastro-hippopotamus nerve into action, but Herkimer says it, and he was called to the case first. If you want to
make it a consultation, there's no objection."

Old doc takes the book and looks at it by means of his specs and
a fireman's lantern.

"Well, Mr. Pratt," says he, "you evidently got on the wrong line
in reading your diagnosis. The recipe for suffocation says: 'Get the
patient into fresh air as quickly as possible, and place in a reclining
position.' The flaxseed remedy is for 'Dust and Cinders in the Eye,'
on the line above. But, after all—"

"See here," interrupts Mrs. Sampson, "I reckon I've got something to say in this consultation. That flaxseed done me more good
than anything I ever tried." And then she raises up her head and
lays it back on my arm again, and says: "Put some in the other eye,
Sandy dear."

And so if you was to stop off at Rosa to-morrow, or any other

---

*A purgative drug cultivated from the roots of a Mexican climbing plant.

day, you'd see a fine new yellow house with Mrs. Pratt, that was Mrs. Sampson, embellishing and adorning it. And if you was to step inside you'd see on the marble-top centre table in the parlour "Herkimer's Handbook of Indispensable Information," all rebound in red morocco, and ready to be consulted on any subject pertaining to human happiness and wisdom.

—from *The Heart of the West* (1907)

TELEMACHUS, FRIEND

Returning from a hunting trip, I waited at the little town of Los Piños, in New Mexico, for the south-bound train, which was one hour late. I sat on the porch of the Summit House and discussed the functions of life with Telemachus Hicks,[1] the hotel proprietor.

Perceiving that personalities were not out of order, I asked him what species of beast had long ago twisted and mutilated his left ear. Being a hunter, I was concerned in the evils that may befall one in the pursuit of game.

"That ear," says Hicks, "is the relic of true friendship."

"An ancient?" I persisted.

"No friendship is an accident," said Telemachus; and I was silent.

"The only perfect case of true friendship I ever knew," went on my host, "was a cordial intent between a Connecticut man and a monkey. The monkey climbed palms in Barranquilla and threw down cocoanuts to the man. The man sawed them in two and made dippers, which he sold for two *reales* each and bought rum. The monkey drank the milk of the nuts. Through each being satisfied with his own share of the graft, they lived like brothers.

"But in the case of human beings, friendship is a transitory art, subject to discontinuance without further notice.

"I had a friend once, of the entitlement of Paisley Fish, that I imagined was sealed to me for an endless space of time. Side by side for seven years we had mined, ranched, sold patent churns, herded sheep, took photographs and other things, built wire fences, and picked prunes. Thinks I, neither homicide nor flattery nor riches nor sophistry nor drink can make trouble between me and Paisley Fish. We was friends an amount you could hardly guess at. We was friends in business, and we let our amicable qualities lap over and season our hours of recreation and folly. We certainly had days of Damon and nights of Pythias.[2]

"One summer me and Paisley gallops down into these San Andrés mountains for the purpose of a month's surcease and levity, dressed in the natural store habiliments of man. We hit this town of Los Piños, which certainly was a roof-garden spot of the world, and flowing with condensed milk and honey. It had a street or two, and air, and hens, and a eating-house; and that was enough for us.

"We strikes the town after supper-time, and we concludes to sample whatever efficacy there is in this eating-house down by the railroad tracks. By the time we had set down and pried up our plates with a knife from the red oil-cloth, along intrudes Widow Jessup with the hot biscuit and the fried liver.

"Now, there was a woman that would have tempted an anchovy to forget his vows. She was not so small as she was large; and a kind of welcome air seemed to mitigate her vicinity. The pink of her face was the *in hoc signo** of a culinary temper and a warm disposition, and her smile would have brought out the dogwood blossoms in December.

"Widow Jessup talks to us a lot of garrulousness about the climate and history and Tennyson[3] and prunes and the scarcity of mutton, and finally wants to know where we came from.

" 'Spring Valley,' says I.

" 'Big Spring Valley,' chips in Paisley, out of a lot of potatoes and knuckle-bone of ham in his mouth.

"That was the first sign I noticed that the old *fidus Diogenes*† business between me and Paisley Fish was ended forever. He knew how I hated a talkative person, and yet he stampedes into the conversation with his amendments and addendums of syntax. On the map it was Big Spring Valley; but I had heard Paisley himself call it Spring Valley a thousand times.

"Without saying any more, we went out after supper and set on the railroad track. We had been pardners too long not to know what was going on in each other's mind.

---

*By this sign (Latin); in this context, seal or stamp.

†Diogenes was a third-century B.C. Greek philosopher famous for his stoic self-sufficiency; *fidus* in Latin means "faithful."

" 'I reckon you understand,' says Paisley, 'that I've made up my mind to accrue that widow woman as part and parcel in and to my hereditaments forever, both domestic, sociable, legal, and otherwise, until death us do part.'

" 'Why, yes,' says I, 'I read it between the lines, though you only spoke one. And I suppose you are aware,' says I, 'that I have a movement on foot that leads up to the widow's changing her name to Hicks, and leaves you writing to the society column to inquire whether the best man wears a japonica or seamless socks at the wedding!'

" 'There'll be some hiatuses in your program,' says Paisley, chewing up a piece of a railroad tie. 'I'd give in to you,' says he, 'in 'most any respect if it was secular affairs, but this is not so. The smiles of woman,' goes on Paisley, 'is the whirlpool of Squills and Chalybeates, into which vortex the good ship Friendship is often drawn and dismembered.⁴ I'd assault a bear that was annoying you,' says Paisley, 'or I'd indorse your note, or rub the place between your shoulder-blades with opodeldoc* the same as ever; but there my sense of etiquette ceases. In this fracas with Mrs. Jessup we play it alone. I've notified you fair.'

"And then I collaborates with myself, and offers the following resolutions and by-laws:

" 'Friendship between man and man,' says I, 'is an ancient historical virtue enacted in the days when men had to protect each other against lizards with eighty-foot tails and flying turtles. And they've kept up the habit to this day, and stand by each other till the bellboy comes up and tells them the animals are not really there. I've often heard,' I says, 'about ladies stepping in and breaking up a friendship between men. Why should that be? I'll tell you, Paisley, the first sight and hot biscuit of Mrs. Jessup appears to have inserted a oscillation into each of our bosoms. Let the best man of us have her. I'll play you a square game, and won't do any underhanded work. I'll do all of my courting of her in your presence, so you will have an equal opportunity. With that arrangement I don't see why our steamboat of friendship should fall overboard in the medicinal whirlpools you speak of, whichever of us wins out.'

---

*Solution of soap and alcohol.

" 'Good old hoss!' says Paisley, shaking my hand. 'And I'll do the same,' says he. 'We'll court the lady synonymously, and without any of the prudery and bloodshed usual to such occasions. And we'll be friends still, win or lose.'

"At one side of Mrs. Jessup's eating-house was a bench under some trees where she used to sit in the breeze after the south-bound had been fed and gone. And there me and Paisley used to congregate after supper and make partial payments on our respects to the lady of our choice. And we was so honourable and circuitous in our calls that if one of us got there first we waited for the other before beginning any gallivantery.

"The first evening that Mrs. Jessup knew about our arrangement I got to the bench before Paisley did. Supper was just over, and Mrs. Jessup was out there with a fresh pink dress on, and almost cool enough to handle.

"I sat down by her and made a few specifications about the moral surface of nature as set forth by the landscape and the contiguous perspective. That evening was surely a case in point. The moon was attending to business in the section of sky where it belonged, and the trees was making shadows on the ground according to science and nature, and there was a kind of conspicuous hullabaloo going on in the bushes between the bullbats and the orioles and the jack-rabbits and other feathered insects of the forest. And the wind out of the mountains was singing like a jew's-harp in the pile of old tomato-cans by the railroad track.

"I felt a kind of sensation in my left side—something like dough rising in a crock by the fire. Mrs. Jessup had moved up closer.

" 'Oh, Mr. Hicks,' says she, 'when one is alone in the world, don't they feel it more aggravated on a beautiful night like this?'

"I rose up off of the bench at once.

" 'Excuse me, ma'am,' says I, 'but I'll have to wait till Paisley comes before I can give a audible hearing to leading questions like that.'

"And then I explained to her how we was friends cinctured by years of embarrassment and travel and complicity, and how we had agreed to take no advantage of each other in any of the more mushy walks of life, such as might be fomented by sentiment and prox-imity. Mrs. Jessup appears to think serious about the matter for a minute, and then she breaks into a species of laughter that makes the wildwood resound.

"In a few minutes Paisley drops around, with oil of bergamot on his hair, and sits on the other side of Mrs. Jessup, and inaugurates a sad tale of adventure in which him and Pieface Lumley has a skinning-match of dead cows in '95 for a silver-mounted saddle in the Santa Rita valley during the nine months' drought.

"Now, from the start of that courtship I had Paisley Fish hobbled and tied to a post. Each one of us had a different system of reaching out for the easy places in the female heart. Paisley's scheme was to petrify 'em with wonderful relations of events that he had either come across personally or in large print. I think he must have got his idea of subjugation from one of Shakespeare's shows I see once called, 'Othello.' There is a coloured man in it who acquires a duke's daughter by disbursing to her a mixture of the talk turned out by Rider Haggard, Lew Dockstader, and Dr. Parkhurst.[5] But that style of courting don't work well off the stage.

"Now, I give you my own recipe for inveigling a woman into that state of affairs when she can be referred to as '*née* Jones.' Learn how to pick up her hand and hold it, and she's yours. It ain't so easy. Some men grab at it so much like they was going to set a dislocation of the shoulder that you can smell the arnica and hear 'em tearing off bandages. Some take it up like a hot horseshoe, and hold it off at arm's length like a druggist pouring tincture of asafœtida in a bottle. And most of 'em catch hold of it and drag it right out before the lady's eyes like a boy finding a baseball in the grass, without giving her a chance to forget that the hand is growing on the end of her arm. Them ways are all wrong.

"I'll tell you the right way. Did you ever see a man sneak out in the back yard and pick up a rock to throw at a tomcat that was sitting on a fence looking at him? He pretends he hasn't got a thing in his hand, and that the cat don't see him, and that he don't see the cat. That's the idea. Never drag her hand out where she'll have to take notice of it. Don't let her know that you think she knows you have the least idea she is aware you are holding her hand. That was my rule of tactics; and as far as Paisley's serenade about hostilities and misadventure went, he might as well have been reading to her a time-table of the Sunday trains that stop at Ocean Grove, New Jersey.

"One night when I beat Paisley to the bench by one pipeful, my friendship gets subsidised for a minute, and I asks Mrs. Jessup if she didn't think a 'H' was easier to write than a 'J.' In a second her head was mashing the oleander flower in my buttonhole, and I leaned over and—but I didn't.

" 'If you don't mind,' says I, standing up, 'we'll wait for Paisley to come before finishing this. I've never done anything dishonourable yet to our friendship, and this won't be quite fair.'

" 'Mr. Hicks,' says Mrs. Jessup, looking at me peculiar in the dark, 'if it wasn't for but one thing, I'd ask you to hike yourself down the gulch and never disresume your visits to my house.'

" 'And what is that, ma'am?' I asks.

" 'You are too good a friend not to make a good husband,' says she.

"In five minutes Paisley was on his side of Mrs. Jessup.

" 'In Silver City, in the summer of '98,' he begins, 'I see Jim Bartholomew chew off a Chinaman's ear in the Blue Light Saloon on account of a crossbarred muslin shirt that—what was that noise?'

"I had resumed matters again with Mrs. Jessup right where we had left off.

" 'Mrs. Jessup,' says I, 'has promised to make it Hicks. And this is another of the same sort.'

"Paisley winds his feet around a leg of the bench and kind of groans.

" 'Lem,' says he, 'we been friends for seven years. Would you mind not kissing Mrs. Jessup quite so loud? I'd do the same for you.'

" 'All right,' says I. 'The other kind will do as well.'

" 'This Chinaman,' goes on Paisley, 'was the one that shot a man named Mullins in the spring of '97, and that was—'

"Paisley interrupted himself again.

" 'Lem,' says he, 'if you was a true friend you wouldn't hug Mrs. Jessup quite so hard. I felt the bench shake all over just then. You know you told me you would give me an even chance as long as there was any.'

" 'Mr. Man,' says Mrs. Jessup, turning around to Paisley, 'if you was to drop in to the celebration of mine and Mr. Hicks's silver wedding, twenty-five years from now, do you think you could get it into that Hubbard squash you call your head that you are *nix cum rous** in this business? I've put up with you a long time because you was Mr. Hicks's friend; but it seems to me it's time for you to wear the willow and trot off down the hill.'

" 'Mrs. Jessup,' says I, without losing my grasp on the situation as fiancé, 'Mr. Paisley is my friend, and I offered him a square deal and a equal opportunity as long as there was a chance.'

" 'A chance!' says she. 'Well, he may think he has a chance; but I hope he won't think he's got a cinch, after what he's been next to all the evening.'

"Well, a month afterwards me and Mrs. Jessup was married in the Los Piños Methodist Church; and the whole town closed up to see the performance.

"When we lined up in front, and the preacher was beginning to sing out his rituals and observances, I looks around and misses Paisley. I calls time on the preacher. 'Paisley ain't here,' says I. 'We've got to wait for Paisley. A friend once, a friend always— that's Telemachus Hicks,' says I. Mrs. Jessup's eyes snapped some; but the preacher holds up the incantations according to instructions.

"In a few minutes Paisley gallops up the aisle, putting on a cuff as he comes. He explains that the only dry-goods store in town was closed for the wedding, and he couldn't get the kind of a boiled shirt that his taste called for until he had broke open the back window of the store and helped himself. Then he ranges up on the other side of the bride, and the wedding goes on. I always imagined that Paisley calculated as a last chance that the preacher might marry him to the widow by mistake.

"After the proceedings was over we had tea and jerked antelope and canned apricots, and then the populace hiked itself away. Last of all Paisley shook me by the hand and told me I'd acted square and on the level with him and he was proud to call me a friend.

"The preacher had a small house on the side of the street that

---

*Mrs. Jessup uses bastardized Latin to say that Paisley's attentions are unwelcome.

he'd fixed up to rent; and he allowed me and Mrs. Hicks to occupy it till the ten-forty train the next morning, when we was going on a bridal tour to El Paso. His wife had decorated it all up with hollyhocks and poison ivy, and it looked real festal and bowery.

"About ten o'clock that night I sets down in the front door and pulls off my boots a while in the cool breeze, while Mrs. Hicks was fixing around in the room. Right soon the light went out inside; and I sat there a while reverberating over old times and scenes. And then I heard Mrs. Hicks call out, 'Ain't you coming in soon, Lem?'

" 'Well, well!' says I, kind of rousing up. 'Durn me if I wasn't waiting for old Paisley to—'

"But when I got that far," concluded Telemachus Hicks, "I thought somebody had shot this left ear of mine off with a forty-five. But it turned out to be only a lick from a broomhandle in the hands of Mrs. Hicks."

—from *The Heart of the West* (1907)

THE LONESOME ROAD

Brown as a coffee-berry, rugged, pistoled, spurred, wary, indefeasible, I saw my old friend, Deputy-Marshal Buck Caperton, stumble, with jingling rowels, into a chair in the marshal's outer office.

And because the court-house was almost deserted at that hour, and because Buck would sometimes relate to me things that were out of print, I followed him in and tricked him into talk through knowledge of a weakness he had. For, cigarettes rolled with sweet corn husk were as honey to Buck's palate; and though he could finger the trigger of a forty-five with skill and suddenness, he never could learn to roll a cigarette.

It was through no fault of mine (for I rolled the cigarettes tight and smooth), but the upshot of some whim of his own, that instead of to an Odyssey of the chaparral,[1] I listened to—a dissertation upon matrimony! This from Buck Caperton! But I maintain that the cigarettes were impeccable, and crave absolution for myself.

"We just brought in Jim and Bud Granberry," said Buck. "Train robbing, you know. Held up the Aransas Pass last month. We caught 'em in the Twenty-Mile pear flat, south of the Nueces."

"Have much trouble corralling them?" I asked, for here was the meat that my hunger for epics craved.

"Some," said Buck; and then, during a little pause, his thoughts stampeded off the trail. "It's kind of queer about women," he went on, "and the place they're supposed to occupy in botany. If I was asked to classify them I'd say they was a human loco weed. Ever see a bronc that had been chewing loco? Ride him up to a puddle of water two feet wide, and he'll give a snort and fall back on you. It looks as big as the Mississippi River to him. Next trip he'd walk into a cañon a thousand feet deep thinking it was a prairie-dog hole. Same way with a married man.

"I was thinking of Perry Rountree, that used to be my sidekicker before he committed matrimony. In them days me and Perry hated indisturbances of any kind. We roamed around considerable, stirring up the echoes and making 'em attend to business. Why, when me and Perry wanted to have some fun in a town it was a picnic for the census takers. They just counted the marshal's posse that it took to subdue us, and there was your population. But then there came along this Mariana Goodnight girl and looked at Perry sideways, and he was all bridle-wise and saddle-broke before you could skin a yearling.

"I wasn't even asked to the wedding. I reckon the bride had my pedigree and the front elevation of my habits all mapped out, and she decided that Perry would trot better in double harness without any unconverted mustang like Buck Caperton whickering around on the matrimonial range. So it was six months before I saw Perry again.

"One day I was passing on the edge of town, and I see something like a man in a little yard by a little house with a sprinkling-pot squirting water on a rose-bush. Seemed to me, I'd seen something like it before, and I stopped at the gate, trying to figure out its brands. 'Twas not Perry Rountree, but 'twas the kind of a curdled jellyfish matrimony had made out of him.

"Homicide was what that Mariana had perpetrated. He was looking well enough, but he had on a white collar and shoes, and you could tell in a minute that he'd speak polite and pay taxes and stick his little finger out while drinking, just like a sheep man or a citizen. Great skyrockets! but I hated to see Perry all corrupted and Willie-ized like that.

"He came out to the gate, and shook hands; and I says, with scorn, and speaking like a paroquet with the pip: 'Beg pardon—Mr. Rountree, I believe. Seems to me I sagatiated in your associations once, if I am not mistaken.'

" 'Oh, go to the devil, Buck,' says Perry, polite, as I was afraid he'd be.

" 'Well, then,' says I, 'you poor, contaminated adjunct of a sprinkling-pot and degraded household pet, what did you go and do it for? Look at you, all decent and unriotous, and only fit to sit on juries and mend the wood-house door. You was a man once. I have hostility for all such acts. Why don't you go in the house and count the tidies or set the clock, and not stand out here in the atmosphere? A jackrabbit might come along and bite you.'

" 'Now, Buck,' says Perry, speaking mild, and some sorrowful, 'you don't understand. A married man has got to be different. He feels different from a tough old cloudburst like you. It's sinful to waste time pulling up towns just to look at their roots, and playing faro and looking upon red liquor, and such restless policies as them.'

" 'There was a time,' I says, and I expect I sighed when I mentioned it, 'when a certain domesticated little Mary's lamb I could name was some instructed himself in the line of pernicious sprightliness. I never expected, Perry, to see you reduced down from a full-grown pestilence to such a frivolous fraction of a man. Why,' says I, 'you've got a necktie on; and you speak a senseless kind of indoor drivel that reminds me of a storekeeper or a lady. You look to me like you might tote an umbrella and wear suspenders, and go home of nights.'

" 'The little woman,' says Perry, 'has made some improvements, I believe. You can't understand, Buck. I haven't been away from the house at night since we was married.'

"We talked on a while, me and Perry, and, as sure as I live, that man interrupted me in the middle of my talk to tell me about six tomato plants he had growing in his garden. Shoved his agricultural degradation right up under my nose while I was telling him about the fun we had tarring and feathering that faro dealer at California Pete's layout! But by and by Perry shows a flicker of sense.

" 'Buck,' says he, 'I'll have to admit that it is a little dull at times. Not that I'm not perfectly happy with the little woman, but a man seems to require some excitement now and then. Now, I'll tell you: Mariana's gone visiting this afternoon, and she won't be home till seven o'clock. That's the limit for both of us—seven o'clock. Neither of us ever stays out a minute after that time unless we are together. Now, I'm glad you came along, Buck,' says Perry, 'for I'm feeling just like having one more rip-roaring razoo with you for the sake of old times. What you say to us putting in the afternoon having fun—I'd like it fine,' says Perry.

"I slapped that old captive range-rider half across his little garden.

" 'Get your hat, you old dried-up alligator,' I shouts, 'you ain't dead yet. You're part human, anyhow, if you did get all bogged up in matrimony. We'll take this town to pieces and see what makes it tick. We'll make all kinds of profligate demands upon the science of cork pulling. You'll grow horns yet, old muley cow,' says I, punching Perry in the ribs, 'if you trot around on the trail of vice with your Uncle Buck.'

" 'I'll have to be home by seven, you know,' says Perry again.

" 'Oh, yes,' says I, winking to myself, for I knew the kind of seven o'clocks Perry Rountree got back by after he once got to passing repartee with the bartenders.

"We goes down to the Gray Mule saloon—that old 'dobe building by the depot.

" 'Give it a name,' says I, as soon as we got one hoof on the foot-rest.

" 'Sarsaparilla,' says Perry.

"You could have knocked me down with a lemon peeling.

" 'Insult me as much as you want to,' I says to Perry, 'but don't startle the bartender. He may have heart-disease. Come on, now; your tongue got twisted. The tall glasses,' I orders, 'and the bottle in the left-hand corner of the ice-chest.'

" 'Sarsaparilla,' repeats Perry, and then his eyes get animated, and I see he's got some great scheme in his mind he wants to emit.

" 'Buck,' he says, all interested, 'I'll tell you what! I want to make this a red-letter day. I've been keeping close at home, and I want to turn myself a-loose. We'll have the highest old time you ever saw. We'll go in the back room here and play checkers till half-past six.'

"I leaned against the bar, and I says to Gotch-eared Mike, who was on watch:

" 'For God's sake don't mention this. You know what Perry used to be. He's had the fever, and the doctor says we must humour him.'

" 'Give us the checker-board and the men, Mike,' says Perry. 'Come on, Buck, I'm just wild to have some excitement.'

"I went in the back room with Perry. Before we closed the door, I says to Mike:

" 'Don't ever let it straggle out from under your hat that you seen

Buck Caperton fraternal with sarsaparilla or *persona grata** with a
checker-board, or I'll make a swallow-fork in your other ear.'

"I locked the door and me and Perry played checkers. To see
that poor old humiliated piece of household bric-a-brac sitting
there and sniggering out loud whenever he jumped a man, and all
obnoxious with animation when he got into my king row, would
have made a sheep-dog sick with mortification. Him that was once
satisfied only when he was pegging six boards at keno or giving the
faro dealers nervous prostration—to see him pushing them checkers about like Sally Louisa at a school-children's party—why, I was
all smothered up with mortification.

"And I sits there playing the black men, all sweating for fear
somebody I knew would find it out. And I thinks to myself some
about this marrying business, and how it seems to be the same kind
of a game as that Mrs. Delilah played. She give her old man a hair
cut, and everybody knows what a man's head looks like after a
woman cuts his hair. And then when the Pharisees[2] came around
to guy him he was so 'shamed he went to work and kicked the
whole house down on top of the whole outfit. 'Them married men,'
thinks I, 'lose all their spirit and instinct for riot and foolishness.
They won't drink, they won't buck the tiger, they won't even fight.
What do they want to go and stay married for?' I asks myself.

"But Perry seems to be having hilarity in considerable quantities.

" 'Buck old hoss,' says he, 'isn't this just the hell-roaringest time
we ever had in our lives? I don't know when I've been stirred up
so. You see, I've been sticking pretty close to home since I married,
and I haven't been on a spree in a long time.'

" 'Spree!' Yes, that's what he called it. Playing checkers in the
back room of the Gray Mule! I suppose it did seem to him a little
more immoral and nearer to a prolonged debauch than standing
over six tomato plants with a sprinkling-pot.

"Every little bit Perry looks at his watch and says:

" 'I got to be home, you know, Buck, at seven.'

" 'All right,' I'd say. 'Romp along and move. This here excitement's killing me. If I don't reform some, and loosen up the strain
of this checkered dissipation I won't have a nerve left.'

---

*A welcome person (Latin).

"It might have been half-past six when commotions began to go on outside in the street. We heard a yelling and a six-shootering, and a lot of galloping and manœuvres.

" 'What's that?' I wonders.

" 'Oh, some nonsense outside,' says Perry. 'It's your move. We just got time to play this game.'

" 'I'll just take a peep through the window,' says I, 'and see. You can't expect a mere mortal to stand the excitement of having a king jumped and listen to an unidentified conflict going on at the same time.'

"The Gray Mule saloon was one of them old Spanish 'dobe* buildings, and the back room only had two little windows a foot wide, with iron bars in 'em. I looked out one, and I see the cause of the rucus.

"There was the Trimble gang—ten of 'em—the worst outfit of desperadoes and horse-thieves in Texas, coming up the street shooting right and left. They was coming right straight for the Gray Mule. Then they got past the range of my sight, but we heard 'em ride up to the front door, and then they socked the place full of lead. We heard the big looking-glass behind the bar knocked all to pieces and the bottles crashing. We could see Gotch-eared Mike in his apron running across the plaza like a coyote, with the bullets puffing up the dust all around him. Then the gang went to work in the saloon, drinking what they wanted and smashing what they didn't.

"Me and Perry both knew that gang, and they knew us. The year before Perry married, him and me was in the same ranger company—and we fought that outfit down on the San Miguel, and brought back Ben Trimble and two others for murder.

" 'We can't get out,' says I. "We'll have to stay in here till they leave.'

Perry looked at his watch.

" 'Twenty-five to seven,' says he. 'We can finish that game. I got two men on you. It's your move, Buck. I got to be home at seven, you know.'

---

*Adobe, a red-clay building material common in the Southwest.

"We sat down and went on playing. The Trimble gang had a roughhouse for sure. They were getting good and drunk. They'd drink a while and holler a while, and then they'd shoot up a few bottles and glasses. Two or three times they came and tried to open our door. Then there was some more shooting outside, and I looked out the window again. Ham Gossett, the town marshal, had a posse in the houses and stores across the street, and was trying to bag a Trimble or two through the windows.

"I lost that game of checkers. I'm free in saying that I lost three kings that I might have saved if I had been corralled in a more peaceful pasture. But that drivelling married man sat there and cackled when he won a man like an unintelligent hen picking up a grain of corn.

"When the game was over Perry gets up and looks at his watch.

" 'I've had a glorious time, Buck,' says he, 'but I'll have to be going now. It's a quarter to seven, and I got to be home by seven, you know.'

"I thought he was joking.

" 'They'll clear out or be dead drunk in half an hour or an hour,' says I. 'You ain't that tired of being married that you want to commit any more sudden suicide, are you?' says I, giving him the laugh.

" 'One time,' says Perry, 'I was half an hour late getting home. I met Mariana on the street looking for me. If you could have seen her, Buck—but you don't understand. She knows what a wild kind of a snoozer I've been, and she's afraid something will happen. I'll never be late getting home again. I'll say good-bye to you now, Buck.'

"I got between him and the door.

" 'Married man,' says I, 'I know you was christened a fool the minute the preacher tangled you up, but don't you never sometimes think one little think on a human basis? There's ten of that gang in there, and they're pizen with whiskey and desire for murder. They'll drink you up like a bottle of booze before you get half-way to the door. Be intelligent, now, and use at least wild-hog sense. Sit down and wait till we have some chance to get out without being carried in baskets.'

" 'I got to be home by seven, Buck,' repeats this henpecked thing of little wisdom, like an unthinking poll parrot. 'Mariana,' says he, "ll be looking out for me.' And he reaches down and pulls a leg out of the checker table. 'I'll go through this Trimble outfit,' says he, 'like a cottontail through a brush corral. I'm not pestered any more with a desire to engage in rucuses, but I got to be home by seven. You lock the door after me, Buck. And don't you forget— I won three out of them five games. I'd play longer, but Mariana—'

" 'Hush up, you old locoed road runner,' I interrupts. 'Did you ever notice your Uncle Buck locking doors against trouble? I'm not married,' says I, 'but I'm as big a d—n* fool as any Mormon.[3] One from four leaves three,' says I, and I gathers out another leg of the table. 'We'll get home by seven,' says I, 'whether it's the heavenly one or the other. May I see you home?' says I, 'you sarsaparilla-drinking, checker-playing glutton for death and destruction.'

"We opened the door easy, and then stampeded for the front. Part of the gang was lined up at the bar; part of 'em was passing over the drinks, and two or three was peeping out the door and window taking shots at the marshal's crowd. The room was so full of smoke we got half-way to the front door before they noticed us. Then I heard Berry Trimble's voice somewhere yell out:

" 'How'd that Buck Caperton get in here?' and he skinned the side of my neck with a bullet. I reckon he felt bad over that miss, for Berry's the best shot south of the Southern Pacific Railroad. But the smoke in the saloon was some too thick for good shooting.

"Me and Perry smashed over two of the gang with our table legs, which didn't miss like the guns did, and as we run out the door I grabbed a Winchester from a fellow who was watching the outside, and I turned and regulated the account of Mr. Berry.

"Me and Perry got out and around the corner all right. I never much expected to get out, but I wasn't going to be intimidated by that married man. According to Perry's idea, checkers was the event of the day, but if I am any judge of gentle recreations that little table-leg parade through the Gray Mule saloon deserved the head-lines in the bill of particulars.

---

*Damn.

" 'Walk fast,' says Perry, 'it's two minutes to seven, and I got to be home by—'

" 'Oh, shut up,' says I. 'I had an appointment as chief performer at an inquest at seven, and I'm not kicking about not keeping it.'

"I had to pass by Perry's little house. His Mariana was standing at the gate. We got there at five minutes past seven. She had on a blue wrapper, and her hair was pulled back smooth like little girls do when they want to look grown-folksy. She didn't see us till we got close, for she was gazing up the other way. Then she backed around, and saw Perry, and a kind of a look scooted around over her face—danged if I can describe it. I heard her breathe long, just like a cow when you turn her calf in the lot, and she says: 'You're late, Perry.'

" 'Five minutes,' says Perry, cheerful. 'Me and old Buck was having a game of checkers.'

"Perry introduces me to Mariana, and they ask me to come in. No, sir-ee. I'd had enough truck with married folks for that day. I says I'll be going along, and that I've spent a very pleasant afternoon with my old partner—'especially,' says I, just to jostle Perry, 'during that game when the table legs came all loose.' But I'd promised him not to let her know anything.

"I've been worrying over that business ever since it happened," continued Buck. "There's one thing about it that's got me all twisted up, and I can't figure it out."

"What was that?" I asked, as I rolled and handed Buck the last cigarette.

"Why, I'll tell you: When I saw the look that little woman give Perry when she turned round and saw him coming back to the ranch safe—why was it I got the idea all in a minute that that look of hers was worth more than the whole caboodle of us—sarsaparilla, checkers, and all, and that the d—n fool in the game wasn't named Perry Rountree at all?"

—from *The Roads of Destiny* (1909)

A RETRIEVED REFORMATION

A guard came to the prison shoe-shop, where Jimmy Valentine was assiduously stitching uppers, and escorted him to the front office. There the warden handed Jimmy his pardon, which had been signed that morning by the governor. Jimmy took it in a tired kind of way. He had served nearly ten months of a four-year sentence. He had expected to stay only about three months, at the longest. When a man with as many friends on the outside as Jimmy Valentine had is received in the "stir" it is hardly worth while to cut his hair.

"Now, Valentine," said the warden, "you'll go out in the morning. Brace up, and make a man of yourself. You're not a bad fellow at heart. Stop cracking safes, and live straight."

"Me?" said Jimmy, in surprise. "Why, I never cracked a safe in my life."

"Oh, no," laughed the warden. "Of course not. Let's see, now. How was it you happened to get sent up on that Springfield job? Was it because you wouldn't prove an alibi for fear of compromising somebody in extremely high-toned society? Or was it simply a case of a mean old jury that had it in for you? It's always one or the other with you innocent victims."

"Me?" said Jimmy, still blankly virtuous. "Why, warden, I never was in Springfield in my life!"

"Take him back, Cronin," smiled the warden, "and fix him up with outgoing clothes. Unlock him at seven in the morning, and let him come to the bull-pen. Better think over my advice, Valentine."

At a quarter past seven on the next morning Jimmy stood in the warden's outer office. He had on a suit of the villainously fitting, ready-made clothes and a pair of the stiff, squeaky shoes that the state furnishes to its discharged compulsory guests.

The clerk handed him a railroad ticket and the five-dollar bill with which the law expected him to rehabilitate himself into good citizenship and prosperity. The warden gave him a cigar, and shook hands. Valentine, 9762, was chronicled on the books "Pardoned by Governor," and Mr. James Valentine walked out into the sunshine.

Disregarding the song of the birds, the waving green trees, and the smell of the flowers, Jimmy headed straight for a restaurant. There he tasted the first sweet joys of liberty in the shape of a broiled chicken and a bottle of white wine—followed by a cigar a grade better than the one the warden had given him. From there he proceeded leisurely to the depot. He tossed a quarter into the hat of a blind man sitting by the door, and boarded his train. Three hours set him down in a little town near the state line. He went to the café of one Mike Dolan and shook hands with Mike, who was alone behind the bar.

"Sorry we couldn't make it sooner, Jimmy, me boy," said Mike. "But we had that protest from Springfield to buck against, and the governor nearly balked. Feeling all right?"

"Fine," said Jimmy. "Got my key?"

He got his key and went up-stairs, unlocking the door of a room at the rear. Everything was just as he had left it. There on the floor was still Ben Price's collar-button that had been torn from that eminent detective's shirt-band when they had overpowered Jimmy to arrest him.

Pulling out from the wall a folding-bed, Jimmy slid back a panel in the wall and dragged out a dust-covered suit-case. He opened this and gazed fondly at the finest set of burglar's tools in the East. It was a complete set, made of specially tempered steel, the latest designs in drills, punches, braces and bits, jimmies, clamps, and augers, with two or three novelties, invented by Jimmy himself, in which he took pride. Over nine hundred dollars they had cost him to have made at——, a place where they make such things for the profession.

In half an hour Jimmy went down stairs and through the café. He was now dressed in tasteful and well-fitting clothes, and carried his dusted and cleaned suit-case in his hand.

"Got anything on?" asked Mike Dolan, genially.

"Me?" said Jimmy, in a puzzled tone. "I don't understand. I'm representing the New York Amalgamated Short Snap Biscuit Cracker and Frazzled Wheat Company."

This statement delighted Mike to such an extent that Jimmy had to take a seltzer-and-milk on the spot. He never touched "hard" drinks.

A week after the release of Valentine, 9762, there was a neat job of safe-burglary done in Richmond, Indiana, with no clue to the author. A scant eight hundred dollars was all that was secured. Two weeks after that a patented, improved, burglar-proof safe in Logansport was opened like a cheese to the tune of fifteen hundred dollars, currency; securities and silver untouched. That began to interest the rogue-catchers. Then an old-fashioned bank-safe in Jefferson City became active and threw out of its crater an eruption of bank-notes amounting to five thousand dollars. The losses were now high enough to bring the matter up into Ben Price's class of work. By comparing notes, a remarkable similarity in the methods of the burglaries was noticed. Ben Price investigated the scenes of the robberies, and was heard to remark:

"That's Dandy Jim Valentine's autograph. He's resumed business. Look at that combination knob—jerked out as easy as pulling up a radish in wet weather. He's got the only clamps that can do it. And look how clean those tumblers were punched out! Jimmy never has to drill but one hole. Yes, I guess I want Mr. Valentine. He'll do his bit next time without any short-time or clemency foolishness."

Ben Price knew Jimmy's habits. He had learned them while working up the Springfield case. Long jumps, quick get-aways, no confederates, and a taste for good society—these ways had helped Mr. Valentine to become noted as a successful dodger of retribution. It was given out that Ben Price had taken up the trail of the elusive cracksman, and other people with burglar-proof safes felt more at ease.

One afternoon Jimmy Valentine and his suit-case climbed out of the mail-hack in Elmore, a little town five miles off the railroad down in the black-jack country of Arkansas. Jimmy, looking like an athletic young senior just home from college, went down the board side-walk toward the hotel.

A young lady crossed the street, passed him at the corner and entered a door over which was the sign "The Elmore Bank." Jimmy Valentine looked into her eyes, forgot what he was, and became another man. She lowered her eyes and coloured slightly. Young men of Jimmy's style and looks were scarce in Elmore.

Jimmy collared a boy that was loafing on the steps of the bank as if he were one of the stockholders, and began to ask him questions about the town, feeding him dimes at intervals. By and by the young lady came out, looking royally unconscious of the young man with the suit-case, and went her way.

"Isn't that young lady Miss Polly Simpson?" asked Jimmy, with specious guile.

"Naw," said the boy. "She's Annabel Adams. Her pa owns this bank. What'd you come to Elmore for? Is that a gold watch-chain? I'm going to get a bulldog. Got any more dimes?"

Jimmy went to the Planters' Hotel, registered as Ralph D. Spencer, and engaged a room. He leaned on the desk and declared his platform to the clerk. He said he had come to Elmore to look for a location to go into business. How was the shoe business, now, in the town? He had thought of the shoe business. Was there an opening?

The clerk was impressed by the clothes and manner of Jimmy. He, himself, was something of a pattern of fashion to the thinly gilded youth of Elmore, but he now perceived his shortcomings. While trying to figure out Jimmy's manner of tying his four-in-hand he cordially gave information.

Yes, there ought to be a good opening in the shoe line. There wasn't an exclusive shoe-store in the place. The dry-goods and general stores handled them. Business in all lines was fairly good. Hoped Mr. Spencer would decide to locate in Elmore. He would find it a pleasant town to live in, and the people very sociable.

Mr. Spencer thought he would stop over in the town a few days and look over the situation. No, the clerk needn't call the boy. He would carry up his suit-case, himself; it was rather heavy.

Mr. Ralph Spencer, the phœnix that arose from Jimmy Valentine's ashes—ashes left by the flame of a sudden and alterative attack of love—remained in Elmore, and prospered. He opened a shoe-store and secured a good run of trade.

Socially he was also a success, and made many friends. And he accomplished the wish of his heart. He met Miss Annabel Adams, and became more and more captivated by her charms.

At the end of a year the situation of Mr. Ralph Spencer was this: he had won the respect of the community, his shoe-store was flourishing, and he and Annabel were engaged to be married in two weeks. Mr. Adams, the typical, plodding, country banker, approved of Spencer. Annabel's pride in him almost equalled her affection. He was as much at home in the family of Mr. Adams and that of Annabel's married sister as if he were already a member.

One day Jimmy sat down in his room and wrote this letter, which he mailed to the safe address of one of his old friends in St. Louis:

DEAR OLD PAL:

I want you to be at Sullivan's place, in Little Rock, next Wednesday night, at nine o'clock. I want you to wind up some little matters for me. And, also, I want to make you a present of my kit of tools. I know you'll be glad to get them—you couldn't duplicate the lot for a thousand dollars. Say, Billy, I've quit the old business—a year ago. I've got a nice store. I'm making an honest living, and I'm going to marry the finest girl on earth two weeks from now. It's the only life, Billy—the straight one. I wouldn't touch a dollar of another man's money now for a million. After I get married I'm going to sell out and go West, where there won't be so much danger of having old scores brought up against me. I tell you, Billy, she's an angel. She believes in me; and I wouldn't do another crooked thing for the whole world. Be sure to be at Sully's, for I must see you. I'll bring along the tools with me.

YOUR OLD FRIEND,
JIMMY.

On the Monday night after Jimmy wrote this letter, Ben Price jogged unobtrusively into Elmore in a livery buggy. He lounged about town in his quiet way until he found out what he wanted to know. From the drug-store across the street from Spencer's shoe-store he got a good look at Ralph D. Spencer.

"Going to marry the banker's daughter are you, Jimmy?" said Ben to himself, softly. "Well, I don't know!"

The next morning Jimmy took breakfast at the Adamses. He was going to Little Rock that day to order his wedding-suit and buy something nice for Annabel. That would be the first time he had left town since he came to Elmore. It had been more than a year now since those last professional "jobs," and he thought he could safely venture out.

After breakfast quite a family party went downtown together— Mr. Adams, Annabel, Jimmy, and Annabel's married sister with her two little girls, aged five and nine. They came by the hotel where Jimmy still boarded, and he ran up to his room and brought along his suit-case. Then they went on to the bank. There stood Jimmy's horse and buggy and Dolph Gibson, who was going to drive him over to the railroad station.

All went inside the high, carved oak railings into the banking-room—Jimmy included, for Mr. Adams's future son-in-law was welcome anywhere. The clerks were pleased to be greeted by the good-looking, agreeable young man who was going to marry Miss Annabel. Jimmy set his suit-case down. Annabel, whose heart was bubbling with happiness and lively youth, put on Jimmy's hat, and picked up the suit-case. "Wouldn't I make a nice drummer?" said Annabel. "My! Ralph, how heavy it is? Feels like it was full of gold bricks."

"Lot of nickel-plated shoe-horns in there," said Jimmy, coolly, "that I'm going to return. Thought I'd save express charges by taking them up. I'm getting awfully economical."

The Elmore Bank had just put in a new safe and vault. Mr. Adams was very proud of it, and insisted on an inspection by every one. The vault was a small one, but it had a new, patented door. It fastened with three solid steel bolts thrown simultaneously with a single handle, and had a time-lock. Mr. Adams beamingly explained its workings to Mr. Spencer, who showed a courteous but not too intelligent interest. The two children, May and Agatha, were delighted by the shining metal and funny clock and knobs.

While they were thus engaged Ben Price sauntered in and leaned on his elbow, looking casually inside between the railings. He told the teller that he didn't want anything; he was just waiting for a man he knew.

Suddenly there was a scream or two from the women, and a commotion. Unperceived by the elders, May, the nine-year-old girl, in a spirit of play, had shut Agatha in the vault. She had then shot the bolts and turned the knob of the combination as she had seen Mr. Adams do.

The old banker sprang to the handle and tugged at it for a moment. "The door can't be opened," he groaned. "The clock hasn't been wound nor the combination set."

Agatha's mother screamed again, hysterically.

"Hush!" said Mr. Adams, raising his trembling hand. "All be quiet for a moment. Agatha!" he called as loudly as he could. "Listen to me." During the following silence they could just hear the faint sound of the child wildly shrieking in the dark vault in a panic of terror.

"My precious darling!" wailed the mother. "She will die of fright! Open the door! Oh, break it open! Can't you men do something?"

"There isn't a man nearer than Little Rock who can open that door," said Mr. Adams, in a shaky voice. "My God! Spencer, what shall we do? That child—she can't stand it long in there. There isn't enough air, and, besides, she'll go into convulsions from fright."

Agatha's mother, frantic now, beat the door of the vault with her hands. Somebody wildly suggested dynamite. Annabel turned to Jimmy, her large eyes full of anguish, but not yet despairing. To a woman nothing seems quite impossible to the powers of the man she worships.

"Can't you do something, Ralph—*try*, won't you?"

He looked at her with a queer, soft smile on his lips and in his keen eyes.

"Annabel," he said, "give me that rose you are wearing, will you?"

Hardly believing that she heard him aright, she unpinned the bud from the bosom of her dress, and placed it in his hand. Jimmy stuffed it into his vest-pocket, threw off his coat and pulled up his shirt-sleeves. With that act Ralph D. Spencer passed away and Jimmy Valentine took his place.

"Get away from the door, all of you," he commanded, shortly.

He set his suit-case on the table, and opened it out flat. From that time on he seemed to be unconscious of the presence of any one else. He laid out the shining, queer implements swiftly and orderly, whistling softly to himself as he always did when at work. In a deep silence and immovable, the others watched him as if under a spell.

In a minute Jimmy's pet drill was biting smoothly into the steel door. In ten minutes—breaking his own burglarious record—he threw back the bolts and opened the door.

Agatha, almost collapsed, but safe, was gathered into her mother's arms.

Jimmy Valentine put on his coat, and walked outside the railings toward the front door. As he went he thought he heard a far-away voice that he once knew call "Ralph!" But he never hesitated.

At the door a big man stood somewhat in his way.

"Hello, Ben!" said Jimmy, still with his strange smile. "Got around at last, have you? Well, let's go. I don't know that it makes much difference, now."

And then Ben Price acted rather strangely.

"Guess you're mistaken, Mr. Spencer," he said. "Don't believe I recognize you. Your buggy's waiting for you, ain't it?"

And Ben Price turned and strolled down the street.

—from *The Roads of Destiny* (1909)

THE RENAISSANCE AT CHARLEROI

Grandemont Charles was a little Creole gentleman, aged thirty-four, with a bald spot on the top of his head and the manners of a prince. By day he was a clerk in a cotton broker's office in one of those cold, rancid mountains of oozy brick, down near the levee in New Orleans. By night, in his three-story-high *chambre garnier** in the old French Quarter he was again the last male descendant of the Charles family, that noble house that had lorded it in France, and had pushed its way smiling, rapiered, and courtly into Louisiana's early and brilliant days. Of late years the Charleses had subsided into the more Republican but scarcely less royally carried magnificence and ease of plantation life along the Mississippi. Perhaps Grandemont was even Marquis de Brassé. There was that title in the family. But a Marquis on seventy-five dollars per month! *Vraiment!*† Still, it has been done on less.

Grandemont had saved out of his salary the sum of six hundred dollars. Enough, you would say, for any man to marry on. So, after a silence of two years on that subject, he reopened that most hazardous question to Mlle. Adèle Fauquier, riding down to Meade d'Or, her father's plantation. Her answer was the same that it had been any time during the last ten years: "First find my brother, Monsieur Charles."

This time he had stood before her, perhaps discouraged by a love so long and hopeless, being dependent upon a contingency so unreasonable, and demanded to be told in simple words whether she loved him or no.

Adèle looked at him steadily out of her gray eyes that betrayed no secrets and answered, a little more softly:

---

*Furnished room (French).
†Indeed! Really! (French).

"Grandemont, you have no right to ask that question unless you can do what I ask of you. Either bring back brother Victor to us or the proof that he died."

Somehow, though five times thus rejected, his heart was not so heavy when he left. She had not denied that she loved. Upon what shallow waters can the bark of passion remain afloat! Or, shall we play the doctrinaire, and hint that at thirty-four the tides of life are calmer and cognizant of many sources instead of but one—as at four-and-twenty?

Victor Fauquier would never be found. In those early days of his disappearance there was money to the Charles name, and Grandemont had spent the dollars as if they were picayunes in trying to find the lost youth. Even then he had had small hope of success, for the Mississippi gives up a victim from its oily tangles only at the whim of its malign will.

A thousand times had Grandemont conned in his mind the scene of Victor's disappearance. And, at each time that Adèle had set her stubborn but pitiful alternative against his suit, still clearer it repeated itself in his brain.

The boy had been the family favourite; daring, winning, reckless. His unwise fancy had been captured by a girl on the plantation— the daughter of an overseer. Victor's family was in ignorance of the intrigue, as far as it had gone. To save them the inevitable pain that his course promised, Grandemont strove to prevent it. Omnipotent money smoothed the way. The overseer and his daughter left, be-tween a sunset and dawn, for an undesignated bourne. Grandemont was confident that this stroke would bring the boy to reason. He rode over to Meade d'Or to talk with him. The two strolled out of the house and grounds, crossed the road, and, mounting the levee, walked its broad path while they conversed. A thunder-cloud was hanging, imminent, above, but, as yet, no rain fell. At Grande-mont's disclosure of his interference in the clandestine romance, Victor attacked him, in a wild and sudden fury. Grandemont, though of slight frame, possessed muscles of iron. He caught the wrists amid a shower of blows descending upon him, bent the lad backward and stretched him upon the levee path. In a little while the gust of passion was spent, and he was allowed to rise. Calm now, but a powder mine where he had been but a whiff of the tantrums, Victor extended his hand toward the dwelling house of Meade d'Or.

"You and they," he cried, "have conspired to destroy my happiness. None of you shall ever look upon my face again."

Turning, he ran swiftly down the levee, disappearing in the darkness. Grandemont followed as well as he could, calling to him, but in vain. For longer than an hour he pursued the search. Descending the side of the levee, he penetrated the rank density of weeds and willows that undergrew the trees until the river's edge, shouting Victor's name. There was never an answer, though once he thought he heard a bubbling scream from the dun waters sliding past. Then the storm broke, and he returned to the house drenched and dejected.

There he explained the boy's absence sufficiently, he thought, not speaking of the tangle that had led to it, for he hoped that Victor would return as soon as his anger had cooled. Afterward, when the threat was made good and they saw his face no more, he found it difficult to alter his explanations of that night, and there clung a certain mystery to the boy's reasons for vanishing as well as to the manner of it.

It was on that night that Grandemont first perceived a new and singular expression in Adèle's eyes whenever she looked at him. And through the years following that expression was always there. He could not read it, for it was born of a thought she would never otherwise reveal.

Perhaps, if he had known that Adèle had stood at the gate on that unlucky night, where she had followed, lingering, to await the return of her brother and lover, wondering why they had chosen so tempestuous an hour and so black a spot to hold converse—if he had known that a sudden flash of lightning had revealed to her sight that short, sharp struggle as Victor was sinking under his hands, he might have explained everything, and she—

I know not what she would have done. But one thing is clear—there was something besides her brother's disappearance between Grandemont's pleadings for her hand and Adèle's "yes." Ten years had passed, and what she had seen during the space of that lightning flash remained an indelible picture. She had loved her brother, but was she holding out for the solution of that mystery or for the

"Truth"? Women have been known to reverence it, even as an abstract principle. It is said there have been a few who, in the matter of their affections, have considered a life to be a small thing as compared with a lie. That I do not know. But, I wonder, had Grandemont cast himself at her feet crying that his hand had sent Victor to the bottom of that inscrutable river, and that he could no longer sully his love with a lie, I wonder if—I wonder what she would have done!

But, Grandemont Charles, Arcadian little gentleman,[1] never guessed the meaning of that look in Adèle's eyes; and from this last bootless payment of his devoirs* he rode away as rich as ever in honour and love, but poor in hope.

That was in September. It was during the first winter month that Grandemont conceived his idea of the *renaissance*. Since Adèle would never be his, and wealth without her were useless trumpery, why need he add to that hoard of slowly harvested dollars? Why should he even retain that hoard?

Hundreds were the cigarettes he consumed over his claret, sitting at the little polished tables in the Royal street cafés while thinking over his plan. By and by he had it perfect. It would cost, beyond doubt, all the money he had, but—*le jeu vaut la chandelle*†—for some hours he would be once more a Charles of Charleroi. Once again should the nineteenth of January, that most significant day in the fortunes of the house of Charles, be fittingly observed. On that date the French king had seated a Charles by his side at table; on that date Armand Charles, Marquis de Brassé, landed, like a brilliant meteor, in New Orleans; it was the date of his mother's wedding; of Grandemont's birth. Since Grandemont could remember until the breaking up of the family that anniversary had been the synonym for feasting, hospitality, and proud commemoration.

Charleroi was the old family plantation, lying some twenty miles down the river. Years ago the estate had been sold to discharge the debts of its too-bountiful owners. Once again it had changed hands, and now the must and mildew of litigation had settled upon it. A question of heirship was in the courts, and the dwelling house of

---

*Duties (French).

†The play is worth the candle (French); figuratively, the event is worth the effort.

Charleroi, unless the tales told of ghostly powdered and laced Charleses haunting its unechoing chambers were true, stood uninhabited.

Grandemont found the solicitor in chancery who held the keys pending the decision. He proved to be an old friend of the family. Grandemont explained briefly that he desired to rent the house for two or three days. He wanted to give a dinner at his old home to a few friends. That was all.

"Take it for a week—a month, if you will," said the solicitor; "but do not speak to me of rental." With a sigh he concluded: "The dinners I have eaten under that roof, *mon fils!*"*

There came to many of the old, established dealers in furniture, china, silverware, decorations and household fittings at their stores on Canal, Chartres, St. Charles, and Royal Streets, a quiet young man with a little bald spot on the top of his head, distinguished manners, and the eye of a *connoisseur*, who explained what he wanted. To hire the complete and elegant equipment of a dining-room, hall, reception-room, and cloak-rooms. The goods were to be packed and sent, by boat, to the Charleroi landing, and would be returned within three or four days. All damage or loss to be promptly paid for.

Many of those old merchants knew Grandemont by sight, and the Charleses of old by association. Some of them were of Creole stock and felt a thrill of responsive sympathy with the magnificently indiscreet design of this impoverished clerk who would revive but for a moment the ancient flame of glory with the fuel of his savings.

"Choose what you want," they said to him. "Handle everything carefully. See that the damage bill is kept low, and the charges for the loan will not oppress you."

To the wine merchants next; and here a doleful slice was lopped from the six hundred. It was an exquisite pleasure to Grandemont once more to pick among the precious vintages. The champagne bins lured him like the abodes of sirens, but these he was forced to pass. With his six hundred he stood before them as a child with a penny stands before a French doll. But he bought with taste and

---

*"My son!" (French).

discretion of other wines—Chablis, Moselle, Château d'Or, Hochheimer, and port of right age and pedigree.

The matter of the cuisine gave him some studious hours until he suddenly recollected André—André, their old *chef*—the most sublime master of French Creole cookery in the Mississippi Valley. Perhaps he was yet somewhere about the plantation. The solicitor had told him that the place was still being cultivated, in accordance with a compromise agreement between the litigants.

On the next Sunday after the thought Grandemont rode, horseback, down to Charleroi. The big, square house with its two long ells looked blank and cheerless with its closed shutters and doors.

The shrubbery in the yard was ragged and riotous. Fallen leaves from the grove littered the walks and porches. Turning down the lane at the side of the house, Grandemont rode on to the quarters of the plantation hands. He found the workers just streaming back from church, careless, happy, and bedecked in gay yellows, reds, and blues.

Yes, André was still there; his wool a little grayer; his mouth as wide; his laughter as ready as ever. Grandemont told him of his plan, and the old *chef* swayed with pride and delight. With a sigh of relief, knowing that he need have no further concern until the serving of that dinner was announced, he placed in André's hands a liberal sum for the cost of it, giving *carte blanche** for its creation.

Among the blacks were also a number of the old house servants. Absalom, the former major domo,† and a half-dozen of the younger men, once waiters and attachés of the kitchen, pantry, and other domestic departments crowded around to greet *"M'shi Grande."‡* Absalom guaranteed to marshal, of these, a corps of assistants that would perform with credit the serving of the dinner.

After distributing a liberal largesse among the faithful, Grandemont rode back to town well pleased. There were many other smaller details to think of and provide for, but eventually the

---

*A blank slate (French); figuratively, permission to do as one pleases.
†Head servant.
‡Mr. Big (French).

scheme was complete, and now there remained only the issuance of the invitations to his guests.

Along the river within the scope of a score of miles dwelt some half-dozen families with whose princely hospitality that of the Charleses had been contemporaneous. They were the proudest and most august of the old régime. Their small circle had been a brilliant one; their social relations close and warm; their houses full of rare welcome and discriminating bounty. Those friends, said Grandemont, should once more, if never again, sit at Charleroi on a nineteenth of January to celebrate the festal day of his house.

Grandemont had his cards of invitation engraved. They were expensive, but beautiful. In one particular their good taste might have been disputed; but the Creole allowed himself that one feather in the cap of his fugacious splendour. Might he not be allowed, for the one day of the *renaissance*, to be "Grandemont du Puy Charles, of Charleroi"? He sent the invitations out early in January so that the guests might not fail to receive due notice.

At eight o'clock on the morning of the nineteenth, the lower coast steamboat *River Belle* gingerly approached the long unused landing at Charleroi. The bridge was lowered, and a swarm of the plantation hands streamed along the rotting pier, bearing ashore a strange assortment of freight. Great shapeless bundles and bales and packets swathed in cloths and bound with ropes; tubs and urns of palms, evergreens, and tropical flowers; tables, mirrors, chairs, couches, carpets, and pictures—all carefully bound and padded against the dangers of transit.

Grandemont was among them, the busiest there. To the safe conveyance of certain large hampers eloquent with printed cautions to delicate handling he gave his superintendence, for they contained the fragile china and glassware. The dropping of one of those hampers would have cost him more than he could have saved in a year.

The last article unloaded, the *River Belle* backed off and continued her course down stream. In less than an hour everything had been conveyed to the house. And came then Absalom's task, directing the placing of the furniture and wares. There was plenty of help, for that day was always a holiday at Charleroi, and the Negroes did not suffer the old traditions to lapse. Almost the entire population of the quarters volunteered their aid. A score of picca-

ninnies* were sweeping at the leaves in the yard. In the big kitchen
at the rear André was lording it with his old-time magnificence
over his numerous sub-cooks and scullions. Shutters were flung
wide; dust spun in clouds; the house echoed to voices and the tread
of busy feet. The prince had come again, and Charleroi woke from
its long sleep.

The full moon, as she rose across the river that night and peeped
above the levee saw a sight that had been long missing from her
orbit. The old plantation house shed a soft and alluring radiance
from every window. Of its two-score rooms only four had been
refurnished—the large reception chamber, the dining hall, and two
smaller rooms for the convenience of the expected guests. But
lighted wax candles were set in the windows of every room.

The dining hall was the *chef d'œuvre*.† The long table, set with
twenty-five covers, sparkled like a winter landscape with its snowy
napery and china and the icy gleam of crystal. The chaste beauty
of the room had required small adornment. The polished floor
burned to a glowing ruby with the reflection of candle light. The
rich wainscoting reached half way to the ceiling. Along and above
this had been set the relieving lightness of a few water-colour
sketches of fruit and flower.

The reception chamber was fitted in a simple but elegant style.
Its arrangement suggested nothing of the fact that on the morrow
the room would again be cleared and abandoned to the dust and
the spider. The entrance hall was imposing with palms and ferns
and the light of an immense candelabrum.

At seven o'clock Grandemont, in evening dress, with pearls—a
family passion—in his spotless linen, emerged from somewhere.
The invitations had specified eight as the dining hour. He drew an
armchair upon the porch, and sat there, smoking cigarettes and half
dreaming.

The moon was an hour high. Fifty yards back from the gate
stood the house, under its noble grove. The road ran in front, and
then came the grass-grown levee and the insatiate river beyond.
Just above the levee top a tiny red light was creeping down and a

---

*Pejorative term for black children.
†Main accomplishment (French).

tiny green one was creeping up. Then the passing steamers saluted, and the hoarse din startled the drowsy silence of the melancholy lowlands. The stillness returned, save for the little voices of the night—the owl's recitative, the capriccio of the crickets, the concerto of the frogs in the grass. The piccaninnies and the dawdlers from the quarters had been dismissed to their confines, and the melée of the day was reduced to an orderly and intelligent silence. The six coloured waiters, in their white jackets, paced, cat-footed, about the table, pretending to arrange where all was beyond betterment. Absalom, in black and shining pumps posed, superior, here and there where the lights set off his grandeur. And Grandemont rested in his chair, waiting for his guests.

He must have drifted into a dream—and an extravagant one—for he was master of Charleroi and Adèle was his wife. She was coming out to him now; he could hear her steps; he could feel her hand upon his shoulder—

"*Pardon moi, M'shi Grande*"*—it was Absalom's hand touching him, it was Absalom's voice, speaking the *patois*† of the blacks— "but it is eight o'clock."

Eight o'clock. Grandemont sprang up. In the moonlight he could see the row of hitching-posts outside the gate. Long ago the horses of the guests should have stood there. They were vacant.

A chanted roar of indignation, a just, waxing bellow of affront and dishonoured genius came from André's kitchen, filling the house with rhythmic protest. The beautiful dinner, the pearl of a dinner, the little excellent superb jewel of a dinner! But one moment more of waiting and not even the thousand thunders of black pigs of the quarters would touch it!

"They are a little late," said Grandemont, calmly. "They will come soon. Tell André to hold back dinner. And ask him if, by some chance, a bull from the pastures has broken, roaring, into the house."

He seated himself again to his cigarettes. Though he had said it, he scarcely believed Charleroi would entertain company that night. For the first time in history the invitation of a Charles had

---

*Excuse me, Mr. Big (French).
†Dialect (French).

been ignored. So simple in courtesy and honour was Grandemont and, perhaps, so serenely confident in the prestige of his name, that the most likely reasons for his vacant board did not occur to him.

Charleroi stood by a road travelled daily by people from those plantations whither his invitations had gone. No doubt even on the day before the sudden reanimation of the old house they had driven past and observed the evidences of long desertion and decay. They had looked at the corpse of Charleroi and then at Grandemont's invitations, and, though the puzzle or tasteless hoax or whatever the thing meant left them perplexed, they would not seek its solution by the folly of a visit to that deserted house.

The moon was now above the grove, and the yard was pied with deep shadows save where they lightened in the tender glow of out-pouring candle light. A crisp breeze from the river hinted at the possibility of frost when the night should have become older. The grass at one side of the steps was specked with the white stubs of Grandemont's cigarettes. The cotton-broker's clerk sat in his chair with the smoke spiralling above him. I doubt that he once thought of the little fortune he had so impotently squandered. Perhaps it was compensation enough for him to sit thus at Charleroi for a few retrieved hours. Idly his mind wandered in and out many fanciful paths of memory. He smiled to himself as a paraphrased line of Scripture strayed into his mind: "A certain *poor* man made a feast."

He heard the sound of Absalom coughing a note of summons. Grandemont stirred. This time he had not been asleep—only drowsing.

"Nine o'clock, *M'shi Grande*," said Absalom in the uninflected voice of a good servant who states a fact unqualified by personal opinion.

Grandemont rose to his feet. In their time all the Charleses had been proven, and they were gallant losers.

"Serve dinner," he said calmly. And then he checked Absalom's movement to obey, for something clicked the gate latch and was coming down the walk toward the house. Something that shuffled its feet and muttered to itself as it came. It stopped in the current of light at the foot of the steps and spake, in the universal whine of the gadding mendicant.*

---

*Wandering beggar.

"Kind sir, could you spare a poor, hungry man, out of luck, a little to eat? And to sleep in the corner of a shed? For"—the thing concluded, irrelevantly—"I can sleep now. There are no mountains to dance reels in the night; and the copper kettles are all scoured bright. The iron band is still around my ankle, and a link, if it is your desire I should be chained."

It set a foot upon the step and drew up the rags that hung upon the limb. Above the distorted shoe, caked with the dust of a hundred leagues, they saw the link and the iron band. The clothes of the tramp were wreaked to piebald tatters by sun and rain and wear. A mat of brown, tangled hair and beard covered his head and face, out of which his eyes stared distractedly. Grandemont noticed that he carried in one hand a white, square card.

"What is that?" he asked.

"I picked it up, sir, at the side of the road." The vagabond handed the card to Grandemont. "Just a little to eat, sir. A little parched corn, a *tortilla*, or a handful of beans. Goat's meat I cannot eat. When I cut their throats they cry like children."

Grandemont held up the card. It was one of his own invitations to dinner. No doubt some one had cast it away from a passing carriage after comparing it with the tenantless house of Charleroi.

"From the hedges and highways bid them come,"[2] he said to himself, softly smiling. And then to Absalom: "Send Louis to me."

Louis, once his own body-servant, came promptly, in his white jacket.

"This gentleman," said Grandemont, "will dine with me. Furnish him with bath and clothes. In twenty minutes have him ready and dinner served."

Louis approached the disreputable guest with the suavity due to a visitor to Charleroi, and spirited him away to inner regions.

Promptly, in twenty minutes, Absalom announced dinner, and, a moment later, the guest was ushered into the dining hall where Grandemont waited, standing, at the head of the table. The attentions of Louis had transformed the stranger into something resembling the polite animal. Clean linen and an old evening suit that had been sent down from town to clothe a waiter had worked a miracle with his exterior. Brush and comb had partially subdued the wild disorder of his hair. Now he might have passed for no

more extravagant a thing than one of those *poseurs** in art and music
who affect such oddity of guise. The man's countenance and demeanour, as he approached the table, exhibited nothing of the awk-
wardness or confusion to be expected from his Arabian Nights
change. He allowed Absalom to seat him at Grandemont's right
hand with the manner of one thus accustomed to be waited upon.

"It grieves me," said Grandemont, "to be obliged to exchange
names with a guest. My own name is Charles."

"In the mountains," said the wayfarer, "they call me Gringo.
Along the roads they call me Jack."

"I prefer the latter," said Grandemont. "A glass of wine with
you, Mr. Jack."

Course after course was served by the supernumerous waiters.
Grandemont, inspired by the results of André's exquisite skill in
cookery and his own in the selection of wines became the model
host, talkative, witty, and genial. The guest was fitful in conversation. His mind seemed to be sustaining a succession of waves of
dementia followed by intervals of comparative lucidity. There was
the glassy brightness of recent fever in his eyes. A long course of it
must have been the cause of his emaciation and weakness, his distracted mind, and the dull pallor that showed even through the tan
of wind and sun.

"Charles," he said to Grandemont—for thus he seemed to interpret his name—"you never saw the mountains dance, did you?"

"No, Mr. Jack," answered Grandemont, gravely, "the spectacle
has been denied me. But, I assure you, I can understand it must be
a diverting sight. The big ones, you know, white with snow on the
tops, waltzing—*décolleté,*† we may say."

"You first scour the kettles," said Mr. Jack, leaning toward him
excitedly, "to cook the beans in the morning, and you lie down on
a blanket and keep quite still. Then they come out and dance for
you. You would go out and dance with them but you are chained
every night to the centre pole of the hut. You believe the mountains
dance, don't you, Charlie?"

"I contradict no traveller's tales," said Grandemont, with a smile.

---

*Show-offs (French).
†*Décolleté* is the French word for a low-cut dress.

Mr. Jack laughed loudly. He dropped his voice to a confidential whisper.

"You are a fool to believe it," he went on. "They don't really dance. It's the fever in your head. It's the hard work and the bad water that does it. You are sick for weeks and there is no medicine. The fever comes on every evening, and then you are as strong as two men. One night the *compañia** are lying drunk with *mescal*.† They have brought back sacks of silver dollars from a ride, and they drink to celebrate. In the night you file the chain in two and go down the mountain. You walk for miles—hundreds of them. By and by the mountains are all gone, and you come to the prairies. They do not dance at night; they are merciful, and you sleep. Then you come to the river, and it says things to you. You follow it down, down, but you can't find what you are looking for."

Mr. Jack leaned back in his chair, and his eyes slowly closed. The food and wine had steeped him in a deep calm. The tense strain had been smoothed from his face. The languor of repletion was claiming him. Drowsily he spoke again.

"It's bad manners—I know—to go to sleep—at table—but— that was—such a good dinner—Grande, old fellow."

Grande! The owner of the name started and set down his glass. How should this wretched tatterdemalion whom he had invited, Caliph-like,‡ to sit at his feast know his name?

Not at first, but soon, little by little, the suspicion, wild and unreasonable as it was, stole into his brain. He drew out his watch with hands that almost balked him by their trembling, and opened the back case. There was a picture there—a photograph fixed to the inner side.

Rising, Grandemont shook Mr. Jack by the shoulder. The weary guest opened his eyes. Grandemont held the watch.

"Look at this picture, Mr. Jack. Have you ever—"

"My sister Adèle!"

The vagrant's voice rang loud and sudden through the room. He

---

*Company (Spanish).

†Powerful Mexican liquor.

‡In Muslim countries, Caliph is the title given to the head religious and civilian ruler.

started to his feet, but Grandemont's arms were about him, and Grandemont was calling him "Victor!—Victor Fauquier! *Merci, merci, mon Dieu!*"*

Too far overcome by sleep and fatigue was the lost one to talk that night. Days afterward, when the tropic *calentura*† had cooled in his veins, the disordered fragments he had spoken were completed in shape and sequence. He told the story of his angry flight, of toils and calamities on sea and shore, of his ebbing and flowing fortune in southern lands, and of his latest peril when, held a captive, he served menially in a stronghold of bandits in the Sonora Mountains of Mexico. And of the fever that seized him there and his escape and delirium, during which he strayed, perhaps led by some marvellous instinct, back to the river on whose bank he had been born. And of the proud and stubborn thing in his blood that had kept him silent through all those years, clouding the honour of one, though he knew it not, and keeping apart two loving hearts. "What a thing is love!" you may say. And if I grant it, you shall say, with me: "What a thing is pride!"

On a couch in the reception chamber Victor lay, with a dawning understanding in his heavy eyes and peace in his softened countenance. Absalom was preparing a lounge for the transient master of Charleroi, who, to-morrow, would be again the clerk of a cotton broker, but also—

"To-morrow," Grandemont was saying, as he stood by the couch of his guest, speaking the words with his face shining as must have shone the face of Elijah's charioteer when he announced the glories of that heavenly journey[3]—"To-morrow I will take you to Her."[4]

—from *The Roads of Destiny* (1909)

---

*"Thank you, thank you, my Lord!" (French).
†Temperature, fever (Spanish).

THE THING'S THE PLAY

B eing acquainted with a newspaper reporter who had a couple of free passes, I got to see the performance a few nights ago at one of the popular vaudeville houses.

One of the numbers was a violin solo by a striking-looking man not much past forty, but with very gray thick hair. Not being afflicted with a taste for music, I let the system of noises drift past my ears while I regarded the man.

"There was a story about that chap a month or two ago," said the reporter. "They gave me the assignment. It was to run a column and was to be on the extremely light and joking order. The old man seems to like the funny touch I give to local happenings. Oh, yes, I'm working on a farce comedy now. Well, I went down to the house and got all the details; but I certainly fell down on that job. I went back and turned in a comic write-up of an east side funeral instead. Why? Oh, I couldn't seem to get hold of it with my funny hooks, somehow. Maybe you could make a one-act tragedy out of it for a curtain-raiser. I'll give you the details."

After the performance my friend, the reporter, recited to me the facts over the Würzburger.*

"I see no reason," said I, when he had concluded, "why that shouldn't make a rattling good funny story. Those three people couldn't have acted in a more absurd and preposterous manner if they had been real actors in a real theatre. I'm really afraid that all the stage is a world, anyhow, and all the players merely men and women. 'The thing's the play,'[1] is the way I quote Mr. Shakespeare."

"Try it," said the reporter.

---

*Brand of beer.

"I will," said I; and I did, to show him how he could have made a humorous column of it for his paper.

There stands a house near Abingdon Square. On the ground floor there has been for twenty-five years a little store where toys and notions and stationery are sold.

One night twenty years ago there was a wedding in the rooms above the store. The Widow Mayo owned the house and store. Her daughter Helen was married to Frank Barry. John Delaney was best man. Helen was eighteen, and her picture had been printed in a morning paper next to the headlines of a "Wholesale Female Murderess" story from Butte, Mont. But after your eye and intelligence had rejected the connection, you seized your magnifying glass and read beneath the portrait her description as one of a series of Prominent Beauties and Belles of the lower west side.

Frank Barry and John Delaney were "prominent" young beaux of the same side, and bosom friends, whom you expected to turn upon each other every time the curtain went up. One who pays his money for orchestra seats and fiction expects this. That is the first funny idea that has turned up in the story yet. Both had made a great race for Helen's hand. When Frank won, John shook his hand and congratulated him—honestly, he did.

After the ceremony Helen ran upstairs to put on her hat. She was getting married in a traveling dress. She and Frank were going to Old Point Comfort for a week. Downstairs the usual horde of gibbering cave-dwellers were waiting with their hands full of old Congress gaiters and paper bags of hominy.

Then there was a rattle of the fire-escape, and into her room jumps the mad and infatuated John Delaney, with a damp curl drooping upon his forehead, and made violent and reprehensible love to his lost one, entreating her to flee or fly with him to the Riviera, or the Bronx, or any old place where there are Italian skies and *dolce far niente.**

It would have carried Blaney off his feet to see Helen repulse him. With blazing and scornful eyes she fairly withered him by demanding whatever he meant by speaking to respectable people that way.

---

*Sweet idleness (Italian).

In a few moments she had him going. The manliness that had possessed him departed. He bowed low, and said something about "irresistible impulse" and "forever carry in his heart the memory of"—and she suggested that he catch the first fire-escape going down.

"I will away," said John Delaney, "to the furthermost parts of the earth. I cannot remain near you and know that you are another's. I will to Africa, and there amid other scenes strive to for—"

"For goodness sake, get out," said Helen. "Somebody might come in."

He knelt upon one knee, and she extended him one white hand that he might give it a farewell kiss.

Girls, was this choice boon of the great little god Cupid ever vouchsafed you—to have the fellow you want hard and fast, and have the one you don't want come with a damp curl on his forehead and kneel to you and babble of Africa and love which, in spite of everything, shall forever bloom, an amaranth, in his heart? To know your power, and to feel the sweet security of your own happy state; to send the unlucky one, broken-hearted, to foreign climes, while you congratulate yourself as he presses his last kiss upon your knuckles, that your nails are well manicured—say, girls, it's galluptious*—don't ever let it get by you.

And then, of course—how did you guess it?—the door opened and in stalked the bridegroom, jealous of slow-tying bonnet strings.

The farewell kiss was imprinted upon Helen's hand, and out of the window and down the fire-escape sprang John Delaney, Africa bound.

A little slow music, if you please—faint violin, just a breath in the clarinet and a touch of the 'cello. Imagine the scene. Frank, white-hot, with the cry of a man wounded to death bursting from him. Helen, rushing and clinging to him, trying to explain. He catches her wrists and tears them from his shoulders—once, twice, thrice he sways her this way and that—the stage manager will show you how—and throws her from him to the floor a huddled, crushed, moaning thing. Never, he cries, will he look upon her face

---

*Marvelous.

again, and rushes from the house through the staring groups of astonished guests.

And, now, because it is the Thing instead of the Play, the audience must stroll out into the real lobby of the world and marry, die, grow gray, rich, poor, happy or sad during the intermission of twenty years which must precede the rising of the curtain again.

Mrs. Barry inherited the shop and the house. At thirty-eight she could have bested many an eighteen-year-old at a beauty show on points and general results. Only a few people remembered her wedding comedy, but she made of it no secret. She did not pack it in lavender or moth balls, nor did she sell it to a magazine.

One day a middle-aged, money-making lawyer, who bought his legal cap and ink of her, asked her across the counter to marry him.

"I'm really much obliged to you," said Helen, cheerfully, "but I married another man twenty years ago. He was more a goose than a man, but I think I love him yet. I have never seen him since about half an hour after the ceremony. Was it copying ink that you wanted or just writing fluid?"

The lawyer bowed over the counter with old-time grace and left a respectful kiss on the back of her hand. Helen sighed. Parting salutes, however romantic, may be overdone. Here she was at thirty-eight, beautiful and admired; and all that she seemed to have got from her lovers were reproaches and adieus. Worse still, in the last one she had lost a customer, too.

Business languished, and she hung out a Room to Let card. Two large rooms on the third floor were prepared for desirable tenants. Roomers came, and went regretfully, for the house of Mrs. Barry was the abode of neatness, comfort and taste.

One day came Ramonti, the violinist, and engaged the front room above. The discord and clatter uptown offended his nice ear; so a friend had sent him to this oasis in the desert of noise.

Ramonti, with his still youthful face, his dark eyebrows, his short, pointed, foreign, brown beard, his distinguished head of gray hair, and his artist's temperament—revealed in his light, gay and sympathetic manner—was a welcome tenant in the old house near Abingdon Square.

Helen lived on the floor above the store. The architecture of it was singular and quaint. The hall was large and almost square. Up one side of it, and then across the end of it ascended an open stairway to the floor above. This hall space she had furnished as a sitting room and office combined. There she kept her desk and wrote her business letters; and there she sat of evenings by a warm fire and a bright red light and sewed or read. Ramonti found the atmosphere so agreeable that he spent much time there, describing to Mrs. Barry the wonders of Paris, where he had studied with a particularly notorious and noisy fiddler.

Next comes lodger No. 2, a handsome, melancholy man in the early 40's, with a brown, mysterious beard, and strangely pleading, haunting eyes. He, too, found the society of Helen a desirable thing. With the eyes of Romeo and Othello's tongue,[2] he charmed her with tales of distant climes and wooed her by respectful innuendo.

From the first Helen felt a marvelous and compelling thrill in the presence of this man. His voice somehow took her swiftly back to the days of her youth's romance. This feeling grew, and she gave way to it, and it led her to an instinctive belief that he had been a factor in that romance. And then with a woman's reasoning (oh, yes, they do, sometimes) she leaped over common syllogisms and theory, and logic, and was sure that her husband had come back to her. For she saw in his eyes love, which no woman can mistake, and a thousand tons of regret and remorse, which aroused pity, which is perilously near to love requited, which is the *sine qua non*** in the house that Jack built.

But she made no sign. A husband who steps around the corner for twenty years and then drops in again should not expect to find his slippers laid out too conveniently near nor a match ready lighted for his cigar. There must be expiation, explanation, and possibly execration. A little purgatory, and then, maybe, if he were properly humble, he might be trusted with a harp and crown. And so she made no sign that she knew or suspected.

And my friend, the reporter, could see nothing funny in this! Sent out on an assignment to write up a roaring, hilarious, brilliant joshing story of—but I will not knock a brother—let us go on with the story.

---

*Indispensable thing (Latin).

One evening Ramonti stopped in Helen's hall-office-reception-room and told his love with the tenderness and ardor of the enraptured artist. His words were a bright flame of the divine fire that glows in the heart of a man who is a dreamer and a doer combined.

"But before you give me an answer," he went on, before she could accuse him of suddenness, "I must tell you that 'Ramonti' is the only name I have to offer you. My manager gave me that. I do not know who I am or where I came from. My first recollection is of opening my eyes in a hospital. I was a young man, and I had been there for weeks. My life before that is a blank to me. They told me that I was found lying in the street with a wound on my head and was brought there in an ambulance. They thought I must have fallen and struck my head upon the stones. There was nothing to show who I was. I have never been able to remember. After I was discharged from the hospital, I took up the violin. I have had success. Mrs. Barry—I do not know your name except that—I love you; the first time I saw you I realized that you were the one woman in the world for me—and"—oh, a lot of stuff like that.

Helen felt young again. First a wave of pride and a sweet little thrill of vanity went all over her; and then she looked Ramonti in the eyes, and a tremendous throb went through her heart. She hadn't expected that throb. It took her by surprise. The musician had become a big factor in her life, and she hadn't been aware of it.

"Mr. Ramonti," she said sorrowfully (this was not on the stage, remember; it was in the old home near Abingdon Square), "I'm awfully sorry, but I'm a married woman."

And then she told him the sad story of her life, as a heroine must do, sooner or later, either to a theatrical manager or to a reporter.

Ramonti took her hand, bowed low and kissed it, and went up to his room.

Helen sat down and looked mournfully at her hand. Well she might. Three suitors had kissed it, mounted their red roan steeds and ridden away.

In an hour entered the mysterious stranger with the haunting eyes. Helen was in the willow rocker, knitting a useless thing in cotton-wool. He ricocheted from the stairs and stopped for a chat.

Sitting across the table from her, he also poured out his narrative of love. And then he said: "Helen, do you not remember me? I think I have seen it in your eyes. Can you forgive the past and remember the love that has lasted for twenty years? I wronged you deeply—I was afraid to come back to you—but my love over-powered my reason. Can you, will you, forgive me?"

Helen stood up. The mysterious stranger held one of her hands in a strong and trembling clasp.

There she stood, and I pity the stage that it has not acquired a scene like that and her emotions to portray.

For she stood with a divided heart. The fresh, unforgettable, virginal love for her bridegroom was hers; the treasured, sacred, honored memory of her first choice filled half her soul. She leaned to that pure feeling. Honor and faith and sweet, abiding romance bound her to it. But the other half of her heart and soul was filled with something else—a later, fuller, nearer influence. And so the old fought against the new.

And while she hesitated, from the room above came the soft, racking, petitionary music of a violin. The hag, music, bewitches some of the noblest. The daws may peck upon one's sleeve without injury, but whoever wears his heart upon his tympanum gets it not far from the neck.

This music and the musician called her, and at her side honor and the old love held her back.

"Forgive me," he pleaded.

"Twenty years is a long time to remain away from the one you say you love," she declared, with a purgatorial touch.

"How could I tell?" he begged. "I will conceal nothing from you. That night when he left I followed him. I was mad with jealousy. On a dark street I struck him down. He did not rise. I examined him. His head had struck a stone. I did not intend to kill him. I was mad with love and jealousy. I hid near by and saw an ambulance take him away. Although you married him, Helen—"

"*Who Are You?*" cried the woman, with wide-open eyes, snatching her hand away.

"Don't you remember me, Helen—the one who has always loved you the best? I am John Delaney. If you can forgive—"

But she was gone, leaping, stumbling, hurrying, flying up the stairs toward the music and him who had forgotten, but who had known her for his in each of his two existences, and as she climbed up she sobbed, cried and sang: "Frank! Frank! Frank!"

Three mortals thus juggling with years as though they were billiard balls, and my friend, the reporter, couldn't see anything funny in it!

—from *Strictly Business* (1910)

TOBIN'S PALM

Tobin and me, the two of us, went down to Coney one day, for there was four dollars between us, and Tobin had need of distractions. For there was Katie Mahorner, his sweetheart, of County Sligo,* lost since she started for America three months before with two hundred dollars, her own savings, and one hundred dollars from the sale of Tobin's inherited estate, a fine cottage and pig on the Bog Shannaugh. And since the letter that Tobin got saying that she had started to come to him not a bit of news had he heard or seen of Katie Mahorner. Tobin advertised in the papers, but nothing could be found of the colleen.†

So, to Coney me and Tobin went, thinking that a turn at the chutes and the smell of the popcorn might raise the heart in his bosom. But Tobin was a hard-headed man, and the sadness stuck in his skin. He ground his teeth at the crying balloons; he cursed the moving pictures; and, though he would drink whenever asked, he scorned Punch and Judy, and was for licking the tintype men as they came.

So I gets him down a side way on a board walk where the attractions were some less violent. At a little six by eight stall Tobin halts, with a more human look in his eye.

" 'Tis here," says he, "I will be diverted. I'll have the palm of me hand investigated by the wonderful palmist of the Nile, and see if what is to be will be."

Tobin was a believer in signs and the unnatural in nature. He possessed illegal convictions in his mind along the subjects of black cats, lucky numbers, and the weather predictions in the papers.

---

*In Ireland.
†Young Irish girl.

We went into the enchanted chicken coop, which was fixed mysterious with red cloth and pictures of hands with lines crossing 'em like a railroad centre. The sign over the door says it is Madame Zozo the Egyptian Palmist. There was a fat woman inside in a red jumper with pothooks and beasties embroidered upon it. Tobin gives her ten cents and extends one of his hands. She lifts Tobin's hand, which is own brother to the hoof of a drayhorse, and examines it to see whether 'tis a stone in the frog or a cast shoe he has come for.

"Man," says this Madame Zozo, "the line of your fate shows—"

" 'Tis not me foot at all," says Tobin, interrupting. "Sure, 'tis no beauty, but ye hold the palm of me hand."

"The line shows," says the Madame, "that ye've not arrived at your time of life without bad luck. And there's more to come. The mount of Venus—or is that a stone bruise?—shows that ye've been in love. There's been trouble in your life on account of your sweetheart."

" 'Tis Katie Mahorner she has references with," whispers Tobin to me in a loud voice to one side.

"I see," says the palmist, "a great deal of sorrow and tribulation with one whom ye cannot forget. I see the lines of designation point to the letter K and the letter M in her name."

"Whist!" says Tobin to me; "do ye hear that?"

"Look out," goes on the palmist, "for a dark man and a light woman; for they'll both bring ye trouble. Ye'll make a voyage upon the water very soon, and have a financial loss. I see one line that brings good luck. There's a man coming into your life who will fetch ye good fortune. Ye'll know him when ye see him by his crooked nose."

"Is his name set down?" asks Tobin. " 'Twill be convenient in the way of greeting when he backs up to dump off the good luck."

"His name," says the palmist, thoughtful looking, "is not spelled out by the lines, but they indicate 'tis a long one, and the letter 'o' should be in it. There's no more to tell. Good-evening. Don't block up the door."

" 'Tis wonderful how she knows," says Tobin as we walk to the pier.

As we squeezed through the gates a nigger man sticks his lighted segar against Tobin's ear, and there is trouble. Tobin hammers his neck, and the women squeal, and by presence of mind I drag the little man out of the way before the police comes. Tobin is always in an ugly mood when enjoying himself.

On the boat going back, when the man calls "Who wants the good-looking waiter?" Tobin tried to plead guilty, feeling the desire to blow the foam off a crock of suds, but when he felt in his pocket he found himself discharged for lack of evidence. Somebody had disturbed his change during the commotion. So we sat, dry, upon the stools, listening to the Dagoes* fiddling on deck. If anything, Tobin was lower in spirits and less congenial with his misfortunes than when we started.

On a seat against the railing was a young woman dressed suitable for red automobiles, with hair the colour on an unsmoked meerschaum.† In passing by Tobin kicks her foot without intentions, and, being polite to ladies when in drink, he tries to give his hat a twist while apologizing. But he knocks it off, and the wind carries it overboard.

Tobin came back and sat down, and I began to look out for him, for the man's adversities were becoming frequent. He was apt, when pushed so close by hard luck, to kick the best dressed man he could see, and try to take command of the boat.

Presently Tobin grabs my arm and says, excited: "Jawn," says he, "do ye know what we're doing? We're taking a voyage upon the water."

"There now," says I; "subdue yeself. The boat'll land in ten minutes more."

"Look," says he, "at the light lady upon the bench. And have ye forgotten the nigger man that burned me ear? And isn't the money I had gone—a dollar sixty-five it was?"

I thought he was no more than summing up his catastrophes so as to get violent with good excuse, as men will do, and I tried to make him understand such things was trifles.

"Listen," says Tobin. "Ye've no ear for the gift of prophecy or

---

*Term used, usually disparagingly, to refer to people of Italian or Spanish descent.
†White, clay-like mineral used to make tobacco pipes.

the miracles of the inspired. What did the palmist lady tell ye out of me hand? 'Tis coming true before your eyes. 'Look out,' says she, 'for a dark man and a light woman; they'll bring ye trouble.' Have ye forgot the nigger man, though he got some of it back from me fist? Can ye show me a lighter woman than the blonde lady that was the cause of me hat falling in the water? And where's the dollar sixty-five I had in me vest when we left the shooting gallery?"

The way Tobin put it, it did seem to corroborate the art of prediction, though it looked to me that these accidents could happen to any one at Coney without the implication of palmistry.

Tobin got up and walked around on deck, looking close at the passengers out of his little red eyes. I asked him the interpretation of his movements. Ye never know what Tobin has in his mind until he begins to carry it out.

"Ye should know," says he, "I'm working out the salvation promised by the lines in me palm. I'm looking for the crooked-nose man that's to bring the good luck. 'Tis all that will save us. Jawn, did ye ever see a straighter-nosed gang of hellions in the days of your life?"

'Twas the nine-thirty boat, and we landed and walked up-town through Twenty-second Street, Tobin being without his hat.

On a street corner, standing under a gas-light and looking over the elevated road at the moon, was a man. A long man he was, dressed decent, with a segar between his teeth, and I saw that his nose made two twists from bridge to end, like the wriggle of a snake. Tobin saw it at the same time, and I heard him breathe hard like a horse when you take the saddle off. He went straight up to the man, and I went with him.

"Good-night to ye," Tobin says to the man. The man takes out a segar and passes the compliments, sociable.

"Would ye hand us your name," asks Tobin, "and let us look at the size of it? It may be our duty to become acquainted with ye."

"My name," says the man, polite, "is Friedenhausman—Maximus G. Friedenhausman."

" 'Tis the right length," says Tobin. "Do you spell it with an 'o' anywhere down the stretch of it?"

"I do not," says the man.

"*Can* ye spell it with an 'o'?" inquires Tobin, turning anxious.

"If your conscience," says the man with the nose, "is indisposed toward foreign idioms ye might, to please yourself, smuggle the letter into the penultimate syllable."

" 'Tis well," says Tobin. "Ye're in the presence of Jawn Malone and Daniel Tobin."

" 'Tis highly appreciated," says the man, with a bow. "And now since I cannot conceive that ye would hold a spelling bee upon the street corner, will ye name some reasonable excuse for being at large?"

"By the two signs," answers Tobin, trying to explain, "which ye display according to the reading of the Egyptian palmist from the sole of me hand, ye've been nominated to offset with good luck the lines of trouble leading to the nigger man and the blonde lady with her feet crossed in the boat, besides the financial loss of a dollar sixty-five, all so far fulfilled according to Hoyle."*

The man stopped smoking and looked at me.

"Have ye any amendments," he asks, "to offer to that statement, or are ye one too? I thought by the looks of ye ye might have him in charge."

"None," says I to him, "except that as one horseshoe resembles another so are ye the picture of good luck as predicted by the hand of me friend. If not, then the lines of Danny's hand may have been crossed, I don't know."

"There's two of ye," says the man with the nose, looking up and down for the sight of a policeman. "I've enjoyed your company immense. Good-night."

With that he shoves his segar in his mouth and moves across the street, stepping fast. But Tobin sticks close to one side of him and me at the other.

"What!" says he, stopping on the opposite sidewalk and pushing back his hat; "do ye follow me? I tell ye," he says, very loud, "I'm proud to have met ye. But it is my desire to be rid of ye. I am off to me home."

"Do," says Tobin, leaning against his sleeve. "Do be off to your home. And I will sit at the door of it till ye come out in the morning. For the dependence is upon ye to obviate the curse of the nigger

---

*Meaning according to authority; the English writer Edmund Hoyle (1672–1769) wrote books establishing the rules for many card and board games.

man and the blonde lady and the financial loss of the one-sixty-five."

" 'Tis a strange hallucination," says the man, turning to me as a more reasonable lunatic. "Hadn't ye better get him home?"

"Listen, man," says I to him. "Daniel Tobin is as sensible as he ever was. Maybe he is a bit deranged on account of having drink enough to disturb but not enough to settle his wits, but he is no more than following out the legitimate path of his superstitions and predicaments, which I will explain to you." With that I relates the facts about the palmist lady and how the finger of suspicion points to him as an instrument of good fortune. "Now, understand," I concludes, "my position in this riot. I am the friend of me friend Tobin, according to me interpretations. 'Tis easy to be a friend to the prosperous, for it pays; 'tis not hard to be a friend to the poor, for ye get puffed up by gratitude and have your picture printed standing in front of a tenement with a scuttle of coal and an orphan in each hand. But it strains the art of friendship to be true friend to a born fool. And that's what I'm doing," says I, "for, in my opinion, there's no fortune to be read from the palm of me hand that wasn't printed there with the handle of a pick. And, though ye've got the crookedest nose in New York City, I misdoubt that all the fortune-tellers doing business could milk good luck from ye. But the lines of Danny's hand pointed to ye fair, and I'll assist him to experiment with ye until he's convinced ye're dry."

After that the man turns, sudden, to laughing. He leans against a corner and laughs considerable. Then he claps me and Tobin on the backs of us and takes us by an arm apiece.

" 'Tis my mistake," says he. "How could I be expecting anything so fine and wonderful to be turning the corner upon me? I came near being found unworthy. Hard by," says he, "is a café, snug and suitable for the entertainment of idiosyncrasies. Let us go there and have a drink while we discuss the unavailability of the categorical."

So saying, he marched me and Tobin to the back room of a saloon, and ordered the drinks, and laid the money on the table. He looks at me and Tobin like brothers of his, and we have the segars.

"Ye must know," says the man of destiny, "that me walk in life is one that is called the literary. I wander abroad be night seeking idiosyncrasies in the masses and truth in the heavens above. When ye came upon me I was in contemplation of the elevated road in conjunction with the chief luminary of night. The rapid transit is poetry and art: the moon but a tedious, dry body, moving by rote. But these are private opinions, for, in the business of literature, the conditions are reversed. 'Tis me hope to be writing a book to explain the strange things I have discovered in life."

"Ye will put me in a book," says Tobin, disgusted; "will ye put me in a book?"

"I will not," says the man, "for the covers will not hold ye. Not yet. The best I can do is to enjoy ye meself, for the time is not ripe for destroying the limitations of print. Ye would look fantastic in type. All alone by meself must I drink this cup of joy. But, I thank ye, boys; I am truly grateful."

"The talk of ye," says Tobin, blowing through his moustache and pounding the table with his fist, "is an eyesore to me patience. There was good luck promised out of the crook of your nose, but ye bear fruit like the bang of a drum. Ye resemble, with your noise of books, the wind blowing through a crack. Sure, now, I would be thinking the palm of me hand lied but for the coming true of the nigger man and the blonde lady and—"

"Whist!" says the long man; "would ye be led astray by physiognomy? Me nose will do what it can within bounds. Let us have these glasses filled again, for 'tis good to keep idiosyncrasies well moistened, they being subject to deterioration in a dry moral atmosphere."

So, the man of literature makes good, to my notion, for he pays, cheerful, for everything, the capital of me and Tobin being exhausted by prediction. But Tobin is sore, and drinks quiet, with the red showing in his eye.

By and by we moved out, for 'twas eleven o'clock, and stands a bit upon the sidewalk. And then the man says he must be going home, and invites me and Tobin to walk that way. We arrives on a side street two blocks away where there is a stretch of brick houses with high stoops and iron fences. The man stops at one of them and looks up at the top windows which he finds dark.

" 'Tis me humble dwelling," says he, "and I begin to perceive by the signs that me wife has retired to slumber. Therefore I will venture a bit in the way of hospitality. 'Tis me wish that ye enter the basement room, where we dine, and partake of a reasonable refreshment. There will be some fine cold fowl and cheese and a bottle or two of ale. Ye will be welcome to enter and eat, for I am indebted to ye for diversions."

The appetite and conscience of me and Tobin was congenial to the proposition, though 'twas sticking hard in Danny's superstitions to think that a few drinks and a cold lunch should represent the good fortune promised by the palm of his hand.

"Step down the steps," says the man with the crooked nose, "and I will enter by the door above and let ye in. I will ask the new girl we have in the kitchen," says he, "to make ye a pot of coffee to drink before ye go. 'Tis fine coffee Katie Mahorner makes for a green girl just landed three months. Step in," says the man, "and I'll send her down to ye."

—from *The Four Million* (1906)

A NEWSPAPER STORY

At 8 A.M. it lay on Giuseppi's news-stand, still damp from the presses. Giuseppi, with the cunning of his ilk, philandered on the opposite corner, leaving his patrons to help themselves, no doubt on a theory related to the hypothesis of the watched pot.

This particular newspaper was, according to its custom and design, an educator, a guide, a monitor, a champion and a household counsellor and *vade mecum.**

From its many excellencies might be selected three editorials. One was in simple and chaste but illuminating language directed to parents and teachers, deprecating corporal punishment for children.

Another was an accusive and significant warning addressed to a notorious labour leader who was on the point of instigating his clients to a troublesome strike.

The third was an eloquent demand that the police force be sustained and aided in everything that tended to increase its efficiency as public guardians and servants.

Besides these more important chidings and requisitions upon the store of good citizenship was a wise prescription or form of procedure laid out by the editor of the heart-to-heart column in the specific case of a young man who had complained of the obduracy of his lady love, teaching him how he might win her.

Again, there was, on the beauty page, a complete answer to a young lady inquirer who desired admonition toward the securing of bright eyes, rosy cheeks and a beautiful countenance.

One other item requiring special cognizance was a brief "personal," running thus:

---

*Literally, go with me (Latin); here refers to a handy reference book.

DEAR JACK:—Forgive me. You were right. Meet me corner Madison and —th at 8:30 this morning. We leave at noon.

                                                                    PENITENT.

At 8 o'clock a young man with a haggard look and the feverish gleam of unrest in his eye dropped a penny and picked up the top paper as he passed Giuseppi's stand. A sleepless night had left him a late riser. There was an office to be reached by nine, and a shave and a hasty cup of coffee to be crowded into the interval.

He visited his barber shop and then hurried on his way. He pocketed his paper, meditating a belated perusal of it at the luncheon hour. At the next corner it fell from his pocket, carrying with it his pair of new gloves. Three blocks he walked, missed the gloves and turned back fuming.

Just on the half-hour he reached the corner where lay the gloves and the paper. But he strangely ignored that which he had come to seek. He was holding two little hands as tightly as ever he could and looking into two penitent brown eyes, while joy rioted in his heart.

"Dear Jack," she said, "I knew you would be here on time."

"I wonder what she means by that," he was saying to himself; "but it's all right, it's all right."

A big wind puffed out of the west, picked up the paper from the sidewalk, opened it out and sent it flying and whirling down a side street. Up that street was driving a skittish bay to a spider-wheel buggy, the young man who had written to the heart-to-heart editor for a recipe that he might win her for whom he sighed.

The wind, with a prankish flurry, flapped the flying newspaper against the face of the skittish bay. There was a lengthened streak of bay mingled with the red of running gear that stretched itself out for four blocks. Then a water-hydrant played its part in the cosmogony, the buggy became matchwood as foreordained, and the driver rested very quietly where he had been flung on the asphalt in front of a certain brownstone mansion.

They came out and had him inside very promptly. And there was one who made herself a pillow for his head, and cared for no curious eyes, bending over and saying, "Oh, it was you; it was you all the time, Bobby! Couldn't you see it? And if you die, why, so must I, and——"

But in all this wind we must hurry to keep in touch with our paper.

Policeman O'Brine arrested it as a character dangerous to traffic. Straightening its dishevelled leaves with his big, slow fingers, he stood a few feet from the family entrance of the Shandon Bells Café. One headline he spelled out ponderously: "The Papers to the Front in a Move to Help the Police."

But, whisht! The voice of Danny, the head bartender, through the crack of the door: "Here's a nip for ye, Mike, ould man."

Behind the widespread, amicable columns of the press Policeman O'Brine receives swiftly his nip of the real stuff. He moves away, stalwart, refreshed, fortified, to his duties. Might not the editor man view with pride the early, the spiritual, the literal fruit that had blessed his labours.

Policeman O'Brine folded the paper and poked it playfully under the arm of a small boy that was passing. That boy was named Johnny, and he took the paper home with him. His sister was named Gladys, and she had written to the beauty editor of the paper asking for the practicable touchstone of beauty. That was weeks ago, and she had ceased to look for an answer. Gladys was a pale girl, with dull eyes and a discontented expression. She was dressing to go up to the avenue to get some braid. Beneath her skirt she pinned two leaves of the paper Johnny had brought. When she walked the rustling sound was an exact imitation of the real thing.

On the street she met the Brown girl from the flat below and stopped to talk. The Brown girl turned green. Only silk at $5 a yard could make the sound that she heard when Gladys moved. The Brown girl, consumed by jealousy, said something spiteful and went her way, with pinched lips.

Gladys proceeded toward the avenue. Her eyes now sparkled like jagerfonteins. A rosy bloom visited her cheeks; a triumphant, subtle, vivifying smile transfigured her face. She was beautiful. Could the beauty editor have seen her then! There was something in her answer in the paper, I believe, about cultivating kind feelings toward others in order to make plain features attractive.

The labour leader against whom the paper's solemn and weighty editorial injunction was laid was the father of Gladys and Johnny. He picked up the remains of the journal from which Gladys had ravished a cosmetic of silken sounds. The editorial did not come under his eye, but instead it was greeted by one of those ingenious and specious puzzle problems that enthrall alike the simpleton and the sage.

The labour leader tore off half of the page, provided himself with table, pencil and paper and glued himself to his puzzle.

Three hours later, after waiting vainly for him at the appointed place, other more conservative leaders declared and ruled in favour of arbitration, and the strike with its attendant dangers was averted. Subsequent editions of the paper referred, in coloured inks, to the clarion tone of its successful denunciation of the labour leader's intended designs.

The remaining leaves of the active journal also went loyally to the proving of its potency.

When Johnny returned from school he sought a secluded spot and removed the missing columns from the inside of his clothing, where they had been artfully distributed so as to successfully defend such areas as are generally attacked during scholastic castigations. Johnny attended a private school and had had trouble with his teacher. As has been said, there was an excellent editorial against corporal punishment in that morning's issue, and no doubt it had its effect.

After this can any one doubt the power of the press?

—from *Whirligigs* (1910)

PROOF OF THE PUDDING

S pring winked a vitreous optic at Editor Westbrook of the *Minerva Magazine*,[1] and deflected him from his course. He had lunched in his favorite corner of a Broadway hotel, and was returning to his office when his feet became entangled in the lure of the vernal coquette. Which is by way of saying that he turned eastward in Twenty-sixth Street, safely forded the spring freshet of vehicles in Fifth Avenue, and meandered along the walks of budding Madison Square.

The lenient air and the settings of the little park almost formed a pastoral; the color motif was green—the presiding shade at the creation of man and vegetation.

The callow grass between the walks was the color of verdigris, a poisonous green, reminiscent of the horde of derelict humans that had breathed upon the soil during the summer and autumn. The bursting tree buds looked strangely familiar to those who had botanized among the garnishings of the fish course of a forty-cent dinner. The sky above was of that pale aquamarine tint that hallroom poets rhyme with "true" and "Sue" and "coo." The one natural and frank color visible was the ostensible green of the newly painted benches—a shade between the color of a pickled cucumber and that of a last year's fast-black cravenette raincoat. But, to the city-bred eye of Editor Westbrook, the landscape appeared a masterpiece.

And now, whether you are of those who rush in, or of the gentle concourse that fears to tread,[2] you must follow in a brief invasion of the editor's mind.

Editor Westbrook's spirit was contented and serene. The April number of the *Minerva* had sold its entire edition before the tenth day of the month—a newsdealer in Keokuk had written that he could have sold fifty copies more if he had had 'em. The owners of the magazine had raised his (the editor's) salary; he had just installed in his home a jewel of a recently imported cook who was afraid of policemen; and the morning papers had published in full a speech he had made at a publishers' banquet. Also there were echoing in his mind the jubilant notes of a splendid song that his charming young wife had sung to him before he left his up-town apartment that morning. She was taking enthusiastic interest in her music of late, practising early and diligently. When he had complimented her on the improvement in her voice she had fairly hugged him for joy at his praise. He felt, too, the benign, tonic medicament of the trained nurse, Spring, tripping softly adown the wards of the convalescent city.

While Editor Westbrook was sauntering between the rows of park benches (already filling with vagrants and the guardians of lawless childhood) he felt his sleeve grasped and held. Suspecting that he was about to be panhandled, he turned a cold and unprofitable face, and saw that his captor was—Dawe—Shackleford Dawe, dingy, almost ragged, the genteel scarcely visible in him through the deeper lines of the shabby.

While the editor is pulling himself out of his surprise, a flashlight biography of Dawe is offered.

He was a fiction writer, and one of Westbrook's old acquaintances. At one time they might have called each other old friends. Dawe had some money in those days, and lived in a decent apartment house near Westbrook's. The two families often went to theatres and dinners together. Mrs. Dawe and Mrs. Westbrook became "dearest" friends. Then one day a little tentacle of the octopus, just to amuse itself, ingurgitated Dawe's capital, and he moved to the Gramercy Park neighborhood where one, for a few groats per week, may sit upon one's trunk under eight-branched chandeliers and opposite Carrara marble mantels and watch the mice play upon the floor. Dawe thought to live by writing fiction. Now and then he sold a story. He submitted many to Westbrook. The *Minerva* printed one or two of them; the rest were returned. Westbrook sent a careful and conscientious personal letter with each rejected manuscript, pointing out in detail his reasons for considering it unavailable. Editor Westbrook had his own clear conception of what constituted good fiction. So had Dawe. Mrs. Dawe was mainly concerned about the constituents of the scanty dishes of food that she managed to scrape together. One day Dawe had been spouting to her about the excellencies of certain French writers. At dinner they sat down to a dish that a hungry schoolboy could have encompassed at a gulp. Dawe commented.

"It's Maupassant hash," said Mrs. Dawe. "It may not be art, but I do wish you would do a five-course Marion Crawford serial with an Ella Wheeler Wilcox sonnet[3] for dessert. I'm hungry."

As far as this from success was Shackleford Dawe when he plucked Editor Westbrook's sleeve in Madison Square. That was the first time the editor had seen Dawe in several months.

"Why, Shack, is this you?" said Westbrook, somewhat awkwardly, for the form of his phrase seemed to touch upon the other's changed appearance.

"Sit down for a minute," said Dawe, tugging at his sleeve. "This is my office. I can't come to yours, looking as I do. Oh, sit down—you won't be disgraced. Those half-plucked birds on the other benches will take you for a swell porch-climber. They won't know you are only an editor."

"Smoke, Shack?" said Editor Westbrook, sinking cautiously upon the virulent green bench. He always yielded gracefully when he did yield.

Dawe snapped at the cigar as a kingfisher darts at a sunperch, or a girl pecks at a chocolate cream.

"I have just—" began the editor.

"Oh, I know; don't finish," said Dawe. "Give me a match. You have just ten minutes to spare. How did you manage to get past my office-boy and invade my sanctum? There he goes now, throwing his club at a dog that couldn't read the 'Keep off the Grass' signs."

"How goes the writing?" asked the editor.

"Look at me," said Dawe, "for your answer. Now don't put on that embarrassed, friendly-but-honest look and ask me why I don't get a job as a wine agent or a cab driver. I'm in the fight to a finish. I know I can write good fiction and I'll force you fellows to admit it yet. I'll make you change the spelling of 'regrets' to 'c-h-e-q-u-e' before I'm done with you."

Editor Westbrook gazed through his nose-glasses with a sweetly sorrowful, omniscient, sympathetic, skeptical expression—the copyrighted expression of the editor beleagured by the unavailable contributor.

"Have you read the last story I sent you—'The Alarum of the Soul'?" asked Dawe.

"Carefully. I hesitated over that story, Shack, really I did. It has some good points. I was writing you a letter to send with it when it goes back to you. I regret—"

"Never mind the regrets," said Dawe, grimly. "There's neither salve nor sting in 'em any more. What I want to know is *why*. Come, now; out with the good points first."

"The story," said Westbrook, deliberately, after a suppressed sigh, "is written around an almost original plot. Characterization— the best you have done. Construction—almost as good, except for a few weak joints which might be strengthened by a few changes and touches. It was a good story, except—"

"I can write English, can't I?" interrupted Dawe.

"I have always told you," said the editor, "that you had a style."

"Then the trouble is the—"

"Same old thing," said Editor Westbrook. "You work up to your climax like an artist. And then you turn yourself into a photographer. I don't know what form of obstinate madness possesses you, Shack, but that is what you do with everything that you write. No, I will retract the comparison with the photographer. Now and then photography, in spite of its impossible perspective, manages to record a fleeting glimpse of truth. But you spoil every dénouement by those flat, drab, obliterating strokes of your brush that I have so often complained of. If you would rise to the literary pinnacle of your dramatic scenes, and paint them in the high colors that art requires, the postman would leave fewer bulky, self-addressed envelopes at your door."

"Oh, fiddles and footlights!" cried Dawe, derisively. "You've got that old sawmill drama kink in your brain yet. When the man with the black mustache kidnaps golden-haired Bessie you are bound to have the mother kneel and raise her hands in the spotlight and say: 'May high heaven witness that I will rest neither night nor day till the heartless villain that has stolen me child feels the weight of another's vengeance!' "

Editor Westbrook conceded a smile of impervious complacency.

"I think," said he, "that in real life the woman would express herself in those words or in very similar ones."

"Not in a six hundred nights' run anywhere but on the stage," said Dawe hotly. "I'll tell you what she'd say in real life. She'd say: 'What! Bessie led away by a strange man? Good Lord! It's one trouble after another! Get my other hat, I must hurry around to the police-station. Why wasn't somebody looking after her, I'd like to know? For God's sake, get out of my way or I'll never get ready. Not that hat—the brown one with the velvet bows. Bessie must have been crazy; she's usually shy of strangers. Is that too much powder? Lordy! How I'm upset!'

"That's the way she'd talk," continued Dawe. "People in real life don't fly into heroics and blank verse at emotional crises. They simply can't do it. If they talk at all on such occasions they draw from the same vocabulary that they use every day, and muddle up their words and ideas a little more, that's all."

"Shack," said Editor Westbrook impressively, "did you ever pick up the mangled and lifeless form of a child from under the fender of a street car, and carry it in your arms and lay it down before the distracted mother? Did you ever do that and listen to the words of grief and despair as they flowed spontaneously from her lips?"

"I never did," said Dawe. "Did you?"

"Well, no," said Editor Westbrook, with a slight frown. "But I can well imagine what she would say."

"So can I," said Dawe.

And now the fitting time had come for Editor Westbrook to play the oracle and silence his opinionated contributor. It was not for an unarrived fictionist to dictate words to be uttered by the heroes and heroines of the *Minerva Magazine*, contrary to the theories of the editor thereof.

"My dear Shack," said he, "if I know anything of life I know that every sudden, deep and tragic emotion in the human heart calls forth an apposite, concordant, conformable and proportionate expression of feeling. How much of this inevitable accord between expression and feeling should be attributed to nature, and how much to the influence of art, it would be difficult to say. The sub-limely terrible roar of the lioness that has been deprived of her cubs is dramatically as far above her customary whine and purr as the kingly and transcendent utterances of Lear are above the level of his senile vaporings.[4] But it is also true that all men and women have what may be called a sub-conscious dramatic sense that is awakened by a sufficiently deep and powerful emotion—a sense unconsciously acquired from literature and the stage that prompts them to express those emotions in language befitting their impor-tance and histrionic value."

"And in the name of the seven sacred saddle-blankets of Sag-ittarius,* where did the stage and literature get the stunt?" asked Dawe.

"From life," answered the editor, triumphantly.

The story writer rose from the bench and gesticulated eloquently but dumbly. He was beggared for words with which to formulate adequately his dissent.

On a bench nearby a frowzy loafer opened his red eyes and perceived that his moral support was due a downtrodden brother.

"Punch him one, Jack," he called hoarsely to Dawe. "W'at's he come makin' a noise like a penny arcade for amongst gen'lemen that comes in the Square to set and think?"

Editor Westbrook looked at his watch with an affected show of leisure.

"Tell me," asked Dawe, with truculent anxiety, "what especial faults in 'The Alarum of the Soul' caused you to throw it down?"

"When Gabriel Murray," said Westbrook, "goes to his telephone and is told that his fiancée has been shot by a burglar, he says—I do not recall the exact words, but—"

"I do," said Dawe. "He says: 'Damn Central; she always cuts me off.' (And then to his friend) 'Say, Tommy, does a thirty-two bullet make a big hole? It's kind of hard luck, ain't it? Could you get me a drink from the sideboard, Tommy? No; straight; nothing on the side.'"

"And again," continued the editor, without pausing for argu-

---

*Zodiacal constellation pictured as a centaur (half-man, half-horse).

ment, "when Berenice opens the letter from her husband informing her that he has fled with the manicure girl, her words are—let me see—"

"She says," interposed the author: " 'Well, what do you think of that!' "

"Absurdly inappropriate words," said Westbrook, "presenting an anti-climax—plunging the story into hopeless bathos. Worse yet; they mirror life falsely. No human being ever uttered banal collo-quialisms when confronted by sudden tragedy."

"Wrong," said Dawe, closing his unshaven jaws doggedly. "I say no man or woman ever spouts 'highfalutin' talk when they go up against a real climax. They talk naturally and a little worse."

The editor rose from the bench with his air of indulgence and inside information.

"Say, Westbrook," said Dawe, pinning him by the lapel, "would you have accepted 'The Alarum of the Soul' if you had believed that the actions and words of the characters were true to life in the parts of the story that we discussed?"

"It is very likely that I would, if I believed that way," said the editor. "But I have explained to you that I do not."

"If I could prove to you that I am right?"

"I'm sorry, Shack, but I'm afraid I haven't time to argue any further just now."

"I don't want to argue," said Dawe. "I want to demonstrate to you from life itself that my view is the correct one."

"How could you do that?" asked Westbrook, in a surprised tone.

"Listen," said the writer, seriously. "I have thought of a way. It is important to me that my theory of true-to-life fiction be recognized as correct by the magazines. I've fought for it for three years, and I'm down to my last dollar, with two months' rent due."

"I have applied the opposite of your theory," said the editor, "in selecting the fiction for the *Minerva Magazine*. The circulation has gone up from ninety thousand to—"

"Four hundred thousand," said Dawe. "Whereas it should have been boosted to a million."

"You said something to me just now about demonstrating your pet theory."

"I will. If you'll give me about half an hour of your time I'll prove to you that I am right. I'll prove it by Louise."

"Your wife!" exclaimed Westbrook. "How?"

"Well, not exactly by her, but *with* her," said Dawe. "Now, you know how devoted and loving Louise has always been. She thinks I'm the only genuine preparation on the market that bears the old doctor's signature. She's been fonder and more faithful than ever, since I've been cast for the neglected genius part."

"Indeed, she is a charming and admirable life companion," agreed the editor. "I remember what inseparable friends she and Mrs. Westbrook once were. We are both lucky chaps, Shack, to have such wives. You must bring Mrs. Dawe up some evening soon, and we'll have one of those informal chafing-dish suppers that we used to enjoy so much."

"Later," said Dawe. "When I get another shirt. And now I'll tell you my scheme. When I was about to leave home after breakfast— if you can call tea and oatmeal breakfast—Louise told me she was going to visit her aunt in Eighty-ninth Street. She said she would return home at three o'clock. She is always on time to a minute. It is now—"

Dawe glanced toward the editor's watch pocket.

"Twenty-seven minutes to three," said Westbrook, scanning his time-piece.

"We have just enough time," said Dawe. "We will go to my flat at once. I will write a note, address it to her and leave it on the table where she will see it as she enters the door. You and I will be in the dining-room concealed by the portières. In that note I'll say that I have fled from her forever with an affinity who understands the needs of my artistic soul as she never did. When she reads it we will observe her actions and hear her words. Then we will know which theory is the correct one—yours or mine."

"Oh, never!" exclaimed the editor, shaking his head. "That would be inexcusably cruel. I could not consent to have Mrs. Dawe's feelings played upon in such a manner."

"Brace up," said the writer. "I guess I think as much of her as you do. It's for her benefit as well as mine. I've got to get a market for my stories in some way. It won't hurt Louise. She's healthy and sound. Her heart goes as strong as a ninety-eight-cent watch. It'll last for only a minute, and then I'll step out and explain to her. You really owe it to me to give me the chance, Westbrook."

Editor Westbrook at length yielded, though but half willingly. And in the half of him that consented lurked the vivisectionist that is in all of us. Let him who has not used the scalpel rise and stand in his place. Pity 'tis that there are not enough rabbits and guinea-pigs to go around.

The two experimenters in Art left the Square and hurried eastward and then to the south until they arrived in the Gramercy neighborhood. Within its high iron railings the little park had put on its smart coat of vernal green, and was admiring itself in its fountain mirror. Outside the railings the hollow square of crumbling houses, shells of a bygone gentry, leaned as if in ghostly gossip over the forgotten doings of the vanished quality. *Sic transit gloria urbis.**

A block or two north of the Park, Dawe steered the editor again eastward, then, after covering a short distance, into a lofty but narrow flathouse burdened with a floridly over-decorated façade. To the fifth story they toiled, and Dawe, panting, pushed his latch-key into the door of one of the front flats.

When the door opened Editor Westbrook saw, with feelings of pity, how meanly and meagerly the rooms were furnished.

"Get a chair, if you can find one," said Dawe, "while I hunt up pen and ink. Hello, what's this? Here's a note from Louise. She must have left it there when she went out this morning."

He picked up an envelope that lay on the centre-table and tore it open. He began to read the letter that he drew out of it; and once having begun it aloud he so read it through to the end. These are the words that Editor Westbrook heard:

"DEAR SHACKLEFORD:
"By the time you get this I will be about a hundred miles away and still a-going. I've got a place in the chorus of the Occidental Opera Co., and we start on the road to-day at twelve o'clock. I

---

*Thus passes the glory of the city (Latin).

didn't want to starve to death, and so I decided to make my own living. I'm not coming back. Mrs. Westbrook is going with me. She said she was tired of living with a combination phonograph, iceberg and dictionary, and she's not coming back, either. We've been practising the songs and dances for two months on the quiet. I hope you will be successful, and get along all right! Good-bye.

"LOUISE."

Dawe dropped the letter, covered his face with his trembling hands, and cried out in a deep, vibrating voice:

"My God, why hast thou given me this cup to drink? Since she is false, then let Thy Heaven's fairest gifts, faith and love, become the jesting by-words of traitors and fiends!"

Editor Westbrook's glasses fell to the floor. The fingers of one hand fumbled with a button on his coat as he blurted between his pale lips:

"Say, Shack, ain't that a hell of a note? Wouldn't that knock you off your perch, Shack? Ain't it hell, now. Shack—ain't it?"

—from *Strictly Business* (1910)

CONFESSIONS OF A HUMORIST

There was a painless stage of incubation that lasted twenty-five years, and then it broke out on me, and people said I was It.

But they called it humor instead of measles.

The employees in the store bought a silver inkstand for the senior partner on his fiftieth birthday. We crowded into his private office to present it.

I had been selected for spokesman, and I made a little speech that I had been preparing for a week.

It made a hit. It was full of puns and epigrams and funny twists that brought down the house—which was a very solid one in the wholesale hardware line. Old Marlowe himself actually grinned, and the employees took their cue and roared.

My reputation as a humorist dates from half-past nine o'clock on that morning.

For weeks afterward my fellow clerks fanned the flame of my self-esteem. One by one they came to me, saying what an awfully clever speech that was, old man, and carefully explained to me the point of each one of my jokes.

Gradually I found that I was expected to keep it up. Others might speak sanely on business matters and the day's topics, but from me something gamesome and airy was required.

I was expected to crack jokes about the crockery and lighten up the granite ware with persiflage. I was second bookkeeper, and if I failed to show up a balance sheet without something comic about the footings or could find no cause for laughter in an invoice of plows, the other clerks were disappointed.

By degrees my fame spread, and I became a local "character." Our town was small enough to make this possible. The daily newspaper quoted me. At social gatherings I was indispensable.

I believe I did possess considerable wit and a facility for quick and spontaneous repartee. This gift I cultivated and improved by practice. And the nature of it was kindly and genial, not running to sarcasm or offending others. People began to smile when they saw me coming, and by the time we had met I generally had the word ready to broaden the smile into a laugh.

I had married early. We had a charming boy of three and a girl of five. Naturally, we lived in a vine-covered cottage, and were happy. My salary as bookkeeper in the hardware concern kept at a distance those ills attendant upon superfluous wealth.

At sundry times I had written out a few jokes and conceits that I considered peculiarly happy, and had sent them to certain periodicals that print such things. All of them had been instantly accepted. Several of the editors had written to request further contributions.

One day I received a letter from the editor of a famous weekly publication. He suggested that I submit to him a humorous composition to fill a column of space; hinting that he would make it a regular feature of each issue if the work proved satisfactory. I did so, and at the end of two weeks he offered to make a contract with me for a year at a figure that was considerably higher than the amount paid me by the hardware firm.

I was filled with delight. My wife already crowned me in her mind with the imperishable evergreens of literary success. We had lobster croquettes and a bottle of blackberry wine for supper that night. Here was the chance to liberate myself from drudgery. I talked over the matter very seriously with Louisa. We agreed that I must resign my place at the store and devote myself to humor.

I resigned. My fellow clerks gave me a farewell banquet. The speech I made there coruscated. It was printed in full by the *Gazette*. The next morning I awoke and looked at the clock.

"Late, by George!" I exclaimed, and grabbed for my clothes. Louisa reminded me that I was no longer a slave to hardware and contractors' supplies. I was now a professional humorist.

After breakfast she proudly led me to the little room off the kitchen. Dear girl! There was my table and chair, writing pad, ink, and pipe tray. And all the author's trappings—the celery stand full of fresh roses and honeysuckle, last year's calendar on the wall, the dictionary, and a little bag of chocolates to nibble between inspirations. Dear girl!

I sat me to work. The wall paper is patterned with arabesques or odalisks or—perhaps—it is trapezoids. Upon one of the figures I fixed my eyes. I bethought me of humor.

A voice startled me—Louisa's voice.

"If you aren't too busy, dear," it said, "come to dinner."

I looked at my watch. Yes, five hours had been gathered in by the grim scytheman.* I went to dinner.

"You mustn't work too hard at first," said Louisa. "Goethe—or was it Napoleon?—said five hours a day is enough for mental labor.[1] Couldn't you take me and the children to the woods this afternoon?"

"I *am* a little tired," I admitted. So we went to the woods.

But I soon got the swing of it. Within a month I was turning out copy as regular as shipments of hardware.

And I had success. My column in the weekly made some stir, and I was referred to in a gossipy way by the critics as something fresh in the line of humorists. I augmented my income considerably by contributing to other publications.

I picked up the tricks of the trade. I could take a funny idea and make a two-line joke of it, earning a dollar. With false whiskers on, it would serve up cold as a quatrain, doubling its producing value. By turning the skirt and adding a ruffle of rhyme you would hardly recognize it as *vers de société*† with neatly shod feet and a fashion-plate illustration.

I began to save up money, and we had new carpets, and a parlor organ. My townspeople began to look upon me as a citizen of some consequence instead of the merry trifler I had been when I clerked in the hardware store.

After five or six months the spontaneity seemed to depart from my humor. Quips and droll sayings no longer fell carelessly from my lips. I was sometimes hard run for material. I found myself listening to catch available ideas from the conversation of my

---

*Grim Reaper; death personified as a man or skeleton carrying a scythe.
†Literally, poetry of society (French); light, entertaining poetry and verse.

friends. Sometimes I chewed my pencil and gazed at the wall paper for hours trying to build up some gay little bubble of unstudied fun.

And then I became a harpy, a Moloch, a Jonah,[2] a vampire, to my acquaintances. Anxious, haggard, greedy, I stood among them like a veritable killjoy. Let a bright saying, a witty comparison, a piquant phrase fall from their lips and I was after it like a hound springing upon a bone. I dared not trust my memory; but, turning aside guiltily and meanly, I would make a note of it in my ever-present memorandum book or upon my cuff for my own future use.

My friends regarded me in sorrow and wonder. I was not the same man. Where once I had furnished them entertainment and jollity, I now preyed upon them. No jests from me ever bid for their smiles now. They were too precious. I could not afford to dispense gratuitously the means of my livelihood.

I was a lugubrious fox praising the singing of my friends, the crows, that they might drop from their beaks the morsels of wit that I coveted.

Nearly every one began to avoid me. I even forgot how to smile, not even paying that much for the sayings I appropriated.

No persons, places, times, or subjects were exempt from my plundering in search of material. Even in church my demoralized fancy went hunting among the solemn aisles and pillars for spoil.

Did the minister give out the long-meter doxology, at once I began: "Doxology—sockdology—sockdolager—meter—meether."

The sermon ran through my mental sieve, its precepts filtering unheeded, could I but glean a suggestion of a pun or a *bon mot*.* The solemnest anthems of the choir were but an accompaniment to my thoughts as I conceived new changes to ring upon the ancient comicalities concerning the jealousies of soprano, tenor, and basso.

My own home became a hunting ground. My wife is a singularly feminine creature, candid, sympathetic, and impulsive. Once her conversation was my delight, and her ideas a source of unfailing pleasure. Now I worked her. She was a gold mine of those amusing but lovable inconsistencies that distinguish the female mind.

I began to market those pearls of unwisdom and humor that

---

*Literally, good word (French); witty remark.

should have enriched only the sacred precincts of home. With devilish cunning I encouraged her to talk. Unsuspecting, she laid her heart bare. Upon the cold, conspicuous, common, printed page I offered it to the public gaze.

A literary Judas,[3] I kissed her and betrayed her. For pieces of silver I dressed her sweet confidences in the pantalettes and frills of folly and made them dance in the market place.

Dear Louisa! Of nights I have bent over her cruel as a wolf above a tender lamb, hearkening even to her soft words murmured in sleep, hoping to catch an idea for my next day's grind. There is worse to come.

God help me! Next my fangs were buried deep in the neck of the fugitive sayings of my little children.

Guy and Viola were two bright fountains of childish, quaint thoughts and speeches. I found a ready sale for this kind of humor, and was furnishing a regular department in a magazine with "Funny Fancies of Childhood." I began to stalk them as an Indian stalks the antelope. I would hide behind sofas and doors, or crawl on my hands and knees among the bushes in the yard to eavesdrop while they were at play. I had all the qualities of a harpy except remorse.

Once, when I was barren of ideas, and my copy must leave in the next mail, I covered myself in a pile of autumn leaves in the yard, where I knew they intended to come to play. I cannot bring myself to believe that Guy was aware of my hiding place, but even if he was, I would be loath to blame him for his setting fire to the leaves, causing the destruction of my new suit of clothes, and nearly cremating a parent.

Soon my own children began to shun me as a pest. Often, when I was creeping upon them like a melancholy ghoul, I would hear them say to each other: "Here comes papa," and they would gather their toys and scurry away to some safer hiding place. Miserable wretch that I was!

And yet I was doing well financially. Before the first year had passed I had saved a thousand dollars, and we had lived in comfort.

But at what a cost! I am not quite clear as to what a pariah is, but I was everything that it sounds like. I had no friends, no amusements, no enjoyment of life. The happiness of my family had been sacrificed. I was a bee, sucking sordid honey from life's fairest flowers, dreaded and shunned on account of my sting.

One day a man spoke to me, with a pleasant and friendly smile. Not in months had the thing happened. I was passing the undertaking establishment of Peter Heffelbower. Peter stood in the door and saluted me. I stopped, strangely wrung in my heart by his greeting. He asked me inside.

The day was chill and rainy. We went into the back room, where a fire burned in a little stove. A customer came, and Peter left me alone for a while. Presently I felt a new feeling stealing over me—a sense of beautiful calm and content, I looked around the place. There were rows of shining rosewood caskets, black palls, trestles, hearse plumes, mourning streamers, and all the paraphernalia of the solemn trade. Here was peace, order, silence, the abode of grave and dignified reflections. Here, on the brink of life, was a little niche pervaded by the spirit of eternal rest.

When I entered it, the follies of the world abandoned me at the door. I felt no inclination to wrest a humorous idea from those sombre and stately trappings. My mind seemed to stretch itself to grateful repose upon a couch draped with gentle thoughts.

A quarter of an hour ago I was an abandoned humorist. Now I was a philosopher, full of serenity and ease. I had found a *refuge* from humor, from the hot chase of the shy quip, from the degrading pursuit of the panting joke, from the restless reach after the nimble repartee.

I had not known Heffelbower well. When he came back, I let him talk, fearful that he might prove to be a jarring note in the sweet, dirgelike harmony of his establishment.

But, no. He chimed truly. I gave a long sigh of happiness. Never have I known a man's talk to be as magnificently dull as Peter's was. Compared with it the Dead Sea is a geyser. Never a sparkle or a glimmer of wit marred his words. Commonplaces as trite and as plentiful as blackberries flowed from his lips no more stirring in quality than a last week's tape running from a ticker. Quaking a little, I tried upon him one of my best pointed jokes. It fell back ineffectual, with the point broken. I loved that man from then on.

Two or three evenings each week I would steal down to Heffelbower's and revel in his back room. That was my only joy. I began to rise early and hurry through my work, that I might spend more time in my haven. In no other place could I throw off my habit of extracting humorous ideas from my surroundings. Peter's talk left me no opening had I besieged it ever so hard.

Under this influence I began to improve in spirits. It was the recreation from one's labor which every man needs. I surprised one or two of my former friends by throwing them a smile and a cheery word as I passed them on the streets. Several times I dumfounded my family by relaxing long enough to make a jocose remark in their presence.

I had so long been ridden by the incubus of humor that I seized my hours of holiday with a schoolboy's zest.

My work began to suffer. It was not the pain and burden to me that it had been. I often whistled at my desk, and wrote with far more fluency than before. I accomplished my tasks impatiently, as anxious to be off to my helpful retreat as a drunkard is to get to his tavern.

My wife had some anxious hours in conjecturing where I spent my afternoons. I thought it best not to tell her; women do not understand these things. Poor girl!—she had one shock out of it.

One day I brought home a silver coffin handle for a paper weight and a fine, fluffy hearse plume to dust my papers with.

I loved to see them on my desk, and think of the beloved back room down at Heffelbower's. But Louisa found them, and she shrieked with horror. I had to console her with some lame excuse for having them, but I saw in her eyes that the prejudice was not removed. I had to remove the articles, though, at double-quick time.

One day Peter Heffelbower laid before me a temptation that swept me off my feet. In his sensible, uninspired way he showd me his books, and explained that his profits and his business were increasing rapidly. He had thought of taking in a partner with some cash. He would rather have me than any one he knew. When I left his place that afternoon Peter had my check for the thousand dollars I had in the bank, and I was a partner in his undertaking business.

I went home with feelings of delirious joy, mingled with a certain amount of doubt. I was dreading to tell my wife about it. But I walked on air. To give up the writing of humorous stuff, once more to enjoy the apples of life, instead of squeezing them to a pulp for a few drops of hard cider to make the public feel funny—what a boon that would be!

At the supper table Louisa handed me some letters that had come during my absence. Several of them contained rejected manuscript. Ever since I first began going to Heffelbower's my stuff had been coming back with alarming frequency. Lately I had been dashing off my jokes and articles with the greatest fluency. Previously I had labored like a bricklayer, slowly and with agony.

Presently I opened a letter from the editor of the weekly with which I had a regular contract. The checks for that weekly article were still our main dependence. The letter ran thus:

DEAR SIR:

As you are aware, our contract for the year expires with the present month. While regretting the necessity for so doing, we must say that we do not care to renew same for the coming year. We were quite pleased with your style of humor, which seems to have delighted quite a large proportion of our readers. But for the past two months we have noticed a decided falling off in its quality.

Your earlier work showed a spontaneous, easy, natural flow of fun and wit. Of late it is labored, studied, and unconvincing, giving painful evidence of hard toil and drudging mechanism.

Again regretting that we do not consider your contributions available any longer, we are, yours sincerely,

THE EDITOR.

I handed this letter to my wife. After she had read it her face grew extremely long, and there were tears in her eyes.

"The mean old thing!" she exclaimed indignantly. "I'm sure your pieces are just as good as they ever were. And it doesn't take you half as long to write them as it did." And then, I suppose, Louisa thought of the checks that would cease coming. "Oh, John," she wailed, "what will you do now?"

For an answer I got up and began to do a polka step around the supper table. I am sure Louisa thought the trouble had driven me mad; and I think the children hoped it had, for they tore after me, yelling with glee and emulating my steps. I was now something like their old playmate as of yore.

"The theatre for us to-night!" I shouted; "nothing less. And a late, wild disreputable supper for all of us at the Palace Restaurant. Lumpty-diddle-de-dee-de-dum!"

And then I explained my glee by declaring that I was now a partner in a prosperous undertaking establishment, and that written jokes might go hide their heads in sackcloth and ashes for all me.

With the editor's letter in her hand to justify the deed I had done, my wife could advance no objections save a few mild ones based on the feminine inability to appreciate a good thing such as the little back room of Peter Hef—no, of Heffelbower & Co's. undertaking establishment.

In conclusion, I will say that to-day you will find no man in our town as well liked, as jovial, and full of merry sayings as I. My jokes are again noised about and quoted; once more I take pleasure in my wife's confidential chatter without a mercenary thought, while Guy and Viola play at my feet distributing gems of childish humor without fear of the ghastly tormentor who used to dog their steps, notebook in hand.

Our business has prospered finely. I keep the books and look after the shop while Peter attends to outside matters. He says that my levity and high spirits would simply turn any funeral into a regular Irish wake.

—from *Waifs and Strays* (1917)

ENDNOTES

"The Plutonian Fire"

1. (p. 7) *Winged Victory*: A common subject among ancient Greek sculptors, the Winged Victory is usually depicted sensuously, tilting slightly forward with her wings flexed as if she has just alighted. The most famous Winged Victory is in Paris at the Louvre museum and is called the *Niki de Samothrace*.

2. (p. 7) *reading the latest copy of Le Petit Journal: Le Petit Journal* was a widely read and highly respected weekly newsmagazine in turn-of-the-century France.

3. (p. 8) *battle of Lookout Mountain*: In this battle of the Civil War, fought on November 24, 1863, Union troops successfully stormed a Confederate stronghold atop Tennessee's Lookout Mountain; the battle was fought in dense fog and later nicknamed the Battle Above the Clouds.

4. (p. 8) *adventures in Picardy*: Picardy is a historical region of northern France stretching north to Belgium and south to the Paris basin.

5. (p. 9) *the recurrent lied-motif of the cash-register*: German composer and author Richard Wagner (1813–1883) developed the concept of the *leitmotif* or *leitmotiv* (from the German: *leiten*, to lead, and *motiv*, motive), a recurrent musical phrase associated with a specific character or emotion. In addition to referencing Wagner, the description of the "lied-motif" of the cash register could be a pun on "lied motive" (false motive) and a jab at the commercialism of the "bohemian" nightspot.

6. (p. 9) *one of them was very fond of Flaubert, while the other preferred gin*: The French novelist Gustave Flaubert (1821–1880) was one of the great realists of nineteenth-century literature, known for his precise writing style and accurate observations.

7. (p. 10) *It [love] may be mixed here with a little commercialism—they read Byron*: The English poet Lord Byron (1788–1824) was famous for his creation of the Byronic hero, a mysterious, melancholy personality central in his poems.

8. (p. 10) *Talk about Shylock's pound of flesh! Twenty-five pounds Cupid got from Pettit*: Shylock is the villainous moneylender who demands a pound of flesh as collateral on a loan in Shakespeare's *The Merchant of Venice*. The money from the loan helps Antonio and Bassanio in their pursuit of love, hence the connection to Cupid.

9. (p. 11) *my bully old pal Montaigne*: Michel Eyquem de Montaigne (1533–1592) was a French writer famous for his *Essays*, which are the earliest form of the personal essay.

10. (p. 11) *"Suffering Sappho!"*: Sappho (c.600 B.C) was a famous Greek poet from the island of Lesbos, sometimes called the "tenth Muse"; she is fabled to have thrown herself off a cliff after the beautiful youth Phaon rejected her advances.

11. (p. 11) *Omar*: Persian poet and astronomer Omar Khayyám (c.1120) is most famous for his collection of poems titled *The Rubaiyat*. O. Henry jokes at Omar's expense in his story "Handbook of Hymen," in which two gold diggers wintering in the Bitterroot Mountains are discussing a "poem book" by "Homer K. M.," a phonetic spelling for Omar Khayyám.

12. (p. 12) *Shakespeare's sonnets*: English playwright and poet William Shakespeare (1564–1616) wrote 154 sonnets, some twenty-five of which are addressed to a mysterious woman critics call the "Dark Lady." The economics of literature were very different in Shakespeare's day, although it is interesting to note that, as far as economics and literature are concerned, O. Henry's short stories did much for the commodification of literature and the increased popularity of fiction in magazines.

"The Princess and the Puma"

1. (p. 14) *shared the fate of the Danaë*: In Greek mythology, the king of Argos imprisons his daughter Danaë in a tower of bronze, after the Delphic oracle prophesies that Danaë will bear a son who will kill him. But Zeus visits her in the form of a shower of gold, and she gives birth to Perseus, who eventually fulfills the oracle's prophecy.

"By Courier"

1. (p. 22) *"Den he's goin' to shoot snow-birds in de Klondike"*: Klondike is a region of the Yukon Territory in northwestern Canada.

"The Gift of the Magi"

1. (p. 26) *Had the Queen of Sheba . . . King Solomon*: In the Old Testament (see the Bible, 1 Kings 10), the Queen of Sheba visits King Solomon to test him with some difficult questions. Moved by his wisdom and majesty, she gives him large quantities of gold, spices, and jewels; in return King Solomon gives her all that she desires.

2. (p. 27) *"he'll say I look like a Coney Island chorus girl"*: Coney Island is an amusement park in Brooklyn, New York, that was very popular during the first half of the twentieth century. In O. Henry's stories, Coney Island rep-

resents the seedy as well as the playful side of human nature. He associates it with the lower classes in his stories "Brickdust Row" and "Tobin's Palm." In "Brickdust Row," the main characters "landed at Coney, and were dashed on the crest of a great human wave of mad pleasure-seekers into the walks and avenues of Fairyland gone into vaudeville" (see p. 147).

3. (p. 29) *The magi brought valuable gifts*: The three Magi, part of the legend of Christ's nativity, followed a low, bright star to the manger in which the infant Christ lay. They bore gifts of gold, an emblem of royalty; frankincense, an emblem of divinity; and myrrh, a symbol for death (see the Bible, Matthew 2:1–12).

"The Love-Philtre of Ikey Schoenstein"

1. (p. 31) *The Blue Light Drug Store . . . cough drops and soothing syrups that wait for them inside*: O. Henry spent three years working as a clerk in his uncle's drugstore in North Carolina. C. Alphonso Smith, O. Henry's biographer, describes the drugstore as the center of the social life in Greensboro and asserts that O. Henry's experience there allowed him to observe the idiosyncrasies of his fellow humans from an aloof, artistic perspective (*O. Henry Biography*; see "For Further Reading"). His familiarity with medicines and drugs, displayed in this story and others, comes from his time at the pharmacy.

2. (p. 34) *the backyard Lochinvar*: Lochinvar is the hero of Sir Walter Scott's 1808 romantic poem *Marmion*. In love with a woman who is promised to another, Lochinvar persuades her to dance one last dance, during which he swings her into his saddle and carries her away before the bridegroom can react.

"Mammon and the Archer"

1. (p. 37) *"You tell me where your exclusive circles would be if the first Astor hadn't had the money to pay for his steerage passage over"*: John Jacob Astor (1763–1848) came to America from Germany in 1784 and entered the fur-trading business with great success. The Astor fortune grew with each generation, as did the family's influence in New York. At the beginning of the story, Rockwall sneers at his foreign neighbor without realizing that he is, like John Jacob Astor, the proverbial American success story. During O. Henry's lifetime, New York specifically and America in general suffered under a xenophobic mentality that was in part due to the vast numbers of lower-class emigrants who came through Ellis Island in pursuit of the American dream.

2. (p. 41) *William A. Brady*: William A. Brady (1863–1950) was an American theater producer and manager.

3. (p. 42) *"It was two hours before a snake could get below Greeley's statue"*: Horace

Greeley (1811–1872) founded both the *The New Yorker* magazine and the New York *Tribune* newspaper and was influential in both national and local politics. There are two statues of Greeley in New York City, one in City Hall Park and the other, to which O. Henry is referring, near the theater district in Greeley Square, at Broadway and Thirty-third Street.

"The Memento"

1. (p. 43) *The Hotel Thalia looks on Broadway as Marathon looks on the sea*: In Greek mythology, Thalia is the Muse of comedy and also presides over the realms of husbandry and planting; she is often depicted holding a comic mask and a shepherd's cane. Marathon is a plain in Greece that borders on an inlet of the Aegean Sea.

2. (p. 44) *wander like a lost soul in a Sam Loyd puzzle*: Samuel Loyd (1841–1911) was a well-known American puzzle maker.

3. (p. 44) *gather in doorways and talk of Booth*: Booth is the name of a family of American theater actors active throughout the nineteenth century. The family includes John Wilkes Booth (1838–1865), notorious for assassinating President Abraham Lincoln.

4. (p. 47) *"I'd have given 'em the real Mrs. Fiske laugh"*: Minnie Maddern Fiske (1865–1932) was a popular American theater actress best loved as a comedienne; she is also known for her part in popularizing Ibsen's plays.

5. (p. 47) *"I've got enough soft-coal cinders on my face to go on and play Topsy"*: Topsy is a young black slave in Harriet Beecher Stowe's novel *Uncle Tom's Cabin* (1852), a book that has often been adapted for the stage.

6. (p. 48) *one of that Round Table bunch*: O. Henry's reference to the Old English legend of King Arthur and the Knights of the Round Table is appropriate, given the fact that Rosalie's paramour shares his name with the King.

7. (p. 48) *John Drew in his best drawing-room scene*: John Drew (1853–1927) was an American stage actor notable for his comedies of manners.

8. (p. 49) *"Recited that 'Annie Laurie' thing"*: "Annie Laurie" was a popular Scottish folk song written around 1700.

9. (p. 51) *"Well, I guess we're all to the Mrs. Bluebeard now and then"*: Bluebeard is the villainous husband in Charles Perrault's collection of Mother Goose rhymes, *Contes de ma Mere L'Oye* (1697), who gives his new bride the keys to his castle with the restriction that she cannot open the door to his secret chamber. Unable to resist her curiosity, she opens the forbidden door and, upon looking inside, finds the corpses of his previous wives strewn gruesomely on the floor, killed for their disobedience.

"Springtime à la Carte"

1. (p. 53) *To account for this . . . she had sworn ice-cream off during Lent . . . just*

come from a Hackett matinée: In many Christian churches, Lent is a period of fasting and penitence during the forty days from Ash Wednesday to Easter. James Henry Hackett (1800–1871) was a comedic actor on the American stage particularly well known for his portrayal of Falstaff in Shakespeare's historical dramas set in the time of King Henry IV.

2. (p. 54) *throw the five baseballs at the colored gentleman's head*: O. Henry is referring to a popular game in which players threw balls at a stationary target; the target was often carved out of wood.

3. (p. 57) *Had Juliet so seen . . . lethean herbs*: In Shakespeare's tragedy *Romeo and Juliet*, Juliet feigns death by drinking a poison given to her by Friar Lawrence. "Lethean herbs" refer to the river Lethe, in Greek mythology the river in Hades that causes drinkers to forget their pasts.

4. (p. 57) *"The Cloister and the Hearth"*: This historical novel by the English author Charles Reade, published in 1861, follows the story of Gerard and his beloved Margaret, who are parted and then, after many years of trial and adventure, reunited.

"The Last Leaf"

1. (p. 60) *an Eighth Street "Delmonico's"*: Delmonico's was a family-run restaurant chain with nine separate locations in New York City from 1834 to 1923.

2. (p. 63) *Michael Angelo's Moses*: Moses was the subject of one of the most renowned pieces of Italian sculptor Michelangelo (1475–1564); in the statue, Moses' beard curls elegantly over his chest.

"The Skylight Room"

1. (p. 68) *"I'm not Hetty if I do look green"*: Hetty Green (1834–1916) was a financier reputed to have been the richest woman in America; notorious for her frugality and stinginess, she lived in a series of cheap boardinghouses in Manhattan and Brooklyn.

2. (p. 69) *"Anna Held'll jump at it"*: Anna Held (1865?–1918) was a comedic actress on the American stage.

3. (p. 70) *let the drama halt while Chorus stalks to the footlights*: In classical Greek dramas, the purpose of the chorus, sometimes played by just one person, was to moralize and comment upon the action of the play.

4. (p. 70) *Falstaff might have rendered more romance to the ton*: Sir John Falstaff is the corpulent, self-indulgent, lustful, unscrupulous, comic figure in three of Shakespeare's plays: *Henry IV, Part I, Henry VI, Part II*, and *The Merry Wives of Windsor*.

5. (p. 70) *might carry off Helen herself*: In Greek mythology, Helen is the beau-

tiful woman whose abduction by the Trojan youth Paris triggers the Trojan War.

6. (p. 71) *in that Erebus of a room*: In Greek mythology, Erebus, the son of Chaos and the brother of Night, personifies darkness; his name was given to the underground cavern through which souls had to walk during their descent into the underworld.

"The Caliph, Cupid and The Clock"

1. (p. 74) *In the shadowed spots fauns and hamadryads wooed*: In Roman mythology, fauns, the equivalent of the Greek satyrs, are immortal woodland goatmen associated with excesses of lust and drunkenness. Hamadryads, or dryads, are tree nymphs who would die when the tree they inhabited died.

2. (p. 74) *A hand-organ—Philomel by the grace of our stage carpenter*: Philomel means nightingale. In Greek mythology, Philomela is the heroine of a tragedy that culminates in her rape and the cutting out of her tongue; unable to communicate in any other way, she weaves her story into the fabric of a tapestry. In the end, the gods change her into a nightingale, a nocturnal bird with a sweet song.

3. (p. 75) *He could have matched gold, equipage, jewels . . . with any Croesus in this proud city of Manhattan*: Croesus (c.560–546 B.C.) was the last king of Lydia, an ancient country of western Asia Minor; he acquired great wealth through trade.

"The Count and the Wedding Guest"

1. (p. 82) *"Laugh, and the world laughs with you; weep, and they give you the laugh"*: Miss Conway is paraphrasing the poem "Solitude," by American poet Ella Wheeler Wilcox (1850–1919): "Laugh, and the world laughs with you; / Weep, and you weep alone. / For the sad old earth must borrow its mirth, / But has trouble enough of its own."

"The Romance of a Busy Broker"

1. (p. 89) *The poet sings of the "crowded hour of glorious life"*: The poet is Sir Walter Scott (1771–1832); the quote comes from his poem "Answer": "One crowded hour of glorious life / Is worth an age without a name."

"The Higher Pragmatism"

1. (p. 93) *The Higher Pragmatism*: The title of this story is play on the poem "The Higher Pantheism" (1869), by Alfred, Lord Tennyson. In the poem

Tennyson offers a belief that God not only transcends the world but can also be found within the world. O. Henry was not the only author to parody Tennyson's poem. The English poet Charles Swinburne (1837–1909) wrote "The Higher Pantheism in a Nutshell," which includes the lines "God, whom we see not, is: and God, who is not, we see: / Fiddle, we know, is diddle: And diddle, we take it, is dee."

2. (p. 93) *The ancients are discredited; Plato . . . Epictetus with a pick*: All of these historic figures are renowned for their wisdom: Plato (c.427–348 B.C.) was a seminal Greek philosopher; Marcus Aurelius (121–180) was a Roman emperor known for his stoic philosophy; Aesop (sixth century B.C.) was the reputed Greek author of a collection of fables; Solomon (tenth century B.C.) was a wise king of Israel; and Epictetus (c.100 A.D.) was a Greek philosopher and stoic.

3. (p. 93) *Chautauqua conventions*: The Chautauqua institution of the late nineteenth and early twentieth centuries provided educational programs for adults in rural settings.

4. (p. 93) *As the poet says, "Knowledge comes, but wisdom lingers"*: The poet is Alfred, Lord Tennyson (1809–1892); the poem is "Locksley Hall."

"While the Auto Waits"

1. (p. 103) *a visiting Prince of Tartary*: No such kingdom now exists. Tartary, or Tatary, is an indefinite historical region in Asia and Europe extending from the Sea of Japan to the Dnieper River. Tartary became known in the West for its leader, the conqueror Genghis Khan; "tartar" now refers to a violent or formidable person.

2. (p. 106) *"New Arabian Nights," the author being of the name of Stevenson*: *New Arabian Nights* (1882), by well-known Scottish novelist Robert Louis Stevenson, is based on the *Arabian Nights' Entertainments* (1450), a collection of tales in which Scheherazade, the wife of a king, tells her husband a new story night after night to delay her execution; eventually the king falls in love with her and pardons her.

"The Social Triangle"

1. (pp. 107–108) *Upon him the Tiger purred, and his hand held manna to scatter*: A tiger was the symbol of Tammany Hall, the headquarters of Tammany, the Democratic Party's controlling, corrupt political machine in New York City. In the Old Testament, manna was the bread that miraculously rained down from the heavens to nourish the Israelites as they fled from Egypt (see the Bible, Exodus 16).

2. (p. 109) *Some one was telling how Brannigan fixed 'em over in the Eleventh*: Patsy Brannigan was an American boxer.

3. (p. 109) *with the eye of Moses looking over into the promised land*: The Hebrew prophet Moses led the Israelites out of Egypt and to the Promised Land (see the Bible, the book of Exodus).

"The Green Door"

1. (p. 117) *Prodigal Son*: The Prodigal Son refers to the New Testament story of a repentant sinner who, after wasting his inheritance on debauchery, returns to his family (see the Bible, Luke 15:11–32).

2. (p. 117) *From the Crusades to the Palisades*: The Crusades were a series of religious wars launched by European Christians during the eleventh to thirteenth centuries to win the Holy Land from the Muslims; the Palisades is an area of steep cliffs along the west bank of the Hudson River in New Jersey.

3. (p. 119) *"Junie's Love Test," by Miss Libbey*: Laura Jean Libbey (1862–1924) was a popular American writer of sentimental novels; Libbey did not publish a book titled "Junie's Love Test," but the title would be typical of her work.

4. (p. 122) *The history sounded as big as the* Iliad: The *Iliad* is an epic poem of the eighth century B.C. that is attributed to Homer; it relates the activities of the Greeks and the Trojans during the Trojan War.

"A Lickpenny Lover"

1. (p. 127) *She curved an arm, showing like Psyche's*: Psyche is Cupid's lover in the myth of Cupid and Psyche, recounted in the second-century satirical romance *The Golden Ass* (also called *Metamorphoses*), by Apuleius.

2. (p. 130) *wonderful temples of the Hindoos and Brahmins*: Hindus are adherents of Hinduism, the dominant religion of India; Brahmins are Hindus of the highest caste. O. Henry uses the names here as examples of faraway and exotic things.

"Lost on Dress Parade"

1. (p. 131) *the Flatiron Building was inferior in design to the great cathedral in Milan*: A historic building considered to be the oldest standing skyscraper in New York City, the Flatiron Building was designed by Daniel H. Burnham and built in 1902; located at the intersection of Fifth Avenue and Broadway between Twenty-second and Twenty-third Streets, it is famous for its bold, triangular design. The magnificent Cathedral of Milan in Italy was begun in the 1380s and not completed until the nineteenth century.

"Transients in Arcadia"

1. (p. 138) *Adirondacks*: The Adirondack Mountains in upstate New York were a common summer destination for those who wanted rusticity.

2. (p. 138) *brook trout better than the White Mountains ever served, sea food that would turn Old Point Comfort . . . green with envy*: Ample brook trout would be found in the streams of the White Mountains in New Hampshire. Old Point Comfort, Virginia, is in the Chesapeake Bay area, which is known for its fisheries.

3. (p. 139) *Hotel Lotus*: The hotel is named after Lotus-land in Homer's *Odyssey* (eighth century B.C.). Odysseus and his men stopped there during their long passage home; upon eating the lotus flower, some of the men forgot family and home, and wanted only to continue to live in idleness in Lotus-land. The name of the hotel implies that it is a place of idle, and ideal, forgetfulness.

4. (p. 139) *Versailles*: Versailles, in northern France, is the site of an extremely grand eighteenth-century palace built by King Louis XIV.

5. (p. 139) *Mrs. Fiske*: Minnie Maddern Fiske (1865–1932) was a popular American theater actress and comedienne notable for her part in popularizing Ibsen's plays.

6. (p. 141) *Lotus is further away from Broadway than Thousand Islands or Mackinac*: The Thousand Islands are a group of about 1,500 islands in the upper St. Lawrence River between New York State and Canada; Mackinac is an island in the Straits of Mackinac, which connects Lake Huron and Lake Michigan. Like Lotus-land, both resort island areas are noted for their beauty.

7. (p. 141) *Ural Mountains . . . Baden-Baden and Cannes*: These are all far-flung destinations: The Ural Mountains are a mountain range in Russia; Baden-Baden is a city in southwestern Germany known for its thermal baths; Cannes is a resort city on the French Riviera.

"Brickdust Row"

1. (p. 144) *North Woods*: This heavily wooded region of northern New Hampshire, Vermont, and Maine is also called the Great North Woods.

"The Furnished Room"

1. (p. 152) *"Home, Sweet Home" in ragtime*: "Home Sweet Home" is a song from the 1823 opera *Clari*, written by American actor and playwright John Howard Payne.

2. (p. 154) *confused in speech as though it were an apartment in Babel*: In the Old Testament (see the Bible, Genesis 11), the Tower of Babel was a visionary plan of the descendants of Noah, meant to be a tower so high it would reach

heaven. God confounded the plan by introducing different languages, thus
making it impossible for the builders to communicate. Now, the word "babel"
is used to mean a confusion of sounds and voices.

"Schools and Schools"

1. (p. 159) *Cyril Scott could play him nicely*: O. Henry may be referring to the
   nineteenth-century British-born actor Cyril Scott.
2. (p. 159) *The writing was asthmatic and the spelling St. Vitusy*: St. Vitus of Sicily,
   the third-century child martyr, is invoked against diseases such as epilepsy
   and nervous disorders. St. Vitus's dance is another name for chorea, a nervous
   disorder marked by spasmodic movements. O. Henry invokes "St. Vitusy"
   here probably to indicate illegible writing and childish spelling.
3. (p. 163) *Mr. Fields*: Lew Fields (1867–1941) and Joe Weber (1867–1942)
   were an American comedy team from New York City. Fields owned two
   theaters in New York, the Lew Fields Theater and the Herald Square Theater.
4. (p. 166) *The Avenue was as quiet as a street in Pompeii*: Pompeii was the ancient
   Roman city destroyed by the eruption of Mount Vesuvius in 79 A.D.
5. (p. 166) *the ragged sierras of cloud-capped buildings*: Sierras are mountain ranges
   with an irregular or serrated outline; perhaps Nevada, being from the West,
   would be reminded of the Sierra Nevada mountain range in eastern California
   as she looks up at the New York skyline.
6. (p. 166) *Adam's rib*: According to the Old Testament, God created Eve from
   Adam's rib (see the Bible, Genesis 2:20–22). O. Henry's use of the phrase
   "sprang from," however, also suggests the Greek story of Athena, a woman
   who literally sprang from her father's forehead.
7. (p. 167) *Gilbert did a Pygmalion-and-Galatea act. . . . with a problem to tackle*:
   According to ancient Greek legend, Pygmalion is the king of Cyprus and a
   sculptor who falls in love with his statue of Aphrodite. Venus brings the statue
   to life and Pygmalion names her Galatea.
8. (p. 167) *Remind Agnes of the time I saved her from drowning in Lake Ronkonkoma*: Lake Ronkonkoma, on Long Island, New York, was a resort area popular for the reputedly therapeutic effect of its waters. A host of Indian legends
   surround the lake, many of which have to do with the subject of love; according to one such legend, the mysterious rising and falling of the lake can
   be appeased by sacrificing a beautiful maiden to its waters.

"The Defeat of the City"

1. (p. 171) *the good poet with the game foot and artificially curled hair*: O. Henry
   is referring to the English poet George Gordon Byron, known as Lord Byron
   (1788–1824), who, despite his short stature and his lame foot, developed an

aura of romantic mystery. The poet was often confused with his poetic personality, especially by his female readers, who assumed that his descriptions of the wild, erotic life of the hero of his poems was autobiographical.

2. (p. 172) *Dawson to Forty Mile*: Dawson City and Forty Mile, in the Yukon Territory of western Canada, were popular destinations for prospectors during the Klondike Gold Rush of the late nineteenth to early twentieth centuries.

3. (p. 173) *The wind followed like a whinnying colt in the track of Phoebus's steeds*: In some versions of Greek mythology, Phoebus Apollo drives the chariot of the sun across the heavens each day.

4. (p. 173) *they floated up in clear Pan's pipe notes*: In Greek myth, Pan was the god of pastures, flocks, and shepherds, who played wonderful music on his reed pipes.

"Madame Bo-Peep, of the Ranches"

1. (p. 178) *I prefer to strike bottom like Beelzebub rather than hang around like the Peri*: In Milton's epic poem *Paradise Lost* (1667), Beelzebub follows Satan in his descent to hell and is one of the chief lords of the region. A peri is a fallen angel of Persian folklore who waits disconsolately by the gates of heaven for admittance; peris are featured in Sir Thomas Moore's 1817 poem *Lalla Rookh*.

2. (p. 180) *"Shall I be a shepherdess with a Watteau hat"*: Jean-Antoine Watteau (1684–1721) was a French painter known especially for his ideal representations of country life.

3. (p. 189) *that should have driven Strephon to Chloe*: Strephon is a shepherd in Sir Philip Sidney's pastoral romance *Arcadia* (1590). His name is now used generically to mean a pastoral lover, usually paired with Chloe as his beloved.

4. (p. 190) *Verlaine*: Paul Verlaine (1844–1896) was a French poet and a forerunner of the symbolist movement in poetry, noted for the elegant style and delicate musical suggestiveness of his verse, as well as for his notorious affair with the poet Arthur Rimbaud.

5. (p. 195) *Little Bo-Peep . . . come home, and*: The five lines of this rhyme read: "Little Bo Peep has lost her sheep, / And can't tell where to find them. / Leave them alone, / And they'll come home, / Bringing their tails behind them."

"From Each According to His Ability"

1. (p. 196) *write a historical novel "around" Paul Jones*: The Scottish-born American naval officer John Paul Jones (1747–1792) is well known for his exploits in the Revolutionary War, particularly for his alleged lines, "I have not yet begun to fight!" as his ship was sinking, during a battle in which he defeated

the British ship *Searpis*. He is the central character in James Fenimore Cooper's 1823 sea story *The Pilot*.

2. (p. 200) *Lilliputian chatter*: The Lilliputians were a six-inch-tall race of pygmies in Jonathan Swift's satirical work *Gulliver's Travels* (1726).

3. (p. 201) *As simply as Homer sang*: The blind poet Homer (eighth century B.C.), presumed to be the author of the *Iliad* and the *Odyssey*, is said to have sung his poems.

4. (p. 201) *Looking-Glass Country: Through the Looking-Glass* is Lewis Carroll's 1871 sequel to *Alice's Adventures in Wonderland*; in the story Alice enters a strange country by slipping through a mirror.

5. (p. 201) *Melpomene, Diana and Amaryllis*: In Greek mythology, Melpomene is the muse of tragedy; in Roman myth, Diana is the goddess of hunting and childbirth; Amaryllis is a generic name for a rustic sweetheart.

"The Caballero's Way"

1. (p. 203) *half Carmen, half Madonna*: Carmen is the fiery, passionate, and tragic gypsy of Georges Bizet's 1875 opera *Carmen*. Madonna, the mother of Jesus, could be described as Carmen's exact opposite: humble, loving, and pure.

2. (p. 205) *when he and Pizarro touched glasses to their New World fortunes*: Francisco Pizarro (1475?–1541) was the Spanish conqueror of Peru; he captured Cuzco and founded the new capital, Lima.

3. (p. 206) *the Basque province*: Basque Country is a region of northern Spain.

4. (p. 207) *he knew he would be nibbling . . . at the end of a forty-foot stake-rope while Ulysses rested his head in Circe's straw-roofed hut*: In Greek mythology, when Ulysses (the Roman Odysseus) lands on the sorceress Circe's island, Circe turns his men into swine; Ulysses resists Circe's sorcery by eating an herb, and she falls in love with him and frees his men. Ulysses lives with Circe for a year before continuing his homeward journey.

5. (p. 208) *Don't you monkey . . . what I'll do*: The final two lines of this song are: "I'll cut out your heart with a razor, / and I'll cut your liver too." According to O. Henry's biographer, C. Alphonso Smith, the author learned this song from his grade-school teacher and aunt, Miss Lina.

"Hygeia at the Solito"

1. (p. 216) *that hollow, racking cough so familiar to San Antonian ears*: O. Henry is referring to the cough associated with tuberculosis. The dry air of the southwestern deserts was thought to have a beneficial effect on the cough; O. Henry suffered from the disease and worked on a ranch in Texas for a time.

2. (p. 217) *But Rus Sage himself would have snatched at it*: Russell Sage (1816–

1906) was a wealthy American financier and politician who had a seat on the New York Stock Exchange.

3. (p. 218) *the account of his Waterloo*: The French emperor Napoleon was defeated at the battle of Waterloo on June 18, 1815. "Waterloo" is now used to indicate a final and crushing defeat or setback.

4. (p. 221) *"Dat's the last simoleon in the treasury"*: Simolean is slang for a dollar.

5. (p. 230) *Dago kid*: Dago is a term used, usually disparagingly, to refer to a person of Italian or Spanish descent. Many cowboys in the Old West were either Hispanic or Black.

"The Higher Abdication"

1. (p. 231) *Menger*: The Menger Hotel in San Antonio, Texas, is adjacent to the Alamo; in business since 1859, it is a historical landmark.

2. (p. 231) *The slings and arrows of outrageous fortune*: This is a phrase from Hamlet's soliloquy on suicide in Shakespeare's *Hamlet* (act 3, scene 1); "to suffer the slings and arrows of outrageous fortune" is to suffer the pain of life, as Curly suffers at the hands of bartenders.

3. (p. 237) *Old "Kiowa" Truesdell*: O. Henry is comparing Truesdell's move from Mississippi to Texas to the Native American Kiowa tribe, which migrated from the Southeast westward to the Great Plains in the late eighteenth century.

4. (p. 240) *the satin poll of a Cléo de Mérode*: The Cléo de Mérode is a hairstyle made famous by the French ballet dancer of the same name; Mérode (1873–1966) was the first woman to dance with a male partner in the Russian Ballet.

"A Double-Dyed Deceiver"

1. (p. 255) *Paradise Lost*: *Paradise Lost* is John Milton's epic poem published in 1667. This reference makes no use of the religious theme of the poem, which follows Adam and Eve from creation to the fall, but only indicates an ideal place that is now unattainable.

2. (p. 258) *"What was I consul at Sandakan for?"*: Sandakan is a seaport town in Sabah, Malaysia, on the island of Borneo; it was the capital of former British North Borneo.

3. (p. 259) *Rio Janeiro*: The commercial seaport city of Rio de Janeiro, the former capital of Brazil, is a popular tourist destination.

4. (p. 260) *the Basque province*: Basque country is a region of northern Spain.

"Friends in San Rosario"

1. (p. 268) *the cattle business had known a depression*: The economy of the cattle ranch depended upon open grazing and the ability to drive the herd to market.

With increasing population density, the open ranges were segmented into private property by barbed wire, which deterred the herd's mobility. In addition, three terribly cold and dry winters from 1887 to 1889 seriously harmed the cattle business.

"The Hiding of Black Bill"

1. (p. 280) *"I was lonesomer than Crusoe's goat"*: Robinson Crusoe is the main character in Daniel Defoe's novel *The Life and Strange Surprising Adventures of Robinson Crusoe, of York, Marine* (1719). In the novel, Crusoe is shipwrecked on a desert island for many years; the island abounds in feral goats, which he domesticates and raises for food and milk.

2. (p. 281) *Joe Weber*: Joseph M. Weber (1867–1942) and Lew Fields (1867–1941) were a popular American comedy team from New York City.

3. (p. 281) *Adriatic Sea*: The Adriatic is an arm of the Mediterranean Sea, between Italy and the Balkan Peninsula.

4. (p. 281) *"Curfew Shall Not Ring To-night"*: "Curfew Must Not Ring To-night" is a sentimental ballad by American writer Rose Hartwick Thorpe (1850–1939), which tells the story of a woman who saves her lover from execution.

5. (p. 282) *"bought a sheep-ranch and hired me to Little-Boy-Blue 'em"*: In the nursery rhyme, Little Boy Blue is a shepherd.

6. (p. 287) *"like Delilah when she set the Philip Steins on to Samson"*: In the Old Testament, Delilah is the woman who betrays Samson by revealing the source of his strength to his enemies, the Philistines (see the Bible, Judges 16); her name has become synonymous with seduction and treachery. "Philip Steins" is a phonetic near-pronunciation of Philistines.

"Jeff Peters as a Personal Magnet"

1. (p. 290) *Ta-qua-la, the beautiful wife of the chief of the Choctaw Nation*: The Choctaw Native American tribe originated in Mississippi and was the first of the southern tribes to be moved to Oklahoma, a journey that came to be known as the Trail of Tears. Ta-qua-la is in all probability a name O. Henry invented to sound vaguely Indian.

2. (p. 291) *Dorothy Vernon*: Dorothy Vernon is a character from Charles Major's 1902 novel *Dorothy Vernon of Haddon Hall*, a love story set in the time of Queen Elizabeth.

3. (p. 293) *"I'm not a regular preordained disciple of S. Q. Lapius"*: A pun on Aesculapius, the Greek name for the son of Apollo and a demi-god healer so skilled he was to be able to bring the dead back to life. He was killed by a begrudging Zeus who felt the half-mortal should not have the power to grant immortality. His symbol is the knotted staff and snake now associated with the medical professions.

4. (p. 294) *"I'm one of the Sole Sanhedrims"*: The Sanhedrin was the supreme council of the Jews from the end of their exile in Babylon to around the time of the birth of Christ; a "Sole Sanhedrin," therefore, would be the only member of the high council.

"The Man Higher Up"

1. (p. 299) *"I was sine qua grata with a member of the housebreakers' union and one of the John D. Napoleons of finance"*: O. Henry is jumbling Latin phrases and names here, to come up with nonsense. *Sine qua grata* comes from the Latin phrases *sine qua non*, meaning something indispensable, and *persona non grata*, meaning unwelcome; John D. Napoleon is a strange mixing of John D. Rockefeller (1839–1937), the wealthy oil magnate and possessor of one of the largest fortunes in American history, and Napoleon Bonaparte (1769–1821), emperor of France.

2. (p. 300) *"I struck a Lewis and Clark lope for the swollen rivers and impenetrable forests"*: Meriwether Lewis (1774–1809) and William Clark (1770–1838) set out on an exploratory mission to find a trade route to the Pacific Ocean. It took the expedition more than two years to travel from St. Louis to the mouth of the Columbia River and back. In America, the names Lewis and Clark have become synonymous with exploration.

3. (p. 301) *"She had sure cut off my locks. She was a Delilah"*: In the Old Testament, Delilah is the woman who betrays Samson by revealing his hair as the source of his strength to his enemies, the Philistines (see the Bible, Judges 16); her name has become synonymous with seduction and treachery.

4. (p. 302) *"I reckon we can't count on them unless we take Luther Burbank in for a partner"*: The American horticulturist Luther Burbank (1849–1926) is famous for developing the Burbank potato, as well as for developing new varieties of plums, berries, lilies, roses, poppies, tomatoes, corn, and squash.

5. (p. 302) *"Didn't you see Colonel Manna drop down right before your eyes? Don't you hear the rustling of General Raven's wings? I'm surprised at you, Elijah"*: These are references to the Old Testament and miraculous supplies of food: Manna is the bread that rains down from the heavens to nourish the Israelites as they flee from Egypt (see the Bible, Exodus 16), and ravens are sent by God to feed the prophet Elijah during a long drought (see the Bible, 1 Kings 17:1–6). To raven can also mean to plunder.

6. (p. 303) *Lake Okeechobee*: Lake Okeechobee, in south-central Florida, is the largest lake in the southern United States.

7. (p. 306) *Masonic temple*: A Masonic temple, sometimes called a lodge, is a gathering place for members of the Order of Masons, a secret fraternal society that originated in England in the seventeenth century and became an influential presence in the United States.

8. (p. 307) *"It's a kind of Industrial Christian Science. . . . both Rockefeller and Mrs. Eddy on the job"*: Mary Baker Eddy (1821–1910) was the founder of the Church of Christ, Scientist, known as the Christian Science Church, which believes in healing by spiritual means rather than by surgery or medicine. O. Henry's reference to her indicates that the sand for the lamp works on faith.

9. (p. 309) *"it will be such a cold proposition that nobody but Robert E. Peary and Charlie Fairbanks will be able to sit on the board of directors"*: These are two men who spent a good deal of time in the cold: Robert Edwin Peary (1856–1920) was an American arctic explorer and the first white man to reach the North Pole (April 6, 1909). Charles Warren Fairbanks (1852–1918), vice president of the United States from 1905–1909, was instrumental in smoothing U.S.–Canada relations over the disputed territory of Alaska; the Alaskan city Fairbanks was named for him.

10. (p. 309) *"you can't get a Pasteur institute to start up within fifty miles of where I live"*: Louis Pasteur (1822–1895), was a French chemist famous for his work in microbiology. O. Henry's reference to him draws a parallel between Mr. Bassett and a bacterium.

11. (p. 310) *the Autolycan adventurer*: In Greek mythology, Autolycus is the son of Mercury and a clever thief who steals his neighbors' flocks and changes their marks. Shakespeare uses the name for his roguish peddler in *The Winter's Tale*. In Greek, the word suggests a meaning similar to "Lone Wolf."

"The Handbook of Hymen"

1. (p. 312) *Walla-Walla*: Walla Walla is a city in Washington state that felt the effects of the Gold Rush in 1861.

2. (p. 313) *if we had studied Homer*: The blind poet Homer (eighth century B.C.) is presumed to be the author of the epic poems the *Iliad* and the *Odyssey*.

3. (p. 314) *Solomon*: In the Old Testament, Solomon is the wisest of the kings of Israel (see the Bible, 1 Kings 2–11).

4. (p. 315) *"a volume by Homer K. M."*: Homer K. M. is a phonetic pronunciation of Omar Khayyám (c.1120), a Persian poet and astronomer known for his series of quatrains, which he collected under the title *The Rubaiyat*. In 1859 Edward FitzGerald published a translation of 101 of the quatrains, bringing them to fame in the English-speaking world. FitzGerald's translation of the poems concentrate on the beauty of the sensual life.

5. (p. 319) *"I'm not in the habit of . . . raising Cain"*: In the Old Testament story, Cain murders his brother Abel (see the Bible, Genesis 4:1–16). The phrase "raising Cain" has come to mean acting wildly.

"Telemachus, Friend"

1. (p. 324) *Telmachus Hicks*: The hotel proprietor is named after Odysseus' faithful son Telemachus in Homer's *Odyssey* (eighth century B.C.). Telemachus worries over his father's return while hungry suitors vie for his mother's hand in marriage; he is instrumental in helping Odysseus reclaim his wife and home upon the latter's return from Ithaca.

2. (p. 325) *days of Damon and nights of Pythias*: Damon and Pythias were legendary friends in ancient Greece. Pythias, condemned to death by the tyrant Dionysius, is granted leave to return home and settle his affairs on the condition that, should he not return, Damon will take his place at the gallows. Pythias is delayed and Damon is led to execution; but Pythias returns in the knick of time to save his friend, and Dionysius, impressed by the display of friendship, pardons them both. O. Henry might have intended a pun here: The benevolent fraternal organization known as the Knights of Pythias was founded in 1864.

3. (p. 325) *Tennyson*: Alfred, Lord Tennyson (1809–1892) was a well-known English romantic poet and author of the much anthologized *In Memoriam*, "The Lady of Shalott," and "Ulysses."

4. (p. 326) *"the whirlpool of Squills and Chalybeates, into which vortex the good ship Friendship is often drawn and dismembered"*: A squill, also called a sea-onion, is a bulbous-rooted shore plant; a chalybeate is a medicine impregnated with iron salts. Both are old medical remedies used as purgatives.

5. (p. 328) *a mixture of the talk turned out by Rider Haggard, Lew Dockstader, and Dr. Parkhurst*: That is, cooing, preaching, and joking. Sir Henry Rider Haggard (1856–1925) was an English author of romantic novels. Lew Dockstader (1856–1924) was a minstrel, vaudevillian, and accomplished comic. Charles Henry Parkhurst (1842–1933) was a Presbyterian clergyman known for his sermons against political corruption.

"The Lonesome Road"

1. (p. 332) *an Odyssey of the chaparral*: The epic poem the *Odyssey*, written by the blind poet Homer (eighth century B.C.) follows Odysseus on his adventure-packed trip from Troy and the Trojan War to his home in Ithaca. O. Henry uses the reference here to indicate a story of epic proportions.

2. (p. 336) *the same kind of a game as that Mrs. Delilah played. . . . the Pharisees*: In the Old Testament, Delilah is the treacherous woman who betrays the hero Samson to the Philistines by revealing his hair as the source of his strength and holding him as they shave his head. The Pharisees were Old Testament ascetics known for their strict observance of rites and ceremonies of the Law.

3. (p. 339) *" 'I'm not married,' says I, 'but I'm as big a d—n fool as any Mormon' "*: Mormons, members of the Church of Jesus Christ of the Latter-day Saints,

were known especially for their practice of polygamy, which became part of the Mormon code in 1852.

"The Renaissance at Charleroi"

1. (p. 352) *Arcadian little gentleman*: Arcadia was an isolated, mountainous region of ancient Greece whose residents were much admired by the Greeks for the simplicity and rusticity of their lives. After the name was used by Sir Philip Sydney (1554–1586) as the title of his pastoral romance, Arcadia entered the lexicon to mean an ideal, rustic place and Arcadians simple, happy people.

2. (p. 359) *"From the hedges and highways bid them come"*: O. Henry is referring to the Parable of the Wedding Banquet (see the Bible, Matthew 22:1–14), in which a king has prepared a wedding banquet for his son, but the guests have not arrived. Furious, he kills the invited guests and sends his servants out onto the streets to invite anyone they find. When a man comes to the banquet not wearing proper clothes, the king has him bound hand and foot and thrown out. The passage ends with the quote "for many are invited, but few are chosen."

3. (p. 362) *his face shining as must have shone the face of Elijah's charioteer when he announced the glories of that heavenly journey*: Elijah was one of the main Hebrew prophets; a chariot of fire brought him to heaven in a whirlwind (see the Bible, 2 Kings 2).

4. (p. 362) *Her*: Capitalization of a pronoun usually indicates a deity (such as Him for God). O. Henry's capitalization of the feminine pronoun here is a bold typographical choice and lends an additional level of interpretation to the reference to Elijah in the previous sentence.

"The Thing's the Play"

1. (p. 363) *"all the stage is a world, . . . 'The thing's the play' "*: O. Henry inverts words in two lines from Shakespeare: from *As You Like It* (act 2, scene 7): "All the world's a stage, / And all the men and women merely players" and *Hamlet* (act 2, scene 2): "The play's the thing / Wherein I'll catch the conscience of the King."

2. (p. 367) *the eyes of Romeo and Othello's tongue*: Although Shakespeare's Romeo, from *Romeo and Juliet*, is second to none with his tongue, he woos Juliet not by words but with a look. The title character from Shakespeare's *Othello*, on the other hand, is renowned for his ability to woo women with words. When Othello successfully woos and wins the beautiful Desdemona, her friends suspect that she had been literally bewitched by his words.

"Proof of the Pudding"

1. (p. 383) Minerva Magazine: The magazine is named after Minerva, the goddess of wisdom and the patroness of trade and the arts in Roman mythology.

2. (p. 383) *whether you are of those who rush in, or of the gentle concourse that fears to tread*: O. Henry is playing with a line from Alexander Pope's *Essay on Criticism* (1711): "Fools rush in where Angels fear to tread." Pope's essay is addressed to writers and critics who, through an explanation of his own artistic philosophy, he hopes to help and guide in their art; the reference aptly applies to "Proof of the Pudding," which attempts a similar goal.

3. (p. 385) *"It's Maupassant hash, . . . Marion Crawford serial with an Ella Wheeler Wilcox sonnet"*: Maupassant, Crawford, and Wheeler are writers of various reputation, skill, and fame. Guy de Maupassant (1850–1893), generally considered to be the greatest French short-story writer, is known for his detached, unsentimental style. Francis Marion Crawford (1854–1909) was an Italian-American novelist who, in contrast to Maupassant, wrote historical romances. Ella Wheeler Wilcox (1850–1919) was an American poet of sentimental verse.

4. (p. 388) *as the kingly and transcendent utterances of Lear are above the level of his senile vaporings*: King Lear, the tragic hero of Shakespeare's play of the same name, transforms during the course of the play from a stately and wise king to a mad, blinded fool who takes refuge in a cave.

"Confessions of a Humorist"

1. (p. 395) *Goethe—or was it Napoleon?—said five hours a day is enough for mental labor*: Johann Wolfgang von Goethe (1749–1832) was a German writer and philosopher. Napoleon Bonaparte (1769–1821) was the French military-man who became emperor. The quote can be attributed to neither.

2. (p. 396) *And then I became a harpy, a Moloch, a Jonah*: In Greek mythology, a harpy was a rapacious creature, half-woman half-bird. A Moloch was a Semitic god to whom children were sacrificed. Jonah was the willful biblical prophet who refused to preach repentance to the people of Nineveh and, as punishment, was thrown overboard and swallowed by a whale.

3. (p. 397) *A literary Judas*: One of the New Testament's twelve apostles, Judas Iscariot betrayed Jesus to his enemies in exchange for thirty pieces of silver. His name has become a synonym for "traitor."

INSPIRED BY O. HENRY

The people of America loved O. Henry . . . he was a
nobody, but he was a nobody who also was
somebody, everybody's somebody.
—William Saroyan

The O. Henry Awards

Between 1903 and 1910 William Sydney Porter published some
300 short stories under the pen name O. Henry. His immense
popularity and mastery of the surprise ending did more to legitimize
the short-story form than did efforts by any writer before him.

As "a monument to O. Henry's genius," the Society of Arts and
Sciences established the O. Henry Awards in 1918, eight years after
the writer's death. Presented annually, the O. Henry Awards celebrate the year's best short stories written by American and Canadian authors and published in American and Canadian
magazines. The series editor chooses twenty stories from the
thousands that are submitted each year and passes them on to a
jury, which often comprises well-known writers; the jury then de-
termines the top three prize-winning stories. The stories are read
"blind"—that is, without knowledge of the author or magazine in
which they originally appeared—and many writers have won O.
Henry Awards numerous times. Over the years, William Saroyan
earned six awards, Eudora Welty eight, and William Faulkner
twelve, and Alice Adams has earned twenty-three. But Joyce Carol
Oates wins the day—she has taken home an astonishing twenty-
eight O. Henry Awards!

The Cisco Kid

O. Henry's story "The Caballero's Way" (collected in *The Heart of the West*, 1907) gave birth to one of the most enduring personalities of American pop culture—the Cisco Kid. The inspiration for several feature films (including a silent titled after O. Henry's story), a popular radio program, a comic-book series, and a successful television show, O. Henry's "Robin Hood of the West" is the stuff of American legend.

Fox Studios launched the first series of Cisco Kid films in 1929 with *In Old Arizona*, which was nominated for a host of Academy Awards—Best Film, Best Director, Best Screenplay, Best Cinematography, and Best Actor, for which Warner Baxter won. Over the next twelve years, Fox produced ten films in the series. United Artists and Monogram followed with more than a dozen motion pictures of the *Don Quixote*-inspired hero and his sidekick. This rich cinematic history is captured in Francis M. Nevins's book *The Films of the Cisco Kid* (1998).

Duncan Renaldo and Leo Carrillo, actors from the United Artist films, went on to star in the television series *The Cisco Kid*, which aired 156 episodes between 1950 and 1956. The Cisco Kid's popularity has not faded; in 1994 the cable television network TNT produced *The Cisco Kid*, starring Jimmy Smits and featuring Cheech Marin as Pancho.

A Twist at the End

In *A Twist at the End: A Novel of O. Henry* (2000), historical writer Steven Saylor builds a mystery around the real-life case of the "Servant Girl Annihilators," one of the first serial-killer cases ever recorded. The "Servant Girl Annihilators," a phrase coined by O. Henry, refers to a string of unsolved ax slayings that occurred near the turn of the last century in Austin, Texas—the time when young William Sydney Porter worked there as a bank teller and was arrested for embezzlement of funds. A canny Saylor casts O. Henry as the hero of the novel. The narrative shifts between 1884, when O. Henry was still known as William Sydney Porter, and twenty years later, when he had become a popular writer of short stories.

In Saylor's novel O. Henry finds himself a victim of blackmail and accusation.

In addition to the central mystery, Saylor juggles several fascinating elements of Texas history. The novel explores the racial crisis of post-Confederacy Texas—six of the eight victims are black. It also probes gender issues of the time, with complex romantic subplots that surround Porter and a genuine, affirmative action-type bill mandating that half of all government clerks be women. Saylor, a sometime-Austinite like O. Henry, takes great pleasure in rendering the Austin of a simpler, bygone era and displays careful research throughout his story. An ingenious mix of nearly forgotten fact and fanciful invention, *A Twist at the End* is beautifully paced and, especially in its finale, deeply rewarding.

COMMENTS & QUESTIONS

In this section, we aim to provide the reader with an array of perspectives on the text, as well as questions that challenge those perspectives. The commentary has been culled from sources as diverse as reviews contemporaneous with the work, letters written by the author, literary criticism of later generations, and appreciations written throughout history. Following the commentary, a series of questions seeks to filter Selected Stories of O. Henry *through a variety of points of view and bring about a richer understanding of these enduring works.*

Comments

THE ATLANTIC MONTHLY

[O. Henry] knows his world well, but he sees it with an eye for its beauty as well as its absurdity. There is imagination as well as vision, and beyond his expert knowledge of our colloquial tongue, he possesses in the background, to be used when needed, a real style. He is not afraid to be leisurely in the shortest sketch, he even risks an occasional introductory page. "The Green Door" actually opens with a charming essay upon adventure and the adventurous to whom once in a while "a slip of paper, written upon, flutters down . . . from the high lattices of Chance." He may talk Bowery, or talk Tenderloin or Harlem with impunity; he also talks the language of civilization. . . .

In noticing all this, it must not be forgotten that "O. Henry" is also exceedingly funny. In a general way the stories suggest the thumbnail studies of Frapié, Provins, and the other flashlight Frenchmen, but without their pessimism and despair. Where their tendency is to forget that they are writing stories, to approximate as far as possible to a literal document, "O. Henry" does not hesitate to round out, to fill in, to take advantage of coincidence, in short, to indulge his reader's weak-minded craving for a little human enjoyment. And after all, since babies still smile and crow, even in courts and alleys, and lads take their sweethearts for an outing, and the rhythm of a hand-organ still quickens tired feet to a waltz, perhaps his picture with its glimmer of arc light and sunshine may be to the full as true as if it were altogether drawn in India ink and charcoal.

—January 1907

THE ATLANTIC MONTHLY

O. Henry seems to possess the happy gift of picking up gold pieces from the asphalt pavement. If occasionally his finds turn out to be tobacco-tags instead, you easily forgive him, it's so clearly a part of the jubilant and irresponsible game he is playing. It is the unpremeditated element that lends half the characteristic charm to O. Henry's writing. His faculty of vernacular observation rarely fails him. "Eight months," he tells us, "went by as smoothly and surely as though they had 'elapsed' on a theatre program." To Raggles, the tramp who was a poet, other cities had yielded their secrets as quickly as country maidens, "but here was one [New York] as cold, glittering, serene, impossible, as a four-carat diamond in a window to a lover outside, fingering damply in his pocket his ribbon-counter salary." O. Henry's stories are as disorderly as the streets of the city he loves so well. This newer collection shows not the least growth in the quality of his perceptions (always shrewd, but never deep), nor any hoped-for attention to good workmanship. Having learned a trick or two of construction,—the three-line surprise ending, for example,—he seems quite satisfied to go no further. Yet there is something irresistible about the stories, with all their crimes upon them; they are so buoyant and careless, so genial in their commentary, and so pleasantly colored by a sentiment which, if as sophisticated as Broadway itself, is still perfectly spontaneous and sincere.

—July 1907

HENRY JAMES FORMAN

For the first time since the eclipse of Mr. Kipling the short story is again beginning to make public appearance between bookcovers.

Publishers still look upon it somewhat askance, as on one under a cloud, and authors, worldly-wise, still cling to the novel as the unquestioned leader. But here and there a writer now boldly brings forth a book of short tales, and the publisher does his part. The stigma of the *genre* is wearing off, and for the rehabilitation one man is chiefly responsible.

Mr. Sydney Porter, the gentleman who, in the language of some of his characters, is "denounced" by the euphonious pen-name of O. Henry, has breathed new life into the short story. Gifted as he is with a flashing wit, abundant humor and quick observation, no subject has terrors for him. If it be too much to say, in the old phrase, that nothing human is alien to him, at least the larger part of humanity is his domain. . . .

It is idle to compare O. Henry with anybody. No talent could be more original or more delightful. The combination of technical excellence with whimsical, sparkling wit, abundant humor and fertile invention is so rare that the reader is content without comparisons.

—from *North American Review* (May 1908)

THE NATION

Of the particular type of short story which he produces, O. Henry is a perfectly assured master. Heeding the maxim of Goethe, he has worked in a strictly limited field. He has attempted no rivalry with Irving or Hawthorne or Poe. It is shocking to find him mentioned in the same sentence with them, for he has so limited his field as to exclude wonder, beauty, passion, terror. On the other hand, he has as sedulously avoided the risky formula of the naturalistic short story which has flourished in France. Never penetrating beneath the surface, he has furnished an astonishing amount of diversion by presenting merely comic aspects of universal rascaldom.

—July 15, 1909

THE NATION

[O. Henry's] unrivalled "timeliness" as a writer of fiction may be suggested by the title of one of these stories—"The Higher Pragmatism." The humor which rises from the juxtaposition of the remote and the immediate can scarcely go further than his comparison of the beauty of a Texas sheep-ranchman asleep to that of a "cab-horse leaning against the Metropolitan Opera House at 12:30 A.M., dreaming of the plains of Arabia." Nor can much advance be expected upon the artifice of construction which makes "No Story" in reality no story till within a dozen lines of the end, where it suddenly becomes, *ex post facto*, as the author might say, an extremely dramatic incident, and forces the reader to think it all through again. Structural cleverness is O. Henry's dark angel.

—December 2, 1909

Questions

1. Can one abstract a coherent philosophy, or set of values, or politics, or psychology from O. Henry's stories?

2. Is there a consistent view of American national character in these stories?

3. Would these stories work if written in a neutral, "objective" style, without the humor?

4. Are O. Henry's characters ever driven by what can be recognized as unconscious motivation?

5. How much does history, national or personal, weigh on O. Henry's characters?

6. How would you characterize O. Henry's typical narrator?

FOR FURTHER READING

General

Brooks, Van Wyck. *The Confident Years: 1885–1915*. New York: Dutton, 1955. Occupying the ambiguous space between general survey and academic study, this book nevertheless provides good information about the period in question.

Callow, James T., and Robert J. Reilly. *Guide to American Literature from Emily Dickinson to the Present*. New York: Barnes and Noble, 1977. A survey of major American literary trends, written in the brief but clear format of a study guide, this book is useful for quick reference.

Gelfant, Blanche H., ed. *The Columbia Companion to the Twentieth-century American Short Story*. New York: Columbia University Press, 2000.

May, Charles E., ed. *The New Short Story Theories*. Athens: Ohio University Press, 1994. Includes an article by the Russian critic B. M. Ejxenbaum. This collection of essays provides a useful mosaic of current and historical readings of the short story, with many of the essays speaking to the general issue of American short-story writing; as a whole, it makes for very interesting reading.

Woodress, James, ed. *Essays Mostly on Periodical Publishing in America: A Collection in Honor of Clarence Gohdes*. Durham, NC: Duke University Press, 1973. An academic survey of American publishing in the late nineteenth and early twentieth centuries. Although O. Henry receives only passing mention, this book is useful for its intelligent analysis of the major (and sometimes minor) movements and players of the period.

On O. Henry and His Works

Current-García, Eugene. *O. Henry (William Sydney Porter)*. New York: Twayne Publishers, 1965. Current-García aims more at literary explanation than biographical exploration, and intelligently analyzes O. Henry's context and work without indulging in the tone of hero-worship that pervades so many other biographies.

Harris, Richard C. *William Sydney Porter (O. Henry), A Reference Guide*. Boston: G. K. Hall, 1980.

Long, E. Hudson. *O. Henry, the Man and His Work*. New York: Russell and Russell, 1969.

O'Connor, Richard. *O. Henry: The Legendary Life of William S. Porter*. Garden City, NY: Doubleday, 1970.

O. Henry Papers; Containing Some Sketches of His Life Together with an Alphabetical Index to His Complete Works. Folcroft, PA: Folcroft Library Editions, 1973. An entertaining and engaging collection of recollections about O. Henry written by people who knew him. This book is as much a period piece as it is part of the literary record, as reflected in the somewhat antiquated language and style. All in all, however, the recollections show a degree of sensitivity to O. Henry and his stories that is largely lacking in recent criticism.

O. Henry (William Sydney Porter). *The Works of O. Henry*. New York: Doubleday, Page, 1911. At the end of this complete collection of O. Henry's stories, there is a substantial section of essays about O. Henry's life and art by his peers. In addition to these essays, which in themselves make the book worth a look, there are excerpts from O. Henry's letters, a selection of his *Rolling Stone* writings, and some of his *Postscripts*.

Smith, C. Alphonso. *O. Henry Biography*. Garden City, NY: Doubleday, Page, 1916. This is the first book any student of O. Henry should read, keeping in mind, however, that because it was written so soon after his death it strikes an odd tone somewhere between admiration and revelation. Smith was the first person to publicly discuss O. Henry's incarceration and the other hidden facts about his life. As such, he was the first O. Henry expert. For an objective view of O. Henry, this book should be read in conjunction with other biographies.

Other Works Cited in the Introduction

Cooper, Frederic Taber. *Some American Story Tellers*. Freeport, NY: Books for Libraries Press, 1968.

Ejxenbaum, B. M. *O. Henry and the Theory of the Short Story*. Translated and with notes and a postscript by I. R. Titunik. Ann Arbor: University of Michigan, 1968.

MacAdam, George. "O. Henry's Only Autobiographia." In *O. Henry Papers*. Folcroft, PA: Folcroft Library Editions, 1973 (see above).

Look for the following titles, available now from
BARNES & NOBLE CLASSICS

Adventures of Huckleberry Finn	Mark Twain	1-59308-112-X	$6.95
The Adventures of Tom Sawyer	Mark Twain	1-59308-139-1	$6.95
The Aeneid	Vergil	1-59308-237-1	$7.95
Aesop's Fables		1-59308-062-X	$5.95
The Age of Innocence	Edith Wharton	1-59308-143-X	$5.95
Alice's Adventures in Wonderland and Through the Looking-Glass	Lewis Carroll	1-59308-015-8	$5.95
Anna Karenina	Leo Tolstoy	1-59308-027-1	$8.95
The Arabian Nights	Anonymous	1-59308-281-9	$9.95
The Art of War	Sun Tzu	1-59308-017-4	$7.95
The Autobiography of an Ex-Colored Man and Other Writings	James Weldon Johnson	1-59308-289-4	$5.95
The Awakening and Selected Short Fiction	Kate Chopin	1-59308-113-8	$6.95
Billy Budd and The Piazza Tales	Herman Melville	1-59308-253-3	$5.95
The Brothers Karamazov	Fyodor Dostoevsky	1-59308-045-X	$9.95
The Call of the Wild and White Fang	Jack London	1-59308-200-2	$5.95
Candide	Voltaire	1-59308-028-X	$4.95
The Canterbury Tales	Geoffrey Chaucer	1-59308-080-8	$9.95
A Christmas Carol, The Chimes and The Cricket on the Hearth	Charles Dickens	1-59308-033-6	$5.95
The Collected Oscar Wilde		1-59308-310-6	$9.95
The Collected Poems of Emily Dickinson		1-59308-050-6	$5.95
The Complete Sherlock Holmes, Vol. I	Sir Arthur Conan Doyle	1-59308-034-4	$7.95
The Complete Sherlock Holmes, Vol. II	Sir Arthur Conan Doyle	1-59308-040-9	$7.95
Confessions	Saint Augustine	1-59308-259-2	$6.95
The Count of Monte Cristo	Alexandre Dumas	1-59308-151-0	$7.95
Don Quixote	Miguel de Cervantes	1-59308-046-8	$9.95
Dracula	Bram Stoker	1-59308-114-6	$6.95
Emma	Jane Austen	1-59308-152-9	$6.95
Essays and Poems by Ralph Waldo Emerson		1-59308-076-X	$6.95
The Essential Tales and Poems of Edgar Allan Poe		1-59308-064-6	$7.95
Ethan Frome and Selected Stories	Edith Wharton	1-59308-090-5	$5.95
Fairy Tales	Hans Christian Andersen	1-59308-260-6	$9.95
Founding America: Documents from the Revolution to the Bill of Rights	Jefferson, et al.	1-59308-230-4	$9.95
Frankenstein	Mary Shelley	1-59308-115-4	$4.95
Great American Short Stories: From Hawthorne to Hemingway	Various	1-59308-086-7	$7.95
The Great Escapes: Four Slave Narratives	Various	1-59308-294-0	$6.95
Great Expectations	Charles Dickens	1-59308-116-2	$6.95
Grimm's Fairy Tales	Jacob and Wilhelm Grimm	1-59308-056-5	$7.95
Gulliver's Travels	Jonathan Swift	1-59308-132-4	$5.95
Heart of Darkness and Selected Short Fiction	Joseph Conrad	1-59308-123-5	$5.95
The Idiot	Fyodor Dostoevsky	1-59308-058-1	$7.95
The Importance of Being Earnest and Four Other Plays	Oscar Wilde	1-59308-059-X	$6.95
The Inferno	Dante Alighieri	1-59308-051-4	$6.95
Jane Eyre	Charlotte Brontë	1-59308-117-0	$7.95

(continued)

Jude the Obscure	Thomas Hardy	1-59308-035-2	$6.95
The Jungle	Upton Sinclair	1-59308-118-9	$6.95
The Last of the Mohicans	James Fenimore Cooper	1-59308-137-5	$5.95
Les Liaisons Dangereuses	Pierre Choderlos de Laclos	1-59308-240-1	$7.95
Little Women	Louisa May Alcott	1-59308-108-1	$6.95
Lost Illusions	Honoré de Balzac	1-59308-315-7	$9.95
Main Street	Sinclair Lewis	1-59308-386-6	$7.95
Mansfield Park	Jane Austen	1-59308-154-5	$5.95
The Metamorphosis and Other Stories	Franz Kafka	1-59308-029-8	$6.95
Moby-Dick	Herman Melville	1-59308-018-2	$9.95
My Ántonia	Willa Cather	1-59308-202-9	$5.95
Narrative of Sojourner Truth		1-59308-293-2	$6.95
The Odyssey	Homer	1-59308-009-3	$5.95
Oliver Twist	Charles Dickens	1-59308-206-1	$6.95
The Origin of Species	Charles Darwin	1-59308-077-8	$7.95
Paradise Lost	John Milton	1-59308-095-6	$7.95
Persuasion	Jane Austen	1-59308-130-8	$5.95
The Picture of Dorian Gray	Oscar Wilde	1-59308-025-5	$4.95
A Portrait of the Artist as a Young Man and Dubliners	James Joyce	1-59308-031-X	$6.95
Pride and Prejudice	Jane Austen	1-59308-201-0	$5.95
The Prince and Other Writings	Niccolò Machiavelli	1-59308-060-3	$5.95
The Red Badge of Courage and Selected Short Fiction	Stephen Crane	1-59308-119-7	$4.95
Republic	Plato	1-59308-097-2	$6.95
Robinson Crusoe	Daniel Defoe	1-59308-360-2	$5.95
The Scarlet Letter	Nathaniel Hawthorne	1-59308-207-X	$5.95
The Secret Agent	Joseph Conrad	1-59308-305-X	$6.95
Selected Stories of O. Henry		1-59308-042-5	$5.95
Sense and Sensibility	Jane Austen	1-59308-125-1	$5.95
Siddhartha	Hermann Hesse	1-59308-379-3	$5.95
The Souls of Black Folk	W. E. B. Du Bois	1-59308-014-X	$5.95
The Strange Case of Dr. Jekyll and Mr. Hyde and Other Stories	Robert Louis Stevenson	1-59308-131-6	$4.95
A Tale of Two Cities	Charles Dickens	1-59308-138-3	$5.95
Three Theban Plays	Sophocles	1-59308-235-5	$6.95
Thus Spoke Zarathustra	Friedrich Nietzsche	1-59308-278-9	$7.95
The Time Machine and The Invisible Man	H. G. Wells	1-59308-388-2	$6.95
Treasure Island	Robert Louis Stevenson	1-59308-247-9	$4.95
The Turn of the Screw, The Aspern Papers and Two Stories	Henry James	1-59308-043-3	$5.95
Uncle Tom's Cabin	Harriet Beecher Stowe	1-59308-121-9	$7.95
Vanity Fair	William Makepeace Thackeray	1-59308-071-9	$7.95
Walden and Civil Disobedience	Henry David Thoreau	1-59308-208-8	$5.95
The War of the Worlds	H. G. Wells	1-59308-362-9	$5.95
Ward No. 6 and Other Stories	Anton Chekhov	1-59308-003-4	$7.95
Wuthering Heights	Emily Brontë	1-59308-128-6	$5.95

𝒜ℬ

BARNES & NOBLE CLASSICS

If you are an educator and would like to receive an
Examination or Desk Copy of a Barnes & Noble Classics edition,
please refer to Academic Resources on our website at
WWW.BN.COM/CLASSICS
or contact us at
BNCLASSICS@BN.COM

All prices are subject to change.

0208